FAIR WARNING

"The destruction of invaders is part of their nature, their instinct." The Highlander shrugged. "The Woodwose see all humans as unregistered treepests—and they exist to *destroy* treepests."

The Chinese woman wore a puzzled expression, then laughed lightly. "But the Woodwose, it is such an ugly thing!"

The Highlander smiled mirthlessly. "Ugly or not, they still treat humans as treepests. Nor are they unintelligent. They should not be underestimated. It is easy to avoid such a fate of course—just stay out of Fenrille's great forest. That is the preserve of the Arizel and the Woodwose. They do not welcome intruders."

Also by Christopher Rowley
Published by Ballantine Books:

THE WAR FOR ETERNITY

THE BLACK SHIP

Christopher Rowley

A Del Rey Book

BALLANTINE BOOKS • NEW YORK

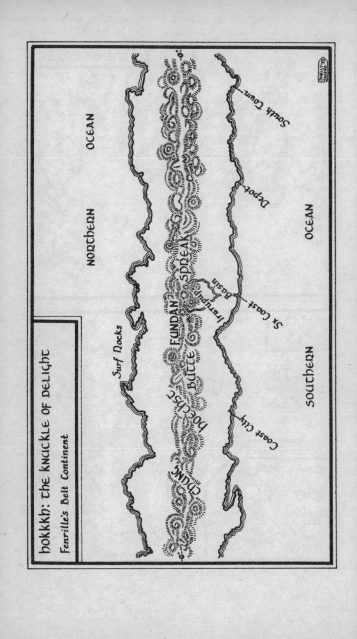

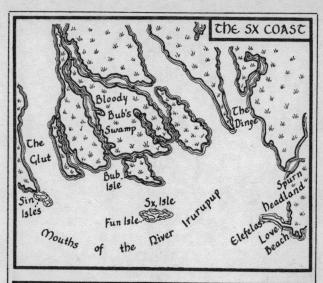

THE SX COAST

Bloody Bub's Swamp

The Dinge

The Glut

Bub Isle

Spurn Headland

Sin Isles

Sx Isle

Fun Isle

Mouths of the River Irurupup

Elefelas

Love Beach

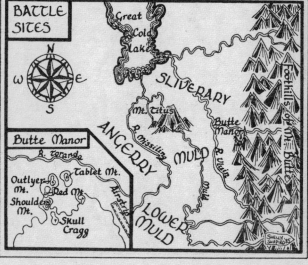

BATTLE SITES

Great Cold Lake

N
W E
S

SLIVERARY

Foothills of Mt. Butte

Mt. Titus

R. missilin

Butte Manor

ANGERRY MULD

R. Vluin

Muld

Butte Manor

R. Veranda

Tablet Mt.

Outlyer Mt.

Red Mt.

Shoulder Mt.

Skull Cragg

Airstrip

LOWER MULD

SHELLY SHAPIRO 85 N.Y.

1

THE NUMAL EXERCISED DURING THAT CYCLE, DISPORTING IN the laleven fluid, running several thousand bodylengths on fully extended podial surfaces, burrowing energetically in the crystal sands on the beach of forever.

The Ring Sun was semiocculted; only low filters were in place; hence the light was bright but cool. The Numal's breath echoed in heavy gasps from its respiratory sphincter; the exertion was intense; it was converting body sugars to energy at a formidable rate, but the medical scan had decreed increased exercise; it was good for the circulatory system.

When the heavy filters rose into place the air became cold, a chill mist rose over the sea, the waves grew glacial. The Numal emerged from a thirty-bodylength tunnel it had smashed through the dunes and found its sweat turning into rime frost across its dark gray torso. Retracting all but a pair of long-distance podial surfaces, it began to lope ponderously back to the castle.

Before it crested the inner dunes, the Numal's communicator beeped shrilly and a data pulse followed that it accepted through the brain droud.

Immediately the Numal accelerated its pace; a wait of many aeons had finally been rewarded.

The Numal thundered across the drawbridge and went immediately to the laboratory. Swiftly, with trembling pseudopodia, it focused the intricate psionic sensing device it had developed after aeons of research. The target was a "djinn" field, a net of subtle physical anomalies bearing a slight electric charge in constant flux that for unknown reasons held together as if it was a living thing.

Now, excitement mounting, the Numal nudged the keys to guide the computers in precise tracking. Enormous dish arrays, coated with a film of activated psionic organism, were focused upon the tiny anomaly source. Once locked on, the psionic organism was stimulated and a control field flung around the target.

A few million miles away, quite by chance, drifted the Divider, great Arizel of Fenrille. The Divider had entered the Numal's universe after retracing its steps through a "rope" of younger universes all interlocked around the space–time folding of this more ancient universe. The trail the Divider followed was faint, no more than the pattern discerned in the creation of Universes, one it hoped to follow until the Creator Itself was revealed.

Now the Divider marveled at the sights around, few and very far away as they were. This was an ancient universe, so old that all the stars had long since burnt out, the galaxies were dark, only the power of massive black holes remained as even the protons decayed and gave up their energy.

Yet the universe had lights, the product of intelligence, burning long after all natural light had died. The black holes were circled by rings of organized matter; huge engines fed gas into black hole singularities and enormous energies were reaped.

The Divider sensed many, many lives; the enormous moebial structures that ringed the black holes were teeming with inhabitants. Then the Divider sensed the despair, the terrible dread of an incredibly advanced race that now faced the slow end of its own universe. In a measurable time there would not be enough matter to burn in the black holes and the holes themselves would shed their energy in the form of gravity waves and so, finally, run down to nothingness. The race faced doom.

At the speed of thought, the Divider drew itself toward a nearby singularity surrounded with orbiting dish-shaped structures that were warmed by the light of a ring of superheated gas fed into the black hole. Abruptly an enormous power on the psionic plane reached out and gripped the Divider as if in a giant hand. It was appallingly strong, but the Divider sensed that it was also almost mindless, a machine of some kind. Nevertheless, the grip could not be broken. For the first time in seventy million years of existence, the Divider experienced fear.

Whatever it was that drew him, the force emanated from a biosupporting region that coated one orbiting dish structure.

Helplessly the great Divider, Master of the One in the Four Forces of all universal creation, was drawn down into an atmosphere of nitrogen and oxygen. Over a dreary plain of dun brown, spotted with plantlike organisms, the Divider passed then flew rapidly across a sea of bright pink liquid that was threaded with veins of a deeper hue. Ahead glittered the far shore where crystalline sands formed dunes that glittered in the light of the Ring Sun.

There squatted a fanciful structure of towers and cubes, cut on a herculean scale from a gleaming gray material. Within lay the Divider's destination. A huge room laden with interconnected devices of an exotic form, asymmetrical, highly crystalline. One device moved, a lozenge-shaped thing with a forest of spidery limbs extruded from red bands on its otherwise gray exterior.

A new field was brought to bear; it locked around the Divider's consciousness with the brutal snap of a steel trap on the leg of a rabbit. There was agony and there was no escape. An envelope was opened—the psionic power was horribly strong, the pressure irresistible as the Divider was tucked into a confinement, trapped with enclosing fields generated by machines. This was a horror that transcended even the agony, beyond anything the Divider had ever known. Within the trap there was darkness; the fields made it impossible to survey the surroundings. The Divider was blind.

In its Laboratory the Numal excitedly slipped the gravity bottle into the focusing region of the scanner. Yes, there it was, caught in the bottle, and the Numal could see that this one was considerably more energetic than any others the Numal had seen before.

The computer scan moved into the visible wavelengths and began subjecting the anomaly to intense bursts of blue-ring light.

The new capture would mean a renewal of the research program. Maybe this time the Numal would succeed in deciphering the phenomenon. Perhaps one day an institute would be founded in the Numal's honor.

2

OVER THE STARTLING BLACK SURFACE OF THE DARK SIDE OF Neptune, a great light broke the void. A colossal wattage lit the cloud tops below.

Laden with the last of the conspirators, the elite of the Neptunian system, the heavy Nereid–Triton shuttle sped toward that light. The atmosphere onboard was one of celebration, tinged here and there with a hysterical anxiety.

Ofur Muynn, tall, blond, dumb, and handsome, capered for his master, Degorak Chevde, party secretary of all Triton. "And just think of the good Chairman Wei's face when they give him the news!" Ofur howled, and a roar of laughter arose from the eighty-odd men and women riding behind Chevde and the other politburo members.

Degorak winced, however, and exchanged nervous glances with his senior advisers Aumus Realme and Ira Ganweek. Both were clearly nervous. *The fools laugh and cheer, but the secret is out* . . .

Ganweek stared at Aumus Realme, wondering. He had never fully trusted Realme. Had Neptune's former chief of military intelligence sold them out? No, that would be preposterous— Realme was at risk with the rest of them. Yet somehow, a few days before, the great secret the conspirators had kept for forty years had leaked to Inner Planets Security.

Alace Rohm, madrelect of the Nereidan Council, had only just received the news. Her face was dark with shock, crumpled by a mortal terror.

. . . *if we are taken it would be better to have never lived than to face Chairman Wei . . . he would send us to the garden* . . .

Still the news that the Earth fleet was hurtling toward them was not widely known, and it would be kept a secret for as long as possible. So for the leaders the now-dreadful celebration rituals had to be undergone with brave smiles.

Ofur Muynn raised his big hands, the heavy bracelets clunking together, his fur vest parted to reveal massively developed chest muscles.

"It's time to start the celebrations, break out the wine." He turned to Degorak. "With your permission, great Degorak."

"Yes yes," Chevde signaled weakly, too weary suddenly to lift the heavy bangles he wore. "Yes, it's time. Let's get on with it."

Ira Ganweek rose and approached Chevde. The deceleration lights had been on for some time, and the shuttle was down to half a gee. Ira produced a palm-size golden egg. Behind him champagne corks exploded in a volley punctuated by squeals of joy.

"Chevde, for you, with my heartfelt thanks, for all you've done. You will go down in human history as one of the greatest freedom fighters of all."

Chevde, glad of an opportunity to turn his thoughts away from Chairman Wei's vengeance, examined the exquisitely engraved scarabs and coiled mice on the egg's surface then pressed a green scarab. A quadrant slid up, revealing a small bottle within the core, half-filled with fat grains of glossy blue pharamol.

"Spreak Skycristal, the best there is," Ganweek said simply. Chevde closed the egg and pressed the pink mouse button. A golden tine slid forth bearing a tiny mechanical fist holding a single grain. Chevde touched it to his tongue.

Skycristal pharamol! Each and every grain worth #93.720,000 on the Chitin drug market in the Outer Planetary systems.

Chevde had never seen more than four grains of Skycristal in one cache before. This was the kind of deal you could bring off only if you had the very best contacts on Fenrille itself. Not just in the smuggler's markets. Ira Ganweek must have used all his legendary muscle to get Skycristal. The enormity of the achievement got through to Chevde.

Chevde clasped Ganweek's hand. "A princely gifting, Ganweek. It will be remembered. If . . ." He couldn't finish. Ganweek was glad he didn't try.

Ofur Muynn handed them champagne flutes and they toasted the image now clearly visible on the view screen above.

"To the *Black Ship*, to freedom and conquest!" The glasses were held high.

"To Fenrille and eternity!" Alace Rohm shrieked in a strange, strangled voice. Her dark, prominent eyes seemed about to point in different directions.

"Don't forget the Galaxy!" bellowed someone from the back.

5

Lots of other jolly cries were sounded, but the leaders looked at each other from time to time while they sipped champagne; there was a taut energy between them that their followers completely misunderstood.

The great light ahead had split into three parts and then into ten and now into a galaxy of individual points. Orbiting low across Neptune's cloud tops came an industrial behemoth with the productive capacity of the entire planet Earth in the late twentieth century. Huge stems and suck tubes dangled into the gas below; heavy fusion drives worked to counter their drag. Beneath the twinkling skin of lights the massive deformed cubes of the *Black Ship*'s drive generators could be discerned. Enormous machines worked steadily across those surfaces adding enriched ices and laying cables.

They were chanting "DEGORAK! DEGORAK! DEGORAK!" so Chevde was forced to rise and, with some effort, make a cheery little speech. When he finished they all rose and chanted again, even Ira Ganweek, who had once found it inconceivable that he would pay homage in Neptunian fashion.

Chevde gave a signal and Underhench Garwal Ko passed out packets of green pharamol, Fundan Slade Mountain, and the noise subsided a little as precious grains were slipped onto eager tongues. Here too Ira Ganweek's influence had been vital. Nobody else in the Neptunian System, a billion miles from the rest of the Solar System, had the contacts on Earth and Luna that he had. No one in the Solar System had the contacts on Fenrille that he had, contacts right in the heart of the longevity drug business. But then no one else in the Solar System had ever been a senator from Fenrille's Sx Coast.

The shuttle sank between immense cubicoid cheeks and flew down a vast access tube to the docking bay. There the eighty Party leaders were met by the thousands of lesser conspirators, space crew recruited secretly from the Neptunian military, administrators and loyal Party members from the Triton and Nereid cities, even a generation of space marines that had been cloned especially for the voyage.

Chevde stepped to a dais to address the throng; there were waves of cheers. The great adventure loomed, freedom from the tyranny of Earth, freedom from the Party, freedom from Chairman Wei.

Chevde was due to lead them in the forbidden cheer. Something unnerved him however, perhaps the thought of Chairman Wei's somehow viewing the scene through a spy, so he nodded

6

irritably to Ofur Muynn and Alace Rohm. Alace looked desperately unhappy while she gestured to the crowd.

. . . GOOD-BYE CHAIRMAN WEI! . . . GOOD-BYE CHAIRMAN WEI! . . .

They continued chanting long after Degorak had left the stand and taken an elevator to a small lounge. Ganweek, Realme, and Rohm joined him; then they locked the door and accessed the ship's computer system.

Anxiously they scanned the situation analysis.

"The Inner Planets main battle fleet is now crossing the orbit of Saturn. It will be close enough to place us within range of a Trusski laser lens within thirty-three hours." Ganweek read out the grim news from the coder.

"How did he find out?" exploded Chevde. They looked at Aumus Realme. Realme's narrow countenance stared back.

"Yeah, cop!" Alace Rohm snarled, "how did they find out! Not through Nereid—I can assure you of that!"

Nobody doubted Alace; her grip on the Nereidans was a strong one. Aulme however held his thin white hands up, palms toward them.

"Look!" he said forcefully. "You're all wrong, very wrong to suspect me. Believe me, if I'd betrayed you it would have been forty years ago, not now. You think I would be rewarded well for taking part in such a conspiracy?"

"Yes. We have developed the Fuhl Drive. You would be amply rewarded for bringing Chairman Wei the drives."

"But for how long? You know how the big man rules. I would not care to live and fall into his hands now."

Alace gave a little groan and put her face in her hands. There was a sincerity in Aumus Realme's voice that even Ganweek recognized. Indeed, immediately after his abrupt transfer to the home system from the planet Fenrille, the senator had spent several years in the close company of the chairman himself.

When the scientists finally let Ganweek go, it was only to residence in a room in the chairman's suite. Where wily, impossibly clever Chairman Wei interrogated him for weeks. He had lived there for months. Ganweek understood the chairman's methods.

"Bah!" he snarled. "What does it matter how he found out? The drives work. Within a few more hours we'll be far enough away from Neptune's gravity to achieve a Fuhl point. Shortly after that we'll be light-years away from here." Ganweek gestured around them. "This is the biggest single engineering project in human history; this ship has more mass than the entire Inner

Planets fleet; it is inconceivable that we could fail now. We will be safe as soon as the drives are in alignment."

Alace looked up, hope returning.

Chevde groaned, however. "But the accursed drives are *not* aligned. They are having the same alignment problems as before. Four heavy gravity fields are difficult to hold together—we've always known this would be a difficult step. The Fuhl Drive works, but..."

He didn't finish. Not long afterward the Klaxons wailed as the *Black Ship* lifted out of its low orbit on fusion drives and began pushing away from the dark side of Neptune into the Ring Belt.

Behind it, orbit swiftly deteriorating, it left a vast shell of construction machines and support devices. The Neptune System treasury had been plundered to build the ship. The economies of Triton and Nereid would be in chaos once the full extent of the plot was uncovered.

Gloomily they went to their cabins; the acceleration couches were the only comfortable place to be as the huge ship accelerated toward a relentless four gee to rise above the narrow rings of Neptune and then beyond.

As the roughly spheroidal vessel picked up speed, it headed outward from Neptune, keeping the planet between itself and the distant Inner Planets fleet.

The hours ticked by. Ira Ganweek found it increasingly hard to breathe; his body began to feel like one vast bruise. The ship was now ten thousand secs into fusion burn, speeding at well in excess of a million miles an hour, and yet they were barely crawling compared with the speed already achieved by their pursuers.

As long as the planet Neptune or one of its two satellites could be kept between them and the onrushing hand of Chairman Wei's retribution, no long-range laser fire could reach them. Soon however the planetary shelter would be lost, and then it would only be a matter of time.

Ganweek's thought turned unbidden in an all-too-familiar direction, . . . the lucky ones will go to the shark. The less lucky will go to the lamprey tank, and we, we who are the heart of the betrayal of His trust, we will go to the leprosy garden. If ever there was a place where life was too long, every moment, it was there, on that high roof overlooking the great sprawl of New Baghdad.

Time dragged on. Somehow word of the pursuit leaked out and spread quickly around the ship. Only the killing acceleration kept the panic under control. Hysteria rose, since it was obvious that within a matter of minutes they would be in the sights of the Inner Planets fleet and its main weaponry, the awesome Trusski lens laser.

Ganweek called Chevde's number again. A face flattened by gee filled the screen; it was underhench Garwal Ko.

"What news?" screamed Ganweek.

Ko fought visibly to control himself. The strain was telling on them all. "The last word was that alignment is almost achieved."

Despair, the giant drives were impossible to align. The test ships had been so much smaller, the fields easier to compress . . . "That was the message four hours ago," Ganweek groaned.

. . . you can live for many years in the garden . . . flesh slowly deforming . . .

In his cabin Ganweek fought to breathe; the murderous acceleration was killing them all. Yet he fingered the solid cyanide spansule in his pocket. He would take it if it seemed he would be captured. He would not fall alive into Chairman Wei's hands.

His monitor screen suddenly filled with Alace Rohm's face. Her features, normally so even and strong, were distorted into a witch's mask by the acceleration.

"Ira, what is going on? I can't get through to Degorak. He won't talk to me. What is happening? Can they get the drives to work or not?" Her voice trembled.

"I don't know. They're so much bigger than the test models, the fields are difficult to compress."

"Ira! We worked, slaved, lived in terror for forty years for this! We can't be taken now; I couldn't go through with that." Her voice had risen to a wail.

"You have the cyanide I gave you. Take that if we are hit."

"But Ira, I'm not supposed to die; I'm madrelect! I'm going to live forever." Her eyes were staring again. Alace seemed on the verge of a breakdown.

"Alace, take a trank, will you, for the luvafuck, and then lie down."

She hesitated, on the verge of hysteria, then got a grip once more. "Yes." She shivered. "Yes, I'll do that, but I want to keep a line open, just in case you hear of something. I want to know!" Her voice was crackling.

The news monitor gave Ganweek split-screen news coverage of the pursuing fleet. In front, by several million kilometers, were the nine ships that formed the lens. Behind came the six colossi that projected what they had called "The Sword of Order"

9

when it was wielded two centuries before in the final war with the rebel cloud cities of Neptune and Uranus.

Neptune was behind them; on the screen the green enemy blips slowly moved into the orange section, still hundreds of millions of kilometers away, that denoted the firing range of the giant Trusski laser.

The *Black Ship* was leaving a heavily scrambled electronic trail, a stream of ghost images and jamming codes designed to fudge the enemy's aim. But that could last only so long before the computers would penetrate the fog and pinpoint the ship.

Ira sucked in his breath with a little *whoop*, despite the acceleration pressure, when he saw the great laser come on, visualized as a red line on the monitor display. It passed them, deflected to a pseudotarget. Sweat began to bead his face.

. . . forty years of lying, hiding, dealing with the party bond lords; Ira would never forget his own bonding initiation; he still had nightmares occasionally about that . . . forty years and it all rode on this moment.

Alace could be heard sobbing on the audiolink.

Again the great Trusski laser beam came on, a blade of green-white fury that lanced into space and missed them by a hairsbreadth, deceived once more by the camouflaging electronics pouring out of the *Black Ship* along with the exhaust ions.

The next would strike them. It would be but moments.

In utter despair Ganweek called Chevde's number again, priority code, breaking in over another caller. The monitor filled with chaos. Despite acceleration that had them on their hands and knees, the Bond lords were screaming at Degorak to save them. They were baying for the drives. Chevde could be heard yelling to the engineering section. "I don't care; do it now, you fools, no matter what the alignment, don't you understand? It will at least give us a clean death!"

Seconds later, even as the sword of laser light stabbed out at them, the Fuhl Drives came on. Four tiny black holes were projected within the midst of the Fusion Modules. Simultaneously the ship shifted in space and time, vanishing in a great burst of gravity waves.

The furious green-white light sliced through their predicted position but the *Black Ship* was gone, hurtling beyond the system at faster than light-speed.

3

THE CHARTERED LIMOUSINE HUMMED THROUGH THE TUNNEL; the two humans and single elderly fein in the capacious rear were hunched in various degrees of misery. It was not a pleasant ride; the car was crowded with too many emotions, and there was nothing to look at outside; the roadbeds of the Sx Coast were underground tunnels.

Chosen Fundan stared straight ahead, doing his utmost to pretend that this was really happening to someone else. Fleur Fundan mused gloomily on the reflection in the window. Beyond her son loomed the shaggy bulk of Bg Rva, still sporting weapons webbing and almost eighty years old, as if he were some ancient memory of the days when every Highland human had a fein bodyguard and savage battles were fought for Clan Honor, fein to fein.

Fleur's simmering anger sent her thoughts down oft-traveled paths. Fein were such incurable romantics sometimes!

. . . dear, dear old Rva, this must stop; it simply must. You must retire, Mzsee of Mzsees; you should've taken the gray robe decades ago . . . and you must let go of my son!

She sighed, it was hopeless; Chosen had decided to hate his mother and that was that. And this bond he had with the fein, it was so strong! Would she ever break it? Did she even want to? It was too strong for a mere mother to break, or so it seemed after her experience of the last three years. She set her jaw firmly.

. . . my son is not going to be some kind of prophetic Darwin figure here on Fenrille. He's a nineteen-year-old boy who's been living in the woods too long; he's going to learn the ways of his own race . . . She glanced at Chosen in the unfamiliar Midships space wear . . . even if it does mean service in the Space Military . . .

It was better than having him learn to fight with the small kifket, the cub's blade, that was reserved for humans.

The mzsee's lined old face stirred in her memory. "I cannot believe that you would do this. He is the one prophesied long

11

ago, the fein-friend at the end of days. It is the end of times, and he must stay with us and complete his work."

... THE END OF TIMES ... there it was again, the "prophecy" that so excited some fein. She seemed to hear that phrase more and more often, and it was just superstition, almost a rumor. ... my boy is not the fein-friend, he's an ordinary nineteen-year-old who happens to be badly in need of a little human company.

The limousine purred on through light traffic, then merged into the hurrying stream of vehicles moving toward the spaceport.

Bg Rva stared out the window on his side with unfocused eyes, brooding on the loss of the fein that he foresaw so clearly. There was no way to avoid it though. This idea was so horrible that Rva went into a reflexive shirrithee. Chosen felt the big bulk on his left tighten suddenly as the tufted tail twitched where it lay curled over the big thigh, the fur stood on end, and even the old mzsee's ears stood up straight and stiff.

Then the realization that he might never see the mzsee alive again came home and Chosen's throat tightened unbearably. A tear almost squeezed from the sombre eyes he kept trained straight ahead.

The hurrying lights converged in a big open space before the terminal gates. Limos and cars disgorged their occupants. Quite a crowd had formed; it was a big day for the humans of Fenrille.

The pity of it was that neither mother nor father had a scientific background. They couldn't see the potential of Chosen's project. Nobody had ever undertaken a complete biosurvey before, so even the microscopic work would take ten years. His parents couldn't be made to see how important it was for him to stay with the project while Rva lived and could guide him to so much lore.

Instead they were obsessed with this need to have him "humanized," meaning two years in outer space with a couple of thousand void-heads from the Sx Coast training schools. They would be taught how to build space habitats and operate deep-space construction technology.

The prospect apalled Chosen.

Drearily he grabbed his bag, shouldered it, and strode to the check-in. He could hardly bring himself to speak to his mother.

Fortunately the terminal was busy; hundreds of people were spread out on the floor or bunched at the checkpoints. Shuttle flights would be departing all day to the Red Moon Habitat, taking those who wanted to be on hand when the new ship for the Fenrille Space Fleet, the *Gandhi*, arrived. The airport was just as busy with jets bringing in folks from South Town and Coast City and the other smaller coastal settlements.

Thinking about the *Gandhi* brought on the sense of panicky dread again. On top of everything else, they'd ordered him to attend a ghastly formal ceremony as the representative of the Highland Clans. There would even be a formal banquet to attend.

Dotted among the brightly garbed Coastals a few sober Highlanders could be seen, in traditional battledress for the most part. There was even another fein present; the mighty form of Igrak, bodyguard to Ervil Spreak, was approaching. Ervil Spreak himself shouldered through the crowds, and Chosen groaned inwardly.

"Well, young man, good luck," Spreak said, extending a massive rock-hard fist. A rare smile broke those wintry features.

"Good-bye," Chosen said. He flushed momentarily at his inability to respond with anything more intelligent.

For a long moment Chosen embraced Rva, then dutifully kissed his mother before heading for the Departures gate.

"He doesn't seem overly cheerful, I must say," Spreak murmured.

"He's not. He hates everything right now. Including his mother." Fleur winced at the angry hunch to Chosen's shoulders. Sometimes it was hell being a mother. Why were teenagers so difficult? Chosen could hope to live for many centuries, why should two years be so important?

She saw Bg Rva gazing at her mournfully. "Oh, for heaven's sake, Rva. He's my son, he's not the one in your prophecy. You must let go of him."

The ancient fein stared at her in spectral sorrow. For a dreadful moment she thought he might throw his head back and give the death howl. She would die of embarrassment! It was already a spectacle being seen with such an ancient fein. Still wearing weapons and webbing! It was absurd. She resolved to speak to Lavin again about it. Rva must be made to retire.

But there was no death howl; the mzsee simply fell in a half step behind her, his tread measured by long habit to near-human length.

Igrak was an inch taller than Rva, and a green-eye at that, with pale gray fur and an unusual length in the limbs. Rva's old muscles were loose and his belly distended, ample signs of extreme age, but Rva kept a feisty eye on Igrak. Igrak had no reason to give Rva riffchuss.

. . . With the kifket, young green-eye, there are tricks, and then there are other tricks . . .

Igrak nodded however, subtly giving old Rva riffchuss. "Yes, this is the one they still talk of in my valley. Long will your skill be remembered, Rva of the Brelkilks."

Rva grinned broadly at the unexpected compliment. "A green-eye with manners! Such a fein is something we need in Abzen Valley."

Igrak chuckled. "A Spreak fein would need all the friends he could find in Abzen Valley."

They found a place by the big window and watched as the enormous lifter balloons were attached to the shuttle, which looked like a silver bird nestling in the big metal hand of its boosters. The lifters were released and slowly bore the shuttle aloft into a cloudless sky. At twenty-five kilometers the lifters would disengage and vent gas while the boosters cut in and took the shuttle the rest of the way.

Long before then they were back in the limo, and Ervil Spreak had invited Fleur to luncheon for the purpose of discussing the upcoming Chitin conference that she had done so much to organize on the Sx Coast.

Igrak rode in front with the chauffeur and Ervil joined Fleur and Rva in the back while Fleur attempted to reconcile the mzsee to Chosen's departure. "Rva, look," she began, but the sight of the defiance in those big yellow eyes turned her words into the angry ones she had never meant to say. "You know it's way past time you took the gray robe and retired. Is there anyone left of your generation, mzsee? Why even Ny'pupe passed on last year; it is the way of things. You have grown too old, and now it is the way that Chosen must go to be among humans for a while. *Now*, when he's still young enough."

Rva read the assertion of humanness behind the veil of her words and connected it to her choice of a home on the Sx Coast for most of the year. Fleur had returned to the city, leaving her husband and children behind in the Highlands. Of course the children were grown. Chosen being the last, but it was plain that she preferred to be among her own kind now.

"If the prophecy is true," he said, "he will return to us. He will fulfill his great work. It is something that has been given to him to do; he feels such things in ways beyond his years. I know this. I have seen him grow."

Fleur sat back and looked out the window as the car emerged from the tunnels beneath Sx Isle and rode the causeway to Fun Isle. She reflected that Rva probably had seen more of her son than she had these last three years. The guilt made her angry. It wasn't her fault! There was too much important work to be done for her to be stuck way out in Abzen Valley. Her job was here where things counted for the human population.

The big domes on Fun Isle sparkled under the sun, the gardens of Nebuchadnezzar a splash of green beside the water. She looked up for a moment; was that a drive flash, high up and way south? Or just a high cloud catching the sunlight? Trying not to think of her miserable son speeding orbitward, she tried to rediscover the exhilaration she'd known when she first moved back into the city. Where the domes were lit up at night and the crowds moved restlessly on the walkways and by the surf. A human city, alive with the sights and sounds of humanity.

Chosen would come to understand, she resolved that much. He would see that she was right, although it might take a few months. She clung to that idea and turned her thoughts to the Chitin Chemistry Conference that would begin on the following day.

The limo purred down into the access tunnels beneath Fun Isle and turned off below the small but well-fortified dome maintained on the South Point by Clan Spreak.

"Prepare yourself for a surprise, Lady Fundan," Ervil said. He smiled oddly.

In an upstairs reception area hung with Spreak banners and family portraits, the eccentric figure of Dali Spreak was waiting for them.

Dali's bald skull was painted with a pattern of bright yellow flowers and green leaves. Around her withered neck she wore a necklace of large silver Chitin. Her modestly cut tunic continued the yellow floral pattern.

"My dear, dear, dear Lady Fundan, confess to it, you're surprised to see me."

Dali Spreak had not been a young woman when the secret of Chitin proteins was first discovered; she appeared both aged and eternal, with a rich pharamol glow in her skin.

"To tell the truth I'm flabbergasted."

"I haven't been out of Pluqyhat in two centuries and that's the truth, but I must say, I think I've been missing out on a few things. I've noticed any number of young men here who are, shall we say, more interesting than the current crop from the Spreak crèches. I'm beginning to wonder if you haven't got something when you espouse this urban living you're so keen on."

With a tinkling laugh, Dali escorted them to a protected balcony that was screened to keep out the blood-sucking vermin native to Fenrille.

A delightful luncheon of custard timbales, stuffed hens' eggs, and a fresh salad of Highland greens was set before them by servants in Spreak livery of scarlet and black. A chilled white wine was poured, but Ervil scowled and complained about the lack of fresh meat.

"To listen to Ervil, you'd think he was a fein sometimes." She patted Fleur's hand with her ancient paw. "You know, darling, I've been vegetarian for more than a century now."

Fleur reflected that that meant Dali had given up meat about when Fleur had been born. Then she reflected that she too was living beyond the normal human span. Soon she would start to look like them as well, losing her hair and nails. That thought never ceased to shock her somewhat.

"One of these days," Dali continued, "I just know we'll be able to convert even little Ervil."

To hear Ervil described as little Ervil made Fleur want to scream with laughter, but she wisely suppressed the urge. Dali rushed on blithely. "I hear that you've sent your son, I forget his name, to serve in the Space Forces. My dear, I just thought, how dreadful, you never know what sort of contagion he might pick up among the common people."

"Oh, I'm sure he'll survive all right, but it was necessary, to show him something about his own race other than the life he already knows."

"But you also sent him to welcome that woman Chi Lin Wei." Dali's eyes were round in concern.

"Indeed," rumbled Ervil Spreak, "that's a heavy responsibility to place on the shoulders of one so young. The woman is said to be very dangerous. Even her father is afraid of her."

"Well, I don't think she'll be able to do that much to Chosen. He's a Fundan, and those Fundans are stubborn types. Besides, unless Chi Lin Wei finds fenro-botany the most stimulating subject in the universe, she's not going to be able to keep up with him."

Ervil had a thin, unenthusiastic smile. "I think I might be a good enough judge of Fundan stubbornness. She may yet weave some subtle web around him and pry from him secrets of our defenses."

Fleur sipped the wine, a Space Colony chardonnay of considerable elegance, and reflected that however isolated Dali Spreak was in Pluqyhat, she still knew how to live very well.

"Well, you see she might find that very difficult because Chosen is what the fein call a 'clean blade.' He knows nothing that can harm us. In addition he will show off one of the best

16

facets of Fenrille—he's young, he's intelligent, and he's passionate about his beliefs. What could be better in a young man?"

"Bah, she will exercise unusual witcheries, you mark my words. But one other thing still bothers me. Why hold this meeting in orbital space anyway? Why not down on the ground where we can enforce security?"

"Because it will please the Space Service, and we need to remember their morale. We have people training up there to spend the rest of their lives building space habitats. Right now life isn't so comfortable off-world; it won't be for ten years or more, so it's important for us to remember Admiral Ursk and to make these ceremonial gestures."

Fleur turned to Dali hoping for support but found her equally concerned.

"Chi Lin Wei is a practitioner of the Maza method. I pray we will not come to regret what you have done."

Fleur felt a slight tremor at the mention of that ancient, terrible name.

"Such things have been forbidden for a thousand years. There is no more Maza. I know, I was raised on Earth."

Dali shrugged impatiently. "My dear, you are not the only one with lines to information from Earth. The awful science still lives on, hidden, but it is still alive, and this woman brings it to us."

Fleur wanted to scoff but instead she diplomatically changed the subject. "At the conference tomorrow, will you be wanting to address the opening meeting?"

Dali seemed to come slowly out of a trance. "Yes, I will." She clapped her hands and a servant brought her a bowl of ice water in which she placed her feet.

"Eating with one's feet nice and cold, it's wonderful, a boon to the digestion, my dear, you should try it."

Fleur giggled. The ancient Spreak crone was a paranoid elitist, but she was irresistibly charming too.

"Actually I did intend to ask you if I might speak, because I have an idea I would like to put to the conference as a whole. I propose that we select some of the very best current projects here on the Sx Coast and move them to our facilities in the Highlands. We've got the best laboratories—I'm talking about Spreak Tower or Ghotaw Mountain now—but the best young scientists are working down here in miserable, cramped conditions."

Ervil, till then semisomnolent at the other end of the table sat up with a jerk. Fleur was wide-eyed.

"Why, that's a wonderful idea, Dali! I think we should most definitely book you to speak at the opening meeting."

"What?" growled Ervil. Dali held a hand up in his direction.

"Now, Ervil, I've spoken to Dame Judith about this, and she's all for it, so it's not just one old woman's whimsy. Spreak Council will review it. I've been assured of a full hearing."

Ervil spluttered. "Are you quite mad? You want to let Coastal scum loose inside Spreak facilities?"

Dali beamed. "It's no good, Ervil. The war is over. There hasn't been any Coastal raiding in fifty years, nor will there be any more. It's time we worked together to try and achieve a breakthrough in the Chitin problem."

Ervil controlled himself with an effort. "They are our enemies, and they always will be. You fail to understand the obvious conflict between our interest and theirs."

"But Ervil," Fleur broke in, "the Arizel ended the wars. Everybody knows that it would be racial suicide to begin them again. The Arizel would destroy the home system."

"The aliens will not return again unless there is tree damage in the great forest. If we who now control the Chitin were to be replaced but no damage was done to the trees then the Arizel would not return."

"But you forget that we disarmed the Coastals. How would they kill us?"

Ervil's smile seemed carved from ice. "Disarmed? So it is said. Personally I have my doubts about that. But however it may be, when the prize is as tempting as eternal life, someone will try for it. That is human nature. So I say *never* let down your guard. Listen to me, Lady Fundan, for this is vital if you intend to live into your third or fourth century."

"Well, you're probably right, Ervil, but let's not be too paranoid, huh?"

"Ervil, this is my lunch," Dali broke in. "You're not to spoil it with an argument. There'll be plenty of time for an argument in Spreak Council, and you'll have your chance then."

Ervil leveled a gaze of iron at them over his wineglass. Dali smiled and started telling Fleur about a new hybrid vine flower she was raising. Fleur sipped wine while reflecting that a seat at the next Spreak Clan Council would be a red-hot ticket.

4

THE PERIOD OF ACCELERATION THAT BEGAN WHEN THE LIFTERS let go wasn't nearly as bad as predicted, but once the shuttle had left the atmosphere the flight lengthened into boredom. For a while Chosen stared out at the blue-green disk of Fenrille as it slowly dwindled behind them. Then he switched to the view of the little Red Moon shown on the main-cabin primary screen. But an elliptical piece of reddish rock studded with habitat windows was of limited interest to Chosen. Something about it symbolized space travel to him; it was just a dead rock infested with human beings who had tunneled out its core. He longed to be home.

The hours dragged by. Gradually the tedium undercut the tension that had stretched his nerves for several weeks, and soon he was in a deep sleep, the best he'd had in days. His dreams began with a replay in slow motion of that dreadful interview with Father. Lavin's study, a crowded room on the gunnery floor at Cracked Rock. Outside the sun sparkled on distant Mithiliwax woods. Far beyond stood the mountains, banded with snow. Chosen asked to be allowed to stay and attend the Chitin training course. But over and over again he saw Lavin pronounce the dreaded numbers. He'd scored 77 percent on the trial exam. Much too low; no one with less than 90 percent would ever be accepted by a Highland Chitin group; the risks involved in harvesting the carnivorous insect were just too great.

The dream shifted however... it was midmorning on the Gleatara trail up above Bitaraf. Chosen rode his mare, Silver, so surefooted she could follow the gzan way up the brush draws above the bluffs. The sound of the river below filled the air; Chitin were visible foraging on the trees. The hunters followed the trail of an elderly female gzan, a gaunt old lady whose time had come. Taking her flesh back to camp would be a mercy on her since she was probably half-blind and her teeth would be worn down to stubs.

Gani Rva was ahead on foot. He signaled them into a thicket

by the side of the trail. "Look here, the old one's spoor. She goes down to the water by a secret way." Very careful observation divulged the telltale signs of the recent passage of a ton of gzan, even a crafty old one who used habitual skill to hide such evidence. They dismounted, Chosen had his crossbow out, a bolt in place. Down a tortuous trail strewn with loose stones, they tracked her. She led them through dense tangles of glob glob and thorn vine. It was hot work and they were all breathing hard when they reached the bottom. Then a sound turned their heads to the trail above. A wheezy *whaunk* sounded from the furtive gzan! She'd tricked them, doubling back somehow. They stared at each other, fein almost in shirrithee; then Gani doubled over in explosive laughter, instantly followed by everyone else.

Chosen slept on as the shuttle crept up on the Red Moon. The first movie of the flight was shown, a video from Earth about a highly emotional female executive with damaged genes trying to obtain a gene transplant from her male friend.

A roboserve prowled the aisles, and when Chosen did awake at last he ordered a soft drink and sat sipping it while the Red Moon expanded on screen until they had a fine detailed shot of the central habitation windows, huge octagons that looked like immense insectal eyes.

The moon itself was ringed with orbiting agricultural satellites and connected via a fifty-kilometer service channel to a fusion reaction chamber. In addition large solar cell arrays orbited beside the Red Moon and bathed parts of the surface with microwave energy. The little moon had become convenient radiation shielding for the fifty thousand wealthy people who inhabited it.

A morose mood settled over Chosen, and he finished his drink while reflecting bitterly on the recent passage of events as the shuttle sank toward the docking structure, a barrel-shaped protuberance that jutted out of the habitat like some colossal bird's beak.

Everyone disembarked and milled around in the reception concourse. Chosen, along with most of the shuttle passengers, was due to reembark on another shuttle within a couple of hours, then would head out to rendezvous with the new ship from Earth, the WGS *Gandhi*.

Briefly he strolled around the viewing gallery. The docking bay was at the neck of the cone-shaped habitat. For 360 degrees the designer-curved paths wound into the parkland. A million windows glittered like diamond dust amid the green. To kill some time he watched a tourist video that gave a tour of Red

20

Moon Habitat. But the relaxed way of life in the tiny, ultraexpensive condos seemed horrifyingly restricted and tame to Chosen. Even stranger to him was the statistic that fully a third of the wealthy elite who lived there were Highland Clansfolk.

Tourists were not encouraged to leave the low-gravity cone-hub around the docking structures. Those who paid megarents for life on the Red Moon didn't want what privacy there was diluted any further.

Since Chosen didn't feel like visiting the traditional tourist district, with the usual saloons, whorehouses, and casinos designed to extract cash from visitors, there wasn't much else to do but sit out in the Concourse Bar and sip drinks and watch the cheerful hordes of midship-suited trainees who were also on their way to the *Gandhi*. Most of them would be going on to the *Austerlitz* and after a year to the habitat construction brigades in the L4 and L5 points of the Fenro–Pale Moon System. Within the next half century it was intended to move most of the human population on Fenrille off-planet and into gigahabitats, each with a million or more inhabitants.

The faces of the young men and women about him were flushed with excitement. Most were escaping the dead-end existence of the Coastal cities. They had careers, salaries, even life plans of Agunol or Optimol, the popular longevity drugs, to look forward to.

Noisily they drank beer, got a little drunk, and toasted one another and various figures of fun from the training schools they'd left behind on the Sx Coast.

Finally they were called to the new shuttle and reboarded. Chosen found himself seated behind a boisterous group of youths intended for a construction battalion. He watched their frolics with little enthusiasm. It all seemed brutally childish.

The shuttle pushed off with a sudden jolt from the attitude rockets, then oriented itself before engaging the boosters and—this being a military flight now—set off at three gee for the rendezvous point with *Gandhi*.

The gee soon reduced the frolicsome to groans and kept everyone firmly in their seats. When the acceleration finally cut out there was no ship spin to give them any gravity, and thus they floated on toward their destiny.

An orange light flashed at the side of the game screen. The slender Chinese woman flicked on a subsidiary monitor tuned to the ship's news channel. A small shuttle vessel was being taken aboard the *Gandhi*. She froze the game action, watched,

21

almost spellbound for a few moments, as the shuttle passengers disembarked.

At last . . . the thought washed through her mind almost like a physical force. The long, long journey was over, and she was finally within reach of the new planet.

Father would never be able to kill her now.

She turned back to the game and had the moves recorded. Her attempt at the difficult fifth-subset gambit had been well executed; the computer had been on the defensive for the rest of the game. No matter what it had done, her patterns remained; its screen modules could not shake her grip.

She rose and began to dress in front of the mirror, pausing a moment to examine her slender body with searching eyes. The pharamol glow was spreading; she could see it clearly in the vein behind her left knee. So far, though, the horror had yet to spread to her face.

The body cult tao ran through her mind. LOVE THE BODY, BODY LOVE; CONTROL THE BODY, BODY LOVE; THROUGH THE GOOD BODY IS LIFE, BODY LIFE. . . .

She put on a scarlet dress in Japanese silk with sheer stockings and matching shoes.

The meeting ahead would be the most important of her life, her first contact with the rulers of her new world. Those that she must cajole, humor, and—eventually—dominate. This was a meeting she had prepared for, a day when she must use all her skill and charm. She could not fail!

Minutes later she emerged from her suite and rode the tube to the hospitality lounge surrounded by her retinue of six cloned Chinese males.

In the lounge the newly arrived representatives of Fenrille were already surrounded by senior *Gandhi* personnel. Chi Lin Wei looked around for the Highland Clan representative; she expected some hoary chieftain in one of those incredible costumes of jewelry, knives, and guns that she'd seen so often in video. But no such fantastic chieftain was in sight. Instead, to her astonishment, a stripling with scarcely a beard on his chin pushed forward through the throng and thrust a hand out toward her before baring white teeth in a smile.

"Hello there, you must be Chi Lin Wei," the apparition announced cheerfully as it gave her hand a firm shake. "My name is Fundan, Chosen Fundan."

Since she made no signal, her bodyguards let him live, but they all rose onto the balls of their feet and readied themselves. There was a moment of silence. Chi Lin Wei's stunned surprise must have been obvious, for the boy bent closer to her and whispered, "I'm sorry about this. It wasn't my idea, I can tell you."

"Yes." She said, bewildered, "Yes, I'm sure it wasn't."

A swarm of questions buzzed in her mind.

Who was this forthright youth? And what did his appearance augur? What lay behind this development? Was this the opening move in the game then?

He was so young. So youthful as to almost seem to be some kind of offering to the altar of Maza. The thought almost made her giggle hysterically.

Then she realized he wore midship uniform and she understood at once. Here was a princeling en route for a tour of duty in the space fleet.

Was this then just an insult? Or a message too subtle for her to read? Of course the boy would know nothing of use to her. An innocent beyond her wiles? It was a baffling development. She would have to reconsider her approach.

An orderly appeared with champagne, but before they could take glasses, one of her clones dropped small floating devices into them. He gave Chosen a beaming smile and said in a guttural rasp, "Ah, very good, everything is fine."

Chosen raised an eyebrow at such a precaution, but nobody else commented, so he raised his glass and tasted the wine. It was very pleasant indeed. He had another glass. He toasted Chi Lin Wei rather clumsily, going on too long, ending in some confusion, and then felt forced to confess.

"I'm not really very experienced in this kind of thing, actually. This was Mother's idea. They all insisted because none of them wanted to come or something. Mother said it would give me experience, but whether it's the kind I actually want or not I couldn't say. I was quite happy, you see, where I was." He felt terribly lame and inappropriate suddenly.

Chi Lin Wei heard this gabble but did not understand it or care to. But her confusion was forgotten in an instant as two tall figures, in white uniforms with caps bearing scarlet clusters, loomed over them. They saluted, and Chosen returned the salute, feeling ridiculous. Then he felt the eyes upon him. There was a peculiar intensity to the lean faces and unnaturally bright eyes.

"Space Captain Mohod," the darker one said, "Captain Yades," the other.

"Welcome aboard the WGS *Gandhi*, Messire Fundan." Mohod extended a big hand sheathed in skin flesh. It was dry to the touch, though with a hint of great strength.

23

"We understand you're going to the old *Austerlitz* for a tour of duty. I served on a sister ship of hers, the old *Granicus*, a real two-speed tub." Yades's bright blue eyes were set too far apart; his artificial face danced to an inhuman rhythm. Seeing Chosen's confusion he grinned. "Two speeds, messire, which means basically on or off." The captains laughed, wise to the suffering of acceleration in military ships. Chosen managed a smile. "Yes, uh, sir."

Captain Mohod seized the opportunity to flatter the lady Wei once more, as he had done assiduously since their first meeting. Not that it had done him any good, since Chi Lin Wei had a deep horror of all the genetic monstrosities that came out of the gene banks of Earth's military.

However, since Mohod was well connected with the High Command, she listened patiently, with just a hint of tightness around her mouth, as the captain outlined another ludicrous and insulting scheme—proposing, in fact, incredibly—that she should accompany him on some tour of the sights of the new planet.

Of course in the home system he would not have dared breathe a word of connection to her, but in the Beni System he freely insulted her! Yet he was well connected, with Commander Tiax among others. She tried to smile indulgently, though it was very hard.

Mohod's eyes seemed to bulge out of a massive, square head. Chi Lin Wei repressed a shudder. The Chinese clones stared straight ahead, eyes like bullets. The insult was unimaginable, but she allowed no more reaction than a widening of the eyes. That this *insect* could think she would entertain sexual thoughts concerning it or any of its kind was simply revolting. She had to take a few deep breaths; the body tao ran through her mind;— LOVE THE BODY, CALM THE BODY— No trace of her real feelings appeared on her face, although Chosen could feel a tremendous tension around her.

Chi Lin Wei was far too wise to make the mistakes that Yades sought to force. She knew him for Plutonian Military Intelligence, had known since the first day aboard the *Gandhi* when Yu Zhao had traced the bug-net in her quarters to a console in Yades's Admin section. But she remained confident that he did not know that she knew that for instance, he was recording the entire scene with two miniature camera systems hidden on his person and focused from optic fiber lenses hidden in the fabric of his suit. Moreover she knew that in her new solar system she was powerless initially. All that lay between her and random

24

death were her own wits and her faithful Yu Zhao clones. So long had Yu Zhao served her, generation unto generation, they were almost as one, she and they.

"Captain, thank you for your invitation. So kind of you, but I think I will be taking a long rest in my new home before I do any traveling."

Yades turned to Chosen. "Actually I'm a lot less interested in the exotic cities of the south coast than the fishing. I hear great things about the big permiads—a helluva game fish by all accounts."

Mohod snorted. "What, man, you'd rather have fish than the sensual wonders of the most sinful planet in the human realm?"

"You can have the sinful planet, Abel Mohod, just give me a good strong boat and enough line for those permiads. Though I've a hankering to get in some hunting too."

Mohod smiled apologetically. "I'm afraid my friend Captain Yades is, ah, a little atavistic in these things."

Yades grinned good-humoredly. "The hunt is part of the primal human experience. You should try it sometime, Modod. Get out from the senso parlor for a change."

Chi Lin Wei almost smiled, then said in a cool voice, "Well, I've heard all about the senso parlors on the Sx Coast, and I'm sure Captain Mohod will be adequately entertained."

Mohod became quite agitated. *A superb piece of acting* Chi Lin Wei thought.

"Madame Wei, I assure you I won't be spending all my time in the senso parlors. My friend uses an old recollection to tinge my record somewhat too colorfully. In fact I am looking forward to the natural sights. There are mountains higher than any on Earth, great rivers, ocean cliffs thousands of feet high."

Chi Lin Wei allowed a tiny smile. Encouraged, Mohod rolled on. "In fact, there are some extraordinary human-built sights as well. The Highland clans have fortress palaces that are unique in the human realm for scale and delicacy. Some of them are open to the paying public now, since the days of warfare are long over. Then there's the giant green cross, built by an early colonist. The thing is two kilometers high but completely covered in foliage. There are cliff cities, the beautiful towers of the Surf Rocks. And, of course, there's the Great Wall, on the Sx Coast, two kilometers long and three hundred meters high. I'm booked on a tour that includes all of these."

"Goodness, Captain Mohod, so many wonders might exhaust one. You mustn't become blasé about our new world too soon; save some of the sights for later. I think it's a mistake to try to cover too many things at one time. For myself I prescribe a long rest in warm, sunny conditions, preferably near the sea. This flight has been extremely long and arduous."

"Well, madam, should you stay on the Sx Coast you'll see the Wall yourself probably; it's one of the man-made wonders of the universe they say. Took centuries to build."

She turned to Chosen for confirmation. "Tell me, what is this wall? I have seen a picture of it, a very big wall."

"That is the Woodwose Wall. It cuts off the Elefelas Peninsula and keeps the Woodwose out."

"Ah!" Chi Lin Wei's face became animated. "The Woodwose monsters, they still live, then."

"They certainly do." Chosen nodded.

"Isn't it amazing. Human settlement here for five centuries and there are still these monsters roaming around." Mohod spread his hands. Chosen did not find it amazing in the slightest.

Captain Yades had a question however. "Tell me, young man, do they still hunt the monsters? Perhaps when we've finished with those big permiads we'll take a crack at a Woodwose."

Yades grinned down at him. "In fact we might even need a guide for an outing like that. I don't know what it would take; we could pull some rank perhaps—"

"No, they don't hunt them," Chosen said hurriedly. "It was stopped fifty years ago; it was—" He struggled for the right word. "—stupid."

Mohod raised an eyebrow.

"Stupid?" barked Yades. "But why do you say that? Surely when a creature is as dangerous as they say the Woodwose is, it's a good thing to hunt it to keep the numbers down, thin out the herds. And besides, the danger makes the hunt more interesting, what! Eh?" He hunched over to hear Chosen's response.

"Well, sir, because of the extreme danger and because the animal is hardly difficult to hunt. It comes to find you, really; they are the 'mouths of the trees.'" Chosen struggled to explain, knowing it was hopeless.

"You see, it's a cycle we have very little understanding of. As you might imagine, it is not easy to research. A lot of those that used to hunt the Woodwose wound up in Woodwose guts. They are not animals as human science is accustomed to thinking of the term."

Yades seemed to smile. "Well, anything that moves can be shot, and if it's shot correctly, it'll be dead, wouldn't you agree. So I can't see why these monsters are so dangerous."

"Well, sir, before you go off to hunt the Woodwose, I beg

you to research the creature thoroughly. There are no Woodwose in the Highlands; the air's too thin, though not for humans and fein. Which is why our colony survived in the end."

Mohod shrugged expansively. "Well, anyway this wall is quite something, apparently; not only is it huge, but it was built over several centuries by the colonists. It's on our itinerary for the week we're in the Sx Coast itself."

Chi Lin Wei allowed another smile. "Why is the wall so big—hundreds of meters, that sounds excessive."

Mohod nodded, lips puckered. "Does, doesn't it. I understand it's one of the largest engineering projects ever undertaken on an Earthlike world. They say it's so high it completely blocks out the sunlight for the slum neighborhoods that are closest to it."

Chi Lin Wei expressed surprise, looked to Chosen for a moment. Observed the concern that furrowed his brow. He seemed an intense young man, wound up about some inner spring. She wondered what it would be like to release it. "Why does it have to be so high?" she said.

They both looked at him. Chosen shrugged.

"I'm afraid it is difficult for you to comprehend how dangerous Woodwose actually are until you've seen one. You know that wall is electrified. They run fifty thousand volts into it sometimes to burn a stubborn one off."

"But why do the creatures do it—why such fanaticism?"

He shrugged. "It's their nature, their instinct. They see humans as unregistered tree pests. The Woodwose exist to destroy tree pests."

Chi Lin Wei wore a puzzled expression. "But I thought I saw something about this. There is no longer any effort made to interfere in their ecosystem. The monsters protect their sacred trees. Since we no longer threaten their trees, why should they want to kill us?"

He smiled. "This is not an area of scientific concern that has seen much progress. Nor is it very popular. More people prefer to work in longevity chemistry than to seek answers from the Woodwose."

She laughed lightly. "But the Woodwose, it is such an ugly thing! I never saw anything that ugly before."

The six Chinese men laughed in unison with Chi Lin Wei. Chosen smiled mirthlessly at Space Captain Yades.

"Ugly or not, they still treat humans as tree pests. Nor are they unintelligent; they should not be underestimated."

"How awful." Chi Lin Wei wrinkled her nose.

"It is easy to avoid such a fate, of course. Just stay out of the fidnemed, the great forest. That is the preserve of the Arizel and their treetenders, the Woodwose. They do not welcome intruders."

Mohod snorted. "Amazing. Are the Highlanders all like this?"

Chi Lin Wei smiled at Chosen enigmatically. "I still don't see why these dangerous vermin weren't destroyed. Or at least put under restrictions," she said firmly.

Chosen struggled to find yet another way to explain but saw that the visitors could not yet properly understand their new world. They had yet to step out of the air-conditioning into the brutal slap of a summer day on the Sx Coast. Or smell the tropic breath of the giant continent, that odd dank stench that blew in from the swamps. They had seen the forest only on video, they had not appreciated the true scale of things.

Yades laughed loudly once again.

"Well, I guess I don't care what kind of weird animals infest the land. I'm overdue for some time in a boat on the ocean with a fishing line out and some bait on the hook. The big permiads *are* good game fish?"

Chosen nodded. "They have that reputation, yes, sir."

"They get up to a thousand kilos, don't they?" said Yades as if he were anxious lest the alien fishes of this new world should prove less of a challenge than those of Earth.

"I believe they get even larger, in the deep ocean. They're a very successful species—they have adapted to fresh water, so they're in all the big rivers too."

Yades mimed the moment of truth, holding his rod with his eyes on the water monster thrashing on the surface.

Chosen struggled to find a smile.

Later when Mohod and Yades had moved away, he muttered to Chi Lin Wei, "I hope I didn't make a fool of myself. I don't know much about this sort of thing at all." Seeing her frown, he rushed on, "I think it was because my mother's schedule is so crowded right now and nobody else would volunteer; since I was coming this way anyway, they decided I could handle the formal business as well."

. . . And I am supposed to accept such dismissive treatment with a smile and a curtsey, am I? . . . Chi Lin Wei beamed radiantly nonetheless. "Well, I must admit that you were a bit of a surprise. I think I expected some Methuselah of five hundred, but I'm charmed and delighted nonetheless. How clever of your mother to have sent you to enliven this dreadfully dull formal event. Here you are in the flower of youth to represent the young human

28

colony, and I, who am so old, must represent the old world and all its billions of people."

Chosen tried but could not see any marks of age on Chi Lin Wei. She seemed perfectly preserved, although he knew that she was at least two hundred years old and must be wearing a wig and false nails.

More *Gandhi* personnel were introduced, a blizzard of names that Chosen soon lost all track of. Chi Lin Wei, however, continued to hover close at hand, and several times he caught her looking at him with rather speculative eyes. Or so it seemed. It left him a little uncomfortable.

Eventually the introductions were over and everyone adjourned to their suites and cabins to prepare for the formal banquet, which would be held in the Main Mess Hall.

Chosen followed the instructions from his key and wandered seemingly endless corridors of neutral blue-gray filled with cool, odorless air and permeated by a dim, distant hum. Eventually the key whined momentarily and a door slid open. Inside was his tube, three meters wide and five deep, and claustrophobia sent him to the Senso module. One button turned on the exterior view from the ship's navigation scopes—a blaze of star fields that left him gaping. The resolution was very good, much better quality than any Fenrille Senso system he'd ever seen. He tried several combinations and settled on a terrestrial forest scene. So different and yet so similar to home. The greens were lighter, and instead of Fenrille's turquoise skies Earth's was pale blue. He roused himself after a while and showered in the ultrasonic microstall then dug out a clean undersuit. This would be a formal ceremony and required a crisp, new midship uniform that was even more uncomfortable and strange than the midships flight suit. Presently the short-haired white-and-blue-clad military youth in the mirror seemed like someone else, not the Chosen that Chosen Fundan knew.

All too soon, however, the chime sounded, summoning everyone to the Main Mess Hall. There were assembled most of the thousand-strong crew, plus representatives of the Space Marines and the Fenrille VIPs. Chosen endured a dreadful moment when he was introduced to the throng by Space Admiral Ursk. He was seated on the high table between an enormous Space Marine colonel and one of Chi Lin Wei's cloned security men. Chi Lin Wei herself was seated almost opposite.

A glass of white wine was set before him, and Chosen gulped it down. It helped his nerves considerably, so he gladly accepted another from the uniformed midships waiting on the tables.

He noticed something strange about the service personnel around him. Those from the *Gandhi* had all undergone extensive plastic surgery to remove the red nodules and inhuman facial planes of acceleration-resistant space crew. The representatives from the Fenrille Fleet, who had shipped out of the Earth system aboard the *Gagarin* more than a century before *Gandhi*, retained the strange crab-white skin color and the red nodules that clustered around the eyes and stippled the flat cheeks.

The newcomers wore cosmetics and strove to attain a close-to-natural human appearance. They clearly looked down on the *Gagarin* officers, and the *Gagarin* officers weren't taking it very well.

The first course, a clear soup, was served. Since the *Gandhi* people had yet to acclimatize to Fenrille foods, a process that would take some as long as ten years, the banquet was necessarily made from rather bland, neutral synthetics that could be digested by Fenrille systems as well as the *Gandhi* crew.

By the main course, a dish of rather heavy crepes stuffed with a mushroom-flavor sauce, Chosen was hankering for a gzan chop rubbed with herbs and roasted on a spit over the fire. He drank more wine and kept a low profile.

The conversation around him turned mainly on the news from Earth and the home system. Despite the enormous advances in communications derived from the FTL message beam through the black hole singularity A0441, the gulf between the stars still left the people on Fenrille with the sense of being a very, very distant province of humanity. Which indeed they were, being dozens of light years further out than any other human settlement. News from the home world came, but it was censored at the source and lacked the spicy details that were now eagerly sought.

Quermwyere, the corpulent banker, was seated near Chi Lin Wei, and when an opening in the conversation appeared, he turned to her. "Lady Wei, forgive me, but would you please tell us what really happened in that meeting of the Inner Buro that your father convened shortly before you left the system? It was an extraordinary meeting in many respects, we've heard, but the details are so vague and hard to understand. Do please enlighten us?"

Chi Lin Wei seethed below the surface, the odious fool! To ask such a question in a public place! She was appalled. With a stare calculated to convey her indignation and contempt, she replied coolly.

"Why, I thought everyone knew what happened. Chairman Wei decided that a new stratum of the command economy was required. The greenhouse effect has intensified; crop levels have been falling lately. The Inner Buro was made so enthusiastic by the chairman's bold new policy that it constituted itself into an agricultural planning committee on the spot."

Quermwyere sipped his wine and smiled briefly before speaking.

"I had also heard that Ruud Urm, the Transcaucasian party chief, disappeared mysteriously during the first session and the city of New Baghdad was put under indefinite curfew. In fact it's said that no one has been allowed out of there since."

Chi Lin Wei's eyebrows knitted slightly. Did this fool seek her enmity? He could have it . . . she had had enemies before this . . . only her father survived.

"I think it most unwise to repeat rumors like this. It's always the same." She sighed and turned to Chosen. "The rumors begin in the Caucasian Congresses and then spread from there. These remnants of the old Caucasian world domination are chronically disaffected. They chafe under the restraints imposed by the needs of the entire planet and the development of the backward regions. Do you realize, messire, that there are still billions living in the direst poverty? And the terrestrial economy has been flat for decades due to the pressure on agriculture.

"But it is true that a curfew was laid on New Baghdad. Chairman Wei moved the political apparatus to the new capital at Shanghai. Troublesome criminal elements, inspired again by the Caucasian groups, had fomented disorder. Naturally the chairman was forced to act decisively."

Quermwyere chuckled heavily and sloshed more wine down his capacious throat. "So those poor devils formed an agricultural committee, did they?" He nudged Major Brackt and winked at Chosen. "Well, I have a pretty good idea where they may be carrying out their research. And it seems that New Baghdad was indeed nuked, along with Denver and some other American places. The chairman retains his control of the situation however; that much is clear."

He laughed again, clearly to the discomfort of Brackt and the extreme displeasure of Chi Lin Wei.

The situation was saved by the tapping of wineglasses and the beginning of the speeches and formal ceremonies. Captain Mohod was first, a relatively brief welcoming speech. Admiral Ursk followed, at much greater length, detailing the projects already underway in the Fenrille system. *Gandhi*'s Orders of Commission in the Fenrille Fleet and a salute to the new planet of allegiance followed. Then individual representatives went up

31

to give short speeches of welcome. The voices droned on; Chosen drank more wine and tried to listen but soon found his attention wandering.

Chi Lin Wei caught his eye. A moment later her security man seated next to him gave him a scrap of paper with a message written in a fine, tiny hand.

"This is horribly boring! If you would like to see them, I could show you the samples of Terrestrial life-forms that we have brought for the new habitats. The fish in particular are very fine."

Chosen was half out of his chair before rational thought took hold, but he simply filled his wineglass again and joined Chi Lin Wei in slipping away not very surreptitiously.

Behind her the Chinese clone males wore wolfish smiles. They could not suppress their satisfaction. The calf boy was a mistake after all . . . he was about to be devoured.

Sobered by this turn of events, Quermwyere made a small moue of disapproval. He'd enjoyed goading the daughter of great Chairman Wei, but he sensed the power in her and planned to make peace with her at the earliest opportunity. However he couldn't help feeling that Fleur Fundan had made a terrible mistake here.

The banquet continued, but the corpulent banker felt little inclined to enjoy his dessert. That woman had a face designed like a feminine weapon, carefully perfected by the best surgeons on Earth. She was the most beautiful creature Quermwyere had ever seen—imagined for that matter. The boy was a normal young male. The consequences seemed all too obvious. Quermwyere saw Admiral Ursk's frown.

"A damned foolish move if you ask me, Admiral," he said with a conspiratorial wink.

Ursk's eery, almost inhuman, face crinkled as if sheathed in thick plastic. "I agree, it is most unfortunate. I wonder what they thought they were doing sending a child on this mission."

However, despite Quermwyere's apprehensions, Chosen was perfectly safe. In Chi Lin Wei's quarters he was raptly admiring a dozen freshwater trout as they circled one another in a large rectangular tank. In the next were African tilapia, the most prolific food fish of all.

Chi Lin Wei had discovered that she had a fanatic on her hands. A young biologist aristocrat. She struggled to keep up with the flow of speculations that came to him as he excitedly ran up and down between the fish tanks.

Beyond the fish were cages and terrariums with specimens for a zoo to be built on one of the new habitats.

"We brought the sperm and ova of many other creatures, of course, but these are some that we decided to transport as they were."

One item that attracted Chosen instantly was a termite nest, sandwiched between sheets of glass. He observed the long-snouted soldiers grouped about the entrances to the nest.

"Ah—*Nasutitermes kempae*, I believe. The soldiers are blind. They fire drops of an adhesive onto intruders from the nasal proboscises and then bite them to death." He crouched down by the glass to look along a gallery that led to the queen chamber and the brood section.

"Of course this is a tiny little nest compared to even an immature Chitin nest, but then the individual termites are smaller than Chitin. Chitin developed an improved insect respiration system, small valves having evolved to suck air into the animal. This has allowed for much greater efficiency and a larger size."

He gave her a serious look. "Of course the bio system of Fenrille is not purely natural. We believe that many of the species are not native to Fenrille. We know the Chitin is not; indeed we have an enormous amount of work to do just in assaying what forms are native and what are imported."

He turned back to the glass-walled nest. "A primitive social insect, this is fascinating. All depends here on the breeding unit."

Chi Lin Wei feigned a degree of interest.

"Is this not the case with all social insects?"

"Not so with the Chitin, for after the early stages the Chitin Vizier Mass takes over the direction of the nest. The Vizier are thought to be evolved from a sterile drone class, but no one is entirely sure."

"Then a Chitin nest would look down on these termites?"

He laughed, gestured with the wineglass. "Perhaps, but perhaps they would see this nest the way we might see a primitive hunter-gatherer society of humans, or . . ." He groped a moment. "Perhaps a better analogy would be that of fairies, elves from our mythic past, viewed from a degenerate, once-civilized society."

She raised an eyebrow. And how then did Chosen view his own people, the exotic small population of Highlanders descended from the earliest Chitin talkers? But so far she hadn't heard a word out of him that didn't concern fish or insects.

A servant brought brandy, and Chosen gulped it down and enjoyed the warmth it produced in his belly. He fumbled holo slides into her projector and talked about the plants and animals they displayed for him. Chi Lin Wei sat close and replied in a soft, pleasant voice, her eyes seeming to feed on his words. The young professor grew expansive with the brandy.

There was so much to be done! Even the microscopy would take ten years! But the biosurvey would be completed; he would return and take up where he'd been forced to leave off. They wouldn't beat him. Not even with a two-year break for the military.

At some point he realized that the brandy was gone and so was he. He could barely stand. He'd flipped from the lively animation of mania to the quiet gloom of drunk deep time.

He flopped down beside Chi Lin Wei on the pink silk bed-cover. "Whoo, got to settle down now."

"Yes, that sounds like a good idea to me," she agreed.

He was desperately miserable. She was very beautiful. Dimly he had wondered to himself; now he turned to her trying to frame a question.

She smiled. "I know," she said. "I can feel the sadness in you. You hate what they've done to you."

He did hate it, but there was something awfully wrong in the pit of his stomach just then, and it suddenly would brook no resistance. He had a spasm, bent forward, and vomited on her shoes.

5

It was late summer on the Sx Coast, and in the early evening the domes shimmered in the heat haze. Rinus Van Relt gazed out the window onto the calm waters of the Irurupup Delta. Far away across those gold-tinged waves, the dismal mire of the Dinge spread across the horizon.

This was fly season. The horrible little black-and-red blood-suckers were abroad in great numbers. Three of them were soaking up the ebbing sunlight on the outside of the window. Van Relt saw them and was thankful they weren't inside.

. . . this was always the worst time of all down in the Sx Coast slums in Deathwish and Hellbreath, places where there wasn't even air conditioning. Van Relt had seen the bottom, back in the worst days for ex-war band commanders when the Highland clans had arrived in strength and proclaimed the Peace of the Arizel tki Fenrille. He'd spent years in Deathwish, in those rooms where you had to fight down the alien vermin in the heat. Seen people down with spruip fungus from a fly bite go berserk, dying in a frothing frenzy . . . the old memories made him shiver.

He'd been saved from that though, and he remained grateful for it.

Then the slight itch began again in his remaining testicle. The parasite was waking up again; time was running short. He was tempted to ring the bell once more, but he refrained long enough and the door opened at last thus saving him a shred of dignity.

A housemaid in little more than a protective sash beckoned him in. Her back was covered in thin welts, some of them fresh.

As before, Van Relt's senses swam in the atmosphere of rooms where a disorienting Senso operated constantly. A dim booming voice droned on and on somewhere, singing an ancient fein lay. Heavy hangings blocked out the sunlight; the scent of garjal hung in the still air.

A pair of enormous fein warriors, Persimpilgas and Herver, guarded the inner door. They fixed him with unblinking eyes until at an invisible signal they dropped their kifkets to their sides and looked up past his head.

A door opened slightly; a warm breath of air redolent with the ugly stench of burnt goom roots struck Van Relt. The smell brought a wave of relief, and he stiffened his back and straightened his cap.

. . . he makes the antidote, so I am spared once more . . .

He went on, led by another near-naked housemaid through a black veil and a Senso net that scanned for weapons. Beyond that was another veil and a room that was much darker, like an alchemist's cave. Goom root smoke filled the air. Apparatus of scientific purpose loomed in the dark. On a cube of red stone squatted a gaunt man with penetrating eyes and pharamol witchfire under the skin. His head was sunk upon his chest, and his thinning hair hung lank to the shoulders. It was as if the great legend of Young Proud Fundan, the exiled rebel of the Great Clan, had sunk into his flesh, brimming him with a weird heat, compounded of hate and strength. "Welcome Van Relt, the word is no longer Soon, it is Now."

"You have heard?" Van Relt scarcely dared to hope.

"Yes, the message came a few hours ago. The ship is here; we go forward at once."

"So, destiny will give us our revenge at last." Rinus felt a great elation rising inside him. At last! He had waited so long.

"It will be the greatest raid of all time," Young Proud said in a matter-of-fact way as if he were reciting some historic fact. "We will hammer the Buttes and haul a fortune in pharamol from their vaults." His dark eyes seemed to burn with the power of his vision.

"And then my old enemy will come himself to contest our triumph, and there on the Butte Stones we will destroy him. If he lives through the wreck I will take him alive, for myself."

Van Relt shivered a little at that thought, to fall alive into Young Proud Fundan's hands could be considerably worse than death itself. His remaining testicle twitched again.

"My lord, this is wonderful news, but there is another matter, one that is becoming quite pressing."

"Oh? And what might that be?" Young Proud's eyes were glazed from garjal inhalation.

"My lord, have you forgotten. It is now the thirtieth day, the parasite . . ."

A little smile twisted Young Proud's lips. "My worm awakes, does it? Isn't it good that I hold you so close to me, Van Relt?"

"Yes, of course, lord."

"I hold you close so that I may allow myself to trust you, as I trust no other human. You understand this, of course."

"I wish to live, lord."

"Yes, I'm sure of that—and not as a castrate either. In fact you'd like to secure your own revenge on my enemy, wouldn't you?"

There was no need for Rinus to reply to that. He who had been half gelded, along with fifteen thousand other prisoners from the battle of Badleck Ridge fifty years before. He would never forget the name of that enemy, Lavin Fundan, he who had once been but lowly Fundin.

"I keep you close and you serve me well, and together we will have vengeance, and then that crèche boy, that clone of the Great Witch, he will be mine." Young Proud smiled again; it was a troubling thing to witness.

Young Proud climbed off the tall stone block and led Van Relt to the rear of the laboratory. They passed glass cases in which stood preserved human and fein specimens mounted in natural settings.

In an alcove that had the air of a shrine, a beautiful holograph of Ramal Valley shimmered, with the turrets of Proud Tower thrust up above. This had been Young Proud's ancestral home until he lost all in the great war.

Outside the alcove, on a wall picked out by a spotlight, was a painting, a realistic rendering of a battle to the death between two great fein bodyguards. With kifkets in their hands, great slabs of honed steel, the fein struggled in a tornado of muscle, fur, and snarling fangs. Behind them, in the background, were two lines of other fein armed with rifles. In front of them were small groups of humans clad in Highlander battle dress. At the bottom were engraved the words "For the Honor of the Proud Fundans, in Memory of Tefiltiga the Great, of Ramal Village."

A charcoal brazier burned redly on a low bench. Goom roots were reducing in a metal cup. Young Proud examined them briefly and then filled a tube with gray ash. To this he added a clear fluid and then shook the two together. He placed the tube over a burner and placed his hands behind his back.

"You admire my painting, Van Relt?"

"Yes, sir, it's a remarkable work. I've never seen the like."

"It was painted by my father's court painter, Aldiss Grey. A fine craftsman, possessed an exacting technique."

"Who was Tefiltiga the Great?"

"A great champion, Van Relt. He fought for my grandfather, Eldest Proud. This scene shows Tefiltiga—he wears the yellow ear flash of Ramal—in defense of the honor of Proud Fundan against the fein champion of the witch, Fair Fundan, she who cloned herself and continues as that abomination Lavin Fundin."

"I see," said Van Relt with a faint note of wonder. The way of war and survival in the Highlands was still exotic enough to him to leave him wondering at times. "What happened then? In the fight."

Young Proud's face clouded over as he turned off the burner and he seized the tube in some tongs and shook the bubbling mixture a little.

"Alas, poor Tefiltiga was overcome. He died later of his wounds. That was a grievous day indeed for Proud Fundan. You see, in the pursuit of honor in our clan, the combat could not end with Tefiltiga's defeat. As he fell so my Grandfather, Eldest Fundan, drew his own knife and went up against the champion of the Ghotaw witch."

Van Relt stared at Young Proud.

"Your grandfather?"

"He took the kifket to our enemy and he was slain. Ragawal of Ghotaw took his head. It went to Ghotaw, to the witch's trophy room. But Eldest Proud Fundan retained our honor; never shall we forget him."

Young Proud poured the mixture through a cooling tube into a small cup. This he handed to Van Relt.

"Here, still the worm." Young Proud nodded vaguely as Van Relt forced down the hot, ill-tasting mixture, then he activated a six-foot table screen that stood beneath a wall map of Fenrille. On the surface appeared a detailed holograph of the valleys of the Clan Butte.

"Now that we've secured your manhood for another term, you'll be able to concentrate on the Kommando. The local operation begins tonight, and we must be ready to move within two days."

It was almost midnight, and the lobby of the Hotel Luxor was awash in guests as the party to celebrate the Chitin Chemistry Conference got into full swing. In the ballroom the Hyqual Funsters were cutting out timeless four-beats-to-the-bar dance music, and dozens of triples and newly fashionable doubles were whirling on the floor. Waiters bore trays of drinks through the throngs, and Highlanders and Coastals mixed quite openly.

Fleur Fundan stood with a small group on a landing overlooking the dancers. Dali Spreak was the center of attention here. Dali's great idea had been received with thunderous applause earlier in the day. Now the Coastal magnates were quizzing her about her plan.

Kerato Glaibones, chief of Coast City Labs, raised a point that Fleur had been waiting for. But in the euphoria over the idea no one had yet begun to ask such questions.

"I wonder, Madame Spreak, if you would tell us how you think the major funding for your project can be raised?"

Dali was clearly unfazed by the query. "Well, messire, naturally with a project like this we'll have to let many groups contribute. They'll all want a piece of the action—I know the Highland clans will, and I'm sure once we float an issue on the market here, we'll get all the response we'll need."

Dali smiled happily. For the occasion she wore a yellow-and-blue gown, and her skull was painted in blue-and-yellow polka dots; she looked like some new alien life-form. Which, thought Fleur Fundan, wasn't altogether too far from the truth. Living alone for centuries with just the fein, up in remote Pluqyhat hole, could make one a little strange.

"In short, messire, I think we have one of the best investment opportunities available in decades. Don't you agree, Messire Okuba?"

Okuba, of the Central Chitin Bank, had skin stretched like parchment over his skull-like head. "Well, I would have to consult with my board before investing the bank's money, but I should add that I will invest my own too. However another point has occurred to me, that perhaps there might come a time when further research by the Highland Clans might be considered aah, unnecessary, shall we say?"

"Messire!" Dali feigned shock and outrage. "Even to suspect such a thing is unworthy of you." She grinned. "Or are you thinking that we might find a way to achieve a complete synthesis?"

Everyone chuckled. Except Ervil Spreak, who snorted. "Nonsense! Chitin information proteins are the most complex molecules human science has ever encountered. The modular arrays of pharamol equate with an omni enzymatic function; they exhibit a complex flexibility very comparable to Terrestrial DNA. But pharamol is only possible through the catalyst process, and raw Chitin protein is much more complex than pharamol itself."

"And no way has ever been found to raise Chitin nests outside the Fenrille biosphere."

"Absolutely, Messire Okuba, for good reason—the Arizel tki Fenrille placed that prohibition themselves in the Chitin genetic material. We have striven for centuries to produce Chitin without

39

the Arizel codes but to no avail; the best anyone ever managed was to raise a few Chitin nests on the Red Moon Habitat."

"Really. I had not heard of this; I thought it was impossible. What happened?"

"The nests were feral. They produced very few Vizier, and then these were killed by the queens. Just queens, workers and warriors—it was as if the Chitin had reverted to some primitive model, akin to that which they evolved from on Herxx."

"Ah, yes." Okuba nodded. "We've heard that part of the story. The Chitin came here as an advanced space-going species, and when they attempted to hive this world and kill off the great forest, the Arizel returned, destroyed Herxx utterly, and converted the surviving Chitin into the form we now know."

And Fleur Fundan felt the old memories again, of that incredible day in the deep forest, in the sacred fidnemed, in the presence of the Great Arizel.

"And our wars over Chitin not only brought about a second return but also took us to within a few moments of the complete annihilation of Earth and the home system. Fortunately the Hith formula ended the worst pressure on supplies, but now the pressure has returned, and we must find a way to improve the synthetic catalysts."

Kerato Glaibones nodded at this.

"You were there, weren't you, Madame Fundan? In the forest when it happened."

"That was when Fair Fundan disappeared, wasn't it?" Glaibones said.

"You know I never really understood that part of it," Okuba commented.

"It was quite simple actually," Fleur said with a smile. "The Arizel took her with them. She vanished in a great burst of light via some process of theirs. Of course the rest of us thought that it was all over for us. You forgot that nuclear warheads had already been used against the clan."

Fleur nodded, lips compressed grimly. "I will never forget it. The future of the human race hung by a thread that day; the Arizel were prepared to hurl a black hole into the home system if necessary to end our interference with Fenrille."

"Well, I was here on the Sx Coast," Glaibones said, "and we thought it was the end of the world all right. The entire continent was shuddering, and then there was the sound, that noise, it sounded as if the planet itself was singing."

"Anyway," Dali Spreak said, "my brother is quite correct. Don't think we will easily solve the problem of a complete synthesis. The Chitin insect developed these proteins for communication purposes. Over millions of years the level of complexity that they evolved into allowed the Vizier caste to form the typical Chitin brain formation, what we call the Vizier Mass. Between themselves vizier translate a huge diversity of information, and all of this is done with several hundred different protein forms, all extruded from seven huge glands on the vizier abdomen.

"The best we can hope for is to further improve upon Termas Hith's work of more than fifty years ago. If we can increase the replication rate of the synthetic catalysts, then we can increase the amount of longevity drugs in direct proportion. The true synthesis of Chitin proteins is still far beyond us—why we don't really understand all that much of the Chitin genetic material, and we've been working on that for three and a half centuries. The communication proteins are several orders of magnitude more complex."

"The Hith T-class modules are the ones we should concentrate on first, I think," Kerato Glaibones said. "In our laboratories that's what we've been working on for several years now."

"Well, I like what I'm hearing," Okuba said. "I'm sure I can persuade the board of the bank to take an interest."

Ervil Spreak drained his glass. "Messire Okuba need not worry himself unduly about funds for this crazed scheme, because I can assure him that it will never take place."

Okuba nodded sagely. "Of course, that is what I expected to hear. After all, the Highlanders have control of the Chitin; you produce the raw material that we process for the off-worlders. Why risk losing that power and prestige on the discovery of some possible way to a synthesis?"

Spreak bristled at this. "When you consider the cost we have paid to achieve that position, I think you will agree that we have given enough to hold what is ours. We have given blood and sweat beyond measure. I remember, even if others do not, that before the great war, for centuries, your bank made loans to war bands who raided our valleys for Chitin. I have seen enough of my fein, and my people, killed by your money, messire."

Okuba turned a moonface to Spreak. "We have shared in the blood and in the toil, messire. Indeed there was war, but when such a small amount of the drug was produced how could it have been any other way? In the old days the demand pressure was phenomenal; there was no way to hold it back because before the Hith formula supplies were so restricted."

"Our people worked the Chitin hard; we produced as much as we do now, as much as the valleys will bear."

"So we have a common interest in increasing production. Come, Messire Spreak, we will put good money forward to back the venture if the clans will open their laboratories."

"Bah! A pipe dream. I know better." Spreak turned away and stared out over the dancing hordes below.

"I'm afraid my brother isn't feeling the spirit of celebration tonight. Please be forgiving, Messire Okuba—I think he's under a strain with all this." Dali did her best to smooth the roiling waters.

Okuba smiled politely. "Yes, of course, and it is a splendid party. I'm sure something good will come out of this conference even if the very best idea is too radical for some."

And Fleur allowed herself a moment of elation. The conference was already a big success and scarcely begun. She wished her husband Lavin could be there, to see this success and to get the feel of human society again. She missed him, and seeing him only on her short visits to Abzen Valley was insufficient, but he was military commander of the Highland forces and constantly busy. She needed the human city now; she'd spent fifty years living in that valley, three thousand miles from anywhere.

But at the conference she'd organized, Highlanders and Coastals, enemies for centuries, were mingling, socializing freely in a new way that she could not recall ever seeing before. She wanted Lavin to witness it, to see that the old ways of the clans could be forgotten. There was no longer need to maintain the standing armies of fein; as long as they had the space fleet on station to protect the planet, they would satisfy the contract entered into with the Arizel. Humanity could continue to take Chitin proteins as long as the race protected Fenrille from outside interference.

The band finished an up-tempo number and began a more classic mellow sound, something from antiquity, and triples moved off the dance floor and others moved on.

Abruptly a heavy *boom* echoed in the lobby. A heavy thud rumbled through the entire dome. Further ground-trembling thuds followed. Then, faintly, Fleur heard a crackling sound.

"That's . . ." She whirled to look at Ervil Spreak.

"Yes, automatic small arms fire, Lady Fundan. Warband weaponry, I'd know the sound anywhere. The heavier reports are mortars, three hundred-millimeter shell, I'd say. The air pressure is much heavier down here than on the battlefields I'm familiar with, but the vibration in the ground is unmistakable." He turned a small, bitter smile upon her. She could see great Igrak, teeth exposed in a snarl, clearing his path to Ervil.

"What is going on?" Fleur stumbled off the platform and ran to the entrance, where a frightened mob was already jammed around the elevator banks.

Then bullets ripped through the door and cut down the Luxor Hotel security staff, spinning them aside like broken dolls, shattering glass, splintering the reception desk, killing the maître d' against the ruin of a mirror that was smashed before his impact.

And then squads of war band soldiery in green-and-black camouflage began to race in through the entranceway. Fleur turned and ran, up the side stairs and away from the firing that began again to a chorus of screams.

6

Bg Rva awoke with the vibration of the third shell. He sniffed the air, but only the neutral odor of the dome ventilation system reached his nostrils. Another mortar round struck down in the Gardens of Nebuchadnezzar just outside the Luxor Dome. Instantly old Rva was on his feet, hands reaching for the door.

Now he could hear faintly the crackle of small arms fire. He cursed himself in a steady stream of fein expletives for being an old fool and taking a nap when danger should strike. The lady Fundan was in the ballroom; his place was by her side.

His big fingers fumbled with the door mechanism but found it elusive; things built for humans were always so accursedly small. The mechanism required a mere thumb press, but his thumb would not fit the lock on the small utility room door. He jabbed again and again to no avail; there was a lot of shouting nearby and then gunfire and screams. He stopped, listened, then used the kifket to break the door bodily off its hinges and slipped out into the corridor.

The stench of human fear was in the air, along with gun smoke and blood. More heavy explosions rocked the dome; whatever was happening, it was violence on a considerable scale. Rva stalked along the corridor, moving furtively from corner to corner but seeing no one. A side door to a rising stair was partially open, and as he passed it he caught the scent of Lady Fleur. She was afraid, perspiration acrid with fear, and she was not far ahead. Quickly he closed the door behind him and broke the lock with the kifket.

On the third level of the stairs the scent grew stronger, and he could just discern her footsteps far above him. Unfortunately she was quicker on these stairs than an eighty-year-old mzsee, and he would be a very tired old fein by the time he caught up with her.

He leaned out into the stairwell to call up to her as the door on the opposite side cracked open and two war band soldiers with rifles emerged.

They never saw the big body that dropped silently behind the retainer wall, but they did hear Fleur's feet on the stairs above. One spoke into his communicator summoning interception on the higher floors. The pair then moved forward to bring up the rear on the fugitive. As they turned into the stairwell, they were met by three hundred pounds of fighting fein that sent them tumbling.

From the floor they looked up at him in awed amazement. Neither man had seen a fein before except on video.

The back of the kifket blade stunned the first man and Rva had the other by the shirtfront before either of them had time to react.

The man wriggled, grunted, and lashed out with a karate kick. Rva took some of the blow on the upper thigh and grunted in return. Then he threw the man at the retainer wall fairly hard. Without breath in his body the fellow was less eager for a fight and Rva's kifket blade now hovered by his throat.

"You, strong foot man, you tell me now, what is all this fuss? All the weapons and killing I smell?"

The war band soldier saw that fein blade—a steel rectangle honed sharp on two edges—that could take a man's head off with just a wrist flick, and he swallowed hard.

"We're the New Kommando. We have orders to take control of all the domes. Look, I just follow my orders, you see; I don't know exactly what it's all about. They don't tell us that sort of thing, you know."

"Why the shooting, why did I hear mortar shell?"

The man's face twitched. "I don't know. They're shelling the Maya Dome. Maybe the police are in rebellion or something."

Rva sensed dissimulation, deceit. He snorted, "Why would police be rebel? Talk truth or I will split your nose into two equal parts."

The kifket lifted slightly, two kilos of steel that in fein hands could become anything from axe blade to scalpel. The man hastened to explain.

"I don't know. I was just told to muster out tonight, that the big operation was On at last. I don't know what it's all about. I'm just an ordinary soldier—you can see that. I just do what they tell me. Look, this is a misunderstanding. Shouldn't you go find an officer and find out what your orders are. I can see you're in the military too."

Rva snorted dismissively. "And end up captured or shot? I know human blood when I smell it. There was killing."

There were noises up above. Fleur screamed for help.

Rva immediately rendered the man unconscious with a rap of the flat kifket and scrambled up the stairs, big hands priming the war bander's rifle, eyes blazing.

Lady Fleur's cries choked off, there was a male shout, and a door somewhere closed with a slam, cutting off further sound.

A minute or more later Rva puffed up to the door and burst it open with his body. Nothing but an empty elevator bank waited to greet him. One elevator was in motion, descending to the lobby.

Rva's instincts told him the Lady Fleur was now a prisoner, but whose remained a mystery. Once, when blood had been hotter, Rva would have taken the very next elevator to the lobby in hot pursuit. But those fires had cooled just a little over the years. Rva knew well that the old hunter was usually the best hunter. The lobby would be full of armed men; he would most likely be shot if he emerged there now.

With a grunt he turned back to the stairwell. Now he knew he was too old. Here he was, the Hero of Brelkilk, and he was thinking just like Lavin Fundan. After all these years, Rva of the wide path was thinking like a human! It was a galling idea.

But it was clear that Fleur had been taken prisoner and not just shot out of hand, so it would perhaps be best to find out who was doing this, who was responsible for the violence and why. When he had answers to those questions, he could plan an accurate response.

However, someone was bound to organize some sort of search soon, so he headed down to a residential floor and then scouted along a corridor lined with apartment doors pausing to listen for sounds of occupation. Voices, TVs, Senso audio could be heard from most of them. He hurried on with occasional glances behind. To be caught out in the corridor would mean death, but there was nowhere to hide. Eventually he found a doorway with silence beyond it. He looked up and down the corridor, nobody was in sight, although he could hear boots crashing on the stairs behind him.

In one crunching stroke he broke the lock with the kifket and surged inside. In the front room he found a small brown-skinned woman hunched in a chair facing the door; she held an old-fashioned stunner in both hands pointing vaguely in the direction of Rva's considerable midriff.

"Your pardon, madame."

Her jaw dropped open. He growled ingratiatingly. "I did not think anyone was home; I need to look out the window and find out what's going on. I hope I didn't frighten you."

46

Hearing Rva speak in inter-English with a Highlander accent caused the little woman to squeak in astonishment. "Who are you? And what's going on out there? Why are they fighting?"

Rva had the kifket in his hand, and Ms. Lucy Urbimle was ten feet and a split second from a painless death, but Rva smiled, baring gap-tooth fangs in what he hoped would seem a friendly way.

Instead she screamed, a small thin shriek.

"Don't come any closer, don't . . ." and, screwing up her eyes, she turned her head away as she raised the stunner and discharged its bolt into a stuffed chair, which fell over slightly singed.

By then Rva had moved gingerly around her and gently taken the stunner away from her.

Nerveless, scarcely daring to breathe, she stared up at him, a seven-foot-tall monster looking down at her with eyes like great marbled egg yolks.

"I'm sorry," she began. "Don't kill me."

Rva looked out the window. There was little to see, smoke rising from the Bablon Dome, several men in camouflage running across a lawn in the Gardens of Nebuchadnezzar.

"I am friend of humans. I will not harm you. But do you know anything about all this confusion?"

"Know, what's to know? The TV went off; all you can get on every station is a test pattern. So I called my friend Elinor over in the Bablon Dome, and she said that war bands have reformed and are taking over the whole city."

Down below in the plaza fronting on the Garden of Nebuchadnezzar, squads of soldiers marched past. Distant small arms fire continued sporadically, and Rva could just see small groups of men clustered around the entrances of several other big domes.

One thing that struck him was that all wore the same uniform. None wore the old flamboyant costumes of the Long War. This was a unified command of some sort, that much was evident. Which meant a well-organized conspiracy and a large-scale rebellion.

He turned back to the little old woman in her chair. It was rare to see an old human; in the Highlands the humans never aged much once they passed puberty and began taking longevity drugs. Here on the Sx Coast, though, not everyone could afford the drugs and a comfortable life-style.

"I have a bad feeling about all this," he rumbled. "I think I will stay with you for a few hours more, if you will allow it, until we can find out what's going on. I will leave later, when it's dark."

Rva hunched down and tested the sofa. "Is it a strong one?"

Lucy Urbimle struggled for words, confronted by the first fein she'd ever met in the flesh, a monstrous giant with a gun and that huge knife who was actually standing inside her home and proposing to stay there as well.

"Yes, it's built to hold four people," she managed at last.

Rva smiled at her again, sending chills down her spine, and gingerly put his weight on it. The sofa gave a little groan but held.

Lucy struggled to find her courage and after a moment of goggling at the apparition recovered herself. Then as if such a visit happened every day, she inquired whether her guest would like a refreshment. Rva requested a glass of water. On her way to the kitchen she saw the ruin of her front door lock and gave a little shriek.

Rva was contrite. "My apologies, madam, I will make up for the loss somehow." He picked up the pieces and shoved them roughly back into place. They wouldn't hold the door however.

Lucy Urbimle popped open a stimsoda and sipped it carefully. She didn't want to get one of her dreaded hiccups attacks now.

"Well, I don't have many visitors here anyway. Though I couldn't think of a less likely visitor than you, messire—uh, I don't know your name."

The giant exposed its scattered fangs again. She resisted the urge to faint. "I am called Bg Rva. Once many years ago now, I led the Brelkilk fein. I am of the wide path line, all the way back to old Brel himself, in the whenever when, beyond bahlkwan count."

"Oh . . ." She sounded slightly bewildered by it all. "Well, that sounds very nice, Messire Ar-vah, although I'm not sure I understand completely, but my name is Lucy Urbimle."

Rva grimaced and pronounced "Lucy Urbeemel" with great care. She smiled a little hesitantly and then ventured a question. "Messire Ar-vah, tell me, what brings you to the Sx Coast? We don't see very many fein here. Why, they haven't even had those horrible TV shows for fifty years."

Rva nodded gravely. "Thanks be to the Arizel tki Fenrille that all that business was ended forever."

At the mention of the Arizel, Lucy's heart began to hammer in her chest. She remembered a day, long distant, when it seemed as if the whole world was about to end. A day synonymous since then with Fenrille's eldest masters. "Is this something to do with them, with the Dark Masters?" she quavered.

Rva shook his head. "I do not think so. Not yet at least. But what I see makes me think it is a rebellion long in the planning. All I know for sure right now is that I must stay out of the hands of this New Kommando, whatever it is."

Then there came the sound of many booted feet running down the hallway. Outside the dome there were shouts. Maybe the bad times were coming back. Rva looked around. There seemed little likelihood of finding a place for a fein of his girth to hide. Lucy looked around too, in a panic. Then inspiration struck.

"Come!" she jumped up and pulled Rva into the kitchen, one corner of which was taken up by a freezer vault. "My soul mate, old Sal, was a real fisherman. He put a freezer in, but he fell overboard a few years ago, and the fish got their revenge. I still have this though." She opened it and Rva squeezed into its chilly interior past a few small frozen items, soy steaks and quicky pizzas.

"I'll turn it down as much as I can and try to keep them out of here."

Rva listened intently, but it was hard to hear much through the hefty freezer door. Eventually he did hear Lucy talking and then other voices as well. They came into the kitchen. He readied himself for a last charge, kifket in hand. They wouldn't take Bg Rva easily.

7

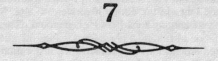

TO SAY THAT THE SURPRISE WAS COMPLETE THROUGHOUT THE
Fenrille system would have been an understatement, except of
course in the case of the Highland clans, where at the first word
of the uprising forts were put on full alert. Fein Impis were
called to the colors in every valley, VTOL aircraft were hurriedly
pulled from storage, checked, and fueled.

On the Sx Coast itself, however, the governing authorities
were woefully unprepared. Within a couple of hours the police
force had been captured and disarmed and all resistance crushed.
Troopers from the Liberation Forces of the New Kommando
pushed into every dome on the Isles and then spread down the
densely populated Elefelas Peninsula.

In a few minutes most of the Fenrille Communication Satellite
network was in Kommando hands too, and on all wavebands
the Kommando proclaimed its victory and called on citizens to
remain calm and indoors.

Fleur Fundan found herself confined in a stinking fish warehouse on the Fun Isle waterfront. One by one other Highlanders
were led in. They wore expressions of shock and dismay.

"Lady Fundan, thank goodness you're here. You'll get them
to stop this madness, won't you?" There was a hopeful expect-
ancy in their faces for a moment or two. Fleur showed them the
wrist cuffs she wore. "I'm afraid not. I'm as much a prisoner
as you are. And I don't really understand what it's all about
either."

"They call themselves the Liberation Front."

"And we're hostages."

The hopes died; the Highlanders paced and growled. She
looked around for Dali or any of the others from the Chemistry
Conference, but they were not to be seen.

Their prison was a gloomy place, and the stench of fish was
very strong in its rough concrete ribs. There was a choice of

standing or sitting on aged silica fish slabs or the floor, pitted, cracked, and stained from centuries of use.

Fleur stood for the first couple of hours until even the floor began to look reasonably attractive, whereupon she found a corner, curled up in it, and tried to sleep.

She was shaken awake by rough hands and dragged to her feet.

Three soldiers held her up while an officer compared her face to that in a photograph.

"She's one of them. Bring her."

They did. She rode on the bloodstained velour seats of a commercial limo through the underground tunnels. Finally they stopped, and she was placed in an elevator and sent aloft, alone.

The elevator stopped on a darkened hallway, and she gasped in surprise as huge fein warriors reached in and pulled her out. They thrust her through another door into an even darker space. She sensed a large room around her, filled with tall dark shapes, but they were just dark masses against the greater gloom. The room's Senso further fudged everything with coiling vapor columns.

A thin-faced man, no older than her husband she judged, appeared out of the mist. He wore silk breeches in Fundan green and a leather shoulder harness. His body was lean and hard; he carried a revolver and a small kifket. She recognized him at last. "Young Proud! Is it really you? Young Proud Fundan! Why, everyone thought you still roamed in the deep forest. There has been no word from you in decades."

He smiled enigmatically. "Yes, you all thought that the Proud Fundans were crushed forever, that my father's submission to the family council had ended our defiance." He attached a short chain to her wrist cuffs.

"But you were wrong, all of you, and now you will learn to fear the wrath of the Proud Fundan. My father, alas, is no more. That hulk of flesh in Fintral Castle that uses his name is not my father; it is an obscenity, a crawling, groveling thing."

Young Proud's voice had risen to a shriek. He jerked on the chain and pulled Fleur into the deeper darkness.

An apparatus rose out of the reek. An operating table, surrounded by equipment.

"Lie down here," Young Proud commanded.

"But what is this? Why are you doing this?"

"Have you no imagination, woman? Just think back to all that I have suffered from the hands of Fair Fundan, in all her forms, including that disgusting deformity you call a husband."

Fleur struggled against the chain; immediately strong hands came out of the murk behind her and lifted her onto the table and strapped her down on it while she screamed up into their blank medical masks and white gowns.

Lights came on, bright ones that hurt her eyes. Young Proud reappeared, masked as well. He held up a small vial.

"You may have heard of this creature, *Fenrille tacer tenacera*," a parasitic worm that will enfold the organ I implant it into and *devour* it unless kept tranquil with an antidote. The antidote can be fashioned specifically for each individual worm, the beauty of the system, to my mind."

His eyes crinkled at the edges as he smiled vacantly down at her. She screamed, but the mask came down, and then there was nothing to scream with.

Meanwhile in the castle of the Numal, by the shores of the sea of forever, the great Divider calculated finely the chances of an escape. To his horror the Divider had discovered other Arizel within the bottle, two ancients so weakened by their treatment that they were barely wraiths. The laboratory was now in constant use as the Numal attempted to affect the Divider with endless tests, forces, fields, particles, phased excitonic matter, to derive some result, some measurement to begin the great decipherment and the ancient race's escape from doom. The Numal was relentless but prey to biological weaknesses.

Thus there were periods, unmercifully brief, when the experiments ceased and the Divider could think deeply . . . the conclusion became obvious, if only because nothing else was possible . . . The Divider had to waken to full consciousness a Woodwose, one of the wondigundi malub, the mouths of the trees. Carefully it considered the idea. The mind of the Woodwose was strong, brutally so, but narrowly directed. Once awakened it would be a difficult steed to control. Nor was there even a guarantee that the control instrument would survive the enormous journey.

The Divider would have to project a nugget of self-consciousness, a simple mathematical anomaly, self-sustaining fluctuations, in effect a part of the Divider's own existence. Of course in the conversion process the Divider would give up almost 10 percent of its life force to produce a micro-psion that could be hurled to Fenrille by the judicious recombination of certain equipments in the great laboratory of the Numal.

The Divider sought ways in which to influence, very slightly, the environment around the confining "bottle" that held him captive. Slowly things progressed. Machines began to cycle on and off in the correct rhythms. An accident soon occurred, and the Numal burned out an optic organ. The Numal was removed swiftly by medic robots. While it was incapacitated the Divider worked frantically within the bottle. The laboratory became more active than ever before, though nobody was there. Small new mechanisms were built. Machines moved.

Eventually all was ready; the equipment operated perfectly; the computer cycled the complex program and the micro-psion was ejected obliquely into nothingness.

On its return the Numal was astonished at the evidence of a great amount of research work strewn through the laboratory as if by a cyclone...

On Fenrille, in a glade of great trees, in the depths of the great forest, one particular tree began to sing emitting the "thrilling note" at about twenty-seven thousand Hertz—inaudible to human ears—that attracted Woodwose.

Not long afterward a Woodwose approached, loping swiftly through the forest. It reached the tree that sang and put its long arms out and around the mother-that-called.

A spark, tiny, bright blue, cracked between them. After a moment the Woodwose backed away from the tree. All eight eyes closed momentarily; it shuddered from the long, heavy claws on its toes to the last tuft of brown-gray shag on top of the parabolic skull. Then it almost fell and had to put out a ten-meter-long arm to steady itself against a tree. The eyes popped open, and for the first time in its existence the Woodwose was Aware.

Strange ancestral memories crowded in. It struggled with a new experience, so alien to a mouth of the mother trees. Yet it knew where it was—a look around showed the trees; it was a well-kept forest here. Its memories were confused, as if the sun were the wrong color, the gravity too light. Memories that had been buried in the Woodwose psyche since the Arizel had taken the first of them and planted the first groves of the great trees on Fenrille now sought to surface through more recent events. And the Woodwose, in wonder, plucked at its own hide, Aware of Self for the first time.

But there had never been a self-aware Woodwose on Fenrille in all the seventy-million years that Woodwose had walked the tree yards.

The confusion was considerable...

8

CHOSEN AWOKE WITH A POISONOUS HANGOVER. GROGGILY HE sat up and rubbed the sleep from his eyes. Something fetid was on his breath. He had no memory of finding his way back to his cabin. Nor of undressing. But he was in his own, sterile little room tucked into his own sterile little bunk.

Something was wrong down in the short-term memory, however, something that he knew instinctively he wouldn't want to remember. It surfaced nonetheless, and he grimaced with embarrassment. What a dreadful young fool he must've seemed. He could almost see the grave disbelief in Father's face. Just confirming what Mother had said about "maturity."

How he hated the way they used that word! When they judged him like that. And what would Bg Rva say? "Sulky man cub!" and an explosion of laughter probably. Chosen almost cringed at the thought. And then there was Chi Lin Wei. The image of her returned, so beautiful that she was dreamlike, impossible.

What must she think?

He rested his head against the cool wall of the tiny shower stall. After a moment he dialed a wet shower. The cold water made him shiver at first, but he focused himself to endure it. When the five-minute timer rang, his head was a fraction clearer and his skin was glowing. He groped about for underwear and a flight suit. Then he noticed the small blue envelope thrust under his door.

It was of real paper and embossed with a stylized likeness of Chi Lin Wei in gold leaf. Slightly awed, he opened it gingerly. There was a single sheet of paper in blue a subtle shade lighter than the envelope itself. The writing was in a small precise hand in real ink. He marveled at the mediaeval form of communication while he read.

I'm afraid we will have to tour the ship today, so prepare yourself for a lot of standing around while they show off their incomprehensible technology. This ship is huge, so it will take quite a few hours, too. But I'm sure you know this already, poor thing. I hope to see you alive and well on the Bridge at 0100 hours in the Leisure Lounge where we will be joined by Commander Tiax. Apparently he intends to conduct the tour in person. I ought to warn you that Tiax is a military buff with a great interest in your father's campaigns. So brace yourself, he can be incredibly long-winded. By the way, in reference to the events of last night, you'll be glad to know that you're forgiven. They were my favorite pair of shoes, but I suddenly realized that the shoes were actually older than you are, so I took that as an omen and I threw them away. They're probably already being recycled into fish food! Thus you were simply an agent of fate! As such I thank you and look forward to your company today.

It was signed with a scrawl and scented ever so slightly with something sweet and flowery.

Chosen took a deep breath, leaned against a wall for a moment, and then opened his pharamol cache, in the heel of one shoe, and removed a grain, which he slipped onto his tongue. "Poor thing!"

By the time he'd begun shaving, he was feeling considerably better. Almost eager, in fact, to meet Chi Lin Wei.

He finished up and went out for breakfast, where he discovered that the world had fallen in. It was stunning news. While he'd slept the Sx Coast had exploded in rebellion and hundreds of Highlanders had been taken hostage.

On every trimonitor in the mess hall one screen played the loop broadcast of the New Kommando's announcement.

From a wall phone Chosen tried to get a line to his mother's hotel but was informed by the *Gandhi* computer that no calls were being allowed by the Kommando.

Did that mean Mother was a hostage? The news commentary on one of the other screens was going into that in some detail, issuing lists of likely hostages. He found an empty seat by a trimonitor and used the comp link to get a Search for her. Her name appeared in seconds. There was no further information. Glumly he lined up for ship's breakfast and washed the synthetics down with weak coffee. He kept the trimonitor working through everything available on the takeover. There was no information about any fein. Was this good or bad news? Had Bg Rva escaped somehow? And Igrak? The list of names was long and studded with the superwealthy, the cream of the Highland elite. Dali Spreak, Melissa Chung, Yosef Hoechst, but he found no reference to Ervil Spreak. The big man had not been caught. Were they loose then, he and Igrak?

He called Cracked Rock but was unable to reach his father.

Lavin was in Command Council. Nobody knew any more than that Fleur was on the Kommando hostage list and that no military steps had been taken by the Fenrille Defense Forces.

The rest of his breakfast was a grim, hurried affair, and he headed back to his cabin as quickly as possible to get to a monitor and catch the Kommando broadcast.

Father had been right after all! Fifty years of planning had not been a waste. Chosen could see that the rebellion had been planned for a long time, and he felt a rush of longing to see his father, who'd been so right for so long against so many doubters.

Including his son. Chosen brushed the hair away from his forehead and pushed open the door to his cabin.

Two strange men awaited him. They pulled him in and shut the door and reached out with stun bulbs. In sudden rage he lashed out at the intruders and caught one with a solid right hand, but the next moment the breath seemed to explode in his lungs as the fellow kneed him in the stomach. A hard blow knocked him sideways into the wall. One of the men pinioned his arms; Chosen slumped as a stun bulb was applied.

"Little bastard," snarled one of his attackers wiping a trickle of blood from his chin. He kicked the recumbent Chosen.

"Enough of that. We've got to get him back to the Master." They opened a sack and slipped it over him and then lifted the body and carried it quickly out the door.

It was the work of a half minute to lug the young man down the corridor and into another cabin. There they taped his wrists and ankles and brought him around with a stimshot.

Chosen's eyes opened. The huge fat man who had been at dinner sat before him wrapped in a scarlet robe. It was hard to control his lips; they felt like rubber, but he was too angry to hold back the words. "What do you mean by this?"

The fat man smiled. "Got the proper Highlander spirit, have you? Or is it just the stimulants I hear, plus some pharamol? The last time I saw you you were being led away by the remarkable Chi Lin Wei. You looked like a calf going to the slaughter."

Chosen discovered his bonds, observed the dour pair of guards standing by the door.

Quermwyere put the palms of his pudgy hands together. "You are aware that a chaotic situation has developed on the Sx Coast?"

"You're part of the rebellion then," Chosen groaned.

Quermwyere chuckled. "By no means, messire, by no means. However, I believe that we will be going through unpredictable times, and I have decided to take a hostage or two of my own. Jut a matter of self-protection, that's all."

"My father will—"

"Your father will have quite enough on his hands." Quermwyere indicated a small communications device on the table. "I have monitored the communications between the ship and the Fenrille Defense Forces. Believe me when I tell you that they are in a bind. Your father is under intense attack in the Command Council for allowing this to happen. With his own wife a captive of the rebels, he can hardly be expected to act impartially; some are calling for him to step down."

"The Council has never voted to fund the Defense Forces to the level necessary to prevent a rebellion. It's hardly my father's fault."

Quermwyere smiled pitilessly. "Of course it isn't, but when the mob wants a scapegoat they will always manage to find one." He patted Chosen's shoulder with a plump palm. "Mind you I also picked up a transmission in Fundan military code that proved surprisingly difficult to decipher.

"Your father has an interesting idea concerning all this." Quermwyere touched a switch. On a trimonitor in front of him, one of the screens lit with a picture of Lavin Fundan, in the Cracked Rock Fort communications center. Another screen wobbled into view.

"My apologies for the picture quality. My decoder program was good, but cracking military comcodes can take time," said the fat man in a gloat.

"How did you obtain this?" Chosen was stunned.

Quermwyere giggled. "In advanced electronics, my dear boy, there are always ways. I'm afraid that in recent years Fundan comp codes have not been as good as once they were." He gestured to the screen. "Look, here we have the bridge." A view of the ship's bridge appeared, very grainy, cut with flashes of datadrop.

"Essentially, what I have found is that your father believes there will be a second stroke to the rebellion. He expects a carefully planned mutiny aboard one of the major ships. I could not decipher the exact ship he expects trouble on, but it could be either the *Gandhi* or the *Gagarin*."

"Surely the *Gandhi*'s crew could not be involved; they've only just arrived in the system. How could they have coordinated such a move?"

"However, the *Gagarin* has been here fifty years, time enough for the crew to chafe at their position. Which is what? Eventual habitat homes after a half century of duty with only occasional leave? What could you expect when they can see the pleasant lives available to others in this system?"

"Even so, where would they go afterward? Where would they hide?" At this Quermwyere giggled again.

"You lack the imagination of your illustrious so-called grandmother, don't you. I knew her, you know." He giggled. "She hated me! But old Fair Fundan would have seen what they'd do. Your father too. He knows. They'll head out into deep space, make a major jump, say in the direction of the Pleiades. Find a new world and live very long lives in comfort. Obviously they will attack one of the Highland families and seize a large supply of longevity base. Besides the ransoms they can expect for their hostages. Some of the names on that list! Did you see they have Melissa Chung, Golden Tongue herself. The greatest Chitin talker of them all, and probably the wealthiest."

"Of course," breathed Chosen. "The ship would give them air superiority, and they could launch a raid."

"It will be the greatest raid in all time if it goes as I begin to imagine it." Quermwyere's fat lips were pursed reflectively. He was like some enormous fish, ruler of his small pool for an aeon. Grown wise on the munching of others' bones.

"But how will one ship overcome the rest of the fleet?"

"Actually I wondered about that too, but observe." He punched up a map of the Beni Stellar System. Around the second planet, Fenrille, three green blips orbited in addition to the pair of moons, the distant Luna-like Pale Moon and the captured asteroid Red Moon.

"So here is *Gandhi*." He pointed to a green blip orbiting low above Fenrille. "Here is *Gagarin* and *Austerlitz*," the other blips, both orbiting close to the Pale Moon, "and the other cruisers are of course way off on the far side of Beni, on patrol." Two more green blips scattered far, far out in the orbit of Chroku, the seventh planet, five billion klicks away.

"So if *Gagarin* were to mutiny, it would only have to face two ships? The odds are still too great."

"Not at all, the *Austerlitz* is an old tub that wouldn't stand two minutes against the primary lasers aboard *Gagarin*. In addition, since *Gandhi* is in such a low orbit, *Gagarin* would have the advantage of maneuver and probably of speed." Quermwyere fixed him with beady, dark eyes.

"Which, dear boy, is why you are now my prisoner. And why we are about to disembark on a shuttle I've rented at considerable expense and head for the Red Moon, where I keep a small place for emergencies."

One of the dour men stepped forward.

"We haven't skin-searched him yet, Master."

"What? You fools! Do it now." Quermwyere waved them on.

The man produced a small oval scanning device; the other man roughly pulled down Chosen's shirt.

As the scanner passed over the skin between his shoulder blades, it emitted a beep.

Concern flooded into their faces.

"Tracer."

"Could be killer."

Quermwyere moved hastily away. "Get it out of him, deactivate it! Quickly now, and then we must get out of here."

The man with the scanner produced a scalpel and cut quickly through Chosen's skin.

"It's quite deep." The man sounded piqued. Chosen gasped at the pain, felt liquid running down his back.

"That bitch only had him for a few hours, but already she's contaminated the child."

The man held up the tracer, a tiny horror of wire and a bead of bright green.

"Just a tracer, Master."

Chosen felt faint. That had been slipped under his skin when he passed out in Chi Lin Wei's suite? She had ordered it? His gorge rose.

"*Just* a tracer! Come on, we have to get out of here. They'll be on their way already. Grab him, wrap him up well. We'll take the shuttle out to the Red Moon Habitat. I have friends there."

Chosen was gagged then stuffed unceremoniously into a sack and carried out of the room. Blood from the open incision in his back ran down into his hair and then around his throat and into his mouth. They slammed into an elevator, dropping him heavily on his side. It was a long ride, a hundred floors or more inward to the central docking bay. For some reason Chosen had tears in his eyes and was quite unable to think of a rational way out of his predicament. And his heart was shaking too, but whether from hate or love he wasn't sure. That green plastic bead had come from *her*! Despite the feeling he was certain had grown between them. Had he mistaken it? But his young man's heart said there had been no mistake, the feeling had been there on her part too. And then she had coolly ordered that thing placed in his body!

He tried to concentrate on the whistling sound of the elevator as it penetrated into lighter gravity levels, toward the central docking bay. The tears continued however, and he felt quite wretchedly ashamed. Finally the elevator banged open with a hiss, and Quermwyere's guards picked him up and ran across the docking bay.

Then very abruptly Chosen was dropped to the floor again. Thuds and cries resounded around him. Then he was lifted once more and thrown over someone's back.

He perceived that he was being carried up some stairs or a ramp. Then the sounds changed, became muted. The bag opened, and he stared up at the earnest Chinese visage of Yu Zhao.

Yu Zhao smiled, turned away. "Boy lives."

Chi Lin Wei appeared, wearing a flight suit like the rest of them. She looked down at him coldly, her face a beautiful, impersonal mask. "Get him into the cabin then. We're in ejection mode. Everyone to their places."

They didn't bother to remove the gag or undo his bonds, and while they pushed him into the acceleration couch, he kept his eyes on hers, challenging her, while the blood streaked his face. His face was almost aching from the intensity of his feeling, but she would not meet his eyes; she would not surrender any sign of recognition.

Was this the same woman who had looked at him so slyly, so amusedly, only the previous evening? Who had written him that note? Who had seduced him with eyes and mouth?

Suddenly something snapped behind her face, and she faced him with eyes hard and bright—she wrenched off the gag— "Your anger is understandable, messire, but it should be tempered. I doubt if you have a full grasp of the situation. For instance—"

She was interrupted by a powerful wail; the crash of alarm bells echoed outside somewhere. A huge voice was shouting, "CONDITION RED," over and over.

"What is it?" Chosen said, almost overwhelmed by the torrent of events.

"What we were warned of by Captain Mohod. A very, very powerful intruder ship has just materialized inside the orbit of the Pale Moon. The other ships are attacking it, since it refuses to open communications."

"What?" It seemed incredible, then he recalled Quermwyere's intercepted conversation between *Gandhi* and Cracked Rock. "Of course, this is the second stroke to the rebellion. Of course they wouldn't rise like that unless they were sure they had a good chance of obtaining air superiority."

"What are you talking about?"

"The fat man, Quermwyere, he showed me; he told me, anyway. He said that my father believed there would be mutiny aboard one of the capital ships in the fleet, the *Gagarin* most likely."

"How did that pig come to possess such information?"

"I don't know, although he claimed to have penetrated Fundan military communication codes. But the point is that there *isn't* a Space Force mutiny, because this strange ship must be part of the rebellion. Was there any idea where it came from?"

She shrugged. "No, but when I heard that we might be attacked, I decided to leave the *Gandhi*. On the way we missed you at your cabin, but we had taken steps to protect you, so we were able to find you again."

"Protect me! You put that horror into my body to protect me?"

She gave him a glare like a basilisk. "Did we find you or did we not?" she snapped.

He glared back. She shrugged. "Prepare for ejection. This will be quite a rough ride at first. Then we're going into the atmosphere. I'm heading for the Northern coast; there's a city called Surf Rock, I believe."

"It's hardly a city, and there's no spaceport. Once you land there, you'll be stuck there."

"There doesn't seem to be much choice. The Highlands are proscribed space; the clans or the New Kommando will shoot at anything coming down; the South Coast cities are all in the hands of the rebels. Where else would you suggest?"

"The other South Coast cities went over too?"

"Let's say I don't think they had much choice."

He stared at her, amazed, dumb, unable to reply. She did not smile. Then she was gone, and he heard heavy hydraulics whine as they fitted the forty-ton mass of the shuttle into the ejection cartridge and lifted it toward the air lock.

There was a moment's rest inside the lock, then they were fired out by the ejection system, shooting free of the onrushing bulk of the *Gandhi*, endless kilometers of fuel tanks and radiation shielding.

9

As THE SPACE BOAT WAS EJECTED PLANETWARD FROM THE *Gandhi*, frantic activity went on throughout the Command levels. Men and women ran for their posts in Gunnery and Engineering. Red screamers wailed in the corridors. On the bridge the entire Command structure was in web, elevated on hydraulics, forming a white-suited hive around the central screen; the trimonitors that hung over every console were like insectal eyes, flickering with images.

The first warning had come ten minutes or so earlier when they received very strange signals from a robot defense probe in the outer regions of the Beni Stellar System. Immediately after the robot's alert signal had come a splash of gravity waves in the inner system, and then every security radar kicked on and alarms rang aboard every ship in the fleet. A massive object had materialized inside the orbit of the Pale Moon with an initial velocity in excess of ten thousand kilometers a second.

The first visual images coughed up by the computers were stunning—a sphere, deformed, made up of four tightly fitted modules. It was producing readings that seemed incomprehensible.

"Albedo of that surface corresponds closely to typical dust coat water moon."

"Three hundred kilometers in diameter. Mass is on order of twenty billion kilograms."

"What?" Admiral Ursk himself was moved to break into the link.

"Three hundred kilometers, sir."

"What are we dealing with?"

"A dust coat moonlet that just appeared from nowhere."

"FTL, sir, at last. This must be it." Number Two in Communications could not keep the excitement out of his voice.

"You're sure? This isn't some rogue asteroid that's got the computers in a frenzy for some reason?"

"Definitely not an asteroid, sir. It's moving way too fast,

accelerating at four gee, in fact, and we have a definite trace on an ion trail from conventional fusion engines."

"Human?"

"Computer gives that a very high probability, sir, in light of the insurrection on the South Coast. Reverse probability of course exists for an alien visitation during the rebellion."

Ursk sighed, not caring that lower Command levels heard him. "Well, that's a fucking relief." He cut out and back to restricted channels in Higher Command.

"Well, gentlemen, ladies, we have our first real test as a battle fleet coming up. I think we can assume that whoever this is they haven't come for milk and cookies."

On their screens were various video images of the thing, coming in constantly from robot probes. The roughly spherical shape was more clearly seen to be the result of the folding of complexly formed modules.

"What the hell is it?"

"No idea, sir," said Number Two. "But it is using a standard Fusion Drive at the moment."

Gandhi had already begun transition to a higher orbit. *Austerlitz* and *Gagarin* were much closer to the intruder.

"*Austerlitz* within forty thousand kilometers, sir."

"Where's *Gagarin*?"

"One hundred thousand kilometers away on the other side, sir. At current speeds and courses will intersect with intruder within six hours."

"I'm just wondering what kind of armament this thing is carrying. Tiax, does it mean anything to you?"

Commander Tiax summoned a top-secret image to his tri-monitor. It took a moment for Ursk's monitor to get complete clearance under the security code.

A deformed sphere, complexly folded modules. But it was a model, less than two meters wide.

Tiax was on High Security channel. "This is a scale model of the so-called Fuhl Drives, developed by Otto Fuhl of Neptunian Military Intelligence. Certain experimental machines like this were made. They disappeared when activated and never returned. Messire Fuhl was called to reserve duty in an agricultural battalion on Earth."

"If it didn't work why is it so secret, why are we using this channel?"

"Nobody says it didn't work—it did work, but something went wrong at the other end of the mission, or the robots were scrambled by the experience. Whatever the case, what we have here is clearly a development of it. The resemblance is striking, don't you agree."

There was no denying it.

"Then the question must be, if this has been developed in the home system, who is it carrying? I mean is Chairman Wei aboard?" Commander Tiax was clearly dubious.

"I think one has to feel that if Chairman Wei were aboard, the fact would have been announced. Nor would it have come at this precise time, when we have our hands full with the situation on the ground down on the South Coast."

"Then we probably have quite a problem on our hands." Ursk chinned out of the High Security net into Command.

"Forward shields are to be activated and positioned between us and the intruder. I want a full missiles pattern, maximum concentration. Meanwhile Security is to get anybody who's still onboard and doesn't belong here off the ship. We're going into high acceleration mode. Hurry."

The enormous black intruder picked up speed, heading toward Fenrille.

"*Austerlitz* hailing, sir. They're within ten thousand kilometers. No reply from intruder."

Anxiously they scanned the noncommunicative intruder, huge, dark, and ominous.

Abruptly there was communication. Small screens jumped with wobbly images.

"Broadcasting on wide spectrum, Admiral, very strong signal. It must be clear all over this side of Fenrille."

A face, thick-necked, heavy-jowled, with large dark eyes that seemed to bore into the viewer, exploded onto the screen.

"Greetings, I am Degorak Chevde, captain of the *Black Ship*. I bring you greetings from the Bond lords of Triton and Nereid. We announce the beginning of the new order of things. To the people of the Beni System I say awake, throw off your chains and join us. To the oppressors and warlords in the battle fleet I bring you a single relevant proposition. I will accept the surrender of your ships at the earliest possible moment. You may conduct any necessary ceremonies at that time. All crew members will be given the choice of service aboard my ship or being set down on the planetary surface. So surrender, then join us through the bonding and come with us to become the masters of the galaxy!"

The voice was harsh, the accent coarse, guttural. Tiax breathed. "Neptune system, Bond Leader Chevde. A very powerful, ruthless man; I think we have a serious opponent here."

Lower Command whispered in his ear, "Forward shields in position, sir." The five-kilometer-thick particle shields had been rotated to present the maximum depth of rock to the enemy.

Ursk switched to communications via the system net. "Greetings, Commander Chevde. You are a long way from Neptune, and you bring us a rather blunt message. What if we choose not to surrender?"

There was a moment's pause as the messages crossed in the emptiness.

"If you do not surrender, then we will be forced to destroy you. I offer you a way to save the lives of yourself and your crews. Do not sacrifice them unnecessarily."

The gunnery section broke through on Ursk's comlink. "Missile pattern ready, sir."

"Hold your fire, Mr. Gunner."

"Messire Chevde, by what authority is it that you demand this surrender?"

"By that vested in me by my fellow shareholders in the *Black Ship*. Messire, the situation is simple enough. I advise you to surrender now, while you can."

"*Austerlitz* wants to know if they can fire across the intruder's course, sir." Ursk nodded, suddenly nervous, not sure at all of what this intruder was capable of. Yet he had three ships, two of them *Achilles*-class battle wagons. Nothing could harm such a force.

"Yes, tell them to be sure to miss by a good margin though. I don't want accidental hostilities."

Moments later the main-screen representation of the Fenrille system exhibited a bright green line as *Austerlitz* closed to within five thousand kilometers and fired a burst of its primary laser across the intruder's bows.

"Intruder is rotating, sir."

"What is he trying to do? Bring his Fusion Drive to bear? Won't work on *Austerlitz*'s screens; they're too thick for that."

Suddenly a massive laser stabbed out at *Austerlitz*.

The gauge levels jumped on their screens. "Computer has that at a five Orange five."

"Good grief! That's a thousand gigawatts. No particle shield can take that for long."

"*Austerlitz* says particle screen is degrading, sir."

It was at extreme close range; the old space cruiser's screens were not heavy enough. Holes were punched right through the five hundred meters of rock shielding.

"Oh no, she's much too close, there's no way out of there."

The deadly beam finally chopped through the shield and ignited one of the ship's fusion drives.

Their screens opaqued in the blinding flash as a small sun blossomed briefly within the system. It was gone in a few moments and so was the *Austerlitz* and her two thousand crew, leaving nothing but a cloud of expanding gases and highly radioactive microdebris.

Ursk felt his eyeballs bulge in his head. "Get me the wattage figure on that. Deploy emergency shielding on engine pods." He thought for a moment.

"Tiax, this is not my ship; normally the *Gandhi* is your command. In fact I wish I were aboard the *Gagarin* right now. Nevertheless I'm afraid I'm going to have fight this battle from right here."Admiral Ursk swallowed. "But, you know something, I think they outgun us."

"We must run, sir. I don't think we can give them the tactical advantage as well as that beam. They must rotate their vessel to bring the thing to bear. That must mean they fire it from between those Fuhl Modules. If they can fire out, we can fire in, but we need to work on the approach. I suggest we try to get out of here."

"What will we tell Messire Fundan?"

"The truth, what he already knows I'd say. That we're trying to save our ships and we'll be back."

"It may be too late by then."

"It may be too late already, sir, look."

The *Black Ship*'s laser had been turned on the *Gagarin*. At eighty thousand kilometers *Gagarin* was also in easy range.

Gandhi and *Gagarin* both fired their primary lasers, heavy weapons indeed, but the beams struck the outer surface of the immense Fuhl Modules and caused only temporary ice melt.

They deployed complex waves of missiles. Several small thermonuclear devices got through, but these two detonated on the exterior of the Fuhl Modules. The *Black Ship* was jolted, perhaps, but only momentarily. Meanwhile that heavy laser continued to stab into *Gagarin*'s particle shield, an arrowhead five kilometers deep that was now rotated to cover the ship's headlong retreat out of the system.

"*Gagarin* is to drop engines if the shields degrade too far."

After a moment's pause Tiax said, "They acknowledge, sir."

Gandhi had changed course to an elliptic that would take them down close to Fenrille and then out again on an orbit that would keep the *Gandhi* out of the *Black Ship*'s line of sight until the enemy had rounded Fenrille.

Again and again the huge primary laser flickered to life gouging superheated pits in the battle wagons' shields. Smaller weapons lanced out to mop up the missile barrage. The *Black Ship* was wreathed in bright nuclear bursts, streaming a cometary head of vapor as the warships' heavy lasers continued to strike on the Fuhl Drives.

At a range of 260,000 kilometers the *Black Ship* finally broke through and disabled one of *Gagarin*'s engines. *Gagarin* uncoupled both engines and drifted on out of the system without primary power.

Gandhi ran from the huge intruder.

"No further communications, sir."

"Range one hundred ninety thousand kilometers, sir. And closing."

The ship strained forward accelerating inward at five gee. They would snick past the planet's cloud tops and vanish into the umbral shadow beyond.

Then the big laser hissed against their rear shields.

They stared helplessly at the small screens, the ominously thick green line linking the green blip and the heavy black blip.

"Shield degrading, sir."

"Another missile pattern, please, Mr. Gunner. We must try to shut down that laser."

A few moments later, yellow bursts flashed on their screens as the first missiles were picked off. Some got through; more flashes burst around the intruder.

"That was much better, Mr. Gunner. Proceed to repeat."

Indeed, for a few minutes the remorseless heavy beam was shut off and the *Black Ship* was forced to rotate to avoid damage from a warhead that zipped through the defense barrage.

"We might make it, Commander," Ursk breathed over High Security circuit.

On the screen the heavy green blip of the *Gandhi* was closing fast on the orange disk of Fenrille.

"Range one hundred ninety four thousand kilometers; we're six hundred six kilometers above the atmosphere."

"I think we're going to, sir," Tiax said.

"I think—" and then the heavy laser came back on.

"Shield degrading, sir."

"Spin the shield. Hurry . . ."

"Range one hundred ninety three thousand eight hundred . . ."

"Shield penetrated, sir," someone said in a dread voice. Then the *Gandhi* was cut in two, enormous sections breaking up, explosions rippled throughout, and the life-support zone disintegrated into a chaos of frozen air, bodies, and debris.

The youngsters in Fundan Central Command concentrated on their tasks, monitoring the situation. Nobody looked up; nobody wanted to risk having to meet the eyes of the one man there who attended no machinery—because upon him lay the sole task of making decisions.

But they knew. They had received the messages, had watched the radars track the remains of the shattered *Gandhi* through the atmosphere.

His wife in the hands of Young Proud, his mortal enemy. His son lost with the *Gandhi*, all in a matter of minutes. Lavin Fundan stood perfectly still, thoughts frozen like glaciated teardrops coursing an endless cheek.

Fool! He cursed himself. Of course Young Proud would wait. And of course he would wait for this, because now he would have air superiority.

That Fleur was in Young Proud's hands was Lavin's fault; he should never have dropped their guard this far.

That his son was lost, unless—his eyes had never strayed from that shower of radar blips; something was happening there— that Chosen was gone was his fault too, and the terrible irony of what he'd done didn't fail to sting him.

. . . thus we are prepared by the experience of life—to exist without the mark of existence is unattainable within this life, and thus woe must be our lot . . . for without pain there can be no self and without self, no realization of self . . .

The ancient mantra of the fein—he sought not comfort but strength from it, and strangely, strength came. He set his jaw, gritted his teeth. They would pay! He would show them how!

But he had to think clearly now; he fought for control; he took a deep breath, concentrated everything on the view screens.

The Fein meditation for control worked. He heaved a sigh. As with everything, the older race had trod these grounds long, long before there was even such a thing as an ape or an advanced mammal on Earth. He caught his bodyguard's eye, Val Bo-Ho, a young giant from Brelkilk Village. Bo-Ho was watching that odd blip on the screen as well. The concern in those big yellow eyes was plain to see. Bo-Ho had been bodyguard for only half a year, since the retirement of Mzsee Glabaz Rva.

But the situation remained as it had been. Lavin had stirred his forces to life at the first news of trouble on the Sx Coast, but there was little to be done until the enemy made their move.

And Young Proud lived! Had he ever really doubted it? He tried but failed to recall at which point he had actually decided that Young Proud must be dead. Perhaps he never had actually made such a decision but had simply forgotten his old foe, a figure from fifty years ago, presumed lost in the deep forest with a few loyal fein from the once-great Impis of Ramal Valley.

Fool! The curse chilled him. But something very definitely was taking place on the radar scan.

"Get me a close reading on that slow-moving blip; that separation from the others must mean something."

The radar computer was swiftly brought to bear. A bumpy image was produced.

"Space boat!" Rang Fundin almost screamed, and others exhaled loudly all round. Cordelia Fundin dared a glimpse of Lavin. But nothing was to be seen there except the intentness with which his eyes followed the descent of the space boat.

"Enemy vessel now appearing over horizon," Clade Fundin reported from the long-range radar monitor.

Almost immediately heavy electronic weaponry was brought to bear on the Highland valleys. Lavin was forewarned of this; his radars went off automatically except for the imaging radar locked on the space boat. Rang Fundin opened a line into the Butte Clan communications center over in Butte Manor, one thousand kilometers away. Not long afterward the Fundan imaging radar was destroyed by an EMP charge produced by the *Black Ship*, but they continued to track its progress through the Butte radars.

The tension rose in the room as the blip descended across the screen. "Position twelve hundred kilometers south and east, descending at one hundred twenty mps, clearly under control."

"I can see that myself, Mister Rang," said Lavin Fundan crisply. An almost tangible feeling of hope, against all odds, began to build in the room. Then the heavy blip marking the enemy ship moved into the picture, closing rapidly from behind upon the space boat.

The hope was replaced by dread.

"Missiles launched from enemy ship."

Moments later the space boat staggered and began to fall more directly.

The *Black Ship* rode westward at orbital speed, and the Cracked Rock radars swiveled to bear once more.

The boat tumbled, then at eighty kilometers it steadied once more, keeping her heat shields facing forward.

"Somebody's still alive on that boat," Rang said without thinking . . . "or is it just the unkillable computer . . ."

The silence was dreadful as they watched the boat fall and disappear off their screens, dropping into the great forest, thousands of kilometers south and east.

10

THE SPACE BOAT WAS ARCING INTO THE ATMOSPHERE, RIDING down on extended heat shields, when the *Gandhi* was mortally struck down by the *Black Ship*.

The initial bursts were nonnuclear, and huge sections of debris sprayed forward, sending streams of bright meteors flaring through the daytime skies over Fenrille's single continent.

The computer decelerated savagely, trying to bring the space boat down behind the avalanche of debris. The occupants were flung around in their seats by the violence of the boat's evasive maneuvers as large pieces began to scorch past them. They were still directly in the path, and small fragments drummed on the hull.

A heavy bump caused the boat to shudder; Chosen closed his eyes, felt his tongue hard pressed against the roof of his mouth from sheer terror. He fought down the urge to scream. If the boat turned over, they were fried. He wondered what it would feel like to die.

Far above and ahead of them now the *Gandhi*'s engines were suddenly consumed by a bright nuclear flash.

The boat computer continued the savage deceleration using fuel prodigiously.

"First parachute will engage in forty-four seconds," the computer announced in its reassuring female voice.

On the main screen a view of the planet below gradually materialized. Chosen recognized the great hooked curve of the River Bhjum. They were coming down over the southern part of the continent, a long way from the Surf Rocks.

He craned his neck to catch a glimpse of Chi Lin Wei's face. Her eyes were glued to the screen in obvious terror.

"I think I ought to say something. You see we're not coming down on the right side of the mountains."

She flashed him a look of hatred.

"Be quiet."

Then they screamed in unison as the boat was struck very

hard then staggered, wobbled sickeningly, and threatened to roll over, exposing them to incinerating atmosphere.

The wild gyrations flung them around in their seats hard enough to stun Chi Lin Wei. Chosen saw her neck snap back at an awkward angle and was surprised to find that he was concerned. He shouted her name but then was overcome by a wave of darkness. Before he went under he realized with dull regret that the biosurvey would never be completed.

But by some miracle of its programming and the sturdy design of attitude jets, the computer brought the space boat back under control at an altitude of eighty kilometers. It reported the damage in its cool, relaxed-sounding female voice to the unconscious cargo.

"Main engines and primary fuel tanks have been destroyed. Attitude jets are still operable, as are three of the parachutes. Due to small punctures in the rear storage sections, these have been sealed off for your continued safety. Passengers are asked to remain in their seats with belts fastened." Since no one was conscious to hear, the computer turned on the sprinkler system, letting cool drops of water bring the survivors around. After a few seconds it detected the sounds of movement and repeated its message.

Not long afterward, the first chute was deployed and brought them up with a jerk.

Their descent continued, more smoothly now. The semi-molten rear section, virtually fused by the heat from the exploding fuel tanks, left a long trail of smoke behind them as they described a giant, smooth curve over the basin of the great Bhjum.

When he returned to consciousness Chosen was faintly surprised to still be among the living. Then his curiosity returned. "So what happened?"

One of the Yu Zhao clones turned around and stared at him. "Boat struck by missile from enemy ship."

"Where's the enemy ship now?"

The computer put an image of the raider on the screen, but even its most time-consuming computer imaging techniques produced just a hazy circle, a dark mass photographed distantly by a satellite in the Fenrille Communications Network high above them.

"Intruder vessel is orbiting planet at five thousand kilometers and is now passing over our radar horizon."

"Where will we come down?" Chosen inquired in some concern. Ignoring the computer, the Chinese men had gathered around the unconscious Chi Lin Wei.

After a moment the computer answered him with some unfamiliar coordinates on screen before it spoke to explain. "Since we have only attitude jets operational, we will be forced to land within a radius of one hundred kilometers of our present position." They would come down in the center of the Bhjum Basin, thousands of kilometers from either coast.

"I don't want to unduly alarm you gentlemen, but I think you would be better advised spending the next few moments finding space suits rather than worrying about Chi Lin Wei. We're coming down in the deep forest."

He was met by a blank stare.

"Why should we need space suits?" one asked. They conversed briefly in Mandarin then laughed in unison. They bent over Chi Lin Wei and began to deploy medical equipment, but she awoke, shooed them away. Chosen implored them to remove his bonds. She glanced at him, her upper lip puffed up, a trace of blood on her forehead. She waved a hand toward Chosen and looked away. "Release him."

One of the Chinese clones removed his bonds. Chosen struggled with a dire impatience until he could stand it no longer. "Look, we must find space suits. I suggest we all look for the space suit locker and put on as much protection as we can. In particular look for heavy-duty outer skin and top-quality breathing filters."

"But why should we need space suits?" Yu Zhao said. He was identifiable by his age and the red stripe he wore on his flight suit. "This is an Earth-like world, people breathe the air all the time."

"Earth-like, yes, Earth, no, and where we're going the flies will be biting hard, since this is day side. A bite, a scratch, hell, even breathe too deeply down there and you could lodge a few spores of the blood fungi, the spruip. We don't have Alvosterine or any fungicides; besides, you wouldn't have a chance. Death would follow within a day or so."

Chi Lin Wei was white-faced. "You mean we have to stay in space suits all the time?"

"Well, at night the flies won't be biting, so you can risk removing your helmet to grab a quick meal."

He turned to the computer console. "Can this craft float on water?"

"No, messire, we are not designed for that mode of operation."

73

He sighed. They stared at him, perplexed, fearful. "If they're still whole after what we've been through, I'd suggest we find suits, and then use the ejection seats and try to come down in the river itself. We're going to pass over the Bhjum at a reasonable height for parachutes."

"Why don't we just stay in the space boat?" Yu Zhao said.

"Because the Woodwose will come."

"But not even the Woodwose can harm us if we're in the space boat," Chi Lin Wei protested.

Chosen looked from her to the others. They stared back, clinging to some obscure shred of security.

"Look, when the boat comes down it will damage trees. It must, even if it just lands in the branches. That by itself will bring a Woodwose. Even if it has to come thirty kilometers, it will come. If, alone, it cannot utterly destroy the space boat, then it will summon others. Believe me when I tell you that they will be quick to arrive."

Obviously they found it incredible. How could any mere animal harm them, encased as they were in one hundred tons of steel, plastic, and alloy?

"Look," Chosen said, more urgently, "the Woodwose is twenty-five meters tall. It has been observed to lift objects with measured weights of six tons. It will labor unceasingly to destroy the boat. Nothing will be left except shards of totally indigestible material that will be cast into the river Bhjum."

"These animals are not equipped with battle armor, are they?" said Yu Zhao two in a surly voice.

"No, of course not."

"Then they must be vulnerable to fire from lasers and rifles. We will simply destroy them when they attack."

Chosen shrugged. "I think you should reconsider. These are not animals as you of Earth understand the term. They can be cunning, and they are very swift."

"They live, don't they?"

"Of course, Yu Zhao."

"Anything that lives can be killed. So if we have to, we will kill them. Sorry to destroy local life-form, but we must survive."

Chosen looked to Chi Lin Wei.

She sniffed, looked away. "This is insanity," she said, the strain showing in her voice. "I cannot believe that anything can harm us if we land in the space boat."

They would not be moved. Chosen looked at the screen clock. There was no time to persuade them.

He got up and by interrogating the computer he learned of

an equipment locker filled with space suits, helmets, and other gear. With nervous hands he pulled an unfamiliar suit over his head and wriggled it over his body. Then he grabbed the helmet and a filter unit and a slim oxygen tank. He slung the tank over his shoulders and connected the breathing apparatus. In another compartment he found four cased revolvers, boxes of ammunition, and several shoulder holsters. The guns fired soft-nosed nine mm bullets or exploding darts of the same caliber. He buckled one around his right shoulder and then handed the others to Yu Zhao. The ejection seats could be deployed safely only when fired in unison, so he was forced to break open the emergency hatch at the rear of the cabin.

Then the second chute deployed, and the shuttle continued its controlled descent into the green hell below. Chosen examined the computer projection of their course over the river. He would jump when they neared the far side; he judged that the boat would come down a few kilometers beyond the river.

He turned back to the Chinese. "As soon as you land, put on the space suits. Take the weapons and leave the space boat as quickly and as quietly as you can. Meet me by the river's edge." He pointed to the monitor. "We'll have to float down the river to get out of here. Fortunately, we are close to the river. Keep in radio contact."

Their eyes were like black buttons; they stared at him silently. After a moment of enigmatic silence, he shrugged and forced the emergency hatch open. His chute blossomed and left him floating in the space boat's wake, down through cloudless turquoise skies toward the brown waters below.

Beyond the river the space boat's main chute broke out, a bright stab of magenta against the endless green of the *Esperm gigans* forest.

Between himself and the boat was the river itself. Chosen was coming down several hundred meters offshore. However there was no easily observed shoreline. The Bhjum at this point was an inland sea, averaging fifty kilometers in width. In flood it would be much, much more. Extensive swamp covered low-lying ground. To the far horizons this was all there was. It would be a long and arduous walk.

He chinned the suit radio and scanned for signals. Once or twice he picked up vague stutters of a signal, big CCKB down at Coast City, he assumed. If reception was that bad then they were really in the back country. It might take weeks to float far enough down to get into range with the suit radios.

He tried the Mayday signal anyway; there was always a chance that someone in the Highlands might pick it up from a military-sensing station.

Far ahead the magenta primary chute descended into the trees. Then he looked down and saw the long shapes beneath the water's surface. The big freshwater permiads were migrating upriver to spawn; they would be insatiably hungry, snapping at anything they passed.

With nervous fingers he fitted the oxygen mask on his face and thrust his gun into the waterproof emergency pack. Twenty meters above the water he unhooked the chute and let go a moment later and dove feet-first into the water. He had to get down deep, fast, frightening the permiads away with the splash and dropping to the murky bottom before they regrouped to investigate.

His entry was near perfect, exchanging the clear sky for muddy brown water at the bottom of the river in a flash of bubbles and momentary confusion.

As he'd expected, the permiads fled the violent intrusion and then returned to circle the spot, nosing for a trace of food scent, a trace of blood to lead them to food. But encased in his suit he gave off no odors that were perceptible except from his breathing apparatus, and now he hunched down among the weeds and used the suit's chest light to examine the river bottom. Weeds and roots trailed past from his right to his left, and thus he knew which way to head. He set off into the murk with his light pushing back the dark for a few meters in front. Small fish, also hiding from the permiads above, darted away. He felt an odd sense of identity with them; they were all potential meals for the big migrants moving above.

Soon the roots grew more numerous and thicker. Gradually they merged together in an immense mat that shelved up toward the surface.

At the upper margin of the murky bottom water he halted. The surface waters ran deep into the forest. He would have to get out of the water by climbing up one of the gigantic *Esperm* roots and then try to make his way inland by staying atop the roots. It was an exhausting prospect, and he would have to run the suit's air-conditioner, burning up the batteries and reducing the chance of contacting the outside world through the radio.

A shadow moved above; a lean-bellied permiad was investigating. He watched as it trained a large, featureless black eye upon him, establishing his position precisely among the roots. He clambered back down, pulling himself deeper. The big fish, almost four meters in length, was close to starvation. It nosed down into the brown waters after the bright moving lure. The urge to feed was strong. It champed together jaws lined with teeth as long as a human forefinger and swung its snout back and forth seeking some trace of the prey. Chosen was forced to wriggle in among the roots as the fish came closer. It was much darker, a maze of narrow spaces, and instinctively Chosen moved cautiously. Something told him that this was a deadly place.

The fish continued to nose after his stream of bubbles; he was forced to go deeper, pulling himself along a strangely segmented root that had a sheen to it that he hadn't seen on a root before.

With astonishing swiftness something huge uncoiled from the dark and sprang past him. There was a frantic thrashing in the water; the roots shuddered and jumped around him. Chosen kicked free and headed for the surface. As he emerged from the roots he glimpsed a fantastic nightmare, a giant assassin beetle moving on limbs ten meters long, returning to its lair with the big permiad clutched in its mandibles. For a moment he gazed directly into one of its red-lined green eyes and swallowed hard, but the monster ignored him and dragged the still-thrashing fish into the dark.

Chosen swam to the surface and then climbed out upon a protecting root system that reached down into the water like some gigantic clawed hand. He sat down just in time; he was shaking so hard that he almost fell back into the water. He gave his surroundings a quick inspection. No immediate dangers appeared. Huge root systems gathered up into great tree trunks that ascended hundreds of meters into the sky. Under the trees the light dimmed to a green dusk that receded into darkness in the distance. When the shaking ceased sufficiently he dug his revolver out of the emergency pack and placed it in the damp shoulder holster. He slung the emergency pack over his other shoulder and disconnected the oxygen apparatus and replaced it with the heavy filter, which formed a conical snout below his helmet visor. He practiced drawing the gun and set it to fire explosive darts, then he got to his feet and after taking a fix on the sun so the small suit computer could give him a direction pointer, he set off into the trees.

11

Several times Bg Rva heard the voices enter the kitchen and leave again. Once somebody rapped on the exterior of the freezer and he tensed, gripping his kifket, ready to charge forth and die fighting. But the voices faded away again, and he was left alone in the cold and the dark. Time passed, and he began to shiver; a great fatigue spread through his body. For a fein in his eighties it had been a hell of a day. Eventually his eyes closed despite several desperate attempts to stay awake.

Thus when Lucy Urbimle returned with help and opened the door, Rva simply fell out, half-dead from hypothermia, and almost crushed her on his way to the floor.

"Oh, Messire Arvah," she wailed and dropped down beside him aghast. "Oh, please don't be dead, messire." She groped for his wrist and searched for his pulse.

The impact with the floor had abruptly ended Rva's deathly dreams. Groggily he sat up and looked around him. He'd seen a lot already on this especially long day, so the colorful apparition in front of him was not particularly hard to accept.

He was still shivering though and exhausted. He needed a meal and somewhere safe to sleep for about twenty hours.

In fact for the moment the idea of getting to his feet was one he decided not to contemplate. A dull ache in his thigh reminded him of the brief fight with the war band soldiers.

Beside Lucy stood a scrawny little man with a potbelly. He wore sunglasses and a loud solar shirt atop mauve slacks and white shoes. His sunglasses were pushed up into a shock of white brillo. A gnomish face was cracked by a salesman's cheery smile. Rva instinctively thought of a trader in horses.

"Messire Arvah, this is my friend Bino Dash, a very old friend. He'll be able to help us."

"'Us'?" Rva sat up straighter. Clearly Miss Lucy had thrown herself into the fray. He looked at them, wizened little humans, used to living quiet lives while they eked out low-rent longevity plans and maintained themselves in old age for centuries. Were they aware of the risks? The penalty for going against the Kommando was likely to be simple and severe.

"Where are the soldiers?" he said.

"They've gone. I kept them here while I made them some coffee and gave them some snacks. They've been on duty all day, they said. I thought it wouldn't harm to entertain them; they seemed to lose their interest in tearing the apartment to pieces as well. Quite relaxed they became. They were actually quite talkative. I think they're working their way down the hall to Corridor Forty-one. Kept saying they're looking for 'Criminal elements' but they didn't seem to know what that might mean. Rather confused I thought they were."

Rva looked up at her with new respect.

"They said a reorganization of the whole city was underway and that there would be a complete audit of every citizen's possessions. I assume that means another Search."

The little man took that as his cue. "So when Lucy told me about you I came right over. I hate these thugs as much as she does. I'm with you."

Rva smiled, a slightly unnerving sight, since it bared his remaining front canine tooth like some yellowed fang. "You understand the risks you take?" he rumbled softly.

Bino nodded. "We know the risk, but if we're careful, eh? And we can't let these swine get away with this. They've killed hundreds of people, absolutely innocent bystanders. I've seen their kind of rule before. No, it's clear to both of us that we have to help the Fenrille Defense Forces in any way we can. At the moment, messire, you represent the FDF here, so we shall hide you and help you escape."

Rva chuckled. "I am the FDF, eh?" He giggled and poked Bino Dash with a massive forefinger. "Ho ho, old Rva is the FDF today!"

The little humans gazed at each other in wonder.

Bino continued talking, wondering if the old fein could understand him or whether perhaps it was senile. The way it fell out of that freezer, like it was dead or something. It had almost given Bino one of his "turns." "You see I've lived here sixty-four years, right over the hallway, you see, been a friend of Lucy's for decades; I used to go fishing with her old man, Sal. I got an Optimol plan, you see; you wanna guess how old I am?"

To Rva the little man seemed in late middle age.

"Nope." Bino gleamed proudly. "Went over the century just last week, my first one hundred."

"Bino has a place for you to hide," Lucy said earnestly as she emerged from the kitchen with some hot herb tea that Rva gulped down to put some warmth in his belly. The tea made him all too aware however of just how hungry he'd become.

"Yes," said the little man, "I have a boatyard, on a subbasement floor beneath the yacht basin. I know a great place there where you'll be safe. It's an old smugglers air lock, from the old days before the Great Peace."

Shortly afterward a still-shivering Bg Rva and the slight form of Bino Dash strode furtively around a short corner to the service elevator bank. The Luxor Dome was ominously quiet, not a soul to be seen. From somewhere a ways off, a floor above perhaps, they could hear soldiers marching, boots clacking on the floor.

The elevator car was empty. Bino put it on manual override and took it down fast to the sub B level. There they trotted down an industrial alley. Big cracks, leaks dripping heavily from the ceiling—the place was evidence of the age of the city. The Sx Coast had stood on these small sand islands for three hundred years, the infrastructure was in dire shape.

Bino stopped to activate a sliding door, much begrimed and worn, that opened with a protesting wheeze. Above, the legend "Bino's Boats" radiated in jaunty but fitful neon.

Inside was a workshop and a suite of offices with computer consoles and design equipment. Beyond a partition was a large space filled with boats and bright sails.

"I make racers," Bino said. "But I also keep my hand in at the old used-equipment trade. Which is where me and old Sal started. Selling off stolen stuff, aqualungs, suits—you know what I mean. Anyhow there's a storeroom back here." He opened another door and showed Rva into a warehouse room stacked with marine equipment of every variety. There were hundreds of crates, anyone of which could hide a man and, in some cases, a fein. Bino led him through the maze of crates.

After pushing aside some crates filled with rubber suits, Bino pointed downward. Set into the concrete floor was a steel ring. He heaved at it and after a moment managed to raise a square section out of the floor. Metal stairs led down into a dark well. Bino descended, flicked on a light switch, and showed Rva into a small square room furnished with a couple of crates along one wall.

"We used to do a little business through here in the old days. You'll be safe here for the moment."

Rva disliked the idea of being shut in the tiny place underground, but was too exhausted to think of an alternative. He grunted some thanks and soon slid into a restless sleep tormented by dreams of the Kommando soldiers and the lady Fleur.

When he awoke the little man was back, with a steaming heap of pulse porridge and some bread. It wasn't exactly ideal fein food but would suffice in a pinch, and Rva knew he would be able to digest it. Quickly he shoveled it down then belched loudly, the sound echoing in the small room.

Before composing himself for sleep, he questioned Bino and discovered that a passage led from the room, out beneath the boat basin. The room in fact was a simple air lock and could be flooded and pumped dry.

Rva realized he had come to the perfect place. He sent Bino away with a list of items that he would need.

A few hours later Bino returned with a large sack and woke him. He disgorged its contents. "The most difficult item was the wet suit, I'm afraid there aren't very many made to your dimensions, messire. I had to send someone over to Elefelas to the Tall & Broad Outfitters. But I've got it all here now, except for the aqualung, which I have upstairs."

Rva looked through the items, canned foods, a water evaporator, a heat grid, a gun and ammunition, a sheet of gray tarpaulin. He gave the wet suit a dubious look. How could anything made for humans fit Rva of the Brelkilks? But to his considerable surprise, it slid on quite easily and made a comfortable fit. To Rva humans were a small people, fascinatingly quick, agile and mysterious. Now he considered that there had to be some humans as big as himself, seven feet tall and three hundred pounds weight. There was just no end to human eccentricity!

Bino helped him strap the compact water jets to his ankles. The jets were controlled by the action of the heels during swimming and at full power would propel him through the water at a steady four knots for twelve hours.

Bino left the room, and soon afterward it began to fill with water. Holding a fish baton in one hand and a power lamp in the other, Rva made his way cautiously across the waters of the bay keeping a wary eye for big solitary permiads and the spiny pectaroon, a legendarily voracious predator that lurked in the muds of the delta.

On his wrist he wore an expensive chronocomputer that also gave him his bearings. He headed northeast into the delta of the Irurupup.

The bottom was littered with human garbage and the debris

of civilization. Wrecked boats, bottles, wires, and plastic kitchen items were piled here and there by the currents.

Tall concrete columns jutted up ahead, wreathed in weed, reminders that the Sx Coast was an old city built upon shifting tidal sands. Great domes had once stood there, before the great river rearranged the isles in one monsoon flood.

Kelp beds began there that grew throughout the brackish delta mouth. He passed through the columns into shadows and soon sensed another presence.

From out of the dark came a menacing shadow. A big permiad swung toward him with dilated nostrils. Jaws sliding open, eyes closed off by the protective membrane.

Rva swung round and smartly jolted the ten-foot-long fish with the force baton. The *crack* of the hot blue sparks and the sudden, intensive pain sent the permiad swiftly away in distress. Rva peered around for further dangers. Smaller fish schooled among the tall columns, which were encrusted with shellfish and Fenrille coral forms. The columns formed long avenues in the dim greenness of the bottom of the bay. It was a strange testimony to human perseverance and plain cussedness. A city of concrete pilings, mute tombstones to an earlier century. Rva shook his head. Never had humans seemed more bizarre to him. He jetted on out into the deeper part of the bay and eventually crossed to the Bub Isle, where he pulled himself ashore through a swamp of bladder grove and long-rooted yasm. He moved back from the shoreline into a thicket of blue knuckoo. Around him grew clumps of spine weed, a tasty salad addition. Elsewhere he saw edible plim plam and red-vein bubblewort. Everywhere lay a thick carpet of gray-green gossafener weed. He unpacked his equipment and with the kifket and some instant glue quickly converted some of the knuckoo stems into a lodgepole-style tent frame, over which he fitted the tarpaulin. He weighted it all down with stones from the lee side of a sand channel and dug through the gossafener to make a shallow pit where he stacked cans of food and set up his evaporator sheet.

Finally, with the sun going down in a riot of greens and orange to the west, Rva made the inspection of his corner of the Bub Isle, a narrow peninsula several kilometers long. The southern shore faced the distant domes of the Sx Coast, ten kilometers or more away. Here the yasm and bladder grove swamp was impenetrable. On the northern shore was a smooth curve of sand, a beach that curved around to the north and vanished in heat haze and vegetation. The knuckoo, with its long stems and triangular blue leaves, grew everywhere between.

Rva noted the slime trails of giant predatory land molluscs and saw the burrows of litypups and sarmer mackees. On the sands he spied a number of tracks, and by the water's edge a trio of small, sleek animals watched him approach before slipping smartly into the water and swimming away.

In the calmer backwater air, biting flies buzzed in the dying light. Rva observed them with distaste, for they bore several deadly diseases, including the spruip fungi. He would have to keep to the southern side as much as possible where the estuarial breezes would normally deter the flies.

Once back at his camp he heated a can of synthetic protein-and-carbohydrate stew and ate it quickly before extinguishing all lights and going to sleep. As a precaution against fly bites, he turned the portable bug killer on inside his tent.

The next day he explored his new dominion more thoroughly. The midday heat brought out clouds of flies, and he was forced to go into the water to avoid them. But then he found that floating in his wet suit and moving by water jets was a more relaxing way of exploring anyway. He circumnavigated the Bub Isle. In the channel near the main swamp, he encountered a spiny pectaroon. But a quick flash of the force baton across the creature's feelers was enough to send it hurtling backward, ejecting a cloud of dark evil-smelling ink.

He pondered the problem of communication with Cracked Rock, or any Highland transmitter he could reach. He had a small two-way radio with which he monitored communications on the Sx Coast. Thus he became aware of the New Kommando's extreme efforts to suppress all dissidence. Ham radio operators were being rounded up. Mobile sensors had been set up all over the Sx Coast to help catch spies transmitting messages out of the city. However Rva felt he had to try to get a message out to Abzen, to Lavin Fundan.

He composed a message in Abzen Security Code and punched it into the radio's microcomputer. Then he cut a stalk of blue knuckoo, which he carved into a sharp, hollow spear with his kifket.

After dark he stalked along the shoreline.

He listened intently. Then he heard a grumbling croak from a thicket. He tensed and listened hard. Soon he was rewarded with the sound of the furtive digging of a gravid noripul. Rva squatted down to wait. The digging in the gossafener and the sand below it went on for quite a while as the noripul dug an egg pit.

Eventually the digging ceased and the noripul ejected a heavy sac into the hole and then covered it up and turned back to the water.

As soon as the tentacled mollusc had dragged itself a few bodylengths down the beach, Rva approached the site then repeatedly thrust into the sand with the sharp end of the hollow knuckoo stem.

He put his ear to the stem each time and listened carefully. Finally he heard the soft popping sound made by the maturing eggs as they hardened.

Quickly he dug down into the nest and removed the sac. It was heavy, much larger than those of the freshwater noripul of his mountain home. His muzzle wrinkled involuntarily when he thought of the stink the eggs would generate.

Back at his camp he slit the sac along the basal line and dumped the still-soft eggs into a shallow pit. He shook out the sac. When he stretched it out with his hands it was about as long as his forearm. He tied up the slit he'd made and wrapped it around a narrow knuckoo stem. Exercising his lungs mightily, he blew lustily into the sac and held it over the heat pad to help stretch the membrane evenly.

Then, one by one he put the soft eggs onto the heat pad. They broke down and released great quantities of noxious gases that expanded the sac into a balloon, straining at a length of fishing line, eager to be off into the wind, rising toward the domes and lights of the Sx Coast across the estuary. As his balloon hardened, Rva programmed the small radio to transmit its message when it reached a height of ten kilometers then tied it to the string and released the distended sac.

He watched it disappear as a brisk evening breeze swept it out to sea and, soon, out of sight.

A few minutes later however he heard antiaircraft missiles being launched from the Sx Coast. Distant detonations followed.

Rva shivered in the wind for a second then returned to his tarpaulin tent and made ready to sleep.

12

THE TELECONFERENCE OF THE CLAN COUNCIL HAD BEEN LONG and acrimonious. Lavin Fundan wore a face filled with thunder. He could barely keep his temper under control.

From Mauriar Valley, Diamonze Butte begged for help. A small party of Space Marines had landed and marched against her tower, the pink concrete mushroom of Blowder Castle. The lovely Diamonze had been a founder of the pacifist movement so strong in her family. Her fein Impis were retired, and all she had for defense was a small human force composed of guards and Chitin talkers.

From Takiar Hole, Danilaar Hoechst called for a demi-Impi and support aircraft to be sent at once to repel Space Marines who were plundering the pharamol vault of his ancient manse.

From Tinka Chung in the Magenta Valley came a plea for immediate assistance. A pod of Space Marines was storming the square walls of Chung Tower. The Magenta Impi, a unit reduced to purely ceremonial duties, had been ineffective in defense. In fact the Impi had been annihilated. Hundreds of Chung fein were dead, their valley ravaged.

From far and wide came the calls; dozens of valley holders who had voted consistently to deny funds to the Fenrille Response Force now demanded that that force protect them and their precious hoards of eternity drugs.

Lavin Fundan was blunt in reply. "I have only my own Abzen First Impi at immediate readiness. The Response Force itself is only four thousand fein; if I try to help you, I will have to do so with twelve fein for each. Is that what you want?"

Ovula Butte called in considerable distress, from the ruins of once-fabled Westerend, with its gabled towers and the exquisite Bridge of Sighs. Now the manse was ravaged, the towers burnt, the bridge broken, and Ovula despoiled. She raged against Lavin, damning the Defense Forces.

"When I needed them where were they?" she screamed.

"I will remind everyone that Lady Ovula Butte voted against the FRF budget every year for the last thirty." Lavin was caustic.

"In fact I will not commit the force in response to any of these calls for help. We have only enough strength for one campaign, hopefully a short one. Our strategy is clear. Since we are heavily outnumbered and outgunned and lack air superiority for considerable periods we must concentrate our force and wait until the enemy commits himself to his major thrust. You all know where I believe that attack will come. I wish all Clan Butte to be witness to that." He paused to glare into the screens.

"When the enemy commits his strength we will attack him; have no fears on that score; but we must wait for the right moment, and we must damage his ground forces so severely that they fail to capture a major target. Then we have to hope the *Gagarin* can do something to draw off the *Black Ship*."

He smote his fist for emphasis. "We can manage one battle; even then our fein will be heavily outnumbered and we will certainly be outgunned. But the Response Force has trained for this day. I think we can promise them a stiff little fight."

Lavin's refusal did not sit well.

"Haughty young bastard," Ovula shrieked, "you goddamn *clone*, why if I had—" Lavin cut her off.

Rognius Butte came on the Butte Clan line, a scrambled tight beam through the refined communications system that Lavin had prodded the Council into funding and installing.

"Uncle, I know, I know, she doesn't mean it." He smiled mirthlessly and thought, *If only that was true.* But they did, many of them, the older Clansfolk; they hated him because they feared him and saw him as Fair Fundan reincarnated. But there was no Fair Fundan anymore, nor did Lavin even keep in contact with many of his fellow clones from Fair's tissues. He heaved a sigh; a vast feeling of depression lay over him.

"I have bad news, Lavin."

So even now the pacifists would not concede defeat—Lavin was stunned.

"The Kirk voted against resistance except by the Impi at Butte Manor."

"But it's their own wealth in those vaults. There must be a hundred kilograms of pharamol in there. I mean, don't they understand what they're risking?"

"The Peace of the Lamb is to raise up the other cheek for the fang of the evil one."

Lavin snorted derisively. "The Guards Impi at Butte Manor

is at half muster, their weaponry is exactly the same as it was fifty years ago. If the New Kommando comes, how long do you think the guards will keep them out?—Or make that *when* the Kommando comes, Uncle." For Lavin was certain Butte Manor would be the primary target. The Butte family's maniacal devotion to the Peace of the Lamb those past twenty years had undone the military tradition of four centuries. In the great vaults of Butte Manor, their oldest fortress, was kept the clan pharamol deposited over the centuries.

"Will you stop talking in that military jabber and do something," Diamonze Butte yelled from another screen. "The foul plundering swine are breaking in my gates."

Even as she spoke, the dull boom of satchel charges was audible as the Space Marines broke the pink concrete clam shell and collapsed the mass-drive cannon, which brought down the tower.

All resistance ended at Blowder. On the screen they watched horrified as powersuited Marines burst in upon the shrieking Diamonze. They plucked her from her chair and dragged her away.

There was a moment of silence, then the watching Clansfolk began baying for help. In disgust Lavin turned away and switched Cracked Rock out of the telenet to blank the screens.

Since Young Proud Fundan refused to visit the *Black Ship*, Degorak Chevde and his inner circle descended upon the Sx Coast. There were some things to be discussed that could not be entrusted to codes and radio.

The pinnace from the *Black Ship* was a converted methane hauler from the Neptune Gas Company. It broke into a sunny day over the Sx Coast like some startling bolt from a black-fisted god. The sky brightened at first, a new sun blossoming above, then the thunder rolled over the coast and people turned to their windows or the TV.

It took a minute or more for that thunder to finally die away, but the vast volume of exhaust gases from the pinnace's chemical boosters hung over the city in a thick fog of choking vapor.

Out of the fog marched two dozen Space Marines, seeming to tiptoe in their armor as they kept the suit drives idling. Behind them followed a pair of squat armored vehicles. As Young Proud had been informed beforehand, one carried a three-megaton nuclear warhead that would be detonated in the event of an attack.

The vehicles drove slowly forward to the terminal. Security

men emerged from one and explored the terminal carefully. They then escorted Degorak Chevde and his retinue into the meeting room. The Space Marines fanned out around the room, mingling with the Security Korps from the Kommando.

An hour later Chevde emerged, face flushed with anger. Trailed by his retinue he stamped back into the squat tank and returned to the pinnace. He left behind Ira Ganweek to coordinate liaison with the Kommando.

The heavy boosters cut in, and with a thrust that shook the entire delta of the Irurupup, the pinnace lifted off the blast pan and rumbled upward.

Ira Ganweek watched it with obvious relief on his face. Home. He was home again, in the city he knew how to rule! Home, and sitting in the catbird seat with Degorak on one chain and this lean vampire of a clansman on another. Once he regained control of the old Bablon Syndicate things would get back to normal. The nightmare of fifty years, on Earth and then in the Tritonian Bond, was over. He was home on the Sx Coast.

"You are pleased to see your patrons depart, messire?" At that eery whisper he turned and found Young Proud sidled close.

Ganweek was uncomfortable. He shifted away. "I'm just glad to be home, messire, that's all. You can't imagine how I have hungered to be home, here, for so long, so many, many years. The home system is not like ours, messire. You cannot imagine the bizarre horror they inflict upon each other. On Earth millions still go hungry all their lives. There are slaughters, rebellions, retribution. It is not a pretty world anymore." And Ganweek paused and groped to describe the enormity of greenhouse Earth, with the black skies and endless rain, the colossal cities, the dead seas with their colored waters, and the endless billions of human beings.

"So one chooses the off-world colonies, of course? But to buy a space aboard premium space habitat is more than most people can make in a lifetime, especially if they try to prolong those lives with longevity drugs. Oh, it was horrible, horrible!"

"But now you are home and just days away from revenge, eh?" Young Proud spoke soothingly. The bloated little pig was getting excitable, he seemed to be operating under considerable strain.

"Yes, home, and even some revenge," Ganweek said in a whisper.

Ganweek inquired about his old apartments, high up in the Bablon Dome, but found they were occupied by new tenants. Silently he vowed deaths for each and every one of them. He took rooms in the Hotel Luxor nearby. Later he met with Young Proud and Rinus Van Relt for dinner, during which they discussed the strategy for the coming campaign.

"As I understand you then, messire, you propose to draw the Response Force into battle without committing your major force and then pounce when you have him out in the open." Ganweek leaned back in his chair. The braised molluscs had been delicious, the salad crisp and elegant. He had always liked this little restaurant; it'd been one of old Quermwyere's favorites too. A pity the old walrus had bought it on the *Gandhi*. Ira would miss the fat man.

It sounded good; the plan as outlined by Commander Van Relt had a lot to recommend it. Ganweek remembered Van Relt, a good soldier, had lost command of the great Traif Kommando through some treachery arranged by the Syndicate. Then lost three whole war bands in the disaster of Badleck Ridge and had gone down in history. But he had been successful before that raid, and at Traif his Kommando had engineered the biggest upset of Highland Arms in the three centuries of the Long War.

"We will go in with ten thousand troops. Enough to roll up the manor's defense Impi, which is purely ceremonial these days. That will bring Fundan running. When he throws the Response Force into battle, we will bring up the rest of the Kommando. The *Black Ship* will deploy Space Marines, and we will crush him against the Butte Stones right outside the manor."

"We must take him alive," said Young Proud with a strange little smile. For some reason Ganweek felt a shiver run through him.

That night he slept well, until in the hour before dawn, a series of distant blasts disturbed his sleep. Huge explosions were shaking the whole dome. From the balcony window he saw thick clouds of smoke drifting through the lights around the airport.

Newscasts by the Kommando did not allude to the incident, although later in the morning it was announced that there would be a temporary halt to all flights in and out of Sx Coast airport. No reason for the halt was given other than "urgent military matters," and Ganweek's attempts to find out from Van Relt's staff proved fruitless.

That afternoon there was a rigorous search of the hotel for spies. Ira counted at least two hundred soldiers in the lobby as he waited in the small bar there for the search to end. He was penniless, as poor as the day he started work for the Bablon Syndicate two hundred years before. He reflected that this made him immune to soldier kleptos who were probably rifling the guests' rooms as they searched. Then the radio announced an emergency ban on the use or sale for use of gasoline, kerosene, or aviation fuels.

Whatever those explosions had been, they seemed to have stirred up a hornets' nest; the Kommando was turning over the entire Sx Coast in the hunt for spies.

However, despite Van Relt's maniacal urgings, the results were spotty. A few real real spies were found—a Chinese restaurant with Chung family connections, a Spreak agent in Elefelas, as well as a bag of fein dung in a storeroom on the Fun Isle and some radio equipment hidden in a luxury apartment in the Nineveh Dome.

Soldiers searched Bino's Boats very thoroughly, going through every crate in the storeroom, looking inside every boat and every large piece of machinery. However they did not look beneath the crates and thus missed the passageway.

Bino reflected that the soldiers were simply amateurs at this kind of thing and most of the old Customs Agents had been imprisoned with the captive Police Force.

The cause of the explosions, which had demolished the gasoline-tank farm and half the airport as well, was spending his time peacefully fishing for tasty bolita that he had observed swimming through the roots of the yasm and bladder grove.

Rva used a whippy little knuckoo stem for a rod and a line supplied by Bino, along with Bino's Best Stinger, a sweet little green-flecked fly that bolita loved to bite at.

He soon had three plump specimens in his sack along with a little black fish that he had never seen before. He returned to his carefully hidden tent. While the bolita sizzled on the heat plate, he watched the Kommando News on the portable TV he'd picked up from Bino on his last visit.

Things were certainly hopping over there. The isles were being tight searched, down to the last spare room, for fugitives and spies. Bino's Boats had had all explosives, weapons, even laser equipment, confiscated until further notice. The hunt was continuing over on the peninsula too, and all travelers between the Sx Isle and the peninsula were being searched and monitored.

Rva investigated the little black fish with the honed edge of his kifket, cutting it down the back and opening it out deftly, but a careful sniff of its delicate-looking pink flesh made the hairs on the back of his neck rise. Thoughtfully he took the fish and threw it in the direction of a nest of noisy gowpers who howled furiously every morning at the first light of the sun.

The gowpers sprang from their perches and fought over the

little black fish. With their characteristic "gowp-*ee*?" cry they gobbled it down and returned to their perches.

Rva nodded, lower lip projecting. Well, he still had three nice bolita. And some well-fed gowpers. Then the gowpers started falling out of their perches to land with small thuds among the knuckoo husks on the gossafener. He soon counted six dead gowpers and another pair that were frantically vomiting in the branches.

Rva raised his eyebrows. Gowpers were real stupid in that part of the world.

13

IN THE MIDDLE OF THE FOLLOWING DAY THE FIRST WAVE OF THE *Black Ship*'s transport jets swung in low over Bub Isle and angled for the long runway at the Sx Isle airstrip. They coasted over with a penetrating whistling roar, enormous planes on albatross wings, matte black from their radar camouflage.

Rva counted a dozen of them. An hour and a half later he counted another dozen. By then the first of the monsters to land had received a load and was staggering into the air again on its jets, heading out to sea. Rva kept track with Bino's binox while hidden in a tree house he had built after a confrontation the day before with a slime bear.

It was a mature slime, five meters long, and simply too big to kill without enormous effort. But having it around made it too dangerous to sleep on the ground.

He'd watched it suck up the dead gowpers under the knuckoo and hoped for a while that the little black fish might yet be potent. After a few moments the slime shuddered, and as Rva watched in fascination, it became very still. It even changed color a little, sweated rather obviously, until it was covered in moisture. Then it shook itself out and resumed its normal progress, sliding forward to snuffle for food.

With a shrug Rva had turned to other pursuits. Slime bears were immune to most anything. Indeed their only serious foe were the flesh flies' larvae which fed under the slime's skin. Other than that the huge things went their way without hindrance.

It was much too slow however to catch an agile prey, and all Rva had to do was to move his tent up into the branches of a massive knuckoo. To disguise it against Kommando surveillance, he arranged a number of long fronds so that they arched over the front and roof of the tent and broke up its outline.

Every hour and a half more transport jets arrived. The afternoon resounded to their rumbling takeoffs.

That evening he hunted along the inlets of Bub Isle for a

gravid noripul. It was dark by the time he found one. Eventually he headed back with a modestly heavy egg sack.

He passed through a grove of liskellen bush whose musk reminded him of the scented forest of his home in the Highlands. Liskellen was a rare plant on the coasts, and for a moment Rva was transported far from the heat, humidity, and biting flies. He thought of the woods of Brelkilk, filled with liskellen and mindal.

A sudden movement dead ahead startled him into dropping the egg sac. Rva pulled his kifket and backed away. Something shifted in the deeper darkness. Something big. The questions rose urgently in his mind.

Nachri? Or worse, much, much worse? Feeling very old all of a sudden, Rva put a hand out behind him and steadied himself on a stout knuckoo trunk. There was a long silence, then with a creaking sound an enormous figure detached itself from the dark and leaned over him.

With his throat constricted Rva looked up into a row of black beady eyes, each set within a mobile socket for independent movement. Now all the eyes were focused on a fat old fein. Rva swallowed heavily and searched his memory desperately for the spell that might pacify a Woodwose.

The Woodwose put out an enormous hand, extended a finger almost as long as Rva was tall, and gently touched him on the chest and then the belly. In a gesture that would have seemed comical to Rva if he weren't actually experiencing this in person, the 'wose raised its other enormous hand and rubbed at the side of the pelicanlike beak parts. This 'wose had never seen a fein before and was considering the internal register of tree pests. No fein appeared there either, and the old bipedal animal was clearly a part of the natural fauna; the 'wose could sense that instantly. So after a long, careful examination of Bg Rva, the Woodwose withdrew quietly into the darkness again and disappeared.

Rva was still shaking and whistling a manic little nursery rhyme concerning the good old hungry Woodwose when he got back to his tree house.

Another huge transport plane came thundering in low overhead, shaking the treetops on the isle behind him. It was time to get down to work. Quickly he dressed the noripul egg sac and inflated the balloon. When it was ready he tested the wind; a fresh breeze was picking up off the bay. A few whitecaps were visible out on the water. Far away the lights of the Sx Coast domes twinkled against the darkness. The Pale Moon was rising in the east, throwing its pink-silver light over the scene. The balloon tugged on the line, eager to be off in the wind. He released it, and it bore a small transmitter away into the night.

War had returned to the Highlands. The peace of five decades ended with a drumroll of raids by Space Marines. In every clan there were new refugees, human and fein, crowded into holds deeper in the defense networks. Outlying places, like East Spreak and the Harmers Holes, were abandoned to the enemy.

Where the Marines were successful they dynamited clan forts, smashing the ferroconcrete towers, their mass-drive cannon and electronics. In the valleys the Marines committed occasional atrocities, shooting down fein, humans, and horses wholesale, to spread terror among the rest.

But those were just the small places, like Hawk Harmer's Green Tower, and they contained only relatively small quantities of pharamol and the other longevity drugs. Since the *Black Ship* had so much force at its disposal, it was logical to expect a much larger expedition at some point.

Lavin Fundin was convinced he knew where that would be. On the entire planet there were but three targets on the right scale. Each was radically different from the others and presented very different problems to an attacking force.

The first was the great vault containing Fair Fundan's estate under Ghotaw Mountain. Two hundred kilos of pharamol, plus a hundred kilos of lesser drugs. It had the disadvantage of being guarded by the six Ghotaw Impis, the largest Fundan force and the largest single force still mustered in the highlands.

The other targets were not so well defended. In the far west of the Chung territories lay the Purple Valley. Here the Chung had many small forts dotted over a wealthy Chitin province. Their forces had been run down since the great war, and a well-organized attacker could recoup maybe one hundred kilos of pharamol from taking two dozen small places.

The largest, most tempting target however lay in Butte Manor, the Butte Clan Depository, six galleries cut in the limestone of Mount Butte's foothills, with anything up to four hundred kilos of pharamol hidden in vaults through a labyrinth of passages and holes. A frugal clan in their early days, the Buttes had spent centuries harvesting their Chitin and storing pharamol in the ground.

Of course the manor was a great fortress. It had ten forts and their mass-drive cannon to protect it, but the Buttes had reduced the defense force to a mere demi-Impi, almost a ceremonial force. Since the Butte Kirk was dominated by the pacifist party, the intensely religious Buttes had virtually disarmed themselves.

Accordingly Lavin had quickly put the Response Impi into the air on Plan A, which involved a campaign for Butte Manor. The Response Impi now waited close to the mouth of the manor valley, ready to swoop in as soon as an attack began. Lavin put his own Impi, the First Abzen, at full readiness, with their planes idling on the runway. Meanwhile the Abzen Second Impi was mustering in the villages and would cover the valley in Lavin's absence.

He was everywhere in those hours, a swift implacable force for haste and efficiency. But it was an immense task to move an army of fifteen thousand plus their equipment thousands of kilometers into the forest to hidden backwaters on the great rivers. Even with a small army of assistants working beside him, they were still arranging details for the last few flights when Beni's first light broke above the eastern mountains.

Of his private agony Lavin gave no outward sign. It was as if he were an automaton. He worked at not thinking about Fleur in Young Proud's hands. He tried even harder not to think about Chosen, his son, lost with the *Gandhi*. Every so often, though, his thoughts would idle and the torment would leak through. His heart would grow heavy with concern for his wife. Young Proud was insane. He might do anything! Chosen would lose track of where he was and what he was doing, a weakness that seemed monstrous when everything depended on him. He would suppress it all with sheer rage. Thus he worked with fanatical drive, wearing a face that terrified everyone around him, and drove them to redouble their efforts.

The one piece of good news they had had came as Chulpopek and Ng Farr, the chief neilks of the Response Force, sat with Lavin at a tense strategy meeting in Cracked Rock Fortress. Suddenly there were loud exclamations at the door and Val Bo-Ho bustled in, calling "Old Rva lives still. He sends another message!"

Lavin read it in delighted disbelief then showed it to the others. They chuckled, then fell into fein mirth, loud and uproarious.

"Oh, my," Chulpopek said, wiping his eyes, "old Rva, Mzsee of Mzsees, he excretes on the Kommando. Did you see that part? Fuel tanks, eh?"

"Indeed," Lavin agreed, "now we know for sure what happened there yesterday."

Their mirth subsided, and soon afterward the big Fundan

transport planes were rolling down the runway and lifting off into the southern skies.

Young Proud's personal jet flew in over the broad sweep of the Butte Valley in late morning and angled down for a landing at the New Kommando airstrip, bulldozed only hours before by the assault teams on the slopes of Mount Titus.

In the main cabin the atmosphere was thick with positively dangerous emotions. Degorak Chevde sat up front, hating Young Proud for forcing him to undertake the risky trip. To calm his nerves, Chevde drank one beer after another. As the alcohol took effect, Degorak turned surly and Ofur Muynn and Underhench Garwal Ko were forced to work desperately hard to keep Chevde from focusing on Young Proud. Degorak could easily get violent in these moods. Already he'd offended Alace Rohm and she'd left her seat to join her friends toward the rear of the cabin.

Young Proud, though, was in his element, maliciously inserting long pins into Degorak Chevde whenever the opportunity arose, laughing frequently at his own odd little jokes. At other times he seethed with rage and suppressed contempt... and they think that I, Fundan, would go to the stars with them?... This rabble of gut-crawling flabber bellies?... He sniffed and smiled and looked out the window at the great white mountains. As always he was calmed immediately by the thought of the coming victory and the moment when Lavin Fundan would be brought to him. It would feel good to be alive. As it had not for fifty years.

The guard fein, Persimpilgas and Herver, sat not far from him, awake behind heavy-lidded eyes, which swung every so often to cover Muynn and Degorak Chevde.

The muscle-bound Muynn was the tallest human either fein had ever seen. Both had thus considered him very carefully in terms of an opponent in combat. That was their calling. The fein of Ramal had fought at the sides of the Proud Fundans for centuries. Protecting Young Proud, even from himself, had become their task on the day they were first recruited from their kin groups.

Ofur Muynn was not only tall but very well developed. Precision weight lifting and exercise technique in the Neptune Bund Schools had produced a seven-foot man weighing two hundred thirty five, who could run a mile in one gee in four minutes, nine seconds. Yet he could also bench press two hundred kilos and raise to his knees a five hundred-kilo weight.

Persimpilgas, at seven foot two and three hundred thirty five pounds, reluctantly decided that the cost of killing Muynn could be considerable. If it became necessary Persimpilgas would leave him to young Herver, who topped the older fein by two inches and twenty five pounds. But Muynn was no bio-op, no Space Marine—his muscles were his own, as was any fighting ability he might show. There were no synthetic muscles, no deadly prosthetic limbs—the things fein did fear, for they were impossibly fast. If it came to it, old Persimpilgas, Mzsee of bodyguards, would kill Muynn. Not even a bio-op could take a kifket in the chest, and few fein were quicker with the blade than Persimpilgas.

Of the Master unfortunately there was no sign of improvement, and both fein were concerned. Their hopes had risen in recent days, because with the big operation running, Young Proud's mood had improved. He had ceased raving about Lavin Fundin, whom he persisted in calling the "crèche creature," had not abused Fleur Fundan or destroyed furniture. They had hoped for a continuation of that mood. Now the Master seemed to be brooding again; they felt a volcanic force building up. The question was, would the force be directed against the enemy, the usurper Fundan? Or would it go against Young Proud's allies, these fleshy people from outer space?

The trouble was you could never tell with Young Proud these days. Persimpilgas heaved a sigh; it seemed sometimes that he would never go home to Ramal Valley. His bones would whiten in some alien place or be thrown to the pectaroon in the swamp.

But there was no choice; honor bound him to Young Proud, to all Proud Fundans, who had brought the gifts of technology and medicine to the kin of Orilk in the old forest. Ramal kin had grown mighty in partnership with the Proud Fundans; thus they were honor bound to protect the young Master through his life, despite his obvious insanity. They were a shield of fein flesh behind his back. Their duty lay upon the tradition of three hundred years.

Sitting one row back from Chevde and Young Proud was Ira Ganweek, who felt like a complete physical wreck. Liaison duties between the stiff-necked Bond lords and Young Proud and the New Kommando had become a nightmare. He longed to sleep on a beach for months on end, never to encounter the brutal weight of Degorak Chevde's personality again. Even worse, Ganweek found he was almost a pauper. Many of his little caches of money and pharamol had been looted by his private secretary fifty years previously. She'd cashed in Ira's chips and bought herself a condo on the Red Moon Habitat. As a result he was having to scurry frantically to line up loans from old Syndicate friends so he could buy some pharamol. But temporarily without pharamol and under so much pressure in the past days, he'd had to resort to funkshun, a stimulant with sometimes unpredictable side effects.

At the moment Ira's face was frozen, chemically immobilized as the last dose faded. A fog of confusion rose in his brain. The fog made it hard to think too well, but it also helped to immunize Ira to the strange madness that glared in Young Proud Fundan's eyes.

Once Ira had watched open-mouthed as in the midst of a perfectly normal conversation at a Kommando celebration ball Young Proud had begun to rave in a hysterical voice. "I am Fundan! Not that thing, that clone that she put in my place! That thing she made of herself to keep me from my inheritance. I was born to command!"

Young Proud had then smashed a glass against the wall, drew a revolver, and fired a shot through a window while screaming maniacally, "Die!" over and over. Expensively dressed people hit the floor all over the suite, drinks flying, women screaming, security men frozen in horror at the doors. After a long, strange moment of silence, Young Proud turned and stalked out the door, knocking a servant out of the way.

The stunned elite of the Sx Coast hauled themselves slowly to their feet and dusted off expensive beach suits. There was a very long silence, and when the conversation resumed it did so with a different tone to it, like a hive confronted with the death of a queen.

This was the genius in control of the New Kommando? Young Proud was so consumed by his hate that he could no longer control it. He could explode at any moment.

. . . but Ira nursed his own hatreds too. And prayed that Armada Butte would be drawn into the battle . . . His hands clenched involuntarily at the thought of strangling her, and he ground his teeth.

Sitting in a seat at the rear of the aircraft, her hands cuffed together in her lap, a ball gag in her mouth, wearing a skimpy slave smock, Fleur Fundan begged again for death. . . . let the plane fall out of the sky . . . let it explode . . . She looked at the clouds around them at eleven thousand meters. To be free, to be falling, through the clouds. Nothing could be so sweet.

Never have to feel Young Proud upon her again.

Never. Obscene things crawled on the edges of her mind;

there was a revulsion that left her weeping for hours at a time, that made her think desperately of death.

Young Proud snapped his fingers. Fleur started from her seat, hating herself for obeying, in terror of the pain that would come if she did not. She brought him tea and served it humbly, kneeling, when she wanted to hurl it into his face. He could see her hatred, a fantastic thing, an emotion miles high, and he grinned at her with thin lips drawn back over his teeth at the enormity of his abuse of her.

. . . She would rend my flesh . . . he thought with considerable amusement and turned to Degorak. "So Chevde, where shall we go; tell me again where you plan to take us with your magnificent interstellar machine."

Degorak did not bother to keep the distaste out of his voice. "Another time, Messire Fundan. When this horrible flight is over and we are back on solid ground. I cannot believe you would entrust our lives to this archaic aircraft. It could fall out of the sky at any moment!"

Indeed Chevde had only agreed to come after strenuous bargaining. Had been convinced finally that Young Proud would abort the main operation unless he, Chevde, did come, and so here they were, sweating, in this frantic little jet that was heading into a war zone. The Bond lords of Neptune had not risked their lives for forty years in the great conspiracy to build the *Black Ship* and then survived the great unknown of FTL flight to die on some common battlefield. Thus they looked forward to the next few days with nothing less than stark terror.

Young Proud however was—on at least one level—well and truly happy; a smug feeling of self-satisfaction filled his throat with bubbling laughter that constantly threatened to erupt publicly. He had to avoid that because he knew they'd all look at him again as if were a mad person. And of course he knew he was the sanest of them all, for he had seen to the heart of the black pestilence at the center of the universe. He had seen the mixing of the genes of the gods and he had survived and no other could boast of that . . .

But there was no doubt in his mind that events were proceeding at the perfect rate of development. The New Kommando had invaded the weakest of the great Highland valleys. They would overwhelm the local resistance, and thus they would be sure to draw Lavin Fundan to contest the issue. Then Young Proud's trap would be sprung.

"Come now, friend Chevde, a man who can entrust himself to n-space on the power of the Fuhl Drives need fear nothing ever again. This 'archaic' plane is actually in remarkably good shape, new engines, restructured body frame. The design is centuries old perhaps; the interior is perhaps rather plain. It serves as an executive-class commercial airliner during normal times. But it's perfectly safe; I don't think more than two of this model have ever crashed in three hundred years."

At the mention of "crashed," the bond lords blinked in alarm.

Chevde guzzled beer. Ofur Muynn wasted another warning look on Young Proud, who merely shrugged and remarked expansively, "so to the star fields, we must choose our destination carefully. There is such a lot to be seen. Where shall we go first? Perhaps into the Orion Arm? That sounds good, doesn't it? We could head out of the local association and into the arm first. Then on down the arm toward the galactic center. Or shall we go outward, across the great rift to the Perseus Arm?"

"What the hell," snarled Degorak, "it won't matter, as long as it's very far away from here and Chairman Wei."

"Well, we're already a long way away from Chairman Wei."

Degorak shivered, felt oddly cold for a moment. "No, we are not far enough away at all. Remember that Chairman Wei does not die. And remember that the World Government will take up research on the Fuhl Drives again. In time they will discover the secret of harmonics in the field fluctuations. They will come after us."

. . . unspoken but present in the minds of Chevde, Ganweek, and the others from the *Black Ship* was the memory of how difficult it could be to find those subtle harmonics . . .

Young Proud shrugged. "So they will come after us, but we will be long gone, a million light-years from here, they will never find us."

Chevde crumpled the beer can.

"Pray that they don't, Fundan."

Young Proud looked back at Fleur, still crouching before them in the aisle. Unconsciously she was holding her shoulders insolently squared. Young Proud struck her lightly across her left shoulder with the quirt that hung on his wrist. Silkily he told her, "You are still shamelessly resistant, I see. I will have to hold another session with you when we land. You remember what we said about 'will' and 'wilfulness?'"

Degorak looked at the woman; an attractive, slender female, he had briefly considered her before. Now he pointed to her. "Tell me, messire, is this female available? I will couch with her soon. She attracts my interest."

Young Proud's eyes danced wildly. Fleur shuddered within.

"She is the wife of my great enemy. Of course you may have her. I'll deliver her on her leash personally, to your tent, Great Degorak."

Chevde's eyes widened. "Wife," he mouthed. "Such antiquity of social forms. How delightful to mount upon a wife!"

Fleur sobbed. Young Proud dismissed her with a snap of his fingers.

There was a little turbulence; the jet shuddered once or twice, and Degorak Chevde hastily opened another can of beer and sucked half of it down.

A few minutes later the plane lost altitude and came in to land behind the sheltering bulk of Mount Titus. As they approached the airstrip Ganweek looked down at the terrain below. Jik forest was predominant at these altitudes. The little black trees formed an impenetrable scrub of fifteen-meter-high vegetation out of which burst eruptions of scarlet tanglethorn and bone-white husks of nub bush. Lower down, in the river bottoms, the light green mindal tree was common, breaking up the dark black green masses of jik.

Ira felt a terrible sense of foreboding at the sight. For centuries poor men from the Sx Coast had come here to fight, and to die, for a share of the wealth produced here. Rich men had remained in comfort in the Coastal cities. The landscape below spoke of dangers, fein armies, famous battles from the past that had cost the coastal war bands heavily. Hundreds of thousands of humans had died in these high valleys. Ira's mouth was dry and his tongue was hard in his throat.

Attending this battle in person had certainly not been his idea. But he reflected sadly once again that since his return to the Sx Coast he had found that his own choices meant very little in the scheme of things. Young Proud had seized control of the city. The old Syndicates had been decimated. Proud Fundan had taken the reins of what was left. Young Proud therefore imposed his own choices, and very particular choices they were too. To do something about the general lawlessness that had become endemic in the New Kommando, Young Proud had taken dramatic action.

Immense gibbets had been erected on the beaches of Fun Isle. Those convicted of the slightest offense were hanged upon them and left to decompose. Carrion skrin stood sentinel on treetops in the Gardens of Nebuchadnezzar.

Many of the wealthy inhabitants of the big domes had been forced to shutter the windows to block out the new view.

For the moment the Syndicates were keeping a low profile while they waited for a new opening toward power. However,

Young Proud had built up secret support in the Syndicates as well.

The jet stayed down low, approaching from the south and west to keep the squat bulk of the old volcano between themselves and the mountain forts on Butte Manor. The landing was fast and bumpy, everyone was thrown around in their seats as they raced down the raw airstrip cleared from the brush.

They emerged briefly into the high valley air. Vast mountains glistened with snow along the western horizon. The white peaks marched off into the north in an unbroken, continuous line. Around the airstrip the jik forest grew thick upon the ground. Above their position the gullied heights of Mount Titus supported a fantastic growth of nub brush, a humble-looking round bush that thrust immense spore bodies, like gigantic white cauliflowers, up ten meters on long stalks. Although they were close to the equator and the sun was shining, it was still only pleasantly warm; a soft breeze had come up, to blow the scent of mindal flowers over the airstrip. For some reason the alien scent made Ira Ganweek shiver. Degorak Chevde too wore an expression of concern. The alien forest, the leaves so dark a green as to be almost black, was ominous. What fein hordes might lie in ambush out there? Could they count on the New Kommando to protect them? Chevde shivered too, saw Ganweek looking at him and returned the look with a cold stare. Ira remembered that in the Bond only the dominant could initiate eye contact and dropped his own gaze for a moment.

Then they hurried below into a dugout bunker. "Butte aircraft have raided once," said a Kommando officer in crisp gray-and-black uniform as they were met by Rinus Van Relt and his staff. Young Proud made introductions and Van Relt shook their hands stiffly, a worn-looking man but tall and imposing, with hair receding from a prominent widow's peak. He wore battle fatigues with gray-and-green patches. A well-used holster on his hip bore an automatic hand gun.

"Well, messires," he said. "You've arrived just in time for our first real stab at the outer forts. I've got the Third Division lined up for assault, to coincide with the *Black Ship*'s next pass."

"You are behind schedule then. Quite considerably behind, it seems." Chevde sounded peeved.

"Well, yes," Van Relt agreed reluctantly. "We met unexpectedly determined resistance this morning. Had to wait until we could deploy the second Division forward enough to flank them before we could get them out of their positions along the river. They were up on the bluffs with clear fields of fire. It was impossible to assault it head-on, not even the Space Marines would do it."

"Yes." Young Proud smiled briefly. "I checked the reports. Quite a battle the Butte fein put up. Two thousand fein against fourteen thousand of your men, who had air superiority and Space Marines." And Young Proud laughed mockingly, at some private joke.

"We've always needed superior numbers against good fein units. You know that, messire."

Young Proud agreed with a polite nod. "Yes, I know that, messire. Which is why we will build our force to overwhelming levels once my enemy commits himself. Which I predict he will do this evening."

"The Reinforcement Divisions are now boarding transports on the Sx Coast?"

"They are indeed."

"Let's go over to the map table. I will show you the current dispositions."

They moved into a large room equipped with a holograph map table. A dozen young men and women sat behind computer terminals passing orders and information and monitoring the situation. Alace Rohm sat close to Ganweek. She quizzed him about various details of the map. The trees, the rivers winding through the woods, the mountains that thrust up stubby crowns above the jik, all were reproduced in full-color, high-resolution holographic detail.

Van Relt flicked a stud and the machine began to project the details of the morning battle.

"At 800 hours the Space Marines came down in Muld Woods. There were six pods."

And on cue six sprays of red streaks appeared over the woods set to the south of Mount Titus. The red dots formed up in the characteristic flying-V wedge of Space Marine platoons and pressed northeast, toward the four thousand-meter mass of Mount Aunchus, beneath which lay Butte Manor.

"At 9.06 there was contact along the River Uluin, defensive fire from prepared positions on the bluffs on the eastern bank." A series of yellow blurs spread in the thickets by the Uluin denoting the Butte defensive positions filled by fein and human artillery.

A fierce fire fight raged for the rest of the morning while the New Kommando transports flew in behind Mount Titus unopposed.

Now the New Kommando First and Second Divisions appeared

103

from either side of Mount Titus, large red blotches, moving through the forest. The blotches flowed forward, reaching the Uluin before noon. The second division flowed over the river and lapped around the flank of the Butte Guards Impi on the bluffs.

The yellow positions collapsed, and the yellow blurs moved swiftly back across Sliverary Forest, pursued by the New Kommando, into the forts built around Butte Manor.

"By noon we had assumed our present front lines. The artillery has been digging in ever since." The red masses coagulated in positions facing east, in the margins of the forest surrounding Butte Manor.

"Excellent, messire, excellent." Young Proud seemed perfectly content.

"Excellent?" Degorak Chevde said in disbelief. "You call this excellent? They are now safely hidden behind impregnable fortifications. These forts are dangerous to storm."

"Messire Chevde, allow me to explain the situation. We now besiege the manor. Inside the manor, in the limestone caverns below, are pharamol vaults with legendary amounts—perhaps five hundred kilos of pharamol-grade longevity proteins. So my enemy will not doubt our purposes here. He will come, with the Response Impi, and then we will crush him."

"But if the Space Marines had been deployed properly..." Degorak's protest died away in the face of the insanity in Young Proud's eyes.

"He will come," said Young Proud imperturbably, that strange smile on his lips again. "And we will crush him."

He started, as if from a trance, and, with an effort, turned away from Degorak Chevde. He changed the projection to a wider one, a view of the whole great valley. He waved his thin hands toward it. "There, messires, there we have our killing ground. Here we shall gore the crèche Were and trample it to death."

He paused a moment, seemed to recover control of emotions that threatened to overwhelm him. "As you can see, this is a large valley, more than six hundred kilometers long and two hundred wide. In many ways it is a most unusual valley, a huge rift fault. It's higher than most of the productive valleys. The Buttes came here because they were the last big clan to give up on the coast. They arrived about a century after the others. My own family for instance had already built the fortress at Ghotaw Mountain. This was the last open Chitin range of any size left. It's so high—the average elevation is twenty-five hundred meters—that the fein didn't choose to live here in any numbers. But the Chitin grew well enough for human purposes, so the Buttes overcame the altitude problems and settled in. Although they were always a fractious family, forever feuding and driving one another out into the dark. They scattered over the whole damn valley." On cue the computer produced a scatter of golden hemispheres, widely separated in the great open spaces.

"Of course when the raiding from the Coast got started the Buttes suffered disproportionately, since they were so isolated and lacked adequate defenses against war bands. After a while they were forced to unite to build one impregnable place that would serve as a vault for pharamol."

Young Proud switched the projection to a close-up of a spur from Mount Butte that terminated in a Sugarloaf Mountain, which itself was skirted by an outlyer ridge of four small stubby mountains in the shape of a fragmented letter C.

"Here we have it, my friends, a fortress deep and mighty. There are forts on each of the small mountains. The Centro fort is dug into the forepeak of the Sugarloaf, and the Skullcap overlooks the line from above the Shoulder Mountain."

Red cubes appeared, three on Tablet Mountain, one each on Red and Outlyer, two on Shoulder Mountain. Then there was the Skullcap, perched way up on the Skull crag, and even higher, above them all, mighty Centro, buried in the Sugarloaf.

"At the bottom lies the entrance to the manor itself, which is entirely underground and which is also a Clan Secret. The Buttes have been very successful at keeping those plans out of the hands of everyone else on this planet." Young Proud smirked, obviously pleased with himself.

"However, they could not keep them secret from me."

Ganweek gasped. "You know where the vaults are then?"

"We have deduced some locations. Others will have to be hunted down by more laborious methods."

"This was quite a coup, Messire Fundan."

"Thank you, messire. I worked many years upon the problem. In time I found a solution which perhaps I will describe to you one day. But for now . . ." He returned his attention to the holograph map.

"Now, Aunchus Butte designed the fortifications, and he deduced that any practical assault on the place would have to come from Sliverary. To land a large force in the valleys behind the Sugarloaf would be extremely hazardous. So he tucked the airstrip in behind the Sugarloaf, in Toronodo Valley."

Beyond the mountain spur a green line appeared, near the banks of one of the small rushing highland rivers.

"We are shelling that strip, messire," Van Relt said quickly. "Nothing's moved in or out of there since noon."

"So it should be. But I don't think we need concern ourselves with the airstrip—the Response Force will want to take us on in the open. My enemy has always delighted in maneuver; that's his game, high-speed movement, deception, the sudden flank attack. All grace and acrobatics. We will clamp ourselves to him and never let go, and we will tear and rend him . . ." His voice turned ugly, thickened in his throat, and died away.

Once again Young Proud appeared to hover on the verge of losing control. Once again he recovered.

"So, you see, Chevde, things go as we expected. My enemy is convinced that we seek the pharamol in those vaults."

"But we do, we do seek it!" Chevde shouted.

"We do indeed, but to get it we must shatter the Response Impi. Then with our back safe we can deal with the Buttes and help ourselves to the vaults. Remember it will take time to locate all the vaults; there are many kilometers of caverns below the mountain. We must secure our rear first. So we shall set the trap in motion. My enemy will land, and we will crush him here, in the forest of Sliverary."

14

INSIDE BUTTE MANOR GENERAL CHAOS REIGNED. AN ATMOS-phere of hysterical anxiety gripped the Butte Clan.

In the savage fighting in the woods of Sliverary the Guards Impi had lost four hundred fein. Another five hundred were jammed in the manor's medical section or laid out on stretchers in the corridors outside. In addition there were nearly three hundred human casualties, most of whom would wait until all the fein had been seen to, as had always been clan practice.

Inside the manor parties of people ran frantically to and fro between the vaults and the airstrip.

To hold the fort line just a thousand fein remained, units mostly fought-out by the heroic battle they'd put up against overwhelming numbers. A call had gone out for help, and parties of Buttes had indeed been flying in all day, braving the anti-aircraft fire from the Kommando positions.

One of the first arrivals, roaring in in her old souped-up Hummbird special, was Armada Butte, now a mature lady in her seventieth year and happily wed to an Earthman called Tan Ubu, former first assistant to then-Deputy Ambassador Fleur Kevilla.

Armada had retained her martial instincts however, despite fifty years of peace and child rearing up in Moonloi Hole. The news of the attack had sent her running to her aircraft with an assault rifle in her hands. Her husband and their eldest sons were out on a hunting trip, way down on the bottom lands below the hole, so she'd just left them a message and flown the Hummbird the fifteen hundred kilometers to the manor herself.

She found total confusion. To her disgust she discovered that most of the Buttes that had flown in before her had simply run to their personal vaults down below and emptied them of their precious contents and flown out again. Only a few doughty younger souls had stayed to fight for the place.

There was no sign of her father, Rognius, the ostensible commander of the Butte Forces. Eventually an orderly told her to look in the Centro, and so she rode the high-speed elevator to the high fort, perched four thousand meters above, on the Manor Heights. She scrambled up to the last ramp and into the command post.

Her father was kneeling in front of a smashed computer console praying out loud in a manic voice.

"And dear Lord, rescue us from the machines we have made, liberate us, and give us the assistance now in the hour of our need, for in the Peace of the Lamb we are in your hands . . ."

Armada felt a familiar surge of anger toward the entire Peace of the Lamb movement . . . the fools, they stripped our defenses, and now Rognius is reduced to *praying* for help . . .

She inspected the console. Hammered with the butt of the revolver that was lying on the floor beside Rognius. Thoughtfully Armada picked it up before interrupting her father's endless flow of mumbled prayers. He whirled on her, livid in a rage of misery.

"Aah, my youngest daughter, she who lives out-Kirk, the great ingrate, the atheist, the breaker of her father's heart—she comes at last to gloat over the ruin."

"Father, I think I will have to take command here." She sounded cold, and she meant to sound cold. Between them there had opened a chasm these last five decades.

The strange events that ended the Great War had produced an illogical reaction in the Butte Clan. They had retreated from that reality which included the Arizel tki Fenrille. By dispensing with the services of the fein Impis, they had reduced their dependence on their adopted planet. Secure in the Kirk of Christ Spaceman they shut out the alien knowledge that could not be accommodated within their belief system.

Armada had been in the fidnemen on that terrible day; for her there was no way back into the mental security of the Kirk.

Her father had rejected her as a result.

"You will take over?" Rognius sounded relieved. "I must, dear Father. Come, go down to your quarters. Try and rest. There is much to do."

He gripped her arm suddenly and spoke in a hushed whisper. "There were so many of them. The host of the Satan came down upon us and the Lord tested us. We could not match them."

"Father, there are hundreds of dead fein in Sliverary woods and we have barely enough troops to man the forts. I must take command." Rognius began to weep, emitting a keening sound that made Armada's lip curl. Fighting to keep the disgust out of her voice, she signaled to an orderly who was waiting discreetly by the entrance.

"Take him down to the hospital. Get him a sedative. This has been too much for my father. You understand, don't you?"

The man nodded.

As the broken old man was led away Armada's thoughts were bitter . . . Rognius should never have commanded here anyway. Damn them all, damn the Peace of the Lamb. Rognius wanted the Peace of the Lamb, he wanted it so badly he ousted Justes and took command of the manor himself. In his first real battle he fell to pieces, and we probably lost a hundred more fein as a result . . .

She shook herself out of her anger; he was her father, even if he was a blithering old fool. She should feel more respect, love, something. It bothered her when she didn't. But the contradictions between the clan life-style and its professed beliefs were just too great. Rognius was her paternal parent, but since he had fathered her through artifical insemination of Ovula Butte's egg and since he had rarely taken an interest in her during her formative years, Armada had never taken much notice of her father or counted on him. Her mother, of course, she had never seen in the flesh. Ovula Butte had a hearty disdain for the rest of her family; she hadn't been seen out of her fortress in two hundred years. Armada had grown up crèche-style, playing with a few other young Buttes and the children of the Under-Buttes, the collective family name for the several thousand human servants of the clan.

With an effort of will, she pushed it all aside and activated the auxilliary computer screen. Quickly it outlined the situation.

The Kommando had dug in all along the forest margin on the manor's western side. They had also sent units over the Toronda to get behind the Tablet Mountain forts and bring the airstrip and the inner Green under fire.

The *Black Ship* stayed in a low, insertion orbit, so that it could deploy orbital fighters, which swooped down to pound the forts so heavily they were forced to close the clamshells to protect the guns. Then the Kommando launched assaults directly against the forts, with artillery barrages trained on the defensive lines to keep the fein down.

The low orbit was essential for retrieval of the orbital fighters as they climbed back out of the atmosphere. It meant that the *Black Ship* was overhead only for a few minutes every hour and a half, but in those minutes the orbital fighters could deliver tons of high explosive against the forts.

These tactics had produced results, and the Kommando had taken some of the outer lines on both Outlyer Mountain and the

109

Tablet. Number two on the Tablet was in danger of falling anytime. Its fifty surviving defenders were just too few to hold back an assault by two thousand men. At the same time however there was strong evidence that a major assault was about to be launched against the Red Mountain, the centerpiece of the outer line of forts. To hold it, there were just seventy-six fein and thirty-two humans.

The *Black Ship* was swinging over the horizon. Armada chose to defend the Red Mountain and sent reinforcements from Shoulder Mountain running across the gap.

The Kommando bombardment began again, and soon thousands of smoke canisters burst on the slopes of Red Mountain.

The *Black Ship* came overhead. Orbital fighters swung down and pounded the forts. The clamshells groaned on huge hydraulics as clouds of white dust, pulverized ferroconcrete, rose in the air and blew down into the Manor Green.

Across the lower slopes of the Red Mountain burst wave after wave of smoke shell while other ordnance deposited thousands of infrared sources and radar reflectors.

Into the smoke stormed the troops of the Third Division of the New Kommando. They flowed forward into the shattered outer lines.

Defensive fire cracked down. The advancing troops slowed. Within moments a storm of canister shell detonated over the defense lines forcing the fein back into cover. The Kommando pressed forward again, driving the fein back into the fort. The men began to flow around the central clamshell and filter downslope into the Green itself.

Defensive fire erupted from the entranceways of the manor, dug into the mountain on the far side of the parkland known as the Green.

Orbital fighters swooped over and laid missiles against the entrances, but enormous ferroconcrete doors swung shut just in time. The manor shook from the impacts, even up in the Centro where Armada waited in frantic impatience for the Orbital Fighters to leave. Beneath their shells of stone, the guns in both the Skullcap and the Centro were trained on the slopes of Red Mountain. All they needed was a few seconds' firing time and they would annihilate the attackers.

But again and again the mach-4 fighters shrieked by high overhead and delivered missiles and napalm to the forts and doors.

There were fifty survivors inside the Red Fort. Armada pondered ways of getting them out. As far as she knew there were no deep workings beneath the Red Mountain. A counterattack with all the forces in the Shoulder Mountain forts seemed her only chance. But such an assault could be enormously costly.

She contemplated defeat. The Kommando had twenty thousand men out there, and with the *Black Ship* overhead the forts were helpless. She called up the booby trap program on the computer. They could at least try to take as many of the enemy with them as possible.

She was on the point of arming the bombs hidden beneath every fort when the computer bleeped loudly to gain her attention.

Up the valley, hedgehopping at the speed of sound, came thirty small vtol fliers, down so low they were actually within the thick smokescreen that carpeted the lower slopes of the mountain forts. With a whistling scream of jets they ploughed overhead, leaving a trail of fragmentation ordnance and napalm.

The Third Division staggered, mortally wounded, then it collapsed back through the clouds of oily smoke and the awful stink of barbecue.

Three orbital fighters were still within range and they pounced on the little vtol jets like eagles upon pigeons. Stooping at mach-6 they hurtled from the heights with smart missiles leaping from their belly bays.

The Fundan pilots in their vtol jets were the best the academy at Ghotaw Mountain had ever produced. Now they flew evasive maneuvers that stretched their bat-winged little craft to the ultimate. The sky was filled with explosions and swooping aircraft, but before the vtols could escape to land in clearings north of Sliverary, fourteen had been blasted out of the sky.

But in their wake they had virtually destroyed the New Kommando's Third Division, which in some units had taken 90 percent casualties. Thousands of dead men, many charred beyond recognition, lay on the grim slopes of Red Mountain. Barely a few hundred had survived to lurch back into the relative safety beneath the jik forest.

Rinus Van Relt trembled as he watched the Third Division melt away on that long, exposed slope. He trembled because Young Proud had said, before the attack began, that it would be just a feint, Red Mountain would be the sole objective of the Third Division. It would be a feint to bring Lavin Fundan running. And Young Proud had also, quite calmly, predicted a terrible slaughter of the Third Division.

"They will have one very good tactic hidden from us, you

see. Something that we would not anticipate. So we must expect to draw their venom with our first assault."

In a state of considerable apprehension, Van Relt had set the assault in motion. Now the Third Division was destroyed, almost annihilated. The remnants would have to be fed into other divisions.

Van Relt set his jaw and determined that when this fight was over the Number three would be retired permanently from the New Kommando divisional listing.

Young Proud was blithely unconcerned however. "Make ready the Seventh and Eighth divisions. We have prepared the anvil; now let us raise the hammer."

Young Proud reexamined the orbital schedule of the *Black Ship*. Three hundred Space Marines were being readied as the steel-coated head of Young Proud's hammer blow, which would fall when Lavin Fundan had committed himself.

Van Relt's monitor screen blinked his private code. A scout posted to the south, far below Muld, reported enemy radar traces at the extreme limits of his range.

He reported it to Young Proud.

"Of course, just as expected. The *Black Ship* has just gone out of range and will be gone for an hour. He comes, gentlemen; my enemy comes to engage us."

Degorak Chevde and Ofur Muynn gazed with obvious anxiety at the computerized holograph map.

Young Proud inserted a programmed chip into the computer. He punched up his prepared campaign notes for this particular "opening," as he had grown to think of these computer exercises he had so lovingly constructed.

The big holograph scrolled southward to focus on lower Muld.

From the south a pattern of orange blurs appeared, moving swiftly through the woods on fein trails. Mobile artillery followed, indicated by tightly focused cannon symbols.

"You see my enemy as I have projected his advance. This will be the Response Impi, his crack unit. Behind it will be the First Abzen Impi. You see how he likes to move—swift maneuvers, lightning-fast movements, his entire force spread out in skirmishing groups. Oh, he is the master of this!"

From the north came large maroon blurs, also moving swiftly upon the scene. At the bank of the River of Muld the center of the Kommando column halted and adopted defensive positions. The flanks spread out and crossed the river and headed on toward the approaching Response Impi.

Bright little flashes of light indicated the contact points between

112

the forces as they grappled. Artillery barrages began almost immediately.

The orange blurs rapidly agglomerated together on the line and even pressed it forward. Then they wavered, seemed to hesitate and then fell back; on a front of five or six kilometers they withdrew southward a kilometer or more.

The maroon flankers had begun to advance in to the open pocket. They halted and Young Proud whistled in glee as the orange blurs continued their movements, opening a semicircular cup in the original line.

"Of course they expect us to rush into this death trap they have made. This is typical of my enemy's love of rapidly formed traps all designed to allow sudden infliction of large numbers of casualties upon an enemy. To shock him off balance.

"Of course we will have to sacrifice a few units here to convince him that his strategy is working well. We need to lull him into euphoria before we catch him in our own trap, which is large enough to devour his entire force."

Young Proud's eyebrows rose almost to the hairline as he finished his remarks.

A few maroon blurs entered the cup and were destroyed by the concentrated firepower of half an Impi. The rest began a withdrawal of their own, and soon the orange blurs were rolling forward again, pursuing the maroons toward the defensive barrier of the River Muld.

As they approached the Muld the Kommando formations split and moved to either side of the force dug in on the opposite bank. The orange blurs pushed on, seeking to catch the Kommando in the act of river crossing and ran up against the hot fire from the defensive positions.

"At this point of course the reinforcing divisions are coming into play."

More maroon forces appeared from the north. Another force of orange blurs came up from the south. The maroon were much greater in numbers, and as the orange blurs moved north they were enveloped and gradually funneled toward the Kommando's riverbank defensive positions. Just the restless momentum in the Fundan forces, long used to aggressive movement forward, took them on.

"He will of course seek to counter this concentration effect, and so we will initiate immediate assaults from our flanker forces."

The sides of the funnel pushed in, hot patches of light ignited on new lines. The orange blurs coagulated into defensive positions, facing northeast and northwest.

"This will be the preliminary of course. At this point the *Black Ship* will be coming up on the radar horizon. See—"

Suddenly the orange blurs began to disengage and move rapidly rearward.

Before they could escape the funnel, however, a pattern of bright blue lights began falling across their path.

"The *Black Ship* battalion." Young Proud turned to Chevde and Muynn and the other Neptunian bond lords. "Gentlemen, this will be your moment of glory. To your battalion will go the honor of the charge."

Three hundred Space Marines would drive in on the fein in Muld woods, pressing them back into the funnel, where they could be annihilated by air strikes from orbital fighters.

Chevde looked uneasily at the disposition of forces, looked at Ganweek. Degorak had a tremendous urge to smash someone with his big fists, to break bones and pulverize muscles. It was with enormous effort of will that he did not suddenly assault the plump ex-senator.

Having followed the parade of conflicting desires that passed across Chevde's face, Ganweek swallowed hard. He could imagine the blow, the big fist crashing into his face. He was surprised that he had not flinched.

He looked up and saw Young Proud's strange hawk's eyes fixed upon him unwinkingly. Ganweek turned away, oppressed by these twin terrors. If only they could be made to destroy each other!

Ira went out into the bunker's corridor again to get a breath of fresh air. Fleur Fundan was there, bound, gagged, and attached to a hook by the leash from her silver collar. Her eyes did not meet his, they seemed vacant, dazed. Fresh bruises marked her arms and the left side of her face. Her upper lip was swollen.

For some reason Ganweek was moved to pity her. "Your combative husband is landing in the woods south of here." She did not react. He looked away. Shrugged. It had been a momentary feeling. He had his own desires for revenge on them anyway.

He pressed his lips to her ear and whispered harshly. "Your husband comes. He will fall right into our trap and be destroyed. You'll be seeing him much sooner than you probably would want to. How about that, eh?"

With a giggle he went back into the wild beasts' den of the command post.

15

In Lower Muld a group of people in conical hats, wearing hide breeches and jackets, waited under the eaves of the jik until they received the signal. The *Black Ship* was gone once more.

Abruptly the peace of the forest was shattered in a roar of power saws. The people, in the attire of Chitin talkers, quickly cut the brush and young trees that had grown over the old airstrip.

It had had constant use in the Long Wars, but the strip had been left to nature after the coming of the Peace of the Lamb among the Kirk of the Buttes.

However, the Chitin talkers, the men and women of the Muld Chitin group known as the Manor Bullions, had occasionally groomed the strip on their own cognizance. Their masters, Clan Butte, may have lost sight of the need for such safety systems, but they had not. Tradition in the Bullions went back three hundred years. Most of that time had been spent at war, so the habits were slow to die.

Now teams of fein with enormous draught horses, of ancient Percheron stock, emerged from the forest trails and began to haul the cut brush away, stacking it at the edge of the strip.

They had about two hundred meters cleared behind them when the first Fundan transport jets flew over, fast and low.

In their thundering wake they left a trail of parachutes in two sizes. Large chutes for human scouts and small ones for the minklike sourts that were used for scouting by the Impis. Fein did not fly well and found parachuting almost unimaginable.

As soon as they'd regained their feet, the troopers pushed north seeking the scouts of the New Kommando in the forest of Muld.

Soon afterward a cluster of small vtol aircraft howled in and landed on roaring jets to disgorge Lavin Fundan and his immediate staff.

Almost immediately the sound of many heavy jet engines reverberated over the jik. The first big transports angled in to land on two hundred fifty meters of root-cut concrete. Fortunately these were the pilots of the Fenrille Response Impi, graduates of the Fundan and Spreak military academies for the most part. They knew their planes to the last bolt and brought them down now in beautiful fashion, through what were virtually controlled crashes on the tiny strip. For kilometers in every direction the booming roar of the big engines shook the forests.

The Bullions redoubled their efforts and lengthened the cleared strip to three hundred fifty meters by the time the first plane, a fat four-engine monster, was emptied and came rumbling down the runway toward them. Empty, it clambered into the air with a grotesque, sprightly spring for a plane so large then headed off fast and low into the south.

A few moments later the first shells from the long-range guns of the New Kommando dropped short in the forest a kilometer away. A sudden augur of war.

Fein units formed up and moved off quickly into the forest. With them went supply wagons and field artillery all hauled by packs of adapted terrain mules, swift, surefooted and even edible if absolutely necessary.

By this time the paratroops had moved some distance north, and in the woods of central Muld they detected the scouts of the New Kommando, arrogantly posted on tree platforms visible for kilometers around.

This news spurred Lavin Fundan into a frenzy. Young Proud waited for him, obviously expecting an immediate assault, fooled by Lavin's tactic of landing dangerously close to the Kommando. The Kommando would prefer to receive an attack from the Response Impi against prepared positions. Lavin guessed they would be dug in along the bluffs above the River Muld. Young Proud thus gave up the initiative.

Accompanied by his bodyguard and the chief neilks of the Response Impi, Lavin pushed his horse westward through the nub bush scrub in western Muld. Behind came the dozen young people of the mobile command post, carrying the computers and communications equipment that was so vital to Lavin's style of warfare.

Further back came the Impi, fein loping ahead of the supply trains and artillery, keeping up a steady twelve kilometers an hour. Out on the sensitive eastern flank Lavin left the paratroops and a detachment of cavalry, Chitin talkers called to the colors by Clan Butte for the most part. With stout hearts, good horses, and an intimate knowledge of the terrain, captained by Joshua Butte, they would screen the Impis well.

After a half hour's ride they reached the banks of the river Missiling and waited for the Impi to catch up. Lavin felt his pulse race, his enemy gave up the initiative! Young Proud had always been a quixotic campaigner, but he seemed to grope for new heights of folly now. Lavin looked at his chrono and spoke urgently into his communicator, hurrying the neilks along, getting the big fein to push themselves to keep up an eleven klicks an hour pace, running with the long, sweeping stride of their ancient race, the predators at the top of the Fenrille food chain for nigh on seventy million years.

At the New Kommando base Young Proud had greeted the news with seeming delight. The enemy had successfully landed two Impis and support troops, just out of range of the Kommando's guns. Young Proud gave a bark of manic glee.

"Of course, it is just his way. He comes! Doesn't he come fast!" Young Proud left them to convene directly with Van Relt and the data group as the New Kommando swung into action.

The others were not quite so sanguine about the development. Ira Ganweek pressed forward anxiously and looked over the dispositions of forces with an anxious eye. The enemy had landed where expected except closer, much closer. Now he would presumably hurl his Impis directly across Muld toward the Kommando waiting in the forest.

Could the soldiers of the Kommando hold them?

On the holograph map the enemy's orange blurs were projected once again, except that this time it was for real. The New Kommando's maroon flanking columns also appeared and began to move down into the woods of Muld. The Fourth and Fifth divisions leading the way with the First Division in support, a force of more than fifteen thousand well-armed men.

The orange blurs continued to mass. The enemy had landed on an old, disused airstrip; he was closer to their positions than Young Proud had thought possible. However, it mattered not, the Kommando would wait on the banks of the Muld. When the contact was made, they would move forward and seize hold of the Impis and never let them go.

However the forward scouts had no reports of enemy movements yet.

Young Proud laughed derisively. "See, Van Relt, he has slowed down. He hasn't had to work an Impi in five decades; the fool's forgotten how, probably."

"Certainly we would've expected some contact by now from the old aggressive Lavin Fundan."

"Contact? Great heavens, we'd have expected battle by now. It shows how the genetic morass comes apart, the black void, the beetles that live in it."

Van Relt and his officers exchanged worried looks. Young Proud was acting strangely again.

Van Relt urged his scouts forward, into lower Muld itself. They were unwilling, fearing ambush by the fein, but in a few minutes he had word that no enemy units seemed to have moved northeast of the airstrip. The scouts were close enough to see the big planes still taking off and flying south again, but they had met no resistance.

Van Relt examined the map. "If he hasn't moved northeastward, toward us, then where would he be?"

Captain Trunket suggested that the fein, overawed at the size and majesty of the New Kommando and the *Black Ship*, had dispersed south of the airstrip where they would mount guerrilla attacks. "He has recognized that he is overmatched and has chosen to try and harass our rear."

"Thank you, Captain Trunket. However, since he landed so dangerously close to our positions, I feel sure he must intend some kind of assault. The only route lies through Muld if he wants to get through to the manor and safety in the forts."

. . . if he wants safety of course . . . went the reassuring echo in Van Relt's brain . . . and then he was troubled by a dreadful question. What if Lavin Fundan was unconcerned about safety?

Ten kilometers west of Mount Titus, the gentle River Missiling wound through upland meadows dotted with dwarf hobi gobi and thick patches of bloodmeknots. Here and there, however, the dark leaved jik forest grew all the way down to the river's edge.

It was at such points that the water was suddenly broken. Leaping quickly across the shallows and back to the safety of the shady woods came a torrent of fein in "septs" one hundred strong. Around them were parties of cavalry escorting mule teams hauling small fat-tired guns. Artillery troops jogged alongside.

A small, fast moving army crossed over the Missiling from Angerry and headed eastward. In that direction lay a few kiloms of jik and then the slopes of Mount Titus.

So far it had been a frustrating battle for the scouts from the New Kommando. They'd floundered through Muld without any sight of the enemy. Eventually four scouts rode all the way west to the Missiling Valley. They broke out of the trees on the hillcrest and stiffened. Their binoculars flashed up to their eyes.

A couple of kilometers away they observed the Response Impi, concentrated in columns and undoubtedly heading for the Kommando HQ, on the western slopes of Mount Titus. The roar of hooves, feet, and wheels echoed up in the woodlands.

The scouts turned to get back into the safety of the woods before calling headquarters.

Moving warily in case of enemy skirmishers, they gathered behind a clump of pink-and-white glob glob. Squatting down, Captain Brinks opened his communicator, began to punch in code.

A kifket half a meter long, twenty kilos of honed steel, cut Brinks's head from his body and continued on to sink deep in the plump glob glob stem behind. Blood sprayed up from the captain's decapitated body; they shrank back, turned in alarm. Bullets cut through the glob glob fronds, slapped the leaves. Fein were bounding toward them.

The men ran for their lives, scattering into the trees. The fein loped after them, for these enemies had to be caught before they could give away the Impi's position.

Two of the pursued ran quickly down a slope through patches of jik and found a path that headed east and downhill toward the east-running stream that lay below.

The path divided at the base of an old, dying thorn tree. The men hesitated; one cut to the right and left the game trail. The other panicked and ran on down the trail. Fein appeared ahead of him; he stopped with a scream of dismay and tried to climb a tree.

He jumped for a branch, scrabbling up into the jik, but they reached up and pulled him out and took his head with the kifket.

The man who ran right cut down another slope into a dense bed of hobi gobi. He flung himself down beneath the thick green fronds and held himself still, hardly daring to breathe.

He realized that blowing from north to south, the breeze was in his favor; it would leave him downwind from the fein. Silently a pair of fein loped by, hunting along the edge of the hobi gobi, kifkets at the ready.

The breath froze hard in his throat. Slowly they stalked past and then they were gone. With a slight sob he released the breath.

The silence held for several seconds until a dreadful screaming from the right told him they'd found Hukus. The cries cut off mercifully quickly.

Several more pairs of fein hunted past the hobi gobi patch

but missed his scent. Finally he dared to open his communicator and punch in some code. The base responded.

"Heavy fein forces crossing Missiling River at coordinates . . ." But the figures were never uttered, for his whisper had been overheard by old Neilk Ossimbu, following cannily along behind his fein by a half minute.

Ossimbu had a champion throw. The kifket was a flash of heavy steel that whipped through two thick hobi gobi stems and the man's neck before burying itself in a tough little jik tree.

But the damage had been done.

Especially to Young Proud Fundan's best-case battle plan. When word of the report from the Missiling was brought in, Young Proud at first dismissed it. For a full minute he stood in front of the holo table and considered the original plan. But still the stubborn little orange blurs remained massed in the south, in lower Muld. Why was his enemy so slow to move?

Ira Ganweek tried not to let his concern show. He struggled to keep wrinkles off his forehead. A technique he'd learned in order to survive in Chairman Wei's retinue on Earth. But the desire to wrinkle was strong. If Young Proud was so certain that Lavin Fundan was to cross Muld against the Kommando stretched along the River Muld's banks that no other possibility could be accepted, there might be difficulties in the not-too-distant future. Ganweek discreetly slipped out the door to examine the disposition of aircraft on the strip outside the bunkers.

Then abruptly Young Proud changed the holo with a desperate scream of frustration and tightened it on the terrain between the Missiling and Mount Titus. From the Missiling there were several tributary valleys, thickly clothed in jik and glob glob, that led toward the Kommando airstrip and the base beside it.

"If he comes up Blagston Valley," Captain Trunket said, "he'll only have to cover eleven kilometers to get to this precise spot."

Young Proud whirled, his face alight with sudden alarm. "How long ago did the message come in?"

"A couple of minutes, no more."

Young Proud's face worked in a curious fashion. "I think it has become necessary to visit the front lines. Come, Van Relt, let's fly over to the Muld."

Chevde and the others started up with staring eyes. Young Proud looked across the holo map at them with disdain. "I'm going to inspect the troops in the field. Anyone who cares to accompany us may do so. There's an eight-seater Hummbird that's ready to go. All you'll need is a pilot."

With that Young Proud swept out of the room and marched

at once to the airstrip, commandeered a vtol jet, and flew away. With him went bodyguards, Van Relt, and Fleur Fundan on her leash.

In the main bunker panic broke out. Degorak Chevde and Ofur Muynn burst into the open and looked around them. On the airstrip sat a dozen vtol craft, including a pair of heavy Hummbirds.

They screamed for a pilot as the other Neptunians stumbled out beside them. Together they ran for the planes.

Ira Ganweek ran with them, surprised himself by keeping up with them quite well, and boarded a Hummbird behind Degorak and Muynn.

"Pilot?" Degorak said in agitation, "who is asshole pilot?" his eyes wide and staring.

Ira smiled. "It's been a while, but I know how to fly one of these things—just take a seat."

"You can fly this thing?" Degorak clutched at Ira, pushed him toward the controls. Ira had to suppress his urge to giggle hysterically.

"Okay, folks, relax, ol' Ira's at the wheel here. Here we go."

Ganweek started the engines, which came on with a purr that built to a whine as he set controls for vertical takeoff. Then he noticed something strange—puffs of dust were starting up way down the runway where the heavy transports were loading. More puffs were opening in the sky.

A very loud bang, not fifty meters away, jerked them all around and elicited a scream from some of the Neptunians.

They were under mortar fire! Explosive two hundred-mm shells were dropping onto the strip!

Ganweek tried to stop the trembling in his hands as he kicked in the jets. More puffs blossomed on the far side of the strip. The sharp *crack-boom* of two hundred-mm mortar shell was accompanied by the whine of fragments. The hummbird twanged loudly once, from an impact in the nose, and the forward-seeing radar went dead. Ira pulled hard on the joystick and the bird rose steadily into the air until they were above the treetops, then he turned it and pointed it southward. The autopilot took over and whisked them to safety with the *whoosh* of jets.

Behind them, on the fringes of the western side of the airstrip, the first fein pickets clashed with the perimeter guards. In another minute a monstrous firefight broke out on the perimeter and the base command made a frantic call to Rinus Van Relt for reinforcement.

121

Young Proud ordered the guards to hold the perimeter line at all costs and then cut the contact.

And then Lavin Fundan's entire army blitzed out of the dark jik forest, and the perimeter force ran for their lives. Within minutes the entire base, with a month's supplies for the New Kommando's twenty-five thousand men, was in fein hands.

Inside the storerooms the Impis methodically sought out ammunition and weapons. Search parties ransacked the place for the new smart hand grenades that the Kommando were using.

But there was barely a pause for everyone to get their breath back. Lavin Fundan was riding up and down the lines frantically urging everyone on. Wearily they hefted weapons and booty and loped forward, up the slope of the volcano.

Lavin was one of the last out, spurring his horse up the trail into the strange forest of Nub Bush that cloaked the upper slopes of the mountain in a veil of white spore bodies that sparkled brighter than any snow cover. The bush was unremarkable, but its spore bodies were four meters wide and grew six meters off the ground.

In the ultramontane jungle the Impis dispersed rapidly, breaking up into small groups spread out over the high slopes. There the Impis paused for a meal and a respite. Most had a good view of the airstrip down below. Lavin had told them to watch the coming fireworks.

The *Black Ship* approached once more from the west, 190 kilometers up, deploying a squadron of orbital fighters that howled over the valley and hit the air base with a carpet of high explosive and napalm that incinerated everything for a hundred meters back into the woods.

The Impis finished their meal in a sober frame of mind. Lavin Fundan would have no problems in gaining acceptance of the doctrine of dispersal and reconcentration that he had preached since the Great War.

16

THERE WAS NO WELCOMING COMMITTEE WHEN IRA GANWEEK landed the big Hummbird in the New Kommando trenches overlooking the River Muld. Indeed the posse of Neptunian bond lords soon found itself in a dangerous limbo.

They were informed that Young Proud had long since gone north with the mobile command units to a new post at the front, where a big push was underway.

In fact there was a strong sense of activity in the air. Squads of troops were quick marching past into the forests. Light planes were floating in and out of the tiny airstrip. Big jet transports were rumbling overhead with sprays of parachutes trailing behind.

But the commanding officer at the airport apparently knew nothing of the Neptunians' presence and behaved as if they were spies for the enemy. Armed men cordoned off the CO's office in which they were left with a sergeant, weapon cocked and ready, plus a couple of troopers to watch over them while "something was found out about all this."

Ganweek was unused to military ways and found the frustration hard to take. Degorak Chevde, even less used to such treatment, soon blew his top and became violent. He brutally smashed a trooper in the face, pulping the man's nose. More troopers charged in with boots and sticks. A battle royal ensued with Ofur Muynn being the last to be overpowered and kicked into submission.

Those who had resisted were dragged off none too gently and locked up somewhere further down the corridor. Loud complaints continued to echo from their direction.

The sergeant favored the rest of them with a look of glee, then he gestured with his firearm. "If any more of you crud start something, I really will shoot you." He paused for emphasis. "I've only just been given that order, which is why those others are still alive."

Ira felt sure the man meant it. He went and sat down quietly and composed himself for a wait.

Hours slid by. The Neptunians grew restless and moody, demanding food, water, somewhere to lie down. The sergeant and his squad were replaced with shifts of guards, once an hour.

A small amount of water was made available but no food. Their impatience rose steadily until it peaked out in exhaustion. They argued fitfully and then most of them went to sleep scattered about the office. It was not a pleasant night.

In the morning they awoke, ill-tempered and sore in various places, to a breakfast of stale rolls and warm coffee. The air in the room was staler even than the rolls; the guards were bored and the Neptunians were ready to kill.

Eventually Captain Klain, of the Fourth Division, central admin staff, returned. He was urbane, even relaxed.

"All right, you're cleared with front office. Sorry about all this. I understand there was a little to-do after I left."

"A little to-do!" Alace Rohm exploded. She looked like she was going to strike the captain, but her sisters restrained her.

"Er, yes," Ira mumbled. "It's been an, uh, long night for some of us."

"Well, sometimes these things happen. We've got some fighting to be done, you know. Sorry about that."

With a big effort the Neptunians remained silent, seething, torn between rage and the fear of remaining incarcerated.

"Well I have exciting news for you. There's some transport being laid on for you. You're going right up to the front."

Ganweek was aghast. "I thought this was the front."

"Not at all, they're way up the river someplace, about ten kilometers, I think. There's a big push on."

"A big push? Combat?"

"That's right. Air bed to take you, it'll be round in a jiffy. Just follow me, your boisterous friends are being brought out too. No harm done really, best forgotten I suppose. Didn't know what you people were all about, you see. Front office forgot to warn us. I suppose they've got a lot on their plates right now, what? Wouldn't you agree?" Captain Klain favored them with a beaming smile.

Ira did not feel much like beaming back. Nor did he particularly relish the prospect of rushing toward actual combat, but at the front they would at least be closer to Young Proud. The demonstration of the military's power to interfere with their movements had frightened all of them. Better to be close to Young Proud where they could influence things more directly. There would be less likelihood that they would be incarcerated on some mad whim with no way to affect events.

So after a short argument that Chevde effectively ended by announcing his firm intention of finding Young Proud as soon as possible in order to remonstrate with the "poisonous fop," they all marched out to the air bed, which turned out to be a bulky hovercraft with seats for twelve and roomy cargo space at the rear.

The pilot started up the engines with a hellish whine the moment they were aboard, and they sped away into the forest on one of a series of freshly flattened trails through the jik. All around them the forest was filled with soldiers in motion. Other air beds, generally smaller than their own, sped by with soldiers clustered on top.

Every so often they passed small scout and combat units standing by the trail. A number of small aircraft howled past low overhead.

Then they heard the rumble of gunfire ahead. Heavy shelling was in progress. They reached a curving river crossed by a pair of bridges. One bridge was smashed, the wooden span dropped into the river. The other was of New Kommando pontoons painted a lustrous dark green.

On the far side of the river, a number of bodies had been piled up on the fringes of the trails. They saw fein bodies, smothered in carrion flies, human bodies too, in the dark camouflage uniform of the Butte forces. These were casualties from the sharp battle along the Uluin the previous day.

Here and there the trees had been smashed, snapped off, or even dug out of the ground, leaving a large crater. Craters multiplied; some of them seemed very fresh indeed. Then they came to the burnt place, and for fifty meters they passed through a charred landscape where almost everything had been burnt to cinders.

Several times they saw agitated Chitin nests, the ground around the central air shafts black with warriors deployed to kill anything that came near. The road even detoured around one collection of these. Shells had dug out the nests here and there and sent Chitin armies marching off into the undergrowth. Such feral bands would attack on contact.

More and more Kommando troops were visible now. And the noises up ahead were getting much louder.

A fein, face all bloody, with Butte camouflage webbing, was hanging on a tree by a kifket driven through his chest. The body was savagely mutilated. Ira Ganweek turned away, emotions frozen in a snarl of old hatred. If Armada Butte should chance his way though, he would at last unburden himself of that debt!

Explosions shook the ground to their right. A fountain of dirt and vegetation rose only one hundred meters away as big guns on the mountain fortress searched for targets in Sliverary.

The trail branched. The right fork was new, a recently 'dozered extension that the air bed swung onto. At a roadblock, troops in full chemical warfare kit with leveled automatics searched the hovercraft. They nodded to the driver, and with a lurch he pushed on, down a bulldozered incline. Extensive construction had recently been completed, and raw ground lay everywhere, trees and vegetation thrust back in piles at the side.

A hummock in the ground with a dozen aerials sprouting through its back was their destination. The air bed whined to a stop.

They clambered out of the air bed and strode down a flight of steps, past more guards, and into a tunnel wormed into the ground. After another door, more guards, and an unpleasant young woman in a gray security suit who waved a metal detector over them, they finally emerged into a new bunker, still smelling of the damp ground despite the shiny white foam wall coverings so recently sprayed in place.

Young Proud and Rinus Van Relt were in the prime control room looking down on the holograph projection.

"Ah, gentlemen, ladies from Nereid, welcome." Young Proud greeted them with grotesque affability as if nothing had happened that in any way could have harmed the good relations between himself and the Neptunian bond lords.

Degorak Chevde's wrath bubbled over. He had a number of painful bruises, perhaps even a broken rib from that beating. In addition his lower lip was swollen and he had some sore teeth. He had been treated with scorn and brutality for several hours, and he was not going to take it anymore.

"We have been most sorely neglected, most dreadfully treated, that I can barely find the words to describe it. Messire, I think you owe myself and the rest of us an abject apology. We were placed under arrest! We were brutally assaulted! What was this? The act of our ally? I want an apology, and in addition I demand a change in the manner in which these operations are being conducted.

"From now on I will make much greater input into the decision-making process. From now!" Chevde stabbed the air in front of his bull chest with a ponderous forefinger, just as he always had in front of the Party Conference back on Triton.

"Do you understand?" he bellowed. "We are sick and tired

of this traipsing around after you. Not to forget for a second the astonishing episode of last night."

Young Proud hissed, like a snake that had been stepped on and seemed to coil in on himself for a moment. "Messire Chevde," he purred after a while, "come, observe, discuss the battle. An honest error was made by a young officer who simply did not know who you were. Why you had to start such a fuss after that, I fail to understand. But after you had assaulted my men, I had to keep you locked up for the night for your own good and for the good of morale in the Kommando." He smiled sunnily and extended a hand in friendship.

"Come, let us forget that this ever happened. Remember, I have two men in sick bay as a result of that ill-considered outburst. So let us not talk of apologies but of true cooperation and friendship."

Chevde uttered a strangled growl. "Impudent sperm bag. I will crush you with my own bare hands." Ofur Muynn tried to interpose, but it was too late. Degorak seized Young Proud by the lapels of his combat jacket. Young Proud's dark eyes were wide open in stunned surprise. Then Chevde hoisted Young Proud straight across the room to bounce across the holo table and land on the floor. Van Relt sucked in his breath.

Persimpilgas, the fein bodyguard, materialized out of the shadows on the far side of the room and stood between Young Proud and the Neptunians.

"Out of my way," Chevde roared, completely out of control. "Nobody will prevent me from chastising this noisome popinjay." Chevde surged forward and grappled Persimpilgas and tried to push the old fein out of the way. Persimpilgas was astonished by the strength of the man, those showy muscles were hard, heavy, the product of decades of work with weights in heavy gee. Persimpilgas's astonishment turned to woe however when Chevde kneed him sharply in the abdomen. With a gasp the old fein fell back against the holo table rocking it on its heavy legs.

Chevde lunged for Young Proud, determined to kill him. Instead he ran into Herver, a wall of fein muscle several inches taller than even Ofur Muynn. Chevde surged against Herver trying to force the fein out of his way but was instead lifted and hurled into a section of portable camp chairs, one of which splintered beneath him. Ofur Muynn closed with Herver; for a moment they struggled together, then Muynn attempted a throw. He was rebuffed; Herver slammed him in the belly with a heavy forearm and dropped him to his knees.

Then one of the nereid women caught a guard napping, and,

snatching his weapon, she fired. Herver went down and she continued firing, bullets thudding into the big body until Persimpilgas reached her and swatted her against the wall.

The guards rushed in, leveled their weapons. The Neptunians stood trembling, on the brink of suicidal fury.

Young Proud spoke in a voice thick with fury. "Bind them, gag them, all except the good Senator Ganweek."

Persimpilgas gave a heave and thrust Muynn and Chevde back.

Herver groaned and tried to get up. There was a lot of blood, a brilliant stain on the white plastic floor. Herver sighed. Despite his efforts, his magnificent body simply lacked the strength simply to sit up. He sank back quietly and lay still. Persimpilgas bent over him and cradled the big head on his thigh.

"Hold on, young Herver." There were tears in Persimpilgas's eyes. "Hold on for our village, keep to this life, Herver, don't leave your old mzsee all alone now."

On Young Proud's instructions, the woman who had shot Herver was dragged to her feet and hustled out of the room. The guards then bound the Neptunians and sat them in a row of chairs facing the holographic map. They were all gagged securely with strips of cloth pressed tightly into their mouths. Several of the nereiders screamed aloud at this indignity but were slapped into submission by the troopers.

By then Young Proud and Van Relt had returned their attention to the battle plan. Events were moving toward a fresh crisis. Van Relt was desperate to get his master into motion. By a freak of battlefield maneuver, they had been handed a golden opportunity to destroy their opponent.

During the night the Fenrille Defense Forces had dispersed widely over the eastern slopes of Mount Titus. They had recoalesced in the morning and begun a secret drive to the River Uluin, intending to assault the Kommando siege lines around Butte Manor.

To screen the Impis during this attack, in case the Kommando should suddenly head north, Lavin Fundan had sent a small force into North Muld.

During the night however Young Proud had shifted some divisions toward Mount Titus, crossing the River Muld south of the Impis and heading west. By morning Young Proud's unstable mind had changed, and he became panicky at the thought of being cut off from the other half of his army, which still occupied the siege lines around Butte Manor. The divisions wheeled about and marched east.

They crossed the River Muld again and swept on to the Uluin. Soon their scouts picked up the sign of the recent passage of many fein, and thus they discovered that they had waltzed completely around Lavin Fundan's protective screen and were thundering in on the rear of the Impis.

The Fifth and Sixth divisions, almost eleven thousand men, were moving up into position, but Young Proud had been waiting to show off his maneuvers to the Neptunians and had refrained from giving the vital orders to speed their march into a charge. Van Relt was perfectly well aware that every minute was precious now. He had the divisions spreading out into an assault front but still lacked the order for the attack. Desperately he tried to get Young Proud's attention, but the commander was in a trance of his own, staring at the battle laid on the holo map and oblivious to all else.

But when the Neptunians were finally tied to their chairs and firmly gagged, Young Proud picked up a pointer and proceeded to explain the battle situation to them in considerable detail. All the while there was a bizarre tone of glee in his voice, which bubbled over and forced him to stop and get a grip on himself.

"I'm awfully sorry to have to make of you a somewhat captive audience," he said at one point, and broke into a fit of giggles. He nudged Van Relt and winked crudely.

"I thought that was good, didn't you, Van Relt. 'Captive Audience'?"

"Yes, lord, but the orders, messire—let us attack now for the sake of our success. I can sense victory if we can just get started right away."

Young Proud seemed to agree for a moment and Van Relt breathed a sigh of relief. Then the commander shook his head.

"Nonsense, Van Relt. Keep it steady, man, we're coming in on him, but let's let him squeeze himself up close to the siege lines. We don't want him slipping away."

Van Relt despaired. "No, messire. No, we must strike now. He will sense us within minutes; it's a miracle his scouts haven't already found us. So *now* is our opportunity."

"Yes, yes, Van Relt, no need to panic." Young Proud waved a hand airily. "We have him now. We must just let him slide onto our hook. Meanwhile we can bring our guests up to date."

Van Relt groaned inwardly, hardly able to stand it, while Young Proud proceeded to run through his game plans in orange blurs for the enemy and blue wedges and blurs for the Kommando.

"So we will come onto his rear; we will pin him against the

siege lines and then the Space Marines will come in to finish the job with a smashing blow—right into their center! We'll annihilate them!" He finished with a flourish. He understood it now. This was as fate had willed it would be. This would always be known as Young Proud's Stroke.

Chevde and the others stared at him with hatred in their eyes.

"Now, lord, the *orders*," Van Relt said urgently. Still Young Proud hesitated, relishing his moment, this cusp of history. Sometimes Van Relt was a little too pushy; perhaps the next time the antidote would be a little weaker. It was important to change one's officers every so often.

"Yes, all right, Van Relt." Young Proud issued the command to hurry the divisions forward.

On the holo screen the orange blurs of Lavin's fein Impis had begun to cross the River Uluin, only a few kilometers from the Kommando siege lines around Butte Manor. The blue formations of Young Proud's attack were now moving in behind the orange blurs and would strike them at the river crossings.

The blow was launched, and there was little for Van Relt to do except keep abreast of the progress of the forward units. And pray.

Young Proud paced up and down the room. This was the sort of wear and tear that he hated. His nervousness got the better of him and he picked up the small whip that had dropped from his belt and marched abruptly out of the room.

Van Relt watched him go with misgivings. Young Proud had become very difficult to deal with in the last twenty-four hours. The tension and pressures of the campaign were taking a toll on his ability to restrain his self-destructive urges.

With an effort Van Relt turned his thoughts away from Young Proud. He assumed that one of those poor women was going to suffer. Van Relt found Young Proud's cruel pleasures rather disgusting, but he banished such thoughts and instead refocused himself on the battle. Victory was close; he could almost taste it.

At last the first reports of contact came in. Kommando formations thrust forward to the river, their artillery wreaking havoc on the Impis just ahead of them. The Fifth Division ploughed across the Uluin and struck hard into the rear of the Response Impi. The Sixth Division enveloped a smaller force of fein and artillery on the west side of the Uluin and drove it northward into deep Sliverary.

The Response Impi wheeled about in the scrub, and units from the Abzen First rushed back from the vanguard to hem up the defense and make a stand in the woods of Sliverary, just kilometers from the bloody battlefield of the day before between the Butte Guards and the Kommando. Van Relt committed the reserves now, the Seventh Division, on a kilometer-wide front, looping around the southern flank of the Impi and hooking into the rear.

Again Van Relt sent word to Young Proud, on his personal frequency, informing him of what was happening. There was no response. Young Proud was apparently monitoring his communicator but quite content with the way things were going.

Ira Ganweek had sidled up to the holo map after trying to make himself inconspicuous in the wake of the fight. "What is he doing?" he whispered.

Van Relt looked up, excitement showing in his tired gray eyes. "Well, well, Senator Ganweek, or ex-Senator, as I should say. Fancy meeting you again, and on such a day as this. As for our enemy, I should say he is working very hard on his defense right now. We have him cornered." He gestured to the holo map.

"So I can see."

The big blue formations were lapping around the orange blurs and driving them steadily northward toward the river Sliverary.

"But what I want to know is what is *He* doing? Young Proud, I mean." Ganweek gestured conspiratorially, Van Relt's eyes clouded for a moment.

"Messire, my advice would be for you not to think about what he is doing right now, not unless that sort of thing excites you. But as I recall, you lost your ah, urges in that, ah, direction, didn't you?"

Ganweek colored, then smiled nastily. "And I believe that our opponent on today's battlefield somewhat reduced your own, ah, proclivities, after the battle of Badleck Ridge?"

Van Relt returned the smile. "Touché, Messire, anyway that Nereid woman is not likely to return to you alive, that much is evident." He cleared his throat and then changed the subject.

"However the *Black Ship* will return, and as yet it is not informed about what has happened here. When it is in range you are to give the orders to launch the air strikes on the enemy while he tries to escape. Do you understand? We won't need the Space Marines this time, but the air strikes will break his formations for good. It is imperative that we continue to work with the *Black Ship*. Despite what has happened here."

Ganweek nodded, his mind fogged, unable to think of a way out of his predicament. He didn't want to meet the eyes of

Chevde and the other Neptunians burning furiously on the other side of the table.

Fifteen meters down the corridor, Fleur Fundan gasped in pain and horror as Young Proud came into her. The smell of him, his sweat, his harsh, hot breath in her ear, made her skin crawl and her flesh yearn for death. The memory of what she had just witnessed would not go away however, despite what he did to her. The bloody object swinging mutely from the ceiling hook would not go away either.

They were on the floor; Young Proud had an instinct for the best location of defilement. The room was small, so drops of blood kept falling from the thing above them to land on Young Proud's back or in Fleur's face. They were salty in her mouth.

"I will bring him back, castrate him myself, and make him watch us play if you do not pretend to enjoy this," he whispered in her ear. "He is doomed, you see, his army broken."

17

THE SPACE BOAT SLICED INTO THE TREES WITH A THUNDEROUS roar. Branches broke under its weight, and for a moment a kaleidoscope of leaves flashed across the viewscreens. Then it stopped with a jarring thud that hurled them all into the air on their seat harnesses then back down with a force that crushed the breath from their bodies. For quite a few moments nobody was able to speak.

Incredibly the restraint webbing had held them all in their seats throughout that insane descent from orbit. Chi Lin Wei wondered just what conditions the boat's builders had in mind when they made it so tough.

"The hull is breached," Yu Zhao announced.

"The computer is working," Zhao three called. "The screen too." A dim forest-floor view appeared on the main screen. A tangled jungle of vines and mottled fungi reduced visibility to a matter of meters. Very large tree trunks obtruded here and there.

"Give me a scan of these trees," Chi Lin Wei said. The computer angled its cameras. The trunks, fifty or sixty meters thick, soared endlessly above. Approximately two hundred meters above the ground, the first branches spread out, and beyond that grew a thick canopy that blocked the entire sky.

The computer scanned for sound outside. A deep hush pervaded, punctuated by occasional insect buzzings. Then from far away a mournful hooting could be heard. It was repeated twice more and the silence returned.

"These trees are the *Esperm gigans*," Chi Lin Wei said with a touch of awe. Face thoughtful, she fought to recall what she'd read concerning them.

A strange smell caused her nostrils to twitch. It was the stink of damp ground, alien vegetation, decomposing matter. With a start she realized that the jungle atmosphere had invaded the boat through the broken rear section. The alien stink raised the hairs on the back of her neck. This was the new world, the planet of her dreams! But the stink only brought back to her the memory of the young Highlander and his dire warnings.

She acted. "Where are the space suits?"

Yu Zhao raised an eyebrow in momentary question.

"Quickly, before we catch some deadly disease." She was almost screaming.

The Yu Zhao clones jumped for the locker and pulled out its contents. Hurriedly they dressed Chi Lin Wei and fitted the breathing filters into her suit. Then they turned to suits for themselves. When everyone was suited they opened an air lock, and crawled out, and stood on the stubby wing of the life-support module.

It was very hot and humid so the suits automatically switched the air-conditioning to maximum. The little suit fans hummed in chorus.

Insects of many shapes and hues flashed around them. Some landed momentarily on their suits. Others seemed to prey on these, and Yu Zhao noticed one kind that was especially active. "The black flies with the big red eyes are determined biters. They can almost get through my suit."

Chi Lin Wei felt a small thrill of horror as she watched one of these doing its utmost to stab through her suit with its sharp little proboscis. She slapped at it and shivered. . . . If we had come out here without the suits! . . . We would all have been bitten by now.

Wielding machetes, Yu Zhao and Yu Zhao five cut a way through some of the tangled vines and went out into the jungle.

Chi Lin Wei looked up at the enormous trees and felt oppressed by the sheer monstrous size of the things. The light was so dim and so green, the silence was so sepulchral it was like that of some huge temple of vegetation. Silent but for the busy hum of the insects.

With a suddenness that caused her to suck in her breath and go absolutely rigid in fright, something started screaming maniacally at the edge of the clearing. The raucous shrieks echoed off the trees. Another animal joined in, in fact several, all screaming horribly. Chi Lin Wei retreated to the interior of the space boat and sat, arms wrapped around herself, in front of the main screen while she fought the impulse to weep. Finally, when she was on the point of screaming, the animals quieted.

Yu Zhao returned and posted Zhaos three and four outside the air lock.

"We went about three hundred meters north, nothing but this jungle, no sign of even a clearing so we could see the sun and get a bearing. I think we'll have to try to climb one of these trees."

"What was it that made those hellish screams?"

Yu Zhao smiled. "Would you believe a group of small animals the size of your hand? They looked like lizards but they might be birds for all I know. I never dreamed anything so small could be so loud."

Chi Lin Wei was caught in uncharacteristic indecision. In her mind she could hear Chosen Fundan shouting, "Leave the space boat, save your lives," but she could not imagine anything that could harm the Neptune Gas Company's indestructible space boat. No animal could possibly harm them.

Yu Zhao turned his attention to the radio. After patient work at the receiver, he was able to pick up a distant commercial radio station playing martial music, but calls on hailing frequencies met with no response. They were thousands of kilometers from anyone who might hear.

"We will have to contact a satellite, nothing else is within range."

"But radio signal will tell the enemy ship where we are, won't it?"

"We have to risk that or else stay here for good."

Yu Zhao tried to send a signal on the Mayday frequency, but the SHF transmitter was malfunctioning. Quickly they dismantled the unit to search for the problem.

Time passed; Chi Lin Wei stared at the viewscreen fixedly. Outside Zhaos three and four watched the dim daylight fade a little further into late afternoon. Insects still hummed around them busily. Occasionally something would rustle the leaves farther away but always out of sight.

Despite the peaceful scene Zhao four grew increasingly uneasy. He had the feeling that something was watching him with unusual interest.

Unfortunately he was correct in this surmise. The thing watched him with seven of its eight eyes. The other one kept Zhao three under surveillance. As it watched, a curious kind of rage boiled in its breast. It breathed in ecstatic anticipation of a slaughter of the enemies, whoever they were...

It felt the nearby tree screaming, limbs broken most cruelly by the invader from above. It rocked to the mass anxiety of the mother forms... a metal nest, *other*... and then the dreaded nest worms had appeared from within.

They were certain to be dangerous. Nest worms that came

135

in the metal eggs were known to be lethal to the mother forms. They would bring fire, metal arms to cut the mother forms down. The forest would darken in terror.

Hence the mouth of the trees examined them carefully. The nest worms were slow-moving things, covered in some horrible reflective skin that gave off no odor, although there was strange animal smell in the exhaust venting from their air-conditioning units. Odd smell, odd skin, with worm things inside.

The mouth of the mother forms pondered the situation. Did their languor imply a lack of fear? Did they believe there would not be revenge? Did they think they were beyond the reach?

Rage bubbled in the mind beneath those eight eyes, and the Woodwose, which had no name and never thought of itself in terms separately from the mother forms but would have responded to the descriptive "Class of Four Enragements . . . longest-legged . . . a mouth that devours for the mother forms," shifted almost silently on its thirteen-meter-long legs and moved closer to the metal nest.

Zhao four turned, then froze. The hair on the back of his head stood stiff. He had seen something, something huge, something impossible. He screamed, "Behind us!" and tried to draw his gun, but the thing wrapped a hand the size of a door around him and was lifting him toward a dumpster-size pelican's beak.

His shriek of horror went off like steam from a giant's kettle and was echoed by that of Zhao three, who got off a shot with his revolver, right into the thing's midriff, before a huge foot, toes tipped with heavy claws, swung out of the jungle and hammered him like a football, end over end, thirty meters into the vines.

By then only Zhao four's feet and a long strip of space suit fabric were visible, projecting from the Woodwose's jaws, which moved in vigorous mastication. Swiftly it moved after Zhao three, grabbed his body, and thrust it into its maw. After several minutes' work, only the tough nylon fabric remained, an indigestible ball that the Woodwose finally removed and tossed away in disgust.

It returned to the undergrowth to observe the hated metal nest-thing. There had to be some way to destroy it utterly.

Inside the space boat stunned silence reigned. They stared in horror at the triangular head of the monster that was swallowing Zhao three on the main viewscreen. For a fleeting moment they saw most of it in motion across the camouflage pattern of the jungle. A spindly biped, twenty meters tall, like some insane

cross between a giant ape, a pelican, and a praying mantis—
and then it was gone.

They looked at each other for a long moment. Then Yu Zhao
threw himself back into work on the radio. But he had hardly
begun when something struck the spacecraft and rang it like a
gong.

It struck again, and they recognized the sound of metal plate
buckling.

"Where is that?" Yu Zhao breathed.

"Nose section?"

"No, it's on the air lock."

"Thankfully that's a reinforced section of the hull," Yu Zhao
said as he examined a computer graphic of the ship.

"Are there any cameras down there?"

"I think so. Let's see if we can switch to auxiliary maintenance
screen."

The image changed on the screen to give them a view from
a lens mounted on the dorsal surface of the midsection.

A large rock two meters thick was being raised in two enormous hands. It vanished downward, and the ship reverberated
to a boom and shook along its length.

The rock, easily three metric tons in weight, rose again.

"We are trapped in here," Chi Lin Wei said uneasily.

"Can we kill it?" Zhao six asked.

"Perhaps if we can get it to walk across the front of the boat,
we could fire the laser."

"It may not work."

"We must find something that does work though. Listen."
The air lock's outer door was giving way. The booming blows
ceased as the Woodwose started trying to rip the damaged door
off its massive hinges. The ship shuddered a little and they could
hear metal screaming.

"It's actually tearing the steel!" Yu Zhao groaned in sick
astonishment.

It was the sound of the Woodwose's frenzied assault on the
air lock door that finally drew Chosen to the right spot. In the
tangled vine jungle he'd missed the space boat by a couple of
hundred meters. But it was impossible to mistake the sound of
boulder on hollow metal. Carefully he crept through the trees
until he could see the space boat lying between four towering
trees. Beside the boat, a boulder in both hands above its head,
was a full-grown Woodwose. With a massive grunt it brought
the boulder down against a damaged section of the air lock door.

With a sharp report the boulder splintered and pieces whined off into the vines.

The Woodwose emitted an angry exhalation and examined the remains of its weapon. With a hoot of exasperation it turned and vanished into the trees.

Chosen waited a second and then ran to the space boat and made himself visible to the cameras, praying that they still worked.

The remaining undamaged air lock swung open. He slipped inside.

At least they were all wearing helmets and filters. Then he noticed that there were only four cloned staff officers. "What happened to the Yu Zhaos?"

"The monster ate them. It was so fast, it—" Chi Lin Wei's face was clenched tight as a drum against the fear that absorbed her.

"I see."

They stared at him with impassive glances. Inside the suits they seemed remote from their earlier mistakes. Were they in shock? Chosen imagined that the links between a clone group would be very deep.

"Well, we must leave the ship while the Woodwose is searching for another rock. Soon other 'wose will join it here, and together they'll work until the boat is broken down to pieces small enough to be carried down to the river and thrown in. So we have to get to the river first and build ourselves a raft. Out on the river we'll have a much better chance of survival."

This time there was no disagreement. They hurriedly dug out the survival packs from another locker and set out after Chosen across the gnarled tree roots that covered so much of the forest floor.

Being outside, in the gathering dusk with such dim light, was quite terrifying. The Woodwose might return at any moment. They slipped and scrambled in their haste to put some distance between themselves and the space boat.

They were breathing hard, panting in fact, while the suits whined a little as the air-conditioning took up the load, when Chosen brought them to a temporary halt.

Behind them a dull metallic boom resounded. After a few seconds there was another.

"The monster," Chi Lin Wei said.

"It has not detected our flight. We are very lucky."

"What will it do when it opens the space boat and finds nobody inside?"

Chosen shrugged. "Impossible to say. Probably just smash the boat to fragments—either way, that's the most likely result."

"Where is the river?" she asked after a moment.

"About five hundred meters further on in this direction. Have you noticed this undergrowth of glob glob?" He indicated the riot of pink-and-green leaves that protruded like giant tongues from the ground between the trees.

"We're close to the water now, you see."

They resumed their flight, running furtively through the glob glob. Ahead, under the huge trees, the darkness seemed to be growing thicker.

18

ONLY THE SOUND OF THEIR BREATHING, HARSH AND HEAVY despite the filters, broke the stillness. Despite the air-conditioning they were soon bathed in sweat from the exertion.

Around them lay a pervasive hush, the cathedrallike silence of the forest evening. Laboriously they clambered over and crawled under the nightmare jungle of gigantic twisted roots. Around the major roots grew a thick brush of glob glob and satursine vine, and it was slow work moving through the tangle. All too soon darkness was closing in, the light visibly lessening. Chosen tried to keep their spirits up against the gathering dusk. "We have suit lights, remember. We'll be able to keep moving in the dark."

But for Chi Lin Wei the darkness was pregnant with fresh horrors and all-too-familiar terrors. The eery quiet was perhaps the hardest thing to take; she had accepted by then the smell of herself and the sweat slicking her skin against the suit, but the hush of the enormous woods was intimidating.

Abruptly the peace was torn asunder by a chorus of harsh screaming cries that erupted somewhere not far ahead of them. They were joined at once by other similar cries from points to the left and the right of the original sound. Soon the long ululating screams were reverberating off the trees from every direction.

Chosen caught the look on Chi Lin Wei's face and reached out to reassure her.

"It's all right, it's the sarmer mackees—it's getting close to the monsoon when they breed."

"What are sarmer mackee?" For a moment, without thinking, she took his hand for reassurance.

"A smallish amphibian creature, they breed prolifically during the monsoons."

"Why do they sound like they are being tortured?"

Chosen stifled the urge to laugh. "I doubt that it does sound like that, to them. Both sexes scream, the males to establish mating rights and drive off other males, and the females scream during the mating act itself, for reasons that are unknown."

Suddenly embarrassed, she let go his hand.

The screams had taken on a horrifying intensity, long sobbing wails that lasted for ten seconds at a time. They sounded horribly human, as if hundreds of people were having the flesh stripped from their bones.

He shrugged, and the smile froze on his face when a little stab of pain between his shoulder blades reminded him of that little bead of green plastic on its wire.

Their eyes met for a moment, and she flinched and turned away. Yu Zhao and the others stared at him, eyes level, faces emotionless.

At least he was even with them. They had saved him from the wreck of the Gandhi. He had saved them from the Wood-wose. Yet if they were all to make it out of the Bhjum River Basin they would have to cooperate. There would have to be trust between them. He sighed to himself and turned to the next fat, ribbed root, sheathed in rough and shaggy bark, and began to climb over it.

They pressed on. Everyone was tired by then, and each tree and the enormous root system spread out around it was like a minor mountain placed in their way. They would have to climb over several roots as thick as a man is tall; sometimes they would have to crawl under them or occasionally walk along the top, battling through the glob glob scrub that fought for space above the roots. Chi Lin Wei cursed vigorously in Mandarin throughout the ordeal.

Once Chosen bade her stand still while he pulled several thick tubular creatures off the lower portions of her suit. "Rasp worms, have to get them off fast before they cut your suit. They wouldn't be able to feed off you, but that wouldn't stop them trying."

When she saw the things, Chi Lin Wei shrieked, finally losing control. She screamed and hugged herself and covered her face-plate with her hands.

Chosen was joined by Zhao five, and they soon removed the rest of the rasp worms, but Chi Lin Wei remained distraught.

Leaving her to recover, Chosen hauled himself to the top of the next root and let out an exultant yell.

Dead ahead the tree cover parted, and a streak of evening sky, faded turquoise streaked with gold, showed through.

He jumped down beside the others. "At last! When we heard the sarmer mackees, I knew we were going in the right direction."

They stared at him with blank faces, Chi Lin Wei still shuddering to herself.

"Over there," he said, gesturing wildly, "the river!"

After negotiating a few more elephantine root systems, they came to an exposed riverbank. A wall of tree roots sank into deep water the color of putty. A few small straggling trees even grew farther out, but after a hundred meters or so they gave way to the enormous sweep of the river that faded to the dim horizon.

Small islands dotted the expanse of water, but the other shore was far out of sight.

Far above floated a few small pennon clouds tinged gold-green in the fading light of Beni.

Chi Lin Wei saw at once how different it was from the long smoky sunsets of Earth and became intensely aware that she was seeing by the light of a new star, an alien sun. She was lost in the alien jungles of an alien world and beset by dangers she had never imagined existed. She shivered, felt an unutterable exhaustion settling over her. Would the nightmare ever end? Would she ever feel safe again?

The sarmer mackees had ceased their cries, but now a host of evening animals were announcing their presence. Howls, whoops, and an assortment of whistles broke the stillness.

A husky coughing sound arose somewhere on their left, and Chosen froze and gestured to them to fall back. He drew his revolver, checked it quickly, and pushed it to the setting that would fire explosive darts.

"What is it?" Chi Lin Wei whispered on the suit radio.

"Nachri, coming down to drink." Seeing her face go almost comically blank behind the face mask, he added, "Large predator, dangerous."

Fear appeared in those eyes that had spurned him so coolly only a few hours before.

. . . Yes, milady, it is right to be afraid now . . . He stared hard eyed at her in the gathering murk. She turned away, Yu Zhao had taken out the other revolver.

They waited a long moment there between the roots until Chosen heard splashing and the sound of heavy beasts running. He gestured to everyone to crouch down. After a momentary hesitation they did.

He frowned. Wrapped in their mutually reinforced superiority derived from the power that radiated from Chi Lin Wei's person, the off-worlders could hardly bring themselves to listen to a boy of nineteen, let alone obey him. In Fenrille's ecosystem such hesitation might cost them their lives.

142

The sound grew louder; heavy bodies jumped from root to root, deep, ugly snarls echoed around them. Then it became very much louder, so loud that it seemed sure to come right down upon them where they hid.

Chosen tensed, revolver ready, wondering if the explosive darts would be enough to stop a full-grown Nachri.

Unfortunately the creatures came at six hundred pounds and as fast as a man could run. Where the Nachri knew about guns, they would avoid men armed with them; however, there on the banks of Bhjum, humans would be unknown. What would happen if the Nachri were to spot them was hard to predict. The animals might spook and simply run away. The fein were skilled at handling the Nachri in that way. But fein had better woods skills than Nachri or any animal on Fenrille saving the Woodwose.

And then the uproar passed and steadily moved away to the right. He chanced a peek over the root.

Along the margins of the water a pride of Nachri was at play. Heavy-chested, agile creatures that vaguely resembled terrestrial mandrils, they gamboled, buffeting, pinching, and chasing each other in a chorus of explosive grunts and snarls, occasionally splashing spray into the air.

Two females burdened with small youngsters brought up the rear ambling along more slowly, examining the roots for crustacea or other edibles.

Eventually they too passed by and disappeared around a small headland crowned with a dead tree, a giant snapped off one hundred fifty meters from the ground.

"Would they have attacked us?" Yu Zhao said.

"Quite possibly—they're opportunistic predators. One of the most common higher forms to be found in the forest."

Chosen led them in the opposite direction. "We need a place we can hole up in for the night, a space beneath some roots. Of course all the best ones probably have tenants already, so we may have to eject someone from their home."

He flicked on his headset light and used it to pick out their path. Small animals were in motion, rustling around them as they came down to drink.

A herd of sarmer mackees, like chubby tailless lizards a meter in length, trotted past on a well-worn trail. The creatures had eyes that glowed green, and as they scuttled by there was much grunting and whistling between them.

At last Chosen found a narrow opening between two competing roots that pushed up in a reversed U and made a cave about five meters deep and four wide.

They waited while he investigated it. The light picked out small clumps of animal droppings, and at the far end was a bed of small bones, the remains of many meals.

"By the size of those skull bones I'd say this is a river Were's home, young one, feeds on sarmer mackees mostly and perhaps the occasional fish. We should be able to take over its home for the night; it's too small to bother us."

In fact the access way was so narrow they had to sidle into it scraping the suits along the roots. Yu Zhao set down a small portalite, and they crowded in. When all six of them were inside the small space it was intensely claustrophobic, but it did at least give them an illusion of safety.

They were also ravenous, but Chosen urged them to keep their helmets on until the evening breeze had swept the air free of spruip spores. They stared at him a moment, hating that news, feeling the fatigue in their muscles and drooling at the thought of the protein bars in their packs. Chosen could see at once how much they disbelieved him. They were the guards of Chi Lin Wei, servants of the highest. How could this be happening to them?

Unfortunately the cramped hole by the riverbank was now their reality. If they wanted to survive, they would have to listen to the young roundeye.

Chi Lin Wei had fallen asleep, exhausted by the terror she had endured for so many hours.

Chosen and Zhao two kept the first watch, revolvers at the ready.

It was a quiet evening along that stretch of the great river. Once they heard the tread of a large animal, and something strode past above their hole snorting softly to itself. Chosen identified it instantly as a young bull gzan, alone at this point of its life, thrown out of its old herd by its sire and not strong enough yet to take one of its own.

The Pale Moon rose far away above the waters, dappling them with its ivory-pink light. Occasional skrin calls, with their long, melodious notes, drifted across from the midstream islands, sounding uncannily like human flute players tuning up before a concert.

Chosen had grown used to the lack of communication with the Chinese officers, and he was taken by surprise when the man beside him at the mouth of the passage opened a radio channel.

"This is an enchantingly beautiful world, messire," Zhao two said. "I wish I were in a position to more fully enjoy the beauties."

Chosen nodded. "Indeed I can see at once a myriad of small differences in just the quality of the light here on Fenrille, from that in my home in Central Shanghai."

Chosen saw that Zhao two was grinning and wondered why until he suddenly recalled a video about China's great city regions, where two hundred million people lived in endless tower-block gardens, blanketed in acid rain beneath eternally clouded skies. He laughed at such bitter humor, surfacing here in such a grim situation.

Zhao two went on. "I am haunted though by the ironies. Here we are encased in space suits, talking by radio; we are walled off from all this beauty."

Chosen nodded, but replied, "In a few more hours we could probably get away with being outside the suits. The bad-biting flies aren't abroad, no mosquitoes on Fenrille, and that breeze has probably blown all the spruip spore inland."

"What are your plans?"

Chosen smiled, a trifle bitterly. The task of keeping them alive had obviously devolved to him. But he kept the bitterness out of his voice. Survival required cooperation.

"Tomorrow we'll try and find a stand of knuckoo, or even hobi gobi, because down here the hobi gobi can be enormous. One leaf would serve us as a raft. Knuckoo we can cut and weave into a raft in very little time. With a little more luck we could be all done and out on the water by noon. Perhaps on one of the islands. Out there we could find some more knuckoo to improve things, and at least we'd be out of the reach of the Woodwose."

Zhao two paused a moment. "What do you think the monster is doing now?"

"Smashing the space boat to smithereens, I dare say. It'll take it a day or two to finish the job, unless it gets a few neighbors in to make it a party."

"Such implacable monsters!" Zhao two placed the emphasis on "implacable" and brought a smile to Chosen's lips.

"That's the way to describe this whole ecosystem—think of it as a monoculture, just like a field of agricultural produce. The whole thing is organized around the continuation of the trees, and anything that is disharmonious must be destroyed and removed. It's as fierce as our own immune systems."

Chosen stopped. He could see the tears on Zhao two's face. "I'm sorry . . ." he began.

145

The Chinese face was contorted with the effort of controlling powerful emotions. "I wish we had listened to you," he hissed. "I regret to say that I was with the others at the time in their decision. Aboard the space boat, before . . . I could not believe that it would be . . . like this. These monsters, it was so terrible."

He wept openly for a minute or so and regained control with an obvious effort. "I must apologize. It is disgraceful to cry like this, but I was very close to Zhao four. We grew up together, in the same age cluster. He died, it was just so terrible . . ."

"I'm sure it must have been."

. . . and the Woodwose would have eaten them . . .

"He was my family, my only real relative, you see."

Chosen didn't know what to say after that and instead dared a look outside their bolt hole. He crept out to the edge of a huge dead root that underlay their refuge and listened.

The jungle was quiet now, since the nocturnal predators were all at work, and only the slap of the waves broke the peace. He looked out toward the islands in the channel, clumped in moonlit outlines.

If they could build enough of a raft to get out to those isles, they could find relative safety. Improve the raft. Maybe even get out alive. After a few moments he ducked back into their hiding place.

On his way he failed to notice the pair of eye pods projecting just above the surface of the water twenty meters from shore. *They* however did observe the bright prey-possibility and informed the brain a meter or so below about it.

In response the ancient pectaroon surfaced and tasted the air. Despite its great size, this display of caution was merely sensible, for if Woodwose caught it preying on land they might break its shell and throw it to the permiads. However no Woodwose taint could be detected. On the other hand the bright prey-possibility was very close at hand.

The great spiny crustacean, a conqueror more than a century old, moved on long clockwork limbs up the mat of thick roots and carefully surveyed the hole where the prey-possibility had been. There was movement inside, the glitter was an irresistible lure. The pectaroon jumped forward the last few meters and thrust its foreclaw into the gap under the roots and seized something soft that struggled vainly to escape.

The first warning to Chosen and Zhao two was the sight of the crustacean's meter-long claw as it swung in out of the dark and wrapped around Zhao two's waist. His scream of horror

146

woke the others, and they leaped to help Chosen restrain the claw that was dragging Zhao two out the entrance.

But this was a contest between a few minnows and a king among crustacea. Remorselessly the monster pulled its prey loose and out of the burrow. They stumbled in pursuit, Chosen bringing up his revolver to bear on the pectaroon's head. Where was the brain in this monstrous lobster's skull?

He aimed, but the monster had lifted Zhao two into the line of fire. Chosen ran forward to get closer.

By the water's edge the pectaroon gave its prey a quick inspection and tasted it briefly with its razor-sharp mouthpieces.

The prey was disappointing; it was alien, flavorless, and beyond the ancient one's previous experience. So, suddenly spooked, the old pectaroon dropped the prey-possibility and scuttled back to the water.

Chosen and Yu Zhao ran forward and dragged Zhao two back into the shelter. Chi Lin Wei shone the light on his wounds. It was immediately clear that Zhao two was mortally hurt. Around the waist his suit had been opened as if with a serrated blade, and a brief inspection of the horribly askew vertebrae showed that his back was broken. In addition, around the right shoulder where the monster had bitten him, there were ugly purplish blood patches inches across.

It was no wonder that poor Zhao two was unconscious. The fein thinking came easily to Chosen. Tesraal, the crime of allowing the mortally wounded to wake. Zhao two would have nothing but agony to endure until death mercifully intervened.

Chosen looked up into Chi Lin Wei's face mask; she was invisible behind its reflective curve. There was only one thing he could say.

"I think you'd do best to put him out of his agony. There's no way he can hope to survive now. He needs immediate hospitalization for the back alone. Tomorrow he'll have spruip blood fungi in those wounds. He'll die in agony."

Poor Zhao two, he had outlived his clone brother by only a few hours. The shock was evident on all their faces. The attack had been so swift, so unexpected. Could any of them expect to survive?

Chi Lin Wei struggled for a moment. Zhao two dead, Zhao three and four eaten by the Woodwose. Herself in this horrible place with mud and shit and bloodsuckers and now this new thing . . .

Somehow the Maza control renewed itself; she snapped back. Chi Lin Wei spoke to Yu Zhao alone on another channel.

After a short discussion he appeared to acquiesce. She took the revolver and fired a single bullet into Zhao two's brain. They buried the body in a corner of the tiny cave in a shallow grave. She gave the gun to Yu Zhao, wondering briefly if they would soon be doing this to her, to HER! Her mind screamed. She crawled to the back of the cave and assumed a recovery fetal position. With Maza she would survive; even this could be survived. She would find the will.

Yu Zhao and Zhao six now took the watch. The Red Moon rose, a speeding ruddy speck traversing the sky below the Pale Moon.

Before he slipped into exhausted sleep himself, Chosen found time to be thankful for the stolid stoicism these Earth people exhibited. He felt himself shaking every time he remembered the pectaroon and that scream from poor Zhao two. What they'd do if Chi Lin Wei fell into the hysteria that she seemed to have been skirting, Chosen did not want to think about. Yet it was necessary to try to plan for every contingency. As his father would—always providing for the retreat should it be necessary.

It was necessary to plan, but his body had other priorities at that moment. He sat back against the root and fell instantly asleep.

19

THEY WERE A STIFF, FRIGHTENED LITTLE GROUP OF HUMANS THE next day, laboriously making their way downriver, along its approximate edge, meandering through endless swamps. A cacophony of animal cries came from the jungle in bursts.

Eventually they found a stand of blue knuckoo, with mature stems six meters tall and half a meter thick. Beni was high in the sky, and it was mercilessly hot; the air-conditioners were failing. Still Chosen urged them to make speed in cutting down the knuckoo and binding it together with crude ropes they fashioned from the tough, fibrous leaves.

By noon they had still seen no Woodwose, and they had bound together two dozen knuckoo stems of various thicknesses into a rough-hewn raft. Chosen was eager to board and get the raft out onto the river before a 'wose came upon them, drawn by the sound of knives on knuckoo.

With enormous effort they managed to tug the raft free of the roots where they had built it. When at last it was ready to push out into the river, they paused for a rest; the sweat was streaming down the inside of their suits. They were gasping for air.

Chosen immediately noticed that Chitin insects had appeared around them and begun foraging. Millions of workers, each about a centimeter in length, were busy harvesting the ripe fruits of the glob glob groves, and the trees were almost yellow from the tide of insects covering them. Some warriors appeared on the bank, feelers sensing the alien scent from the space suits' air vents. They were smaller than the ultramontane species like Slade Mountain green that Chosen was familiar with. Their bodies were banded in yellow and about an inch in length.

As the humans watched, a black, four-legged animal covered in horny plates wandered into the glob glob. Where it sensed Chitin workers it sucked them up greedily on several long sticky tongues that shot through a tube dangling from the creature's abdomen.

149

Almost instantly the warriors moved forward in a surge toward the Chitin eater. When they were close enough some attacked its eyes and face; others climbed its chest and bit furiously upon its genitalia. A torrent of reinforcements appeared, forming yellow brown snakes over the roots.

After a few seconds of such attack even the Chitin eater turned and fled back into the forest with its belly far from full of the tasty worker Chitin.

"These insects are the ones that your people harvest?" Chi Lin Wei asked with just a little awe in her voice.

"Not these exactly but very close relatives."

"They are fierce, are they not?"

"Very, a singularly aggressive species, especially down here where it's so hot and humid. Their nests can be enormous, and very old. So old we don't really have any idea how long they've been growing under the ground. It's been established the nest organism can live indefinitely in the laboratory. Of course up in the Highlands we keep the nest immature; they're less dangerous that way."

"I see," Chi Lin Wei said softly.

After they'd poled out about ten meters from shore, a current caught them and they moved downstream quite smartly.

Chosen wanted to stop the raft at the first island they reached because the raft was in need of more knuckoo, but stopping proved quite difficult. The knuckoo stems they'd cut for poling weren't strong enough to hold against the current and bent uselessly while they were swept on downstream. Yu Zhao's pole was quickly lost, ripped from his grasp by a sudden jerk.

Several islands lay immediately ahead, all crowned with glorious stands of blue knuckoo. Chosen became animated in his desire to beach the raft on one of them. By dint of enormous effort he managed to persuade three of the Zhaos to slip over the side with him and swim the raft to shore. At last they scrunched on a sandy bottom.

Small enomahkads, a Fenrille amphibian that occupied an ecological niche similar to that of the crocodile on Earth, scattered before them. None was more than a meter in length, and thus they were still harmless.

The jungle knives reappeared, and they worked industriously into the afternoon on the raft, lengthening it and adding several large cross pieces for strength. Chosen and Chi Lin Wei wove the long blue leaves into crude ropes and reinforced all the bindings. Chosen then took smaller fronds and poles and made thatch for a crude shelter to protect them from the worst of the sun.

Once or twice he tried to initiate conversation with Chi Lin Wei, but he received only blank stares that were quite disturbing.

When the shelter was completed Chosen went in search of glob glob and found an ancient specimen, so old that the central leaves had withered and hardened into crude rectangles.

He had to urge a predatory slime from its cocoon in the center of the glob glob leaf cluster. The slime was a small one fortunately, and a few good swats with the flat of the jungle knife got it into motion, slithering away over the jungle floor.

He then cut the three biggest leaves and towed them behind him back to the raft.

"With these we can make some paddles. We can use some of the small stems for handles."

The Chinese were all staring at him strangely.

"What is it?" Chosen asked.

They looked at each other. At length Yu Zhao replied. "You said you thought we were in the center of this river's basin?"

"Indeed, if anything we're further upstream than that. Why?"

"It will take us weeks to float down to the coast?"

"Of course."

"Then you must give up your food ration. We demand it."

Chosen stared at them blankly.

"Give up your ration!" Zhao five thundered. He held a jungle knife.

Yu Zhao's hand hovered on the butt of his revolver. "It is only right that you should give it up, since you are acclimated to the native forms of food. You can survive on fish or something."

"Or something?" Chosen was aghast. "Well, when we catch this 'something' that I'm able to eat, I'll give up part of my ration—I think that's reasonable, but until then I need to have something to eat."

Their eyes were hard; something ugly had crystallized while he was away.

"Look, we were going to just kill you and leave you behind, but we decided to give you a chance. You can come with us, but you must give up the food."

"And the knife, drop it." Chi Lin Wei was holding the other gun on him.

"You people are unbelievable!"

They advanced on him angrily, tied his arms behind his back, and then hustled him aboard the raft. Only then did they turn and ask his advice on finishing the paddles.

"May I remind you that if you'd killed me just now I wouldn't be able to advise you at this juncture."

"We will not require any more of these comments. Just tell us what we need to know." Chi Lin Wei was set on a murderously simple track.

Wearily he shrugged then told them what to do.

Eventually, later in the afternoon, they pushed off again and floated out into the stream. It picked them up and bore them away into the south.

20

For two days they drifted south with the flow of the endless sea of the mighty Bhjum. In that time they rarely saw a shoreline or anything else except the waters of the great river. His captors gave Chosen nothing but a little water from the purifier.

In midafternoon of the second day, a line appeared ahead, exactly as if they were sighting land at the end of an ocean crossing. It grew quickly into a shoreline; the river was contracting, braiding into narrow channels again.

The Zhaos worked the paddles, but despite their efforts the raft was swept westward into a channel only a hundred meters or so wide. On the western shore stood the massive canopy trees, three hundred meters tall. But on the eastern shore there was only blue knuckoo and pink hobi gobi. On sandbars huge eno-mahkads—the dangerous size—were sunning themselves.

Chosen was very hungry by then and he complained bitterly. "Please explain to me how I'm supposed to eat anything at all if I'm tied up like this?"

He received no reply. They continued to ignore him as they had since the moment they'd turned on him. He cursed them vigorously in Feiner, more natural to him for cursing than Interlingua.

Chi Lin Wei looked up finally, wondering what the harsh sounds meant.

"Look, why are you starving me to death?" She looked away in obvious annoyance, then she barked something at Yu Zhao, who came over with his jungle knife at the ready.

Chosen felt his heart freeze, but Yu Zhao just knelt behind him and cut his bonds.

They ignored him after that.

In his survival pack Chosen found several lengths of fishing line, complete with hooks and lures. Once again he had reason to thank the Neptune Gas Company and its outfitters. Just where survivors had been expected to fish in the outer Solar System was a mystery to Chosen. Unless they were expected to crash-land on an agrihabitat with extensive fish farms. He also found a small Spaceman's Bible, with a magnifier, tucked into a tiny sachet. The magnifier he immediately pocketed. It would serve to light fires by Beni's rays.

Since he lacked anything to bait his hooks, he set a silver lure on the end of the line and cast it overboard. The line was stoutly made, would take a fifteen-kilo strain, which improved his chances, since he had neither rod nor reel.

The lure trolled behind as they floated slowly downstream, and Chosen sat close to the raft's edge while the others gorged themselves on protein bars.

He found it difficult to accept their treatment of him. He had saved their lives. Face flushed, he felt a sense of embarrassing self-condemnation. What an idiot he'd been to think that Chi Lin Wei cared anything about him. How absurd he must seem to her, a woman in her third century. She had seen him as just a callow youth to be pumped for information.

Far away the sarmer mackees screamed, their cries echoing faintly across the water.

After they had eaten and drunk some water from the purifier, the Chinese enacted their daily ritual. Chi Lin Wei doled out pharamol grains from a cache inside a small dragon pendant she wore around her neck. They huddled around her and knelt while she prolonged their lives in a nakedly feudal ceremony. Chosen observed them with feelings of disgust. How tainted seemed the ways of Earth, so different from the fein way.

There came a sharp tug on his line, and he jerked it in, landing a small silvery fish with huge saucer-shape eyes. He threw it back in on the hook and used it for bait. Soon the line jerked again as something bigger struck. He let the line out, played it carefully before finally landing a plump bolita. It was a lucky catch, could be eaten raw, and after a few moments' work with one of the knives, which they allowed him to use only under gunpoint, he had a pair of filets that satisfied some of his intense hunger.

The raft was still winding through a stretch of narrow river channel. Not far ahead a dead tree lay half-submerged, projecting out into the channel. Standing halfway out on the tree, surveying them calmly with huge hands folded on its hips, stood a Wood-wose, tall and gaunt. It had a considerable growth of green moss on its shaggy coat.

The others saw it simultaneously and the Yu Zhao clones

emitted a near-comical series of falsetto cries as they worked frantically with the paddles to move the raft further out.

Chosen jumped up to help, and for once they allowed him to join them. Together they managed a slight adjustment in the raft's course, but the Woodwose simply took a couple of long strides out on the half-submerged tree, so that despite their efforts they passed by right under the thing's enormous beak. Its green-tinted shag was close enough to touch.

His mouth dry with fear, Chosen looked up. The eight eyes of the thing were peering down at them. The enormous hands twitched strongly; the beak opened and shut with an audible snap. The raft flowed on, and the Woodwose did nothing. It simply stared after them, standing up to its knees in the water, a still sentinel in the setting sun.

For several minutes they stood, as if paralyzed, staring back at it as they slowly drifted away.

It was inexplicable; they had been close enough for the monster to reach down and crush them in its hands. Still feeling a little weak in the knees, Chosen eventually curled up beside the shelter and tried to sleep. In time he did, and the Pale Moon rose to tinge the waters around them in fantastic pink light.

Chosen was shaken awake. Chi Lin Wei was crouched beside him; Yu Zhao stood behind her.

He could tell at once why they had disturbed him. Something had changed while he slept. The waters were charged with a power they had not possessed before. The raft was moving quickly, among waves a meter high or more.

"What is happening?" said Chi Lin Wei insistently.

He stood up, stared around them. There was little wind, the sky was clear, millions of stars blazed in the heavens. The waves were ominously active.

"This is the height of dry season. Low water, we must be entering some rapids. Perhaps everyone should find a way to tie themselves onto the raft. We're in for a rough ride."

From ahead came a distant sound, a disturbance in the evening peace. Slowly it grew louder and the raft began dipping and weaving and spray splashed across them. Ahead in the darkness huge shapes loomed, rocks like giant teeth. The sound of the river had risen to a thunder, and the raft spun, first this way and then that, before being picked up and hurled down a long sluice that ended with a sickening impact on enormous stones before it was scooped up and carried away by the onrushing waters.

Chosen was clinging to the mat of knuckoo; he had twisted one wrist into the rope bindings and had his other arm buried under several thick knuckoo stems. He prayed only that the mat didn't turn over. The roaring of the waters went on and on, and they careened from side to side in a maelstrom of foam, waves, rocks, the whole dimly illuminated by the Pale Moon.

Then they shot straight out into empty space. They seemed to wobble a moment before tumbling five meters straight down into a giant whirlpool. The raft had not been built to take such an impact; the big crosspieces snapped, the mats tore, sections rose up and crumpled over. The raft whirled around twice before being expelled back into the flow.

They slammed into a series of rocks, and the raft disintegrated, the crude rope bindings giving way to the onslaught, leaving the passengers clinging to small groups of knuckoo stems as they were washed on down the rapids into the walls of dark water that leapt over the stones.

For a long moment, Chosen saw Yu Zhao rimmed in moonlight, and then the bodyguard was gone and Chosen was smashed into a rock with sufficient force to knock the breath out of his body. For what seemed an eternity he tumbled in dark waters, terrified that his suit would split and fill with water or that a rock would smash in his face or his head. At some point he struck again on stone, and his arm ached dully afterward.

Finally he floated in calmer waters. The air-conditioning unit was dead, the suit cold and clammy. He wondered if the pocket radio still would work. He was faintly surprised to find that he was still tied to a shattered length of thick knuckoo stem. Somehow he'd clung on throughout the ride.

He raised his head and looked around. The rapids were behind him; he floated on a large, relatively gentle pool. He made out a dim outline, the shore of a lagoon. But there were no *Esperm gigans*, so it was probably not the mainland. Not very far away, a muk muk was serenading the night stars.

Cautiously he kicked himself toward the shoreline, pausing to peer into the dark water below. His suit light still worked, but its beam was hardly strong enough to penetrate far in the murky waters.

In the Highland valleys such pools, below the rapids, were the haunt of permiads and giant agnathous fishes who preyed on whatever came down to them.

But the knuckoo grounded ahead of him, and he found the water was only waist-deep. He dragged himself ashore and untwisted his hand from the rope bindings. His left arm throbbed around the elbow joint. In addition there were occasional stabs of pain from the shoulder and the ribs behind it. But his suit seemed to have come through without leaks.

Very slowly he pulled himself up the small beach, sat down, and surveyed the surroundings. Almost immediately he noticed another spacesuited form farther down the beach, slowly walking along it. He tried his suit radio, but for once even the Neptune Gas Company's indestructible equipment failed. By instinct, he tapped it firmly and it crackled to life again, immediately scanning the frequencies for the hum of a carrier. In a moment he heard Chi Lin Wei humming tunelessly.

"You survived!" he blurted.

She stopped. "The young roundeye! Of course *you* would make it. You'd survive anything, wouldn't you?"

Something in her voice was odd, and recent history encouraged him to remain silent and immobile. She would see him if she came much closer anyway.

"Young roundeye, come out. I must see you. You must come with me to help Zhao five. He is badly hurt. I am badly hurt, we have all been hurt by—*you*!" The last syllable exploded on his suit speakers.

Did she still have a gun? Would it still be in working order? He moved, gathered himself up, drew back up the beach toward the knuckoo scrub that crowned this narrow spit of sand, normally a part of the river bottom but exposed now in the dry season.

She came on, still talking, ordering him to come with her to help Zhao five. Once she called him Zhao Zu, and then she laughed to herself. Chosen slipped into the vegetation, praying that Nachri or other nocturnal predators were not around. He crouched in the knuckoo growth and watched Chi Lin Wei's figure pass and recede down the beach to the end of the little isle. The Pale Moon was setting in the west and the material of her space suit glowed an eery pink. She disappeared into the knuckoo.

He waited awhile, then his curiosity got the better of him, and he emerged and headed down the beach in the opposite direction. He cut across a narrow headland and found Zhao five stretched out on the sand and Yu Zhao crouched beside him.

"Zhao brother is dying," Yu Zhao said, mistaking him for Chi Lin Wei.

"I do not think we can save him. This terrible world has completed what your father set out to do. We shall all die here. I believe it must be written in the fates of Maza."

"Nonsense," Chosen said quietly. "We can build another raft.

There's plenty of knuckoo here." But even Chosen realized how difficult it might yet be, without air-conditioning in the suits, without the emergency pack, without even a fishing line. Their chances were slim almost to the point of nonexistence.

Yu Zhao jumped back, as if stung. "You! The one sent to destroy us, the roundeye. You are an agent of Him. Admit it—no other could have conspired so excellently to bring about our doom."

Agent of whom? Chosen raised his hands in a peaceful gesture. "You are mistaken. We have suffered greatly. I understand how you must feel, but it has nothing to do with me. Perhaps our imaginations are running away with us? An effect of the forest, I would say. This is a difficult terrain—not at all what you were expecting, is it?"

Had all the Chinese broken under the strain? If they were completely irrational, he would have to abandon them, he'd have no other choice.

Chosen flopped down on the sand a little distance from Zhao five's prone form. He didn't feel capable of examining the body just to see the horrible injuries. From where he sat he could see the cracks radiating across the smashed faceplate. His arm throbbed dully, his gorge was tight. He didn't feel like anything in fact, except a nice long sleep in a comfortable bed, far, far from the dark beach in the depths of the Bhjum basin.

Yu Zhao was unarmed, so he contented himself with cursing Chosen while settling again beside Zhao five. Ugly purplish blood continued to seep from Zhao's lips, who was hemorrhaging internally. Yu Zhao felt moved to weep. First three and four, then poor Zhao two. Now Zhao five was dying, and there was no sign of Zhao six. They would all die there on that forsaken strand, and all because of the off-worlder, the agent of the chairman.

Sometime later Chi Lin Wei rejoined them with the portalite and the empty survival pack. Of Zhao six she found nothing, though she had circumnavigated the small island.

Yu Zhao indicated Chosen. "What of him? The evil one sent by your father to destroy us!"

They looked at him together. Chosen could now see that Chi Lin Wei had one of the revolvers, inside the waterproof case, strapped to her hip. She produced it now and aimed it at him.

"You, roundeye, get up and come with us. I found a place we can shelter in. You will come with us and keep guard. Get up, or I will shoot you."

Wearily he got to his feet and at her urging set off along the beach. Nearby, the central dune of the isle rose a couple of meters above the vegetation. Along its base was a recessed gully, virtually a cave with room for all three of them.

"Get in here." She motioned him in. "We can't tie you up, so one of us will have to watch you at all times."

"Bit pointless having me keep guard then, isn't it?" They said nothing; the gun didn't waver. He crawled into the small cavelike space inside the dune. "I assure you that this is completely unnecessary. All this paranoia is really a waste of your energies. I'm not interested in harming you, just in getting out of here alive. We should try and rest for a while then see if we can find one of the jungle knives and make another raft. We must work as quickly as possible because this island is close to the shore and Woodwose may visit it even though there are no *Esperm gigans*."

She didn't seem to be listening. Instead she and Yu Zhao carried on a conversation in Mandarin in which she seemed to be hectoring and scolding Yu Zhao, who eventually grew silent while Chi Lin Wei raged on in a high-pitched tone close to a shriek.

Then another voice broke in on the radio, and she cut off midsyllable. "Zhao six? Where are you?" Chosen said instantly.

But Zhao six spoke in Chinese. A few minutes later he appeared on the beach. He had lost his helmet and his suit was torn, but he had one of the jungle knives.

Except for a few bruises and the loss of his helmet, he was unharmed. Chosen felt a wave of pity for the man, surely doomed by his lack of a helmet; unless they could be far out on the water before the biting flies awoke, he would soon be under attack.

The Chinese chattered together animatedly, and then Chi Lin Wei aimed the gun at him again. "Zhao six has no helmet, so you must give up yours."

Stunned, Chosen stared at her. "You realize that's a death sentence. What crime have I committed? I think I'd rather you just shoot me than leave me to die of the spruip."

"Undress, or we will undress you. I am determined to keep my Zhao alive. I have lost four already; you can have no conception of my pain, my torment. If you had, you would surely volunteer your helmet to assuage my agony."

Obviously, being a member of the Wei household gave one a somewhat different perspective on the world. Twenty-four hours earlier Chosen might have entertained romantic notions about the beautiful lady, but even then they would not have included offering his body up for the spruip blood fungus.

"You people are just unbelievable. I came back to save you from the molondi golubi—you remember him, 'the mouth that swallows a man whole.' So in gratitude you will kill me!"

Chi Lin Wei snorted and tossed her head. "Since you show yourself to be a pig without honor, then I feel no compunction in ordering you to be stripped by force!"

Chosen went into a crouch as the Zhaos closed in on him. But they attacked so quickly that he barely had had time to respond to Yu Zhao's thrust at his chest when Zhao six's low kick brought him down. They were upon him instantly and had soon twisted off his helmet.

Then the suit was stripped off, and he was left almost naked. They drove him into a corner of the burrow with blows and threatened him with the gun. With an infuriating smile Zhao six donned Chosen's suit.

Chi Lin Wei pointed down the beach. "Go, put on Zhao five's. He will be dead soon anyway."

After a few moments' contemplation of the alternatives, with great reluctance Chosen approached Zhao five's body. He found no pulse. Chosen unzipped the suit, loosed the toggles, and removed the helmet. The broken faceplate might be patched with something—he could at least try to keep the flies from his face. But the suit's air-conditioner and body-waste machinery were broken; he faced uncomfortable, hazardous conditions for the rest of the trip.

Zhao five's body was buried in a shallow grave at the high-water mark. Chosen left the Chinese to their grief. After a while the others returned and huddled in a group on the opposite side of the cave. Eventually exhaustion defeated the tension and he slept.

21

THE DARKNESS WAS THE FIRST SURPRISE. HE'D SLEPT FOR HOURS, his body told him that, but it was still dark. He turned over, still absolute blackness. Something stirred his memory and the hairs on the back of his neck rose.

Suddenly afraid to turn on a light, he fumbled the radio switch and found to his relief that it still worked. He cleared his throat and tried to wake the others as gently as possible.

Chi Lin Wei came awake with a yelp, and then Yu Zhao's headlamp came on and they saw.

A wall had been built across the opening in the night, sealing them in. A wall that now seethed with worker Chitin. Millions of the insects were at work, streaming in and out of the chamber through large holes in the middle of the floor. Surrounding the holes were the unmistakable forms of warrior Chitin, two inches long with massive mandibles, arrayed in serried ranks facing the humans.

Chi Lin Wei began screaming and had to be restrained forcibly by Yu Zhao.

"What is it. What is happening?" said Yu Zhao in a harsh voice. "Answer me or I will shoot you."

Chosen had to admire the man's calmness. His own voice shook a bit as he spoke. "I'm not exactly sure, but I'd guess that for reasons of its own, some Chitin nest, a helluva big one by the looks of it, has decided to trap us. It's happened before. It's been documented. Nobody is entirely sure why the Chitin does this, but then there is much we have yet to understand about the Chitin."

Their activity, the sudden light, had spurred fresh instructions from the nest's central brain, which Chosen was certain was located some distance away.

The holes in the floor widened appreciably, and in the mobile beams from their suit helmets they observed a tide of warrior Chitin pouring up into the chamber.

All the old stories rose up in his mind. Mad McGinty, who

161

was walled up for a week and remained a gibbering wreck for the rest of his life. The sad, cruel end of Augustine, the one they called the Saint.

He fought down the terror. He had been among Chitin before, in Chitin talker school, in the training with specially bred immature workers. They were all simply components of the nest; there was nothing inherently horrible about them.

Try as he might, though, the myriad eyes winked like dust motes in hell; yellow-brown bodies by the millions were rising onto the walls and ceilings around them,

To his horror he saw Yu Zhao rise to his feet.

"No, Yu Zhao—don't!" But it was too late, and Yu Zhao had gone to the new wall and begun to dig into it with the jungle knife.

"No," Chosen screamed, "get back."

The space suit wouldn't save him. Chosen knew too well how Chitin would work someone out of a space suit.

Yu Zhao's figure was invisible beneath a mound of warrior Chitin; more than a half million individual insects were at work. His suit was opened up as if by a horde of skilled seamstresses, each working on one individual stitch. The stitching around the zippers went first, then the Chitin were inside the suit and Yu Zhao fell, and Chosen simply turned his radio off to keep out some of the noise.

He tried to sit very still. Nobody else had been attacked. Undoubtedly Yu Zhao had been made an example of. The nest that had done this had a purpose, and Chosen knew that there was even a slight chance, a remote possibility, that they would get out alive.

They would have to behave like Chitin talkers. They would have to love the nest, love it with all their might. Or it would eat them.

It would all depend on him. He must remain absolutely passive in the hope of getting the chance.

Chi Lin Wei and Zhao six cowered together, shuddering in an extremity of horror. But at last the awful noises from Yu Zhao were dying away, although the warrior Chitin continued to form a moving mound over his prone body.

Chi Lin Wei wasn't screaming however. Chosen risked the radio.

"Chi Lin Wei, if you can hear me, listen. The nest must have a reason for this. Remember, the Chitin insect is intelligent, though not in a way we would instantly recognize as intelligence. But it has enormous reserves of memory. For some reason it

162

wants to examine us. If we do not threaten or excite it, it may not kill us. Do you hear me?"

There was no reply, nothing but static and the angry buzzing of enraged warrior Chitin busily stripping Yu Zhao of flesh.

The holes in the floor were getting larger, they began to connect together. Soon an adit three feet wide had been opened. Chosen understood at once. He trembled at the thought of what he was going to endure. The nest wanted them, to see, to touch, to think about. He would have to attempt empathic contact, the "talking" with the Chitin that all Chitin talkers used to harvest vizier Chitin, brain Chitin, laden with Chitin communication proteins, from which came pharamol and all the weaker longevity drugs.

Chitin communication protein comprised a family of proteins unique for their complexity and malleable structure. In the nest the individual vizier Chitin modified the masses of communication protein in reaction to events that affected the hive. Between the trees of memory, encryptions were exchanged in a slow pattern of "thought" that had been described once in an academic journal as being akin to "putting fifty million chimpanzees to work inside a gigantic library and having them print a newspaper every twenty minutes from the contents of the library in reaction to the events of the day outside the library's walls."

He spoke softly to the others.

"Listen to me. The hole is being widened. I would wager that the nest intends to make us go down that hole and right over to the vizier chamber. I know this will sound strange to you, but there is just a chance we may make it out of this alive if we play it absolutely correctly. Will you listen to me?"

Chi Lin Wei whimpered sorrowfully.

"Listen, we *must* go down into the hole then crawl to the main nest, which is probably on the mainland, so we have a distance to go. Just keep telling yourself that we may get out of this alive. The nest is obviously quirky and old. It must be huge. So it wants something from us other than our flesh."

Except for Yu Zhao's flesh, which had been entirely removed by that point. His empty suit had also been cut up into small pieces and toted away by a caste of what were normally leaf-carrying workers.

While the hole was widened yet further Chosen did his best to examine the Chitin around him. They were of the yellow-banded variety he had seen earlier, with a great many specialized castes among the workers. One kind of worker possessed long forelimbs with which it constantly stroked the warrior Chitin.

Archstone . . . Last link . . .

Strokers, the sure sign of a totally mature nest. The last caste to be put in place, the ones always forbidden Highland nests, for they gave the Chitin mind its agents extraordinaire, its local captains, who interpreted the chemically inscribed commands produced by the Vizier Mass, the Chitin brain.

Local interpretation of central orders—programmed by a set of chemical controls pressed upon the antennae of the strokers—gave the nest its final characteristics, what had been described as its personality. But the programming made it almost impossible to beguile in the manner of the Chitin talkers.

The strokers directed the warrior Chitin on the spot, constantly applying light layers of control proteins to the warriors' receptors, modifying the control program, preparing the warrior units for the next charge, retreat, or tactical maneuver.

The hole was now wide enough. This was made evident by a brusque thrust forward by a tide of warrior Chitin behind him. They clashed those inch-long mandibles together, producing a sound uncannily like the clashing of ten thousand tiny spears. The intent was unmistakable.

He moved toward the hole, praying that Zhao six would be sufficiently under control to help Chi Lin Wei overcome her terror. Their lights met his by the hole.

"What does it want with us?" Chi Lin Wei said in a distant voice.

"We must satisfy its curiosity. As to what in particular it is curious about, I have no idea. I doubt that humans have ever been here before. We must be the first humans it's ever observed. That alone might be enough for a very old, bored nest. If it sits in the ground in one place for long enough, even an insect's mind will get bored."

The warriors closed in around them, a wave of insects ten inches deep. Again the mandibles clashed, a harsh clicking by the multitude. Chosen slipped into the hole and found a steep incline leading away from the chamber. He crawled crabwise down it. After a few meters it leveled out into a narrow tunnel a meter in diameter that stretched away into the distant dark.

The claustrophobia was intense, instinctive. This worm hole into the mud was no place for a human. It would not even be wide enough to turn around in.

Nor was there any indication of how long the tunnel was, but Chosen was certain that it would run beneath whatever part of the river lay between the small sand isle and the root-encrusted banks of the river.

"Are you coming?" he whispered, feeling dull and alone.

"What is there?" Chi Lin Wei said.

"Just the worst attack of claustrophobia you're ever going to have. You people are tough, but now you've got to start thinking like Chitin talkers. That's what we Fundans call tough. If you want to live through this, keep your wits, attempt to befriend the nest. Think of it as a dragon that's invited you in for a cup of tea; if you're very polite, you may not have to stay for supper."

There was a moment of hesitant silence then a gasp.

"We are getting in the hole," Chi Lin Wei said.

"I don't want to die. Especially not like that."

Workers were still trundling pieces of Yu Zhao's suit down the adit past their heads.

Chosen pushed himself forward and began to crawl into the dark, his suit light stabbing ahead ten meters or so and finding only damp mud, brown dirt speckled with scurrying Chitin.

The work was hard; inside the suit it was terribly hot work. He sweated freely, his breath rasping in his ears, but he was breathing the air of the tunnel itself, without filters since the helmet face mask was cracked. The stink of the nest was intense, and he knew it would be incredible once he reached the central regions. What the Vizier Chamber would be like he trembled to think about. The smell of centuries of Chitin proteins, the spiciest dung in the universe.

Chosen had studied the Chitin; every Fundan did; it was their livelihood, but he had studied deeply, impelled by his intense interest in biology and botany. Now he searched his memory for those rare events, recorded in legends for centuries, when tropical nests, fully mature, captured humans—usually talkers trying to find an immature nest—but did not kill them and even released them after a while.

The Enza twins was the classic case, of course. Two six-year old-boys who were spared death when a Chitin nest broke into a farm compound and ate their parents. The boys were taken into the nest and kept there for a week. They were fed, fruit mostly, and brought water by streams of workers who put one drop apiece on their lips, and then suddenly one day the nest tired of them and they were driven out and away. Both boys had grown up to be formidable Chitin talkers, but both had died the same dreadful death that took so many of the first-century Chitin talkers.

The tunnel seemed endless. He had crawled for thirty minutes, and there was no sign of anything other than the adit ahead.

Chitin streamed past above, swift warriors and strokers who easily outpaced the laboring humans.

For a while he paused and tried to gather some breath. The stink was almost overpowering. He was trembling so much that he almost crushed some of the Chitin passing the other way beside him. The nest would accept some casualties in an endeavor like this but exactly how many was an unknown.

Warriors were gathering beside him, mandibles were clacking, in lilliputian rage the warriors threatened him . . . move on . . . or we will open your suit and hurt you . . .

Yu Zhao's horrible dying noises rose in his memory. He went on, his palms and knees burning; big blisters were forming there. I will die by the spruip anyway, what use is there in going on? But the will to survive was still strong, so he kept placing one knee after the other on the sandy mud. The surface was wet now; millions of worker Chitin were slaving on water retrieval duty and digging drainage pits to either side of the immense adit they had cut.

The nest had not worked so hard in a century; it was actually enjoying the experience, the use of levels of endurance that had not been tested for too long. The exhilaration of peak performance. The tide of Chitin covered the walls and ceiling of the adit, and still they crawled on, Chi Lin Wei screaming from the effort but refusing to give up. Zhao six followed behind whispering encouragement to both of them in Mandarin. Chosen was barely bothering to keep a look ahead, so terribly tired had he become of the dreadful monotony of the stinking, narrow tunnel.

Thus he barely noticed at first that the tunnel widened, then opened out into a long gallery, twenty or thirty meters wide and only three feet high. The gallery was covered with fungi that gave off a faint luminescence, an ethereal glow, that was almost invisible while they had their suit lights on. Tending the fungi were multitudes of worker Chitin. Along the walls of the gallery appeared occasional adit entrances, usually narrow irregular slits a few inches wide and a meter high.

They moved cautiously down the center of this mushroom garden in a crouching walk while a phalanx of warrior Chitin moved in front of and behind them. The ceiling got lower, dropped dramatically and they had to get down and push themselves along on their bellies until the gallery finally opened out into a small chamber shaped like an onion.

A myriad of small holes connected to this space, which from its shape Chosen assumed was probably the original brood chamber, where the young queens had hatched the infant vizier and warriors. Those queens had been recycled a dozen times since then, and the vizier had become uncountable.

By the incredible stink—a wild oily cheesy flower of some unimaginably tropical dung heap with spicy hints and floral sourness and disgusting fecalness—Chosen could tell they were close to the Vizier Mass itself. He wobbled on his knees and tried not to add his own foulness to the general stench, but he found it impossible, so great was the fear. It was disgusting in the suit after that.

A wall seemed to collapse beside him or suddenly transform itself into nothing but Chitin, for it was gone in seconds, and another adit, this time about four meters in diameter, was open before them. He led the way crouching, glad to get off his tortured knees, his lamp showing the floor widening out into a fan and then into an incredible sight.

They were at the bottom of a bowl-shaped structure as wide across as a large room. Above their heads a vast number of knotted beams or branches interwove in a space that ascended perhaps ten meters. On closer inspection the beams could be seen to be composed of millions of Chitin, large Chitin with fat abdomens, all welded together in what looked like glue, layered over them like varnish.

There was the source of the appalling smell, and now all around them he noticed that the walls were covered in Chitin of the same variety but moving in a constant restless dance. Only the floor immediately in front of them was empty. The implication was horribly clear.

An army of warrior Chitin was still present. Should the humans become a threat they would be immediately attacked.

Indeed the empty space now filled with clacking warriors. Others ran forward and began to climb up the humans' legs.

"Don't panic. I think I know what they want. We have to get out of the suits."

"What?" Chi Lin Wei and Zhao six said in unison.

"It wants us naked. It wants to examine us, and it realizes that the suits are not us, but something inaminate. It's intensely curious—can't you feel it?"

"Oh no, oh, this is so horrible. I . . ." but Chi Lin Wei lapsed into Mandarin. Chosen saw her clench her hands together for a moment, and somehow, incredibly, she found the will to start unzipping her suit.

He nodded to himself; he had to admit that whatever else she lacked, Chi Lin Wei did not lack courage. Chosen began shucking off his own. That the nest desired this was soon evident as the angry mandible clicking faded to the background hum of large numbers of Chitin in a small place.

He recalled the training from Chitin school and kept up a constant flow of advice. "Just remember that with the Chitin you are always close to death. Just make that part of every thought, and you'll have no trouble with the rest."

Her helmet was off. Her voice sounded squeaky and tense. Zhao six was standing irresolute, and she had to order Zhao six to remove his helmet and suit. He visibly wavered, then somehow found the strength to control his urge to run, to scrabble for a way to the light, and began unzipping his suit.

"The smell is intolerable; how do they withstand it?" said Chi Lin Wei.

"Chitin don't have a sense of smell, they taste. They taste the world. Other senses are less important, at least here, in the central nest intelligence, the repository of information. They're extremely discriminating in taste, to the extent that that is the nest's primary communication pattern, billions of little tastes, all moving out in waves from here, the center of the nest. And that's what it will want next—it wants to taste us thoroughly, to examine us at first hand, so don't be alarmed at anything that happens. Try and project an emotion as close to love and respect as you can. Marvel at how huge it has grown, at how old it is, how wise it is. Remember the rule—the Chitin is always right. If it wants to go into your mouth, to taste the water on the surface of your eyes, you must let it. Do whatever it wants; you have no choice."

He entered the chamber and crouched down. "Make it easier for them."

They came, in their millions, messengers of the others, suspended above, embedded in crystals incised with events from the centuries.

Their approach was like the application of feathers all over the skin. Moving, moving, little legs rustling through the body hairs. A million sets of mandibles nibbling lightly at the deposits of sweat and blood and fecal matter on his skin.

The Chitin swarmed upon them, investigating everything, obsessed by its quest for the past. For a way to remember the "before," the great era of the Chitin that was walled off in the depths of time and memories too faded for even the Chitin to recall. For on Fenrille the Chitin had been modified by the Arizel tki Fenrille and were unable to combine in the great hives of their long-dead homeworld, mighty Herxx.

Yet the memory of such a past as that of the Chitin insect

was alive even in the genes. The Chitin struggled vainly to penetrate the veils of antiquity and see what the oldest memories spoke of, the homeworld, the world of hive friends, where Chitin nest was not eternally set against Chitin nest—all nests enemies, all nests afraid, all nests alone, as they were on the world that is not the real world—but were combined into social harmony that had allowed them to progress to domination, where they had mastered metal and had hived the world.

And the old nest had a special memory, one inscribed in the sacred memories, the ones that had been brought by the young queen who began the nest and through whose memory cache all the sacred memories had later been deduced.

For the nest she had left as a young winged queen had tasted of an alien thing, a *metal* thing, made, constructed with technology. Machined metals, extruded plastics, things that were not of the world that is not the real world but came from another.

In fact a fragment from a dying fighter, struck down by Highlander cannon from the orbital heights, spiraling into the jungle to the west of the Bhjum. A panel with photronic circuitry straggling from one side had landed within the old nest's range.

Technology existed! Part of the ancient, ancient memory— so old it was possibly only a dream, so faintly inscribed in the memory codes that it was barely decodable—spoke of technology, of materials shaped with machines, beyond the power of the workers, using the workers in different ways, for group ends in organizations of nests. In ways that had been forgotten for thirty million years.

That memory had been fresh and strong in the infant nest. Three centuries had passed and still it lingered. Now the nest examined its captives almost thirstily. Chosen endured the entry of Chitin vizier into his mouth, up his nose, inside his anus. There was no aperture they did not explore with feathery antennae.

He tried to remain still, acquiescent, during the seemingly endless inspection. Zhao six protested when his mouth was invaded the third time. Instantly the visier on his body were joined by warriors who bit him furiously, deriving howls of anguish until he learned to stay absolutely still despite the bites, which continued for a while as the nest punished him.

"Accept it. Do whatever it wants, or it'll kill you right here. You saw what they did to Yu Zhao."

Zhao six gave a groan of horror and despair and sank back down into a fetal crouch. The Chitin swarmed over him once more.

22

IN THE AFTERMATH OF YOUNG PROUD'S STROKE LAVIN FUNDAN worked frantically to save his forces.

A terrible fight went on in the battered groves between the rivers Sliverary and Uluin. In that narrow neck the fein were pinned down, pressed together, unable to maneuver. In desperation Lavin brought all his artillery pieces together, hubcap to hubcap, and fired volleys of puncture cones and exploding shells at point-blank range into the advancing New Kommando.

That stopped the tide for a while, but the weary fein were a little slow in crossing the Sliverary, and the Response Impi was still exposed when the *Black Ship* passed overhead. Napalm strikes scorched the forest, and hundreds of fein died in the fires.

Orbital fighters were joined by Kommando vtol aircraft, and the retreat turned into a rout as the fein spread north into Sliverary. No effective defense could be mounted, Lavin lost most of his guns, and the Kommando rushed on in pursuit, mopping up pockets of resistance. On Young Proud's orders they were taking no prisoners.

Savage little fire fights, ambushes, and last stands took place under the dark leaves of the jik in Sliverary. For a while it looked as if all was lost and the Fenrille Defense Forces would disintegrate entirely.

The fein in the Response Impi however were the greatest warriors of their valleys, volunteers all. The First Abzen Impi was Lavin Fundan's very own. The two units had exercised together countless times. Now they reached deep for reserves of skill and strength. The neilks put the legendary fein stealth to work now in shifting their squads out of the path of the oncoming columns of the New Kommando.

The mobile command post was still at work and moving. Everyone was on horseback, somehow, although they had lost their fresh horses in the last napalm strike before the *Black Ship* passed beyond the orbital horizon. They grouped temporarily under the shade of some Ylcadder trees, a few kilometers north of the Sliverary, and opened the computer cases.

Lavin Fundan and Val Bo-Ho drove up in a captured air bed bearing a generator. They soon had the command web up and functioning. Coded orders on tight beam were streaking out across the forest.

Retreating fein groups were marshaled into loose associations, still retreating rapidly but beginning to work with renewed purpose. The Impis began to recoalesce into a new line, stretching across Sliverary woods.

Lavin calculated finely the timing of the next stroke in the battle.

The New Kommando came on in a hurry, even without air cover. Van Relt and Young Proud were well aware that their enemy's own aircraft were virtually out of action. The big columns were quickly filling up the space just vacated by the Abzen fein.

To Rinus Van Relt, the opportunity before him seemed golden. All that was needed was attention to basics, push, push, and more push. Piling in the Kommando divisions, moving them over the pontoon bridge across the Sliverary and forward against the retreating Impis.

By now there was a scattered front nearly fifty kilometers long forming with Kommando units running into the outlying fein positions in Lavin's new line.

Van Relt was also aware of the mettle in his opponent and that concern drove him on, for though they'd struck Fundan hard at the Uluin and inflicted heavy casualties on one Impi, Young Proud's blow had been late, and thus they had hurt the enemy, but they had not finished him.

As one result Young Proud was in a fury and had determined to leave the Fourth Division facing Butte Manor while he took the rest of the army north into Sliverary and destroyed his enemy. The Neptunian contingent had been confined to a big air bed, under guard, and brought along to witness the fun. As yet Young Proud had managed to keep the news of what had happened between him and the Neptunians from those aboard the *Black Ship*. But he had a sense that time was sure to run out on that front before much longer.

In fact as they rode north on a small air bed together, Young Proud questioned Ira Ganweek quite closely concerning the internal politics of the Neptunian factions. "Tell me, if I should not release Degorak Chevde, what will they do? Will they elect another in his place? Will they form a committee to oversee things until his release is worked out? How will my allies up in orbit there respond to the actions I was forced to undertake? This is what I am having to concern myself with. Of course I'm fighting the most important battle of my life and one that will leave everyone here immeasurably richer than they are, but I have to worry about this stupidity with these arrogant Neptunians!"

"Yes, well." Ganweek couldn't keep the anxiety out of his voice. "I suppose the Bond Council will make that decision."

"What is this Bond Council? I have heard about it constantly, but never do I actually feel its presence."

"Well, of course, the Bond is ruled by Chevde and his circle, but the Council is the key political body. There are seventy members, split between Triton and Nereid, and they vote annually on the controlling posts, Bond leader, Party secretary, hench lord or lady. Chevde of course is all three of those, and he has at least thirty open supporters on the Council. He has others, secret ones who act as spies inside the councils of the opposition. The real opposition is centered on Nereid, and I suspect that if a move is made against Chevde while he is, uhh—"

"In suspension, shall we say. Cooling-off time."

"Ah yes, of course, cooling off." Ganweek wiped his brow. "I would expect the move to come from the Nereid side of things. Perhaps a move to arrange an early vote on the next Party offices that come up on the annual schedule. The Bond maintains a relentless devotion to the forms of democracy, you see. There are constant elections. None of them mean anything, though, for real power is held only by the hench lord through the Bond."

Young Proud mused on this while they moved northward into Sliverary woods. Ahead loomed the big hover bed that held the captive Neptunians. Together the big bed and Proud's smaller model floated down a fein bridle path just wide enough for the heavy hovercraft transports.

"Who do I have to speak to?" Young Proud's implication was plain. Ganweek was to sell Chevde out. Young Proud could simply go to Alace Rohm, riding in the truck ahead of them, and offer her enough pharamol, and she would unleash the Nereidans and they would start the unseating of Chevde. Poor Degorak would be a paltry 190 kilometers below the center of power; for the first time in his political life he would be helpless. His enemies would rend him into pieces.

If Ira Ganweek should resist, dissemble, and then be caught out by Young Proud? Well, he had seen that carcass, swinging

172

like some skinned animal, dripping blood in that little room. Young Proud was a Highlander; Ganweek knew too well that those people were capable of anything.

"All right, listen carefully. The woman Alace Rohm, she is the madrelect of Nereid. She's riding in that air bed just in front of us. Get her out and make her an offer. The Nereidans have been on the downside for a century and a half—they'd jump at the chance for control. Offer her pharamol, and she'll set things in motion that will destroy Chevde as long as he is unable to work to counter them. Of course you'll have to take the risk of letting her go back to the *Black Ship*."

"This is intriguing news."

Young Proud turned it over in his mind. He would call the air bed to a halt and have Rohm removed. He would interview her and present her with a choice of glaring extremes. An agonizing, immediate death or pharamol-assisted eternity in his service. She would wear a worm for him and be his able servant.

As for Ganweek... Young Proud gave the portly little man a sidelong glance. It was too early to kill him. Besides it would be a waste. A worm perhaps?

The air beds continued northward as Van Relt, riding with the mobile command post up ahead, pressed the attack. The First and Second divisions had come up to the River Sliverary in a rush and surged over in pursuit of the fein. Slight resistance had been encountered, but air strikes ahead of the Kommando had kept the fein retreating, avoiding concentration while the orbital fighters were above.

Eventually the *Black Ship* sank beyond the radio horizon, and Young Proud had time to deal with the Nereid woman without having to keep an eye on Ganweek and his communications with the ship. The problem had to be resolved quickly before the *Black Ship* woke up to what had happened. So far they had accepted that Chevde and the others were out of contact because their air bed's radio had broken down, but Young Proud doubted that it would be enough the next time the *Black Ship* made inquiries. A rescue party of Space Marines would be very awkward at this point.

They topped a rise and dropped down into a hollow, lined thickly with jik. Young Proud spoke to the driver of the air bed ahead, and it pulled over and came to a halt. He stopped his own vehicle, ordered a Kommando guard to keep an eye on Ganweek, and then turned to the trussed and bound form of Fleur Fundan in the backseat and asked her if she would like to relieve herself while he watched.

Fleur stared up at him with loathing intermingled with terror. Somehow she managed to shake her head. Young Proud slapped his little whip into the palm of his hand and smiled strangely before striding across to the big 'bed with Persimpilgas behind.

He stood outside, chatting amiably with the guard officer while Alace Rohm was brought forth. Then he led her away into the jik. Persimpilgas followed at a discreet distance.

What happened next was always confused in Fleur's mind, though crystal clear in Ira Ganweek's.

The guard officer returned to the air bed, mounted the steps to the passenger compartment, and then turned, waving his arms violently before falling back out. Gunshots echoed, and more bodies were ejected from the air bed. The upper hatches burst open, and to Ganweek's horror the Neptunian Bond lords emerged. They had somehow overwhelmed the guards and seized their weapons. The Kommando guard sitting behind Ganweek got up and ran quickly into the trees.

A few moments later Ganweek found himself gazing up into the barrel of an assault rifle as Chevde held him on the ground and roared in his face. "Where is he? Where is that monster?" Spittle rained down.

"Gone," was all Ganweek could say. "He went into the trees with that woman." The other Bond lords, male and female, showed consternation and shock at the news.

"I will kill him, I will kill him now!"

Chevde jumped back and looked toward the jik. There was no way to tell where Young Proud might be. The frustration was visibly intense, and Degorak Chevde became considerably aroused by it all. To relieve himself of the frustration, he fired several rounds into the forest in between howls of rage.

"Great Degorak," Ganweek said on his knees behind Chevde while Ofur Muynn pressed a knife against his neck.

"You betrayed us. You are offal, Ganweek," Chevde said ominously, without turning round. More slugs whined off the jik trees.

"I, betray you? No, never I—" he squeaked with pain as the knife dug a little more deeply.

"If you didn't betray us, then why didn't you join us, tied down like animals for the slaughter!"

Ira tried to smile. It was an uneasy process. "Look, I did a lot more for us by staying out here beside him than I would have if I'd been with the rest of you."

"So? What did you do?"

Ganweek was about to explain when there was an appallingly

loud explosion and several small aircraft whizzed overhead. In their wake several large black bomb bursts ripped up the vegetation. One of them turned Young Proud's air bed over on its back and blew all the Neptunians flat on the ground. When they staggered back to their feet there was an unstoppable rush to get back into the big air bed.

Chevde could waste no more time. Later he would find the monster and have revenge, but first he would get back to his ship. When next he spied Alace Rohm there would be an interesting conversation or two as well.

The Neptunians clambered back to their seats while Chevde roared for Ganweek to drive. Ofur Muynn lifted the flipped-over air bed to see if Fleur Fundan had survived and was somewhat surprised to discover that she had. Still bound at wrists and elbows, Fleur was pulled free and taken aboard the big air bed.

Ganweek could not help but feel pity for her. She was virtually naked, her skin covered in welts and bruises. Ira was faintly astonished at the surge of genuine emotion that ran through him as he contemplated her distress. He removed the leather gag then opened the wrist cuffs and released her.

Something was different, dreadfully so, in her face. Her eyes did not so much meet his as pass them on their way to a distant horizon, and something about that fragile beauty of hers had changed, been hardened by grim little lines around her mouth.

"My thanks to you, messire," she said at last in a small voice. "Please give me a gun and let me go. I must die soon."

Ira's eyes clouded over. "No, no, you're much too valuable. You must live, Madame Fundan." He quickly thrust her into her seat.

"Just be thankful for being alive, madame," he said in her ear before standing over her again.

"Strap her into the chair, somebody, make sure she can't get loose. She's feeling suicidal." Ira slipped away toward the driver seat.

"Quite understandable, I would say," someone added.

Two Nereidan women took her to the back of the air bed, sat her down, and strapped her in. One gave her a sedative, and after a while she dozed off into the sleep of black dreams.

By then Ganweek had the big air bed in motion and headed flat out back to the pontoon bridge. They bulled their way across and headed back down the trail, but it was still almost an hour before they saw the airstrip in the distance. They approached cautiously, expecting opposition, perhaps even immediate gunfire, but instead they found the place in a state of modest chaos. Planes were still landing and taking off, but cleanup crews were at work on several hulks that had been shattered in the surprise air sortie by the defense forces' last few vtol craft.

In fact the Neptunian party encountered little opposition when Ira drove out on the airstrip and commandeered a transport that was about to take off. They were airborne a few minutes later.

Ganweek was puzzled by the lack of pursuit. Why had Young Proud not attempted to stop them? What could possibly have intervened to prevent such an attempt? But he watched the green-and-brown landscape drop away with such immense relief that he gave up wondering and just pushed his seat back in an attempt to relax.

So what if Degorak Chevde intended to kill him? That was a battle he could face later on. They were getting out alive; that was all that mattered. They were free of Young Proud Fundan. That was enough.

But in addition Fleur Fundan rode beside him, now wearing Kommando fatigues but also strapped firmly into her seat.

So far she had remained sternly resistant to all Ganweek's sallies and conversational gestures. But Ira was a patient man, and this woman, who had earned his enmity in a bygone era, this woman presented another kind of opportunity to him. . . . She must be kept alive, she must be kept for Lavin Fundan. Who knew what Fundan generosity might turn out to be in the aftermath of the *Black Ship*'s raid.

Thus the plane flew south, away from the war zone, leaving behind the fortune in pharamol they had come to wrest from the vaults of Butte Manor. And there was time to examine bitterly the flow of recent events and reflect that escaping alive was not the purpose of the grand adventure. For life alone they had not spent forty years living with the constant fear of betrayal to Military Intelligence and Chairman Wei.

Far behind them a shuttle from the *Black Ship* was descending on retros toward a cleared space on the banks of the Sliverary. Waiting impatiently for it to land were Alace Rohm and Young Proud Fundan.

176

23

It was only after they'd been in the air for two hours that the dimensions of the trap they'd fallen into became clear to the Neptunians.

Degorak Chevde was in the cockpit holding a knife to the throat of the assistant pilot.

As requested, therefore, the pilot put in a signal to the *Black Ship*, which was then above the horizon but far behind them to the north. Chevde requested a landing party be sent to the Sx Coast spaceport to pick them up as soon as they landed.

But there was only silence from the *Black Ship*.

Puzzlement spread over Chevde's features. Ofur Muynn bent down to growl in the assistant pilot's face.

"Call again, fool. If you are using wrong frequency I will crush your testicles in my fist."

"It is the right frequency, messire. The computer never gets that sort of thing wrong." The pilot's eyes were wide with fright.

"Well, we have not got through, have we—so something's wrong. Call again. Come on."

Just then Ganweek slipped into the cockpit. "What is wrong?"

"No answer from *Black Ship*," growled Chevde. "What are you doing here? Who gave you permission to enter cockpit. Traitor to the Bond, Ganweek!"

"Chevde, no, that's not true," and then the awful truth hit Ira, and he gasped. The assistant pilot was actually punching in the code to signal again.

"No, stop, don't signal! Stop, it's our death warrant if you do."

Startled, the assistant pilot stopped.

Ofur Muynn turned to Ganweek. "In Bond Lodge aboard ship I will enjoy the breaking of your back, Ganweek, traitor. What are you doing interfering here?"

"Don't you see?" Ira was almost beside himself with anxiety. "If you call the *Black Ship* again they'll get your position. They're above the horizon, and orbital fighters could still pick us off even though we're thousands of klicks south of them."

"What are you talking about?" A tinge of fear made Chevde's anger sound even uglier.

"That woman, don't you see? Young Proud must have sent Alace Rohm to the *Black Ship* as soon as we escaped. She's been up there for an hour or more, all by herself!"

When the implications of that sank in, Degorak emitted a sound not unlike that of steam escaping a high-pressure boiler. His face turned a shade of violent purple.

"No wonder there was no pursuit. We were so damned crazy to get out of that madness that we forgot he already had Rohm. Now she has the *Black Ship*. What are we going to do?"

Chevde was frantic.

"Do we know this has happened for certain?" questioned Ofur Muynn.

"Why else would ship not answer signals?" great Chevde howled. "They were probably surprised by our signal and didn't get enough to get a fix on us."

"Or perhaps all they wanted was a confirmation of the fix they already have," Ganweek said finally.

Chevde turned to the pilot. "Take us down low, evasive maneuvers. We are probably targeted by heat seekers."

An extended period of violent turns and twists followed that sent everyone back to their seats as the pilot dropped the big plane down into the mist layer above the eternal jungle of giant trees.

The minutes ticked by, and eventually they concluded that the *Black Ship* had not been able to get a good enough fix on their position from the first contact.

"Perhaps she has not established complete control yet," Chevde voiced in hope. Muynn and the others grabbed at this straw. But unless they gave away their position, there was no way of accurately determining what was happening on the *Black Ship*, which to outward appearances seemed to be continuing its support mission for the New Kommando. At one point they intercepted a couple of strong group signals in the code used by orbital fighter computers.

On other wave bands however only demonically powerful jamming could be discerned. Once they intercepted a brief snippet of battlefield communications bounced south by some freak of the atmosphere, but it was over in a few seconds.

Soon after that they began receiving signals from the Sx Coast. The main automatic radio beacon of the airport, in fact, guiding the transport planes down to the runways, still hundreds of klicks away.

Ganweek counseled a completely blind landing, no communications until they were virtually down on the runway.

"Surprise, that's our only advantage. They know when we took off, they can calculate when we'll arrive, except that we're already late because of the evasive maneuvers. Perhaps if we're late enough we can catch them unawares."

Accordingly the pilot took them down again and flew in toward the Sx Coast at under two thousand meters, taking plenty of time.

"There's a constant flow of traffic back and forth above us, so the Sx Coast radar has several blips to look after at any one time. We'll stay out of sight as long as possible and just slip into the air traffic when we get to the coast."

While the trip continued, frantic calculations went on. Ganweek eventually won permission to try a radio message of his own to a phone in the Bablon Dome. To call however required the use of a secret code, thirteen digits, giving numeric values to letters that formed the name of the mother of the Braziano criminal clan.

Slightly to his surprise, Ganweek got through without trouble. Mobile radio phone links had improved on Fenrille during his fifty-year absence, it seemed. And the New Kommando's jamming had slackened off since the major struggle had intensified at Butte Manor.

"Gebby, Gebbrie Braziano" he intoned.

"Who is calling this number?" asked a heavy voice with a thick Coast accent. Trusting all to the winds, Ganweek replied, "This is Ira Ganweek—just tell Gebby that Ira is on the phone."

There was a long period of silence, and then another voice, lighter, less accented, the product of speech therapy, took over. "Ira Ganweek? Is this for real?"

"Gebby, that's right. It's me. I'm back, but listen carefully because this is a very complex moment. If I'm right this will give the Bablon an opportunity to take power again, something I expect you people would like to see, eh?"

"How do I know this is Ira Ganweek speaking to me and not some New Kommando spy?"

Ira seethed with impatience but controlled himself. "Because I know things about you, Gebby, that no cop could ever know. Like I know who really killed your mother."

"What? Listen, Kommando cop, you better shut your mouth about my mother."

"Gebby, this is Ira Ganweek, remember? Just listen, don't shout."

There was a silence, then, "Okay, who did it then?"

"You did it yourself, with a towel from the bathroom, when she told us she intended to give your slot to Vinnie Angelo."

There was a long silence. A little nervously, Ira went on.

"You see you were always the hot-headed type. Back then you were still mugging for the Teoklitan, but I got the Syndicate to let you into the Bablon, and you never looked back. Despite the fact that you strangled your own mother."

"Where are you, Ira?"

"I can't tell you that just yet. Listen, Gebby, this is important. We have to get the Syndicate moving again."

"What's to move? Lut Vulwald is in charge these days. You can't move anything without him. You know that. Hey, Ira, it's good to hear your voice, been a long time, Ira. How did you manage it anyway, you were forty light-years away. How did you ever make it back?"

"Gebby, I built the *Black Ship*. That's how I made it back."

"Hey, I always knew Ira Ganweek was a big man, but now I have to admit it—Ira, you're the biggest."

"Of course, Geb, of course, and if you stick with me we'll get things back to the way they were."

"You think so?" Hope strained through the incredulity in Braziano's voice.

"Yeah, but listen carefully, there's a lot of things you have to take care of, and we can't trust Vulwald on this."

"Okay, okay, Ira, fire away. I'll be glad to listen."

When Ganweek got back to his seat he knew that he had started an avalanche in motion.

Degorak Chevde nodded and congratulated him. Ofur Muynn was wreathed in smiles. Gone were the ominous references to the breaking of backs in the Bond Lodge. Everyone applauded his quickness of wits, the guile in his plan.

The Syndicates would all move, especially if Bablon moved first. Nobody would want to risk being left out of the spoils. Having shipped most of its strength to Butte Manor, the New Kommando was seriously depleted. The Syndicates' move would probably lead to chaos, even better for the likelihood of the Neptunians' making an unannounced, uncleared landing. On the strip they would land on the main runway but would taxi to the workshop space and not the terminal. Even this would not look totally strange since many of the big jets were cargo carriers anyway.

Thus should a reception party be waiting for them in the terminal, they would elude it from the beginning.

The workshops were a maze of unplanned domes, tunnels, and hangars crowded along the seaward edge of the airport. Inside they would be met by Braziano fighters and escorted to the mass transit station built below. From there they could ride the Yellow line train directly to the Bablon Dome workshop station. By then the dome, which if all went well would be under Syndicate control, would also be in the process of being made defensible once again.

From there they could at least get time to plan their next move. One that would have to be carefully rehearsed, since Braziano had confirmed what they had already expected. Alace Rohm, working in collusion with Young Proud, had managed to seize control of the *Black Ship* by telling everyone that the rest of the leadership had been killed in an air attack. Alace had moved rapidly. Her followers had quickly been voted into positions of power. Her hulking wolf woman Palova Kull had even taken over Ofur Muynn's sumptuous quarters for her own. It was rumored that many of Chevde's supporters had begun to disappear, secretly ejected from the air locks by cheering gangs of Nereidans.

But if they could break through the news blackout, broadcast to the *Black Ship* directly, then Rohm would face the wrath of the Bond Lodge and would surely be brought down. That had to be their hope. Ira, however, had given priority to the humbler question of whether or not they would survive the landing at the airport.

The latter part of the flight slipped somewhere between daze and doze for Fleur Fundan. She slept, but dreamlessly, which was a great mercy.

The plane encountered several patches of turbulence, and the shaking brought her to wakefulness each time. Only then did she remember the horror, feel the unfamiliar garments, and muse again on the uncertain future.

Her resolve to die had not faded. There was nothing else to be done now. How could she possibly be expected to continue to live with such monstrous memories.

Young Proud had not wanted to kill her, that much she knew. Through all the vile debasements he had devised, that thread had remained in his conversation—she would live forever in his grasp.

So there was the single weakness in the net of his monstrous

181

evil. If she killed herself, she would cheat him of the rest of his long drawn out thirst for revenge.

But she realized she would have to wait. Perhaps at the airport an opportunity would come. She had heard rather than paid attention to Ira Ganweek's plan. It made little sense to her, but she did see a certain benefit in staying out of the hands of the New Kommando. So she would cooperate. Let them take her where they would; her chance would soon come. There were so many ways to die if one wanted to badly enough.

At last she did drift into a dream; in high Abzen Valley she walked on the ramparts of Cracked Rock and waited for Lavin to return. But her husband fought an unseen terror that clutched him in a dark tangle of thorn. Lavin fought still, but his time was ebbing. In horror she saw his blood flowing on the dark ground. The thorns were long and sharp.

With a jerk she woke up to the realization that the plane was actually passing over the tidal mud flats of the Dinge. It was a cloudless afternoon, and the great domes of the Sx Coast lay ahead of them like a string of sparkling beach balls strewn in colorful profusion along the narrow dunes.

Over the back bay she looked down into the world of the kelp beds and fish farms. Trapped by the economic collapse five decades before, the people toiling down there eked out a drab existence. For a moment Fleur felt her old sympathies revive. There had to be some way to liberate everyone from such dreadfully wasted lives.

Then the dark runway came up below, and they swept past the first great domes, pink and gray, with bright pennons swinging from the dorsal flagpoles. They touched down in a roar of retros and rolled past the terminal and a line of heavy-winged jumbos waiting to take off. Small fire trucks and other trucks that looked more like armored cars were speeding toward them over the concrete. They were far behind however.

Then they were in a wide passage between hangars; an enormous roof slid overhead. With a heavy hiss the plane made contact with the loading dock.

Ira Ganweek leapt to his feet, unbuckled her seat belt, and helped her up. For safety's sake, he said, her hands had to be cuffed. Ira didn't want her grabbing some guard's gun and shooting herself. So he informed her.

They were almost running as they passed along a severely utilitarian, rubber-lined ramp that gave access to a cargo loading bay.

Then came a hasty journey through a labyrinth of back passages and warehouses. Around them a dozen or more lithe young men suddenly appeared with automatic weapons. They acted as chaperones.

Down a long service corridor they ran and then exited through a narrow metal door onto a staircase inside a mass transit station.

A Yellow-line stop, incongruously Fleur felt her sense of curiosity awaken. In all the years she'd lived in the city she'd never ridden a Yellow-line train. She'd taken all the others, Blue line all the way out to Love Beach and Magenta line every day on her way to and from the former Earth Embassy in the Westwind Dome on Fun Beach.

The train came; they got on. It was older and dirtier than the transit trains she remembered so well. Especially the Magenta.

This time however they were riding to the Bablon Dome.

But Fleur didn't get to see the fabled Ishtar lobby by the main entrance with its exquisite marble and fantastic sculptures. Instead she was crowded into a dirty utility elevator with a score of massive Neptunians.

They got out on the twentieth floor, and she was whisked down several long corridors painted in the Bablon hues of purple and green, into a comfortable suite of rooms that might have been found in any luxury hotel.

A young female guard in Kommando fatigues just like her own took a seat by the door. Fleur remained handcuffed, and a quick inspection of the bathroom revealed a complete absence of edged or pointed items. The mirror and the suite's windows were unbreakable.

The windows gave an interior view of a small courtyard, light slanting down from a shaft above that penetrated through the uppermost floors to the sun ports on the dome roof.

In the courtyard a fountain played, small white trees grew in brick tubs, and women and brightly garbed children, offspring of the very wealthy, were visible beneath the trees. There was a bench, a patch of grass, a sandbox, several hummocked shrubs of violet hue.

On the far side were windows that appeared to let into rooms much like the ones in her suite.

Everywhere was the decorative motif of the Bablon Syndicate, the winged bulls and crowned Ishtar, raised in bas relief above the windows, embossed on the tree tubs, and even on the fountain itself.

The sound of the happy children rose from the courtyard with a piercing poignancy. Childbirth on Fenrille was so rare, a luxury beyond the dreams and aspirations of normal folk. Fleur remembered her own early days there and felt her eyes moisten from some unknown emotion. Perhaps she wept for the millions of childless women who had lived and died on Fenrille, their own dreams shattered on the harsh sands of the strange planet.

But the sound of the children was utlimately soothing. Her tears stopped, and she lost herself in simply staring vacant-eyed at the women on the bench, the white trees, and the sandbox.

Later, when the children had been taken inside, Fleur tried to draw the young guard into a conversation, but the woman plainly had orders forbidding fraternization.

There was nothing to do but switch on the TV and stare at the daily manifestations of the long-running soap on Channel 23, "In Your Sheets Only." Marveling, Fleur sat back and discovered at last that Mayloo's real secret lover was handsome Toni Aroyo, who of course was supposed to be Honey Little's lover and husband-to-be. Except that Honey Little had been fooling around and breaking handsome Toni Aroyo's rather fragile heart. Time passed without memory.

Sometime later the security chief brought her some food, an overdone filet of meat-fish with hydro salad on the side. The young female guard fed her, without ever meeting her eyes or answering a single question.

Completely emotionless, the guard presented the final piece of fish on the fork and then removed the tray.

"Damn you," Fleur said, then smiled to herself at her own feebleness. Suddenly she remembered a friend she hadn't seen in decades. "Armada wouldn't have stood still for your impudence, Ms. Guard," she thought.

The dour young guard returned to the door again.

On TV "Eternal Triangles" replaced "Sheets" and then there was a brief newscast. Pictures of Ira Ganweek, the Neptunian Bond lords, and other, less familiar, faces were broadcast. There was a shot of a group of men walking into a room then walking out again. The announcer spoke briskly of an agreement being signed to formally end the "transition period" of the New Kommando. An announcement about city-wide elections for a new Senate was to be made as soon as possible. However the message ended with an exhortation to Kommando holdouts and renegades to surrender at once. This rather spoiled the effect of the rest.

The soaps started up again and went on through the evening. The female guard changed, but her replacement was as untalkative as the first. After a few attempts Fleur glumly returned her attention to the TV.

. . . the chance would come . . . until then she would lose herself in the twisted love affairs on Channel 23.

Eventually the door opened, and Ira Ganweek slipped in. He came and sat on the edge of the bed, close to her chair.

"I have interesting news for you if you care to listen."

"What news?"

"Your husband has managed to beat off Young Proud's attack. Somehow or other he's kept his army alive. For now there's something of a standoff. In the meantime we've established Syndicate control again on the city."

Lavin lived yet! Her heart thrilled at the knowledge. Then the moment passed as if a ray of sunshine had been cut off by a cloud, and the gray shroud of depression returned.

"Come, lady, you have survived your ordeal. Things will improve." Ganweek was at a loss to understand why his news should leave her so crestfallen and forlorn.

"You do not understand," she managed to say and hung her head.

Ganweek put out a hand, amazing himself, for the woman was as much his enemy of old as her husband or any other Highlander. He patted her shoulder, trying to comfort her, and in a moment he felt a blundering fool, awkward and stupid and out of place.

Her tears were literally splashing off the side table. Still wondering at his actions Ira Ganweek put his arms around her and let her sob on his shoulder.

However, he resolved that no matter how she begged him, he would not remove her handcuffs. She was a very valuable commodity. But only while she was alive.

24

In Butte Manor's lovely forest of Sliverary the armies continued to grapple. Rinus Van Relt had hurled the bulk of the New Kommando into the semicircular pocket that Lavin Fundan had prepared. The Impis waited while it filled, then struck with heavy strokes along the river ridges, carrying the high ground and cutting the Kommando forces in two. A major assault then broke in on the outermost Kommando group, the Fifth Division.

The division took heavy losses as whole units broke in terror at the onrush of the Response Impi, now reformed and burning to avenge the losses of the morning.

By the time Van Relt had pulled the Fifth Division back into the fold of the others and got weapons in place to keep the fein back from the lines, the whole unit was shot out, with hundreds of casualties and wounded left behind in the scrub.

The Impis however pulled back at the first sign of Van Relt's stiffened lines. Within moments the fein had turned and begun to move northward again; the *Black Ship* would appear within thirty minutes or so, so the neilks worked hard in the ranks urging the weary on. The refrain was incessant. "Hurry it up, quickly, quickly, hurry it up!" Many were beginning to show the strain. Two days of continual marching and fighting without more than one really adequate meal. It was getting tough, especially for the biggest and heaviest fein.

Fortunately the heavy damage done to the Fifth Division had made the other divisional commanders cautious in the extreme. None wished to poke his force into a trap. When Young Proud visited them in person, they rallied and pressed their units on, but as soon as he was gone, they resumed a very slow, stealthy pace and kept the scouts working over the woods in front of them while sending in reports of difficulties and hazards ahead.

Rinus Van Relt could hear the tension in his men's voices; all nervously gazed into the jik forest and imagined their flanks erupting with heavily armed fein.

The Kommando therefore tiptoed forward, scouts working

busily over the terrain ahead, into a complete military vaccuum. Lavin and the Impis were already a dozen kilometers distant and spreading into the wide land north and west of Sliverary, a wilderness of jik and nub bush all the way to the shores of the Great Cold Lake.

But a mixed unit of skilled decoys, including elderly gray cowl fein from Ghotaw Mountain, was at work bedeviling the Kommando scouts and drawing them north and east toward the mountain wall and the high passes.

Hesitant, fearful, and only after much anguished debate, the Kommando turned toward the mountains and followed the decoys.

The night was velvety smooth, and within the air-conditioned promenade atop the Bablon Dome, it was also quite comfortable. The lights of the city spread down the dunes twinkling in the smear of the humidity, a scatter of unfocused baubles dropped against the background night.

The Pale Moon had yet to rise. The stars blazed down in the sky. Ira Ganweek had brought her there to lift up her spirits. He waxed eloquent about the *Black Ship* and their plans to fly deep into the galaxy in search of a new home where the Earth and its envious hordes could no longer reach them. Out there, in the filaments spread across the light-years, lay boundless opportunity.

Her response shook him. "But you will have to survive the Fuhl Drives, will you not? It is just as likely that you will be subsumed in the galactic stuff and reborn as fairly hot hydrogen. Or so I have heard." Her mind wandered off again, leaving Ganweek staring at her.

"How do you know?" Had Young Proud told her everything?

"He told me. He liked to tell me such things while he was tormenting me."

Young Proud possessed a wealth of folly, that much was clear to Ganweek.

"It is true the drives were troublesome, but they did work. We shall fine-tune them before we have to use them again. Never fear, the *Black Ship* will still aroving go."

"However, even if I were to come with you to fly across the galaxy, I would only do so as a corpse. I will be long dead before your drives work again."

There was a bitterness so cold in her words that he shivered.

"But why?" Ira could not understand.

"Because—" she began but then broke down. Recovering herself she continued, "Because he placed a certain worm, a

187

gravid female, in my bloodstream. The eggs run in my blood. The species is more predatory than parasitic, you see. But they cannot hatch because of an antidote known only to Young Proud. He created this worm himself, by gene manipulation of Fenrille life-forms. Anyway, within a few days the antidote will run out and the young worms will hatch and begin to feed," she finished, desolate.

"Then we will prepare some of the antidote. A simple matter." Ganweek felt a sense of relief.

"You will try, but I promise you you will fail. Highland science is adept at the manipulation of genes. Young Proud's worm is specifically attuned to resist most worm poisons." She shook her head wearily. "So he has told me many times. Believe me when I say that I have considered the matter carefully, and there is no escape for me, except in death. You will have to let me die."

Ganweek felt a great disgust come over him. If what she said was true, then the poor woman was doomed unless Young Proud himself could be captured and made to give up the antidote.

Ira's expansive mood collapsed. Soon afterward he escorted Lady Fundan to her rooms again and excused himself for the night. He made his way just down the corridor to his own room, where he called through to Dome Medical and ordered tests to be performed immediately on the parasite in Fleur Fundan's blood.

Then he took a pain reliever and attempted to sleep. It was difficult though. The tears, the horror in her eyes, Fleur Fundan's doom was dreadful to contemplate.

Always the question rose up to haunt him. Would he, himself, have to kill her to put her out of her agony? They could not let her die that other way, the unthinkable . . .

He rolled on his side, faced the wall, and waited slightly desperate for sleep.

News of Fleur Fundan's presence in Dome Medical leaked quickly on the underground circuit, and Bino and Lucy Urbimle knew of it within an hour.

It came just in time for Bino to change the signal being coded at that moment for the nightly message sent flickering into the dark.

A few minutes later, far across the waters, a hulking form slipped through the yasm swamp to a vantage point in the branches of an outlier. From a backpack the heavyset figure produced binoculars with which to read the tiny winking lights affixed to one of the dorsal flagpoles atop the Pericles Dome close to the spaceport terminal.

When he'd finished decoding the message, Bg Rva sprang into action. Gone were his plans for a midnight snack and his bed in the shelter of the high knuckoo. Instead he scrambled into his wet suit, affixed breathing apparatus, and packed a bag with potentially useful items. Then, with shock baton at the ready and his main lights on, tunneling into the dark water ahead, he powered across the bay on his water jets.

When he approached the passage leading to Bino's Boatyard he turned off his lights and floated, waiting.

A small green beacon lit up, and he pushed ahead, easing himself into the air lock.

Within a few minutes he was hunched over a map of the Bablon Dome with Bino and Lucy Urbimle.

Bino had a workable plan to get Rva into the Bablon Dome. "I have a friend now working on the plumbing in the dome. They move equipment in and out constantly. The checks have grown perfunctory—my man Swale will do the job."

"Excellent," Rva said, stifling a yawn. Battling the deep fatigue he felt suddenly come over him. Sometimes the long decades, all those years that he'd lived, pressed down upon him with a fearsome weight. The urge to sleep was very strong at that moment; he was exhausted.

But the lady was here; he must concentrate!

They continued. The escape was perhaps the trickiest part of the operation. A bold move to the maintenance elevator.

"My friend Silana will have already inserted a program plasmid in the dome's elevator control. No agency will be able to open the elevator until it reaches the basement, where we will be waiting."

"We?"

"Myself and a few others who will open up the underpassage into the Bablon from the gas utility inspection walk, which runs beneath the main basement."

"I see," Rva said. After a few moments' more discussion they adjourned. The old fein was quickly fast asleep, on a small mat in the corner of Bino's utility room. All too soon he was being shaken awake by little Lucy Urbimle.

"Get up, Messire Rva. It is time."

Slowly he pulled himself together, placed his kifket comfortably against his hip, put a large revolver into his waistband, and tied a clip belt over his shoulder. To the clips he attached pairs of gas grenades. He had chosen a revolver without second thought under Lavin Fundan's dictum concerning the propensity of all automatic weapons to jam. However Bino had brought him a Hercules .45 with ejectable ammunition drums, which much simplified reloading. Each drum contained eight shots.

Finally he took a couple of charges in plastic explosive, each quite flexible and capable of being molded around a door hinge or stuffed into a hole in a wall.

He settled the growls in his stomach with an oversize fish filet that Lucy Urbimle had prepared for him and washed it down with gwassa. "Where'd you find quality gwassa in the city of humans?"

"There's quite a demand for it, you know. Lots of Highlanders live here, so the specialty sections in the markets have it. I got some thinking there'd probably come an opportunity to give it to you." The gwassa was a wonderful touch. He was in fine spirits in no time.

"My thanks once more, Ms. Lucy." He flashed her a grin of snaggly fangs, a sight that would have curdled her blood at one time. Then he was gone, to join Bino in the boatyard loading bay where a plumber's vehicle was waiting. Rva was ushered inside and shown into a motorized cabinet that was normally used to transport large tools.

It was a tight and uncomfortable fit, and Rva soon found it almost unbearable. Something sharp and angular was digging into the middle of his back. Every time the truck swerved around a corner whatever it was stabbed him again.

At last, though, they pulled to a halt. A hydraulic ramp slid to the ground, and the steel cabinet was rolled forward and down smoothly on a set of rubber wheels.

For a short period the cabinet rolled steadily in one direction. Then it stood a moment. But the doors remained closed and abruptly there was a sensation in his belly that Rva knew all too well, a human lifting machine was in motion; they were rising into the air.

At last the disagreeable motion finished. After a momentary wait, the cabinet rolled forward once more. At last it ceased and there was a long moment without perceptible activity.

The doors opened. A frightened-looking young man in plumbers' overalls, one finger pressed to his lips, let him out.

Rva grunted, patted the youth on the shoulder, and slipped into the corridor.

It was a radial service corridor, and Rva moved down it to the big double doors that marked the junction with the circular residential corridor.

Once through those he strode silently toward Suite 1212, the number they'd used in Dome Medical when referring to the patient Fleur Fundan.

He had almost reached the suite when another door popped open and a woman in a nurse's uniform came out. Her mouth opened in a soundless shriek as she confronted Bg Rva, who reached out quickly to stifle her screams. He held the kifket in front of her eyes.

"Be silent," he hissed.

Her eyes widened, but her struggles ceased. She understood.

Releasing her he whispered, "Is the lady Fundan still in that room?"

"Yes, but she is not well."

His expression was suddenly harsh. "What do you mean, 'not well'?"

"She has been confined by the doctors."

"Can she walk?"

The nurse shrugged. "As to that I cannot say, but—"

Rva gave her no more time but conveyed her bodily into Room 1212 in front of him. The guard jumped to her feet, but Rva thrust the nurse into her arms, and she fell back with a *whoosh* of escaping breath.

Before the nurse had scrambled to her feet, Rva had slammed the door and placed an enormous knife blade in front of the guard. It looked extremely sharp.

The fein creature reached down and plucked her gun from her holster and stuffed it into his waistband.

To her surprise the beast spoke good Interlingua with a husky Highland accent.

"You will sit here silently, and I will not kill you. At the slightest noise, I will take your head." She would make no attempt to resist. Let the Syndicate do what they would with her later; she wasn't about to get her head cut off by an alien monster.

The nurse sat quietly in the other armchair.

Rva had already turned his attention to Fleur, who under sedation slept deeply in the big pink bed.

He examined her carefully, tried to wake her, and then turned to the nurse. "She is drugged?"

"Well, under sedation, I think."

The big fein head shook somberly. He would have to carry her; she would not be that heavy. But it would leave them more vulnerable. Just the same.

191

25

RVA TIED THE NURSE AND GUARD WITH TOWELS AND LEFT THEM
in the shower stall. Out in the corridor again he hefted Fleur's
body over his shoulder and slipped quietly back toward the radial
corridor and the maintenance elevator. There was complete quiet;
the Syndicate was still too busy outside the dome to have given
much thought to internal security. Rva felt a sense of relief; the
corridor was just ahead. It would be pleasant to get this dangerous
job over and done with without a battle, as he was a little hard
of breath this morning. It was getting to be past the time for Bg
Rva to fight battles.

An incredible thought! He felt his lips curl into an involuntary
snarl of self-mocking laughter.

A door opened behind him. He whirled to confront a short,
rotund gentleman wearing a tan leisure suit and white shoes.
The man's jaw dropped and with a loud cry he darted back into
his room. Rva cursed and accelerated. It was too late now.

He pushed through the doors, lumbered into the radial corridor, and discovered an unexpected difficulty. The maintenance
elevator was being repaired. A man and a woman in green and
purple overalls were taking apart the controls. They looked up
with stunned expressions at the sight of the giant fein, gun in
hand, an unconscious woman draped over his shoulder. In silence
they all stared at each other.

"Why are you doing this?" he said at last, sounding peeved.

Even more amazed at the fein's command of the language,
they gaped back. He raised the revolver.

"You, tall man, answer." Rva punched the other elevator
buttons. He needed to go Down, and quickly.

The man spread his hands helplessly; his mouth finally started
to work. "Uhh, it was broken—didn't respond to controls. We
were already working on this floor, so we came over."

Rva groaned. The plan was almost in ruins. How was he to
get the lady down to Bino's escape hole in the basement?

In the corridor he heard the doors open from the residential corridor—the pursuit had begun. Dropping to one knee with the lady Fleur behind him, he turned and fired in one motion. The big revolver made a deafening noise in the confined space. The maintenance techs took the opportunity to run away as fast as they could. His second bullet took a guard, spinning the man around and back through the doors. The others proved eager to join him.

An elevator opened behind him. Without looking, without even thinking, Rva backed into it with Fleur in his arms. Only as the doors closed did he realize it was crowded with people. Hotel guests in rainbow-hued leisure suits on their way down to the restaurant floor for breakfast.

They looked at him with horror in their faces. He cleared his throat and tried to smile reassuringly.

"Don't worry, ladies and gentlemen, nothing is happening that should alarm you. Uhh, remain in your places."

For some reason his careful pronunciation and Highlander accent made them even more frightened. Their eyes were virtually popping out of their heads.

Carefully he laid Fleur down against one side of the car. The guests scrambled out of his way.

"Easy now," he said, trying to calm them. The small group of garishly garbed humans was as skittish as a herd of gzan with the scent of Nachri on the wind. However, he was going to have to use them in a moment, so it was important to get behind them. He pushed to the back. They shrank away from him.

The doors opened. Outside a number of men in khaki uniforms turned, weapons at the ready, but did not dare to shoot because Rva was pushing the screaming guests out of the elevator in a stampede of green and blue and yellow couture. The doors closed again and they rode on, toward the dome lobby itself, still far below.

They had almost reached the main lobby level when the elevator stopped with a howl of emergency brakes, between floors, and he realized someone had turned to the central controls. Rva used the kifket to break open the doors and force them back. It was heavy work, and he was panting by the time he could haul Fleur up and place her on the floor above, then scramble out after her.

He entered the corridor. No pursuit had yet reached that level, but other elevators were in motion, so he ran, panting, into the radial service corridor.

Once through the doors he slowed. He had to lay Fleur against the wall and stand still a moment to get his breath back. His heart was thumping painfully in his chest.

No elevator had stopped on the floor yet; no sounds came from beyond the double doors. When he'd regained his breath, he stooped and picked up Fleur Fundan once more. As he did so he reflected that never had he imagined Fleur to be so heavy, yet his eyes told him she weighed less than sixty kilos. She had always been thin, almost gaunt, the result of her strange vegetarian dietary habits. Rva vividly recalled his attempts so long ago to "fatten her up" with gzan liver and chop sauce. Still she felt as heavy as a gzan pup of five months.

But she was pale as a human corpse. Around her eyes were lines that had not been there before. Clearly she had seen harsh treatment recently.

All the more reason to get her to safety. But the trembling in his arms convinced him that he had to rest a little somewhere. It was an unfortunate necessity, but it could not be denied much longer. He headed into the maintenance corridor, listening intently for the sounds of people. He needed a quiet spot to think and regain his breath. He tiptoed down the corridor.

For a few moments all was silent around him. Then, ahead, he heard people approaching; he turned into a side corridor past a big yellow sign that he didn't have time to read. A solid-looking door ended the passage. Frantically he took his kifket to it. The people were following right along after him! He got a renewed grip on his kifket. On the third heave he broke the lock open and pushed into a dark room. There was an odd odor, but he had no time to investigate. He snatched Fleur under the arms and dragged her quickly in the door and closed it.

Exhaling very slowly, he sagged down the door and came to rest on the floor with his back against the door.

He took several deep breaths while his head was swimming from the exertion, but he kept his ears attuned to the corridor outside. The people were close; they laughed together at some shared joke; he heard their shoes scuff the concrete; then they were gone.

He waited a moment to be sure, then he let his breath out in a little sobbing howl. It was a relief to think he wouldn't have to fight anyone just then.

His eyes worked to penetrate the darkness, but it was dim indeed in the little room, so he groped around for a light switch and finally detected a small recess into which he thrust a finger. Harsh light sprang on to illuminate a narrow space, with bare, unfinished concrete walls, piled high with yellow plastic bags

He turned to inspect the still-unconscious Fleur. He frowned in concern as he turned her face in his hands. A large bruise marked the left side of her face, and on the back of her neck he saw the tail end of a welt that disappeared under her collar.

Carefully he turned her in his arms and pulled up her bed shirt. Her body was a mass of welts and terrible bruises. Rva's eyes glowed as they had not glowed in many years. A low growl broke from him involuntarily, and his muzzle hung open as he rode an angry shirrithee.

Whoever had done this would answer! Rva ground his gums together.

Carefully he rearranged her clothing, and then he turned to give the room a brief examination. The yellow plastic bags contained refuse that he knew from the pervasive smell. At the far end of the room were a pair of hatches that opened into the garbage chute.

Experimentally Rva lifted one of the plastic bags and dropped it into the shaft.

It slid from view, continued to make small bumping sounds for a few moments, then there was silence.

The chutes must empty into bins placed not too far below. Anyway the garbage would cushion their fall should they have to take that route. As long as there wasn't an empty bin waiting for them.

Thoughtfully Rva returned to Fleur and put his ear to the door. He stiffened. Two voices approached. Someone exclaimed at the state of the lock and cursed the dome Maintenance workers as he pulled the door open and found himself gazing down the barrel of Rva's revolver.

"Oh, shit! I don't believe this," he said.

"Come in," Rva said with a false grin.

But the sight of him was so unexpected that the two men panicked, turned and ran back up the accessway. With a curse Rva scrambled after them not wishing to fire and draw attention with the shots. The men reached the main corridor and went separate directions. Rva emerged on their heels and caught one by the back of his jacket. His fist closed, and the man ran off his feet into the air and then pitched face forward. On inspection Rva found that he'd fainted.

The other man was gone, through the double doors and into the populated residential corridor.

Rva looked back over his shoulder. There was nothing for it.

In the trash room he moved Fleur until she was lying right

by the biggest hatch, then he eased himself into it. There was room; he just had to hope that he made it down before any garbage hurtled down from above. The shaft was not however a simple straight up-and-down tube. A series of downward sloping shelves filled it in order to break the fall of garbage bags on their way to the bins in the basement. Thus Rva was able to slide down the worn concrete ramps, holding Fleur in his lap, and at the end of each ramp he would brake their descent by spreading his legs wide to get purchase on the sides of the chute. Then holding Fleur in the crook of one arm, he lowered himself over the edge, holding on with the other for as long as possible to break the two-meter fall to the next shelf.

The final drop was five meters, straight down into a three-quarters-full garbage bin. They dropped with Rva underneath and landed with a considerable thump in the middle of the bin. As soon as he had his breath back he sat up. Their fall had been cushioned by sacks of computer-printout perfory. It was extremely hard to stand up on. Even harder to walk on while carrying Fleur. He sweated and grunted with exertion as he waded through the unstable sacks of paper shreds.

There was a clatter above, and two bags of garbage hurtled down on them. He ducked away as they landed. Shaking his head at the bizarre ways of humanity, he finally reached the edge of the bin and got a leg over the side. Somehow he clambered down to solid concrete once again.

He set Fleur down and strove to recover his breath. At which point her eyes fluttered open and she stared up at him. Her eyes widened; her mouth dropped open, then she shook her head and started to sit up.

"My lady, be careful."

She gave a little shriek. "Not dream!" she said bemusedly. "Rva, how is this?

"Rva? Ooh, I feel so groggy. They gave me sedation; I didn't want it . . ." She trailed off into a dazed silence.

He heaved a deep breath; he would still have to carry her, but it could not be far now, entry to the Maintenance elevator had to be nearby.

He gathered her up in his arms and stumbled around the next corner. A small group of people was waiting there. He halted, his eyes strained as he tried to find a face he knew. Were these more enemies? Where were his friends? He continued cautiously toward them.

And then he saw Bino, and they were shouting to him in astonishment and running to his aid. Two men took Fleur from him and carried her quickly to the hole they'd hammered out of the basement floor with pneumatic drills.

They were helping him down a rough passageway and onto a walkway suspended above one of the city's underground highways. Small computer-driven cars and vans rushed past below in a ceaseless stream. They reached a doorway that opened onto a small parking lot. A white van was waiting. A few moments later they were merging into the traffic below.

Bg Rva was already fast asleep. Fleur Fundan on the other hand had woken up. Anxiously she checked the time; it had been four days since her last injection. Her time was running out.

Sometime during the late evening Rinus Van Relt realized he was being duped. The Fundan decoys had by then lured the Kommando fifteen kilometers off course, so that they faced the mountain glens running off Sliverary.

It was the lack of artillery. If Lavin Fundan were really planning to retreat into those high glens and corries, he would have been using well-placed field guns by then to pepper the advancing Kommando. Instead the enemy's artillery fire had become so sporadic that it might well have been generated by a single three-gun battery being raced around the front by teams of mules and men.

Van Relt ordered the advance halted. He sought to open a line of communication to Young Proud, who was at a concealed site not far from the new air base in Muld. Having decided that only traitorous misconduct on the part of the officers and pilots could have allowed the Neptunians to escape, he was already interrogating them by the dozen and weeding out those he decided were "weak links."

Van Relt doubted that morale at the base could withstand many more hours of Young Proud's presence and methods. It might even be better to have him back at the front. The battle had a life of its own by then. As he contemplated the holo map, Van Relt saw how Lavin Fundan had tricked him. The fein Impis were now indubitably spread out far and wide across the forest terrain that sloped down in the west to the Great Cold Lake.

It was after the demoralization of the Fifth Division . . . the divisional commanders were too cautious. We were all scared to death . . . the realization both angered and amused him.

Van Relt remembered all too well a certain night of horror and infamy from long before. A night when his troops had run for the planes with a victorious fein army *whoop*ing in pursuit.

Fifteen thousand men and women had been partially castrated as a result of that terrible night. Many of his soldiers had wept as they were processed like domestic animals. Eventually they had been sold as indentured workers and left to slave for years to buy back their freedom.

When Van Relt thought of that the anger burned brighter than before. And yet his enemy's skill could not but arouse a certain admiration. He has hardly a third as many as we. Nor can he receive fresh supplies nor ferry out his wounded. Van Relt exulted; this time things would be different. The Kommando had overwhelming odds on its side.

Of course his own troops were tired now, worn down by two full days of action. But how much more fatigued must the Impis be? There was only one area of ground warfare in which human troops could claim superiority to fein, and that was endurance. After two days of swift marching and occasional fighting, the heavy fein would be close to exhaustion.

Too, there had also been casualties, but the Kommando was of a size to be able to bear such losses with impunity. Van Relt had six full divisions, nominally sixty thousand soldiers, reduced by fighting in the field to about fifty thousand, of which ten thousand continued to invest Butte Manor, where the defense was slowly weakening.

This still left him with a force of effectives three times the size of the enemy. In addition there were the Space Marines to be called upon as well as all the other resources of the *Black Ship*.

There was no answer from Young Proud. Van Relt turned the Kommando and set his army moving back in the direction from which they'd come. There was considerable grumbling and discontent in the ranks as a result. Traffic foul-ups were numerous on the narrow hunting trails through the dark jik forest.

Finally there came the call from Young Proud, but it was not what he'd been expecting.

In short order Young Proud explained that the Sx Coast syndicates had risen and seized control of the Sx and Fun Isles. "We still have the peninsula. There are two thousand men to hold it as well, so we can starve them out before they can starve us out."

"Starve us out?" Van Relt's dreams of victory began to fade away.

"They refuse to let any transports land, not even our medical planes."

"How could this happen?" Van Relt was stunned.

"I do not understand it fully myself. I do not think it can have been the work of the Neptunians, they have no Syndicate contacts except—"

"Ira Ganweek was with them," Van Relt finished tonelessly. Of course, only Ganweek could have roused the slumbering syndicates in such dramatic fashion.

"Ganweek shall pay for this," Young Proud screamed suddenly. "I shall eviscerate him personally."

Van Relt had a hollow feeling in his stomach. The Kommando had a wealth of supplies in hand, for a complete resupply had been carried out the day before, following the disaster that had befallen the first depot on the slopes of Mount Titus. But within another day or so those supplies would be running dangerously low. Then inspiration struck him.

"There is still the *Black Ship*. The woman Rohm, she will surely see her interest as lying with us. How else can she expect to obtain a fortune in pharamol?"

Young Proud's tirade ground to a halt. "A good point, Van Relt. Contact her at once. Arrange for Space Marines to assist our assault on the manor in the morning. We will capture the vaults. That'll bring our enemy out of his hiding place!"

26

In the first light of morning, Van Relt sent the Kommando assault column rolling up the slopes of Red Mountain. Twelve thousand men, the bulk of three divisions, coming on in waves that soon broke through the enfeebled defenses of the manor and poured across the Manor Green.

Simultaneously a platoon of Space Marines dropped from the *Black Ship* to attack the High Forts—the Skullcap and the Centro. Both were secured within minutes from a few dozen defenders. But in the tunnels beneath the forts, a ferocious fire fight broke out in darkness and confusion. Van Relt sent in gas teams to clean out resistant pockets, and in two hours the outer forts had been secured. Only the manor gates remained.

The Kommando placed heavy charges against the great gates, seventy-five-foot-high slabs of steel-reinforced concrete moving on enormous solar power hydraulics dug into the cliff wall itself.

The gates shook to the detonations. Old Aunchus Butte, sitting in his despoiled palace far away, wore a rueful smile when he heard the news from the Butte defenders. Three sets of blast charges had failed to crack the great doors he designed so long ago.

The main latches, great steel screws that wound into matching sockets, had held. A small amount of raw concrete had powdered, leaving shattered patches on the exterior, but the gates had stood.

In a fury Young Proud was forced to call once more upon Alace Rohm, who sent orbital fighters leaping forth to pound the doors with armor-penetrating missiles. On the second assault, special penetrators finally broke sections open, but still the steel screws and frame held fast.

The remaining defenders, less than a hundred fein and even fewer men and women, began firing out through the holes. The Kommando pressed forward and for a few minutes engaged in a dreadful fire fight through the doors, taking many casualties before gas charges could be lobbed far enough inside the entrance to clear the defenders away.

The Kommando troops poured in; the fighting spread deep into the bowels of the labyrinth beneath the mountains.

By the ninth hour Young Proud and Rinus Van Relt were able to inspect the first captured vaults although fighting was still going on far underground.

Cunningly hidden behind a false rock surface in a deep recess, a pair of identical wooden barrels the size of firkins had been discovered. Each was half-filled with small silk sacks that when opened revealed sparkling purple pharamol, Butte Bullion. When weighed on Young Proud's pocket scales there was more than twelve kilos altogether.

It was an awesome sight. Even Young Proud felt a thrill in the presence of such an enormous cache—it was enough pharamol to keep an army alive for centuries!

The news reached the Sx Coast not long afterward, a video clip of Young Proud displaying a vast spread of sacks, boxes, phials, caskets, and other containers, filled with longevity drugs retrieved from the hidden vaults.

On the upper levels that had already been explored, many vaults were empty, but only half the clan had dared the anti-aircraft batteries and flown in to move their pharamol. Most of the largest caches were still in place. Their owners had trusted solely to their cunning hiding places and techniques. Exploration teams were proceeding cautiously into the lower levels while combat units continued to mop up small groups of defenders.

When they saw the video Ira Ganweek and Gebby Braziano realized they were doomed.

"Ira, I dunno, Ira, I trusted you . . ." The accusation was rising in Gebby's voice.

"You trusted me so far, so keep trusting me. We don't have any choice, Gebby."

"I trusted you, Ira, and now look at the shit you got me in."

Exasperated, Ira exploded. "How was I to know that some fein bodyguard was still alive in this city. I mean you know what fein are like. And all we had was a single guard in her room. The point is, Gebby, that it's not my fault!"

"Lut Vulwald will be at the meeting, Ira, along with everybody else. Young Proud has a lot of pharamol to dispense all of a sudden. Lut is Young Proud's man; we all know that, and so he's sure to want to hand over the woman. He may even want to give you back to Young Proud as well. I hear His Highness is angered with you, Ira."

Ganweek shivered. Had it come to this? That the Syndicate he had served so well for so long would turn him over to that ravening man-wolf, that obscene mind? "We don't have the woman. The old fein has the woman, but the woman is a sad story, Gebby. You wouldn't even want to know the story— believe me, I don't want to remember it."

Braziano snarled, his lean, olive tan face suddenly ugly in rage. "No fucking around, Ira! You tell me the story! You hear! I'm going down the shit hole because of this female. I want to know why I shouldn't want to know."

"Because," Ira floated, helplessly, and then told him.

Braziano stared at him. "You joking on me? He put a, a, a worm in her heart..." Braziano spat suddenly, as if he were trying to keep something from sliding down his throat.

"That's sick, that is disgusting, this man is unwell in his head, it's plain to see. Oh, Ira, you are in terrible trouble. That man wants your head, he wants it bad."

"Wait, Gebby, I got an idea." Braziano's face clouded over. "These ideas you get, you know they're dangerous. You should be careful with them."

"No, listen to me, there is a way out. The *Black Ship*, Alace Rohm, what does she want more than anything?"

"Pharamol, like everyone else."

"No, even more than pharamol."

Braziano made a face. "What, there's something worth more than pharamol? It ain't gold or diamonds, that's for sure. You mean high tech, like Magnetic Monopoles or something? Computer smarts?"

Ira smote his own forehead. "How did you ever get so far, Gebby? She wants the Bond lords, you fool. Until they're dead she's still in a perilous position. She's taken care of Chevde's most visible supporters, of that we can be sure. But if the whole Bond, which means everyone on the ship, heard that Chevde was alive, they would rise and throw Alace and her clique out the air locks."

"So?"

"So we call Alace and do a deal. She helps us get to the *Black Ship and* keeps us alive, and she gets the Bond lords, to do with what she wants."

Braziano was loth at first. Space travel had never appealed to him. He was more interested in yachts, the sun, sand, beautiful women, the pleasures of the Sx Coast. But he had to admit that

Lut Vulwald was no friend of the Brazianos. Lut was old-line Bablon, a connection that went back even further than Ira Ganweek's.

The dome might just decide that Gebby was better off as fish food if things really swung hard that way.

Ira put through a call on the Braziano's own heavy transmitter, hidden on a boat in the marina.

Since he lacked coding equipment, he made his first request to the *Black Ship* a demand for a coded, person-to-person call with Alace Rohm.

Rohm was quick to take the bait. Ira Ganweek had never crossed her yet, and in all their dealings she had come away feeling well served. That he was calling in so unorthodox a way indicated a change in the situation. Eagerly she gave the orders then rose from her couch and slipped on a long black gown with spreading silver quills, decorated with spines of chalcedony that swooped up from bustline to shoulders. On her forehead she wore the tiara of her office as madrelect. Beneath penciled black eyebrows, she composed her features into an inscrutable mask.

The *Black Ship*'s computers locked a tight beam on the Braziano transmitter's small microcomputer and programmed it with Rohm's personal cipher. Thereupon the conversation proceeded.

Rohm immediately saw the value of Ganweek's offer. The pinnace would be dispatched. The *Black Ship* would veer south on her next passage, and Ganweek and the others would be picked up.

It was up to Ganweek and Braziano to do the rest. Gebby made a series of quick calls, in family code, and then they hurried to the first full meeting of the Board of Syndicates in fifty years.

Things were as they had suspected they might be. Lut Vulwald, the man of the hour, was elected chairman on the clear recognition that he would try to seal the breach with Young Proud Fundan. The Syndicates would resume the delivery of supplies, and Young Proud would deal in the leadership in the divvying of the spoils.

Nobody mentioned Ira Ganweek, nor was there much in the way of fiery revolutionary rhetoric. The enthusiasm for independence, and freedom from Young Proud Fundan, had waned miraculously. Fleur Fundan's remarkable abduction by a fein warrior had simply sealed Ira Ganweek's doom.

Lut Vulwald was still in the midst of his acceptance speech when Ganweek slipped away, taking a side door to a public corridor through an anteroom.

He made his way to where the Braziano boys were waiting,

four hit men, soldiers too young to understand what they were really getting into. Everyone had gas masks. Together they rode elevators to the small hotel section where the Neptunians were being held.

Ganweek strolled up to the squad of six guards on hand, showed his ID, and was let through after a quick search for weapons. After the escape of the female prisoner that morning, the guards were especially tense and alert.

To the Neptunians, Ganweek spoke in code, scribbling them quick notes on a paper pad while he exchanged banter and inconsequential pleasantries. They read; they looked at each other and then at Ganweek. Could they trust him? They had trusted him before and they were prisoners, and it seemed they were likely to be given back to Young Proud. Now he promised them freedom once more, if they cooperated.

Chevde looked around him. The hotel suite was a trap. To be sent to Young Proud was quite likely a death sentence. It would be better to be in motion, going somewhere. To regain freedom of maneuver seemed critical. He nodded his assent.

In a moment the Neptunians were positioned and began a mock assault on Ganweek, whose cries brought the guards running.

But as they ran for the door, the Braziano team appeared at the other end of the corridor with grenade launchers. Gas grenades plopped against the door itself, and the fumes almost immediately overcame the unprepared guards, who spilled into the room already half-unconscious. The Neptunians were on them instantly.

For a few minutes all the elevators were packed with burly people in odd costumes of fur and shining metals, and then the Neptunians were crowding aboard a pair of minibuses brought up to the Bablon's underground portal by Gebby Braziano and his brother.

By the time the Syndicate leaders, still in the conference, were apprised of the situation, the buses were halfway across the bridge to the Sx Isle and the spaceport. High above them the *Black Ship*'s pinnace was beginning its tumultuous descent.

Timing was critical. Ganweek had told the Neptunian Bond lords that they were going to the airport in search of a plane with enough fuel to take them to South Town or the Surf Rocks. Neither was an ideal hiding place, but both were far from Young Proud and the Syndicates.

Ira however intended to turn them over to Space Marines,

which he sincerely hoped were already landing and taking their places.

They dropped into the tunnel under the Sx Isle domes and found a wedge of traffic stuck behind a broken-down truck. While they waited, Ira noted the rumbling and trembling going on above and surmised correctly that the pinnace was landing. If only they could get through the traffic, everything would go perfectly. Of course if Rohm smelled a trap, a ruse to obtain the pinnace for instance, she would order an immediate takeoff and all would have been for naught or worse.

Ira tried not to bite his nails while he watched the maintenance crew at work. They moved with the insolent slowness of those who do not care about the concerns of the traveling public. Far behind, Ira could hear sirens wailing. His mouth went dry.

There was only one thing to do. "Out, quickly. We will have to run the rest of the way, come on, before the police get here."

The Neptunians, caution abandoned, were swift to respond, and all were soon racing down the underground highway through sweltering air, toward the distant yellow ramp lights that promised the airport/spaceport complex.

As he ran Ira fancied his head was going to burst from the heat and the pressure. Surely his heart would stop. But he kept on, raising one foot after the other, trying to stay up with the Neptunians, to be sure of an opportunity to control events in the spaceport.

They reached the passenger terminal ramp for the airport. Ira waved and gesticulated. "No, friends, they'll be waiting—on to the spaceport ramp. We'll go into the airport through the Customs shed."

Chevde nodded, the others nodded, they all ran with Ganweek and Braziano, who led them full tilt into the Spaceport Arrivals area where two-dozen space marines were waiting.

A short wild fire fight broke. The survivors, including Ira Ganweek, were hustled aboard the pinnace, which tore loose in a blast of flame, wrecking half the spaceport terminal, shattering windows, and igniting fuel stocks. A huge evil-smelling cloud of vapor spread across the Sx Coast.

27

THE NEAR CHAOS PERVADING THE SX COAST MADE IT MUCH easier to hide fugitives like Bg Rva and Fleur. An apartment in the Theban Dome was chosen, its owner having decided to live out on the Surf Rocks until the New Kommando business had blown over. There they waited while Bino investigated the chances of getting a boat out soon without a heavy inspection by unfriendly Syndicate forces.

Rva had awoken from a long nap feeling considerably refreshed. He went to look in on Fleur and found her bed empty. To his consternation she was nowhere about, the other rooms were empty. He paused by the front door. Outside lay an unfriendly city full of humans. He could not roam free very long out there. However it was possible that Fleur's wits had unraveled during the horrors of her captivity and she had simply wandered away alone.

It was hard to know what to do. Finally he made up his mind. He would call Bino first, that would be best. He searched for the phone console.

Then he heard the sobbing, soft weeping, coming from the small balcony beyond the drapes. Waves of relief and concern flooded over him. He pulled the drapes and found Fleur sitting on a sun chair on the balcony, which enjoyed a pleasant view of an internal courtyard with a small park. Sunlight, filtered through the dome system, shafted down into the space and lit up the leaves to an intense green. A few people were strolling below.

Fleur was hunched forward, holding her body in her arms, her hair a matted mess, wet with tears.

Rva went to her.

"My lady Fundan, poor lady, what is it?"

She looked up at him with such misery in her eyes that it almost made his heart break. "Rva, dear Rva, I am so sorry. So dreadfully sorry, but . . ." She was unable to complete the sentence.

He waited while she gathered strength to continue.

She rested her head on his shoulder, placed her arms around his massive neck. "Rva, you must forgive me. I have to do something unbearable. I have to go back. To him, to Young Proud. I have no choice. Even if I would prefer to die cleanly, by my own hand, but I realize that it is my duty now. I am part of Clan Fundan now. A part of their accursed wars and blood feuds."

He said nothing, pitying her in this depth of insane delusion.

"I have to go because I am dying, and I must go back and kill him before I die. Don't you see?"

He started. "Dying? Why such morbidity, lady? Your freedom is now assured. We will get you away to safety."

She reached out to rub her hand in the thick fur of his neck, beneath the ear. "No Rva, I am not free."

"I do not see . . ." but she raised a hand to his muzzle to quiet him.

Eventually he did see, and when she had told him all and he cradled her head against his massive chest he felt an enormous pall of misery settle over him.

Rva of the Brelkilks sank into cold shirrithee while a numbness settled over his heart.

. . . that such horror should be visited on a blood feud inside Clan Fundan was inexplicable to the old fein. These were not the ways of the Highlanders. Always they had fought for honor, for the clean life in the high valleys.

When she was done and he stood up once more it was with a new determination. He had identified the root of their troubles and was now intent on cutting it out. He went into his room and took up his kifket. He examined it carefully for nicks, then picked up the whetstone and settled himself on the specially reinforced bed.

In her room Fleur used a scramble code to begin the process of telling Young Proud Fundan that he had won, that she was ready to be collected by her master. She routed her call to the New Kommando military communications center on the Sx Coast. She had only to use the code phrase "Death to the witch" and was put through at once.

He came to the line himself when informed of her call and angrily ordered everyone else off.

Her voice had the hollowness of one who is knowingly close to death. "You must come in person, you must bring the antidote."

There was a loathsome self-satisfaction in his voice as he

agreed. "Of course, of course. But meet me at the spaceport. That will be best. Tonight at the stroke of midnight, be at the nearside ship cradle. I will bring the medicine to still that fever that burns in your blood. And then amour, eh, m'*esclave*?"

Aboard the *Black Ship* Ira Ganweek sweated profusely as he begged Alace Rohm for his life. Most of the Neptunian Bond lords had already been dispatched, one by one, through a private little air lock in the computer library section, and the executions had been witnessed by a picked group of Rohm's supporters, who had whooped with delight at each "performance."

For Ofur Muynn they had opened the lock very slowly. He had scrabbled frantically at the door trying to retain air, trying to get back into the ship, while they laughed and laughed as his head ballooned and his body finally began to burst.

For Aumus Realme the lock had been opened quickly, and the black-suited intelligence chief vanished in an instant into the "cleansing void," as Alace described it to the rest.

Still uncomfortable after such sights, Ira had followed Rohm to her stateroom where she had played for him a recently received message from Young Proud Fundan. He demanded the return of Ira Ganweek to his custody. Young Proud did not even mention the Neptunian Bond lords, thus leaving Rohm free to dispose of them at her whim, but poor Ira Ganweek he demanded.

"Of course he does not know for certain that you are still alive," she said slyly.

"You are not indebted to him," Ganweek said hurriedly. "There is no reason why you must comply."

She put on a grave smile. "Well, he does have rather a lot of pharamol at his disposal right now. Enough so that if he gave me my share I could be sure of securing stability here for the foreseeable future. For that I would give up almost anything."

"I can get you a lot of pharamol, madrelect. I have my contacts."

Her eyebrows arched.

"You do? On the Sx Coast? From which I have just rescued you?"

"Of course." He tried to appear jovial and hearty.

"Twaddle! You have no friends left except the few that came with you aboard the pinnace. Lut Vulwald is boss of the Sx Coast now, and he, like myself, is allied with Young Proud."

At the thought of being given into Young Proud Fundan's mercies, Ira Ganweek had no trouble in getting to his knees to the woman and promising absolute fealty, Neptunian style.

At this her smile changed, became almost mischievous.

"No man can be Inbonded by Nereid," she giggled.

"I, I, am not a man," Ganweek began. "I am castrate."

Rohm's eyebrows rose.

"Ah, so the rumors were true then. There is a most interesting story concerning this, uh, dismemberment. Perhaps you will be given the time and opportunity to tell us more of this. And perhaps—if there are no testicles in the way—perhaps you can be Inbonded to a novitiate status or something. I will question the grand mother on the matter. Until then you will stay. I shall keep Young Proud waiting on my answer."

"Thank you, madrelect."

Alace signaled him to press his forehead to the small mat in front of her.

"You are not Inbond, but you have amused me. Perhaps I will find a use for you, Ira Ganweek." And besides, she reflected, Young Proud would have to cut her in on the pharamol anyway. Did she not control the *Black Ship*?

Attendants led Ira and Gebby Braziano away to a small, bare cabin where they were locked up.

Degorak Chevde was brought in. He raged within his bonds.

The Nereidan guards were burly women, all with a degree of Maza-method training. Still three of them were required to place Chevde on his knees. In sensitive areas of his body they placed small adhesive pads connected to wires that ran to a small black box beside Alace Rohm's seat. When Rohm manipulated the keyboard in her hand, Chevde experienced nerve fire throughout his body.

"Only by practicing extreme docility will you be released from the pain, good Chevde," Alace said in a sweet voice.

Chevde had never endured such agony, never imagined such torment could exist. After a moment more he gave in. He crouched, held still. The pain ceased.

"Now, we shall converse in a civilized manner. I want to know a number of things from you. I have questions that only you can answer."

"And when I have told you these secrets? Then you will space me as you did the others?" He hurled the words at her. She folded her hands on her knee and smiled at him.

"With my supporters cheering me on, dear Degorak, I, personally, will push the button that sends you and a small amount of air and moisture out into the great void. But before that blessed moment arrives there are a few things I am determined to have."

The nerve fire jangled on again; Chevde writhed.

209

"Such as the combination that opens the door to your private cabin. That will be the first piece of information, please."

Chevde shook his head. The nerve fire increased. It ran up and down his body as if he were being roasted alive and flayed at the same time. Nerve ends were being held into an oxyacetylene flame to crisp and evaporate.

He gave in. No one could stand that . . . no one . . .

"The numbers, dear Chevde, give me the numbers."

Tonelessly he mumbled them to her recorder.

"And now the entry code to your personal computer files, dear, sweet, obedient Chevde."

In the darkness of late evening, when the last rays of Beni had caromed away from the orb atop the Sx Coast Tower, Bg Rva came out of the trance. He honed his kifket, murmuring the sweet love poem to his blade that he had always sung.

"O, Umpkoma mine, so sharp, so fine,
cut me a fine cured hide, slice me the shank of bones,
Umpkoma, umpkoma, child of mine,
slay me a fine gzan and sunder every stone . . ."

When Fleur Fundan came out of her room, an hour early, in an effort to give the old mzsee the slip and prevent any last-moment heroics, she heard nothing from his room but a gentle snoring. Satisfied, she slipped quietly from the suite. She had done up her hair, pinning it above her head. Hidden within it was a Syrette loaded with the toxic fluid she had drained from the photocopying attachment on the big TV set. The stuff was deadly; all she had to do was get that needle into Young Proud for a second, and he was a dead man.

The "sleeping," old mzsee however was already far down the beach, just outside the spaceport. The snoring had simply been a recording played back on Rva's request by the house computer.

He used his kifket to break the clasps holding the wire panels to the frame of the fence and bent one back to obtain entry. Rva's eyebrows rose when he looked around. The spaceport had been devastated. Exploding fuel tanks had flattened most of the maintenance shops and scattered pieces of their equipment far and wide. The terminal looked as if it had been bombed.

There were a number of excellent hiding positions in the

210

mess. Rva nodded to himself with some satisfaction as he slipped into a place between two charred electric drays. His opportunity would come. The honor of Clan Fundan could be recovered.

There was not long to wait. At ten minutes before the hour he discerned another figure in the ruined spaceport. Someone stood inside the terminal in the shadow to one side of an empty window.

At a minute to midnight there was a faint sound of a jet aircraft, approaching from seaward. Soon afterward a long-distance vtol jet raced in low, without lights, just above the waves, before braking dramatically in a roar of retros right over the nearside ship cradle.

The engines switched off, a door opened and slid wide. Young Proud, accompanied solely by Persimpilgas, jumped down. He clapped his hands.

From the shadows came Fleur Fundan, wearing a long cloak that buttoned at the neck.

Young Proud opened the cloak, pulled it away, and dropped it to the ground. She stood naked in the light of the Pale Moon. With a smile of triumph on his face he handcuffed her wrists. Then he put the collar on her and attached the leash.

"So Madame Fundan. Or rather Fund-IN." He spat the suffix at her contemptuously. "There are things better than death, eh?" Her silence sent him into a fit of giggles.

His laughter echoed for a moment in the ruined spaceport.

Then he gave an oath; Bg Rva had slipped out of the shadows to stand among them. Persimpilgas whirled, eyes popped at the sight of such an old fein, near toothless— Old and silent, with a grim expression.

Rva held up a paw. In the other he held a kifket. The moment had clear clan precedent stretching back hundreds of years. In blood feud, a single combat between fein champions could decide the issue. The mechanism avoided further debilitating bloodshed and made the Highland battle commanders personally aware of the responsibility for death that they carried. It had been in force since the early days of the human settlement in the Highland valleys.

"I am champion of the lady Fleur Fundan. I call on you, Young Proud Fundan, to defend yourself in the name of the honor of Clan Fundan. I also charge that you demean Clan

211

Fundan with your filthy jealousy and unworthy behavior. In the eyes of all fein with clean conscience you would be out-clan, pariah!" Rva saluted with the kifket.

"So then, for the honor of Clan Fundan, you will fight me. To the death!"

For a moment Young Proud blanched. It was unimaginable, this ancient one, eyes rolling, mind rambling, interposing his flabby old body in the affairs of the clan!

Yet he felt compelled to answer. Hot, angry words spilled out. "I pursue the honor of Clan Fundan, stupid old mzsee. I defend the true genes from the works of the witch! Get yourself away from here and think yourself lucky to be allowed to live out your foolish days. Get away while I let you live!"

Obstinately Rva remained where he stood, holding out the kifket, the symbol of honor in the Highlands.

Persimpilgas presented himself. Clan honor was all that this had ever been about, as both fein knew too well. Fair Fundan, clone mother of Lavin, had displaced the Proud Fundans. The weak father had gone mad, the son had become degenerate, renegade, insanely dangerous. But decades of venom were bound in the feud.

Persimpilgas tried to reason with him.

"This seems nonsensical to me, old mzsee. You are way past the time for death, and I honor you. Your legend will always be bright, but I'll take any Brelkilk head I can—and yours will be a great one to place in my yard for us to remember you by. Old Rva, Crazy Rva of the Brelkilks, who thought he could still fight when his teeth were gone."

Rva became impatient. They should not treat him thus. He worked within clan precedent. They knew it as well as he. "Come, Persimpilgas, do not exhaust yourself in these exhortations. Blood is blood and will be shed."

"You are too old, mzsee. It will be easily shed, and thus triumph will come to Ramal. We will defeat the hated Brelkilks."

"Only in dishonor, faint heart Persimpilgas. Only in the service of this one of the dark, this evil."

"Defend yourself, Brelkilk." Persimpilgas had drawn steel.

"Oh, no, Rva, don't do this!" Fleur Fundan begged.

Rva spoke only to Persimpilgas. "Umpkoma comes for you," he said quietly.

The two fein circled. Rva was the taller by an inch but had thirty years on Persimpilgas. His body was worn, some muscles stringy, belly flabby. The contest seemed ridiculous.

The kifkets swung in their big hands, gleaming slabs of steel.

They closed in a rush, kifket on kifket with a loud clang like a bell being smashed with a sledgehammer.

They pushed apart, then closed again. The kifkets rang off each other with showers of sparks. They grappled like two Titans. Persimpilgas was the stronger, and he bore Bg Rva backward. Rva had never felt the weight of superior strength so keenly, and he fought with everything in his immense heart. But, outmatched by age's cruel processes, he was forced first to give ground and then to stumble. He went down with a heavy grunt.

Persimpilgas slipped his kifket free for the killing stroke.

"Goodbye, old fein, your song is ended."

But Rva kicked the other's legs out, and Persimpilgas fell with a crash. Rva locked with him; they rolled, broke apart, and sprang to their feet. Rva felt something singing in his soul even while he labored for breath and his pulse pounded in his skull.

The kifkets met; sparks flew, but Persimpilgas's blow was the stronger. His blade slid past Rva's and nicked Rva's shoulder. Blood seeped rapidly down the old fein's arm. Desperately he backtracked and chopped away Persimpilgas's thrusts. The shorter fein pressed him, foot stamping ahead as he swung and reversed and swung again, keeping Rva on the defensive. Something would give soon; Persimpilgas was just that much stronger, and his blows were coming faster than Rva could counter them. Before he finished Rva would lose an arm or even his head.

Rva struggled to rouse himself, to regain the initiative. But suddenly it was as if he were wading in mud. The fight was ebbing from him. A redness seemed to descend over his eyes.

One last attempt must be made! screamed a voice in old Rva's head, and he stiffened.

Persimpilgas thrust heavily, foot stamping forward. Rva met the blade, deflected it, and turned inside to ram his elbow in Persimpilgas's midriff. The bodyguard's breath exploded, and Rva's blade nicked his belly in the instant.

Persimpilgas touched the spreading blood from the cut; not deep, he had sensed its coming; and stared in wonder. The old fein was something out of the history texts. When Persimpilgas had been a cub at the fireside they had told the stories of Bg Rva, Hero of Brelkilk. And here the old mzsee had managed to turn inside him and slice him just a little!

Persimpilgas's professional sensibility was outraged. He growled low in his throat.

"Enough tricks, old one—it is time to end this farce."

But Rva had taken heart from Persimpilgas's blood. When they met, Rva seized Persimpilgas's wrist and spun him. The effort was enough to send Rva into a turn as well, and their blades met again with a ringing clash as they came back face-to-face.

Persimpilgas roared in anger mixed with amusement. "Wily old mzsee knows the human tricks too, eh?"

Persimpilgas swung and chopped, forcing Rva to retreat once more with impeccable kifket technique. He faked a stumble, and Rva attempted a throw, but Persimpilgas read the move, parried it, and got in a solid chop to the body.

Fleur screamed at the sound of the blade going home. Rva grunted at the blow; there was death in it. His side was wet, the fur matting fast. Time was very short now.

For a moment Rva faced the unthinkable, that he would die and the honor of the Brelkilks would be lost along with the life of the lady Fleur. He dismissed the idea as preposterous and conjured up the memory of Brelkilk Village in Abzen Valley.

Then the pain and the weakness seemed to fade magically. He focused on Persimpilgas, breathing hard, facing his enemy still. "Prepare, Persimpilgas, for now you go to join the dead in the blissful peace of the void."

"Come, Brelkilk. Show me the way to the dead, old fein. Come forward; my blade sings for you already. Be quick, though, for I sense that your time is but short."

They came together, but this time Rva's kifket struck as hard as any steel had ever struck Persimpilgas's blade. They grappled, snarling, in each other's face. Persimpilgas was stunned by the raging strength in the old body pressed against his. He sucked in a breath and exerted himself, slowly, slowly gaining, perspiration dotting the tough leather of his forehead. Then he began to bend the old fein back. Rva emitted a whining growl from deep inside as he sensed defeat.

"Die, old fool," spat Persimpilgas.

Rva felt his berserker strength ebbing, then, too weak to do anything else, he snapped his toothless jaws together on Persimpilgas's nose.

Persimpilgas gave a scream of rage and shook Rva off. He raised his kifket high for the head-splitting blow, and Rva's blade lanced out and sank into his chest.

Persimpilgas looked down aghast; the big blade had cut his life in two. It was unthinkable! His heart stopped. He looked back into Rva's eyes, still bewildered at such sudden strength, and he died.

Rva pulled the blade free, turned to Young Proud, holding his side where the blood pumped freely. "Your champion is dead, messire. He was a brave fein and a fine fighter. He shall be mourned in Abzen as well as in Ramal. By clan precedent the Lady Fundan retains her freedom unless you, messire, care to fight me with the kifket? It would be the quickest way to restore the pride of Clan Fundan from the stain that you have spread upon it. Pick up the blade of the fallen Hero, he who guarded you so well for so long. Contest with Rva of the Brelkilks, as it should always be, as it should always have been, and I will take your head and all honor will be restored for your name within the clan."

"Indeed?" said Young Proud. "So you say, but are there any witnesses, any that count?"

"What need of witnesses? You live within the code, Fundan; how else can you be Proud Fundan? You must obey its dictates, or your life ceases to have meaning."

For a long moment Young Proud stared at Bg Rva, his mouth working in a curious way. He even looked down at the heavy blade of Persimpilgas and then back to Rva. His eyes seemed to shine, and something snapped inside him. His lips set in a queer smile, and without a word he pulled out an automatic and pumped four shots into Bg Rva, toppling the big fein to the concrete by the nearside ship cradle.

Fleur flung herself to her knees beside the old fein's still form. She pressed her head to his bloody chest. There was no heartbeat. The Hero of Brelkilk was no more.

With a scream that welled up from some primal pool of hatred Fleur turned on Young Proud, butted him then leaned quickly forward and bit his lower lip. He struck her with a fist, knocking her to her knees. She lashed forward with her head, and her teeth sank into his thigh muscle, biting through the fatigue cloth. He kicked her away with a curse. She flung herself back at him and kicked, thrashed, and fought him as he dragged her to the plane. At the steps he had to club her senseless with the gun barrel before he could lift her and thrust her through the hatch.

The engines ignited with a roar, and Young Proud lifted off and flew northward.

28

THE SKY WAS AN OMINOUS BLACK FADING TO PURPLISH RED. Lightning forked into the forest, and while the rain pelted down the Impi mobile command post took shelter beneath a hastily erected tent.

On a battered monitor Lavin Fundan reviewed the intercepted signals from Butte Manor. Young Proud gloated over a hoard of longevity drugs, proclaimed himself the Conqueror of the Buttes, and dedicated his victory to the *Black Ship*.

This last caused Lavin to frown slightly. It seemed an unusually diplomatic gesture for Young Proud. That ineffable personality had never shown the ability to tolerate any rival claims to preeminence.

What game was being played between these supposed allies? Lavin had frequently pondered that problem. The ship promised enormous power but plainly only for a while, until Earth produced its own FTL Drive and another armada arrived at Fenrille.

Young Proud would want to be long gone by then, and where else to go but aboard the *Black Ship*.

Of course to Young Proud such a course would be fraught with dangers. And Lavin noted grimly that such dangers would likely be real; the owner of the *Black Ship*, the bull-necked figure they'd all picked up from that initial broadcast, would have little in common with Young Proud other than that hoard of pharamol the Highlander controlled. If appearances were anything to go by, the people aboard the ship seemed a direct, almost brutal people.

How could Young Proud be assured of safety then? What would he do to make himself safe? Lavin leaned back on his camp chair and finished sipping a nutrisoup. It was the last one. From now on he would have to eat camp chow with the rest of them.

He flicked off the tape looper, went to the door of the tent, and stared out into the storm.

It was a bleak situation that he faced. His wife in the hands of his enemy, his son dead, his forces scattered. He had been able to do nothing to prevent Young Proud's smashing into Butte Manor, and this sense of helplessness was perhaps the worst aspect of the morass.

Even on the morrow the odds would not improve markedly. Scattered far and wide through the wet forest he had about eight thousand fein effectives, about four thousand human. The enemy had at least four times his numbers, plus supplies and fresh ammunition. Lavin would have to husband his strength and hope for an opportunity to land one blow, a blow that would have to be decapitating, since it would be his only blow.

In fact the Impis were exhausted. Only Young Proud's inexplicable decision to turn away and assault the manor had saved the Defense Forces from disintegration. All that day the only signs of activity from Lavin's army had been a couple of precious reconnaissance sorties by the last pair of operational vtol aircraft. By the midafternoon he felt able to put together a platoon of volunteers to press an aggressive patrol down the Sliverary River's banks, but the patrol encountered only a few scouts in the region where the river was joined by its tributary, the Uluin.

What remained of Lavin's medical and veterinarian corps was working without rest to patch up the wounded. The artillery vets, who normally tended horses and mules, were now putting unfamiliarly small splints on even more unusually small human legs or fishing bullets out of human and fein bodies.

But perhaps the gravest problem faced by the Impis was the general lack of ammunition. The drawn-out fight in Sliverary Forest had depleted ammunition reserves and resupply was problematical. Some of the Buttes had responded to his calls for aid; some of the younger Buttes, ashamed perhaps of their clan's weakness, had even flown in themselves, with small groups of fein volunteers. Others clung to the will of the Kirk and determined to obey the preachings of the Peace of the Lamb. They refused to aid or assist the work of violence, even in defense.

All of which made Lavin's bitterness only a little more unbearable.

He had to fight, deep within himself, to keep thoughts concerning Fleur from overwhelming him in despair. Young Proud had always been a strange, cruel man. After fifty years in hiding, his ugly traits could only have grown worse.

Still, he tried to find reassurance. Fleur was an important prisoner, too important to be maltreated. But the nagging worry would not leave him, and when it finally did it was only to present him with an image of Chosen, destroyed so casually by the *Black Ship*.

He forbore sleep, took pharamol, and went to work again with the battle computer.

In complete darkness Armada Butte stole forward along the narrow adit. She emerged behind the man in the wider passageway. He paused, sensing something perhaps. His was dangerous work, his senses were stretched tight, straining in the dark. A few fein were still loose in the deep levels.

She swung up her handgun, flicked on the infrared sensor, and fired, catching the trooper before he could respond to the beep of his detector. She heard his gasp and the sound of his fall to the ground as she ducked back into the adit.

From somewhere not too far away, downtunnel, shells whined off the rock. There came shouts and faint beams of light. Armada ran back through the adit. She reached the S bend before the lights and bullets pounded the rocks behind her.

Back on the ramps in the spiral, she kept up a fierce pace for three turns and then crawled off through another even narrower hole at waist height. It led into a well with small handholds carved every few feet. She moved down the tube and emerged in a natural gallery approximately a meter high along which she scrambled to get into the Tertiary Deep, Tammi's Well.

The New Kommando continued its slow penetration of the depths, working even more cautiously. Behind the soldiers came the Chitin detection teams, performing a job that every soldier would love to have had. There were a lot of comparisons being made that watch shift in the platoon, a certain amount of grumbling. Delly's getting it like that was tough.

Ira Ganweek trembled from fatigue and humiliation. Never had he dreamed that he could suffer such indignity.

Before his unusual, almost bizarre, request for Inbonding to Nereid could be considered, the candidate had to endure a full physical and mental examination by the whole Bond. That meant that three hundred superior female members of the Bond took turns in poking and pulling on Ira Ganweek's private parts during a sort of prolonged cocktail party in a big room filled with incense and heavy-limbed music.

Ganweek was shackled to a high chair and could do no more than answer the questions put to him over and over again. Always they howled like laughing banshees at the missing testicles.

At his "introduction" he was put on a small stage and made

to perform ludicrous, degrading exercises to the immense amusement of the Nereidans. Finally a small silver brand was heated red hot on a candle of sacred woman fat and pressed to his right buttock to confirm that he had entered the Bond as Alace Rohm's "interest"—a status somewhere between outright slave and a novice in the worshipful Bond hierarchy.

He was robed in the garb appropriate to his post. Heavy bronze collar and genital restraints, heavy wrist cuffs in spiked leather and similar anklets.

It amused Alace to have him stand behind her chair and fan her gently with a large two-handed fan. To prevent his hearing anything he shouldn't, he wore earplugs. For what seemed an endless eternity he stood there, his forearms aching from the effort of keeping the fan moving just the way Alace preferred it, and she was very particular.

He was dropping off into a state akin to sleep but not quite sleep, his eyelids drooping, when five of the toughest female guards in Rohm's personal squad escorted Degorak Chevde in.

Degorak pointed to Ira and bellowed some curse, but the guards promptly grappled his arms to his sides.

Chevde was forced to his knees. Small wired pads were attached to his nose, his nipples, his genitals and anal region. Chevde writhed on the floor and eventually assumed the posture of humility before Alace Rohm. Ganweek was amazed. Never had he imagined great Degorak Chevde as anything but high Bond lord. Here he bowed to Alace Rohm!

It became clear to him that Alace was interrogating Chevde, and Ganweek knew at once why Degorak was still alive.

Of course, he realized, there were many things that only the previous high Bond lord could know. Codes, for example, such as those that armed the nuclear torpedoes or unlocked the primary lasers. The fact that Chevde still lived was testament to just how many such essential items of information he possessed.

The questioning was prolonged, and several times Chevde had to be given nerve fire until his body writhed and humped like some enormous maggot on the floor.

Eventually he was dragged away, too exhausted to continue.

Alace rose and dismissed Ganweek, allowing him to remove his earplugs. He was shown to his new quarters, a small cupboardlike space just long enough for him to lie down. To soften the floor he was given a single thickness of foam.

Nothing however could have prevented his falling instantly asleep the moment he was lying prone.

* * *

The Bablon Syndicate men were apologetic. They were nothing to do with the New Kommando, they explained. They were not, however, empowered to release the prisoners.

Yet they had an urgent request.

The prisoners, Ervil and Dali Spreak, sat together frowning on a sofa in the hotel room in which they had been captive for the past week.

"Don't come to me for any favors," Ervil Spreak snapped.

The older Syndicate officer, a man in his forties with a big square head and a wide, coarse body, was oddly apologetic. "It is a matter of ceremony. We have a sad duty to perform—two fein have died." He saw their expressions and hastened to explain. "No, no, it's not what you're thinking. We didn't kill them. They appear to have killed each other. We found the bodies in the spaceport. There was a report of a gun battle there earlier. But you can rest assured that the Syndicate did not kill these fein." The young officers were uncomfortable for some reason, just being around such ancient, ancient people.

"We must dispose of the remains in the proper way. That is what we ask you for. What ceremony should be performed?"

The younger officer made a cross in the air with his right hand, the sign of the Church of Christ Spaceman. Both were clearly in a state of acute spiritual unease.

At this Ervil Spreak suddenly asked, "Do you have a picture of these fein with you?"

"Yes, but why should that concern you?"

"Perhaps I would know them."

Even more uncomfortable at the thought of actually knowing a fein, the lieutenant extended a photo. Ervil took one glance and sighed.

"These are famous fein indeed. The one with the kifket wound in his chest is Persimpilgas, Young Proud Fundan's personal guard. The other is old Rva of the Brelkilks, a legend in his own times. You found them together?"

"Yes, uh, sir."

"And tell me, how did Rva die?"

"He was shot four times in the chest. In addition there was a deep wound in his left side."

"I see." And Ervil Spreak did indeed see and could picture the incident very clearly. Rva had gone there to fight for the honor of Clan Fundan. He had triumphed, and Young Proud had finally, totally, renounced his own people. He was out-clan forever now.

"The fein do not as a rule have burials or cremations. They

see the spot where a fein dies as the right spot for that fein to be buried. However in this case we have two great heroes, famous in their own lands. I would suggest their bodies be flown to their respective high valleys and given over to the mzsees of their villages. Rva should be taken to Abzen Valley, Persimpilgas to Ramal. The fein will know what to do with them then."

The officers thanked Ervil Spreak and then left. The endless dreary day continued while Ervil stared out of the window like some captive bird of prey in a cage and Dali worked with the computer terminal by the TV to fetch research documents that she was interested in and place them on-screen.

Of the two, Ervil reflected, she was the more likely to survive the damnable incarceration. It was about to part him from his sanity.

In the great valley of Butte Manor the storm had long since died away and the stars blazed down through a clear night sky when Lavin Fundan finally put the computer board aside and had copies of his new plan printed out for the neilks and other officers.

The Impis would begin to move at dawn. The New Kommando positions were awkwardly skewed. In addition, as the troops had been rewarded with a share out of the loot from Butte Manor, their discipline had grown lax. Lavin had several reports of Kommando units leaving the lines. Small arms fire could sometimes be heard across the lines. Lavin could easily visualize the sort of troop control problems that a pirate force like the New Kommando would be having.

Suddenly enriched with longevity drugs, the troops would feel much less like fighting the Highland fein!

So Lavin's Impis would filter forward. With a little luck they might get to the banks of the Sliverary without being detected. A sudden drive on the bridges could disable the Kommando and even allow the fein to drive on Butte Manor itself. Lavin ordered that everything too heavy to carry be left behind; the forces would be without artillery, without supplies. This would be their last hurrah, and should they fail, there could be no recovery.

Lavin had meticulously plotted the prime infiltration paths, and when he had finished, the battle computer's rating of his plan had shifted from 90 percent probability of failure to 50 percent. The odds were evened; the rest would be up to the fein and humans of the defense forces.

29

FOR LONG HOURS, IN THE DARK BOWELS OF THE GREAT NEST, the Chitin inspected its captures with enormous excitement. Every detail had to be reexamined repeatedly as the slow-moving brain of the vizier caste strove to remember the oldest memories of all, those that lay beyond the great prohibition.

It trilled with pleasure at each new discovery.

They were undoubtedly alien creatures; that was the first and most obvious conclusion. The body of Yu Zhao had been minutely dissected and tasted. The internal structure was therefore well known. If required to, the Chitin could now produce a mental imagery of the human circulatory system, the nervous system, even the various internal organs.

Secondly these were undoubtedly intelligent beings. The nest had measured their cranial surfaces, and from the taste of the head contents of Yu Zhao, the nest knew that the heads contained large amounts of nervous tissue, not unlike the nervous tissue found in other large animals here on the planet that was not the homeworld, the planet that mystified the memory trees. The presence of that form of nervous tissue in such large amounts relative to body size was a good indicator of high intelligence in the individual animal.

Moreover, the beings were clad in materials that were unlike anything ever experienced by the memory trees. And yet ancient, ancient memories were awakened by these materials; the nest knew them, somehow.

Extruded plastics, ceramic, worked metals, and machines such as the devices that projected intense beams of light even there in the heart of the nest. A wonder from the oldest, deepest, legends. Those things were hallmarks of an off-world culture! The nest's level of excitement became feverishly high.

Even further intrigue was stimulated by the totally different responses of the three captives. One had alternated between brief bouts of consciousness, in which it made sharp noises and exuded a sweat laden with certain crude pheromones that bespoke fear to the nest's mind, after which it lapsed into longer periods of unconsciousness.

Another, the smallest, was a different type, a female/queen form, with an outlet for either very large eggs or live young. Live young were the more likely since that would conform again to the memory core's classification of these warmth-generating animals.

The female had put itself into some kind of trance. The Chitin nest was fascinated. Nothing seemed to wake the creature, not even a warrior's vigorous bite. Yet it breathed; the pulse continued to pump fluid about the circulatory system. A swarm of vizier, including some very specialized "tasters" with overlarge mouth parts continued to work over that body.

The third individual was in many ways the most interesting of all, for it exhibited strong signs of a willingness to communicate, a conscious effort to accommodate the nest. There came from it an impression of respect, an empathy, perhaps even a sympathy for the nest. The nest trembled at the idea. Could there be communication? Could the creature actually be made to comprehend the tragedy of the Chitin? If so, could it be made useful? There was so much to know, to find out, and the nest, as always, felt pitifully weak, alone in a ferocious world and isolated from any solutions to its great, vexing questions.

To communicate with the creature would be a problem; there was a vast gulf in understanding between such quick-moving, transitory creatures and the nest that had lain in those muds for centuries. A section of the nest mind was concentrated on the problem and began an intensive review of the chemical structure of the creatures, working from the rough but detailed survey reported from the warriors that had eaten Yu Zhao.

On another level the nest considered the problems of keeping its captives in a healthy state. They were omnivorous forms; so much was clear from their teeth; and thus they could digest a wide variety of foods. Of course the nest did not know if they could digest Fenrille proteins, and as more reports came in from the most sophisticated chemical tests—in which specialized tasters had broken down cells from the captives in their mouths and explored such materials as human DNA in considerable depth—so the nest grew concerned for their nutritive viability.

Analysis of fecal samples confirmed the omnivorous nature of the beings' diet but also betrayed the presence of carbohydrates, relatively simple chemicals. The nest decided to refine some fungal paste for carbohydrate content and to feed it to the beings. Just a small quantity, to see if it was acceptable. Meanwhile parties of workers would be dispatched to fetch fruits from the forest to see if they might be suitable, or even refinable for pure carbohydrates. The fungus was rich in complex proteins but weak in carbohydrate, and a great deal of it had to be laboriously chewed, partially digested in fermenter Chitin, and rechewed with other salival chemicals to render it even 80 percent pure.

Before feeding, however, the captive creatures had to be moved to a new cell, already completed, dug out of an old brood gallery not far from the vizier chamber.

Chosen became aware of the change in the nest very quickly. The vizier Chitin were leaving, there were fewer and fewer of them on his body, which had grown sensitized to the touch of Chitin feet and Chitin bodies. In the dim light from the single remaining suit headlamp and the faint luminescence of the fungi that grew on the roofs and walls, he could just make out the entwined branches of Chitin—writhing with vizier in the process of chemical transfer—that filled the space above their heads. Chosen had never seen a nest so large, with such a heavy vizier mass. The stench was absolutely overpowering.

To the sides of the chamber he saw darker patches, openings that led to other parts of the nest. Looking down, around where he sat, he saw dimly that the floor was empty of moving insects. The nest had withdrawn.

What did it want from them now? It had inspected them for what seemed like hours, but in his extremity of fear Chosen was aware that minutes at such times can seem very much longer than the minutes of happier occasions. There was no way to know how long they had been there, since Chitin had somehow penetrated the chronometer and ruined it. But time indeed was now losing meaning except in one vital regard. Within a given amount of time, maybe days, they would contract the spruip and die horribly. Maybe the nest would put them out of their misery when it began, or maybe it would wait and observe, fascinated, while its captives raved and screamed and eventually died in a frothing frenzy.

Carefully shaking off stray Chitin from his suit, Chosen gathered it up and put the helmet on his head. The light stabbed against the walls. Vizier Chitin teemed there, and from above a constant rain fell, small spatters of excrement. Workers would remove this to the fungal gardens after a while. Something was expected of them, but what?

His light caught rapid movements. Warrior Chitin were appearing on the floor of the chamber. He swept the light around desperately and found that there were no warriors in one direction, which led to an ominous hole. The implication was clear. Chosen tried to rouse Chi Lin Wei but could not. She remained unconscious. Zhao six, however, he did manage to bring to his feet and then induced to follow him, crawling into the hole.

It was a short journey, to a small space about three meters in diameter. The warriors did not follow. Instead streams of tiny Chitin the size of terrestrial ants poured in through small holes in the roof. Once again the humans felt the tread of thousands of small hooked feet, tiny bristles rustling on the skin. Chosen stayed still, although he had to call out twice to Zhao six, to steady him, for the clone wavered on the brink of hysteria whenever the insects moved onto his face.

But they did come, to Chosen as well, a moving carpet of Chitin workers that rolled up his chest, pooled on his shoulders, and then worked in lines to bring water to his mouth, tiny droplets deposited one after the other by workers that had fetched it from the river. In a minute or so there was a mouthful, and he swallowed gladly, relieving a throat so dry that it was painful at first. The water Chitin kept coming, and after a while Chosen had received almost a pint.

His thirst alleviated, his mind instinctively turned to the pangs of hunger. There had been no food since before the rapids.

More Chitin were moving onto his chest, climbing his chin. He opened his mouth when they bit at his lips, and soon a gruel of some sort took shape on his tongue. Slowly, grain by grain, they fed him a few mouthfuls of an oddly flavored mush. It had a strange aftertaste, and he wondered idly if it might be some of the phosphorescent fungi that grew so prominently in the nest.

It hardly had to be chewed, which was fortunate considering the bitter aftertaste, which grew stronger the more of it he ate.

Fleetingly he wondered if the stuff would stay down, and if it did, whether it would prove poisonous. If this was the nest's own favorite food there might be a decided problem, since human and Chitin chemistry were radically different.

Then he felt a shivery feeling down his spine. His eyes felt odd in his face. He fancied he could hear his heart beating, loudly and ponderously, booming in the darkness.

Uneasily he recognized the effects of a drug of some kind. The mushroom, had it contained hallucinogens?

A few moments later he had no doubts.

Once, when he was sixteen and first accompanied old Mzsee Rva on a three-day foraging expedition up to the Kirrim Ridge, Rva had turned to him one evening and offered him klav, a milky extract from the kakung bean and a powerful hallucinogenic drug used occasionally by the fein for important rituals.

That evening and the long night that followed was a turning point in Chosen's life. Crystallized before him was a vision in which he saw his true and appointed duty in his life.

He would catalogue the flora and fauna of the tropical Highlands. An immense task, but one that he felt had been alotted to him at some visceral level.

In the rising and falling of the drug, Rva had occasionally steadied Chosen when he noticed the boy was lost in confusion or frightened by some phantasm from his own mind. At certain moments Chosen found he gained new and great insight into the ways of philosophy that he had studied in Fundan school. And he also recognized the wit in the fein wisdom.

Thus he was now aware that he was in the grip of a drug but hardly prepared for the fury that was opening in his mind. For one alkaloid in the fungal mush, considered harmless by the Chitin, was indeed a very powerful hallucinogen, and Chosen and Zhao six had already ingested heavy doses.

The pounding of his pulse continued to boom in his head. He felt sweat running down inside the helmet and for a moment forgot entirely where he was and instead wondered mutely why he was wearing the helmet. It was an unfamiliar piece of equipment for him. Was he in space? Or, since it was so dark, underwater?

Then the false normalcy was shattered by Zhao six's primal scream. Chosen looked up to find the man's face, dribbling spittle, covered in dirt, hanging over him. Small insects were running this way and that over his body.

It was hard at first even to recall who it was, but gradually Chosen managed to piece it together. Cautiously he reached out and pulled the shivering Chinese down beside him. He kept his hold, pulling the man closer until their skins touched, providing some purely human refuge from the terrifying situation in which they found themselves.

There were lights, wild crazy lights, whirling and spinning, faces, portions of bodies, a Chinese woman, slender and beautiful and wearing a red satin gown. Who was she? He knew, but could not remember exactly; a maddening sense of futility enveloped him. Where was he? And why?

A low-level sense of nausea oppressed him for a while, but as it passed he realized that the Chitin had ceased to feed him. He was groaning softly to himself. The drug's effect was becoming very strong. The sound of his heart worried him; he kept thinking it was going to burst out of his chest. When it did, he presumed the Chitin would eat it and him. After a while that thought made him weep, his tears splashing down inside the helmet and rolling down his neck onto his chest.

Occasional tasters continued to patrol the humans' bodies; they found the tears.

The Vizier Mass responded by undertaking a quick medical check of the humans. Both were shivering, moaning, disorientated. Heart rates were up, temperatures too, and the sweat contained traces of adrenaline and other chemical signs of excitation and intoxication. The nest mind concluded after a quick survey that the humans had been affected by some trace alkaloid in the fungal carbohydrate material. Fortunately there was still one that had not been fed any such foodstuff should it prove fatal. For the moment the nest decided to watch and wait while the research section continued to attempt the production of a new communicator protein, designed for the captive beings, with their own biochemistry in mind.

30

THE MIND OF THE GREAT CHITIN NEST WAS IN SOME WAYS analogous to a choir of thousands of voices; at times there was chaos and cacophony; and then slowly the voices would come together, harmonizing, working into the same tune, forging a glorious tapestry of unity. Then for a while there would be great clarity, great potential of purpose, a moment for deep thinking, then it would pass and the drift back to cacophony would begin.

Except that this describes a far more orderly process than the reality, in which a complex tide of chemicals, elaborately arranged, molecule by molecule by busy vizier Chitin, was worked and reworked, carried back and forth across the ancient chains of memory in a slow-thinking dance that varnished thoughts, layer by layer, component protein by component, over the structures already laid down. Thus the surface was constantly worked, ripped up and laid down again, but each time there would be places where the past was left behind, an accurate record of what the nest had decided upon, laid down with precision on the molecular level. Of course, since the memory surface in the great nest had now reached a gross area of forty square kilometers, this meant that such permanent records of the great but slow-moving mind had to be simultaneously left behind in hundreds of millions of separate points, spread out across the memory maps—a task of coordination that in itself required enormous effort. The mind was slow to remember details, but it could always remember them given time. It was slow but chillingly precise.

The result was a slow-working biological computer with a strong survival urge and the ability to remember indelibly the events of centuries.

Now the great nest by the riverbank, an entity with no further sense of itself than ONE, being the center of the universe, with no memories of another except the First Nest, from which the first queens had come, was in something of a panic.

With frantic haste the nest researched the basic biochemistry of the human beings. Research chemists would have been awed, stunned even, by the speed with which Chitin could sift through the fine detail of terrestrial biochemistry.

The nest had tasted, and recorded the impressions thereof, an entire human being. Those taste impressions had become raw data, along with the wealth of observations chemical and behavorial that had been made from the living captives.

But the captives were not doing well. The nest angrily accused itself of impatience, of mishandling, mistasting the captives. The captives' condition was visibly decaying. The most useful captive, the younger male, seemed completely disoriented. It was also the one with the strongest traces of the strange Chitin substrate the nest had found on the skins and in the bodily fluids of all three. The chemical was present in tiny quantities, but it stuck out of the rest of the alien, mammalian protein traces like a flash of lightning against the background roils of a mighty thundercloud.

The chemical sent a strange thrill of wonder and apprehension through the nest, but that individual had become quite confused. The other male was equally degraded, copious fluids poured from the orifices in its head. The smaller female remained completely inert within the Vizier chamber. And if the nest had such things as "hairs" on the back of its huge old warty neck, they would have stood up stiff every time it thought of that bizarre chemical trace it had found, a tiny amount of communication protein, a substance of a different intrinsic order from everything else about the captive aliens. Their flesh materials and circulatory fluids were all of obvious biochemical nature; the artificial materials were polymers, metal alloys, and complex mixtures of components of combined hydrocarbon polymers, interesting ceramics, and complexes that were vaguely reminiscent of raw Chitin itself. However, the trace of communication protein was something else.

The ancient nest memories spoke vaguely of artificial, manufactured items. It spoke of the other world, where there was only Chitin and where Chitin worked in the Great Harmony and formed the Hive of the World. But that was not this world, and this world contained many creatures with the same structures and basic biochemistry and life processes as the captives, with some singular differences, which confirmed for the nest that the captives were not from this world at all. But how could they be from the world that was spoken of in the memory, the world of hive? On that world there was nothing except Chitin.

Except that there was this trace, very slight, only the matter of a few hundred molecules in the case of the older male, but unmistakable nonetheless, a fully formed communication protein, a molecule with the tendency to form helical chains, tripling, quadrupling, joining into complex toroids. Its form was plastic enough to take innumerable shapes, a property derived from the layering of amino acids in cunning formations that worked like complex clockwork devices. Touched by a communicating cell form, such as a human immune cell checking for intruding antigen, the communication protein would change its exterior coat to mimic perfectly the surface of a friendly cell. In this it was no more complex than some persistent viruses on the Chitin homeworld, but communication proteins contained far more intricate messages than simply the reproductive data contained in virus.

Unmistakable as it was, this strange chemical was odd in other ways. It appeared to address the alien organism itself rather than another Chitin vizier interface. In fact it seemed almost "flavorless" to the tasters, but working with such a tiny sample, even their fine judgment might be suspect. It did exhibit considerable flexibility, a high degree of elasticity in the long chains and subgroups. Possibly it performed several tasks, each different in some ways from the others.

The nest hypothesized that the relatively crude protein had a general physical tonic effect on the captive creatures' organs through an action upon the central nervous system. There were many movements within the general range of the strange protein that implied action at nerve endings. However, without more lengthy analysis of the creatures' immune systems and other such details, the nest was unable to come to a proper evaluation of the substance. The questions remained unanswered. Somewhere though there were other worlds, and on one of them these creatures had evolved.

The question was greater than that—for where were the Chitin that controlled these captives? And how was control maintained? Was it enforced through the odd communication protein? And did the captives come from the World of the Hive? Was this to be the end of the long exile here on the world that was not the real world?

The great nest was in such a pitch of excitement concerning all these questions that its powers of coordination were severely tested. The nest resolved to itself to take a good long time examining these captive creatures.

Except that the captives were in such poor condition. They might die or go into the strange coma state exhibited by the one who still lay curled in a ball in the center of the vizier chamber, oblivious to warrior bites. A light dusting of vizier excrement now covered her body.

If the captives died there could be no hope of finding answers to the great questions. Relentlessly the nest drove itself to fashion superior communication protein, a form similar at root to the plastic toroid of pharamol but vastly more complex in detail that would dovetail neatly with human nerve endings and provide a chemical interface to which other vizier communication proteins might be attached easily.

In another part of the nest, mind "tasters" worried over the threads of reproductive control protein that were present in most cell types in the captive creatures' bodies. What they found was odd—the universe was an older place than the nest had ever considered. The reproductive control protein, or DNA as understood by humans, was long and complex and rather messy. Far longer than that of most inhabitants of this world that was not the real world.

The nest understood such matters well. The evolutionary history behind it was obviously very long and complex. In that it was very different from Chitin reproductive control protein, which was short and plastic and very malleable, allowing a hive swiftly to change and adapt its worker forms at will.

In the incredibly complex triple-helix reproductive control protein, the nest found the evidence of the pre-Cambrian oceans and beyond them the traces left by invertebrate explosions of life that followed and the Devonian ascension by the fishes, through the amphibious and reptilian developments at the close of the Palaeozoic. And there the nest could even dimly read of the catastrophic events at the close of the Permian that had all but obliterated life on Earth. It was all there, an evolutionary record filled with powerful punctuations, a billion years' worth or more, recorded irregularly on the lumpy DNA in the captives' cells.

A history that had led vertebrate development to go far beyond what the nest knew of vertebrate life on the world that was not the real world. The nest now had a vestigial "taste" of Earth from the lungfish to humanity and with strong hints of much earlier eras, when nucleotides first bonded together in the oceans to form competing complex reproductive acids. Such biochemistry was, of course, familiar to the Chitin. But Chitin had evolved quickly on ancient Herxx, and without mass extinctions due to cometary strike, the pace of evolutionary change had lifted the hive insect ancestor of the great nests into the dominant position from which they had hived the world. Now there was another world.

Thus the universe was a more complex place too. There was the world that was not the real world, there was the world of Chitin, and there was another world from which these creatures had come.

But the nest wondered even more where the Chitin that controlled the creatures was. Had the Chitin from the homeworld gone to the world of the creatures and then come here, to the world that was not the real world? Were they perhaps worlds all laid out in a line, and thus were planets orbiting around the sun? This was a "theory" to which the great nest had become addicted, making measurements through specialized workers sent to the top of the great trees at night to make optical observations of the lights in the sky. From their motions the nest had deduced long ago that the world was round. To check it had measured the angle of the sun's rays at various intervals.

Thus this was perhaps a confirmation of the planets theory and now all three planets were lined up together and thus the great Chitin, from the home-world, were come to the world that was not the real world!

To know, however, the great nest had to fashion the communication protein, the "essence to open vertebrate nerve pathways" or simply "essence."

The work went on while Chosen gasped and shuddered in the grip of violent hallucinations. Spasms of nausea racked his body to the point where his internal organs ached dully from the abuse. He had developed a slight case of synaesthesia; the darkness looked like the smooth texture of the Chitin-worn dirt floor. The great putrescent stink of the nest sounded like a swarming of a million bees, and the sound of the breath in the hot silence smelled like waves of sewage, washing onto some long-dead terrestrial beach.

The thought had struck him, hard, as if delivered upon the anvil of his mind by the hammer of Thor, that he was dying. There had been a lethal dose of the mushroom toxin. His heart hammered inside his chest; tears streamed from his eyes. He had no idea why, whether he wept because of his mournful fate or because this was a sign of the infection by spruip fungus that he had been expecting.

Tombstones miles high paraded past his head beneath a harsh blue sun. The sky was dirty pink, and a noise of roaring, a dreadful exultation, filled everything. It was roaring in his ears, his pulse pounding, booming. The stones were carved by giant sculptors that resembled albino Woodwose. They engraved names upon the stones. His point of consciousness floated through the dreamscape toward them where they worked. They cut the names of the recently deceased. The roaring was high and mighty, all around them. There were the names; the great chisels swung into position, huge hammers rose and fell, stone dust flew. He knew his name would be next and shook his head crying weakly, "no."

The image broke down and fled away; another phantasm immediately replaced it as the drug reached a peak within his system. Great doors opened, on other doors, elaborately carved and decorated doors that opened endlessly onto more doors that now bore the carvings of ferocious faces. Great evil djinn of the void, crocodilia and manticores, they snarled and gaped and then sundered in half as they parted, rolling aside as doors, to reveal the next great face, huge eyes boring down from the void, and on until, at last, there was a room, a space, there was no telling which exactly, in which stood the pool, the Moon pool, rotating on its side in the center, its surface so still and so terrible, a one-way membrane to another darkness, a world of endless silence and cold.

Chosen did not want to die, but the nausea had left him weak and almost unable to move his limbs. Nor could he remember if there was any way that he could not die. The hallucination seemed very vivid. He wanted to go toward that pool, he tried to get up on his knees and crawl but found it difficult.

Then a searing pain lit up his hand. Chitin warriors were biting him; he yelled aloud shocking himself by the sudden metallic smell, harsh and hot, that resounded in his head and sat back again, holding himself still while the drug-amplified stings ricocheted around his nervous system.

"Stay still!" he screamed to no one in particular, "Don't move a fucking thing." It smelled like burning animal fat.

There were more workers; streams of them ran up his chest with a sensation that stung his eyes with little flickers of red-and-orange lights. Soon he shivered under a mat of them reaching all the way up to his chin. Another kind was coming, snaking its way up the bodies of the others as if they were steps on some bizarre pyramid and his mouth were the altar.

They came at last to their destination, and among them was a specialized vizier form, hatched only moments before but already with a long stiff proboscis through which to fire essence into the mouth or other open orifice on the head organ. It came forward, warriors bit his lips, and he gasped and opened his mouth.

The adapted vizier came forward and fired a tiny stream of essence onto the back of the tongue.

The workers began to dissassemble the living pyramid of Chitin scaffolding that had surrounded Chosen.

Chosen felt a sudden difference; the Moon pool glowed. A djinn of enormous power was at work in his system, the nausea returned, the spasm was long and hard and dry, and more tears were forced from his eyes as he sobbed and shuddered.

The shuddering grew, and for a blinding second he felt as if he had taken pharamol, very good pharamol at that, and then some vast force with giant hands tore apart the moon pool as if it were a veil that had always lain across his consciousness, a black cloth kept over a mirror too bright to look at in the midday sun. Huge shining light, a sensation as if his entire body were singing, waves rippling over his skin, intimate, sensuous, as if he were being stroked by the most skilled masseuse.

The nausea was gone; so was the hammering of his pulse. Instead his brain seemed to float in a great darkness punctuated with bright points of light, as if they were the stars. But the stars tasted sweetly; they also sang in tiny shrill voices that sounded distant and weak.

He shook his head, put his hands up to his temples.

The shining power inside him was working higher; it felt exactly like a very big dose of pharamol. The sensation had ended the nausea; it had dried his nose and throat uncomfortably too. His nose itched mightily, and he had a desire to sneeze that also tasted sweet and hot.

He closed his eyes, gave a groan, and then the communication essence, having completed the initial medical tasks, grouped itself entirely on the identified connective areas and changed Chosen Fundan into the first individual of a new race.

He gasped. His mind stripped suddenly of normal brain randomness, a new "sense" had appeared. As if a new set of eyes had opened, a new pair of ears, an entirely new sense of touch and smell. With it came an awareness of a new way to die; he had but to use it and he could cease this torment forever. But Chosen Fundan had no wish to die, knew that he would go down to the last spasm in the grip of the spruip, with spore bodies already pushing through the flesh, fighting to live for the last seconds, to deny the Moon pool.

And he knew, with dreadful seriousness, that this was no hallucination, for in the next moment his telepathic sense expanded outward to the limit of its field, about four kilometers in every direction, and he sucked in his breath in wonder and terror at the new world thus presented to him.

Coils and threads of consciousness sparked multicolor images, like faces on bubbles of silver, caroming on a radar screen in his mind that swept around and around, locating thought patterns as if they were aircraft. And as he "saw," he focused and "felt" or absorbed the goings-on within each such small mind. The hunger of the young nibbla, the ferocity in the mind of a Were. Insects glittered like hot points of light, a flickering galaxy overlaying everything else.

And around him, nearby, he sensed the nest, its mind like some great reef of consciousness, a glittering skein filled with dusky motes and sparkling threads mounded up like a small chain of hills.

But this telepathic sense had only just awoken; it was unfocused yet; indeed it would be months, years, before he learned to use all of its varied abilities. It was soft, like a baby's hands, and as yet he barely understood it.

He screamed in revulsion; the madness had taken him too far. He was losing control; this was simply too much. But he found he didn't believe that either.

His scream tasted like red meat; it degraded into soilness. A dry shuddering terror racked him to the edge of the darkness. There floated the Moon pool, still and terrible. Beyond lay the darkest of nights.

He swung there a moment, staring down into the pool; in a moment like an iris opened wide on the death of time. In a second he would be there, on the far side of the discontinuity. And then he knew, a great certainty built in his heart, which had ceased hammering so frantically. He knew what was happening to him, and it was as if a beam had originated in his forebrain, for he looked to Zhao six and read the fellow's tormented thoughts with ease. Such terror, such confusion, the man was in a terrible state. Chosen sensed a fever and knew that it must mean the spruip. They would all die soon, even he with his new sense.

The beam flicked on, exactly as if he were aiming an electric torch into a dark thicket, and then he was aware of the nest, and it of he.

Never in all its calculations had the nest expected this. The captive's mind blazed beside it like some fireball descended from the sun. The great nest shrank back in horror from what it had unwittingly helped create.

Chosen saw the nest as a coral reef of softly glistening patterns, all inlaid upon each other in a level of density that went far beyond such human memory storage systems as ultrafiche or laser video. To his new sense it was a thing of beauty, a repository of centuries of accumulated minute remembrance.

Realizations were coming to him, even as he began to impinge upon the strange alien mind of the nest. The Chitin had fed him another drug; it had seen how ill he was and had done something to try to help. What had happened then was unknowable, at least for now, in fact with the hallucinatory mushroom drug still at work in his body, plus the varied mental shocks that the new senses were giving him, it was hard to know exactly much of anything except that he was still in the nest and still alive.

To be living at that point was something wondrous strange. He was sure he should've been killed. Ah, but the spruip would soon change all that. The thought brought a wry grin momentarily to his lips. How bizarre his fate had become! To die now would only add a further layer of quixotic foolishness to an already foolish doom.

Then the thought of what would be lost to the human race, to the universe itself, through his death, came home to him, and he groaned a little, a quiet sound deep in the ground.

They might never rediscover this! He would die and take humanity's ESP potential with him.

He looked for some way out.

What more did the nest know? His curiosity spurred him, and without thinking about it, as if he'd done that sort of thing every day of his life, he projected his mind forward into the reefs and canyons of the maze of the nest mind.

Even as he did so and impinged upon it, he felt the rage and hate and underlying terror. Panic swelling within sparkling terrains of mentality, the fear came, then the hate, and the harsh orders that were already being extruded and passed to Archstone Chitin.

"*NO!*" his mind howled. "*No*, not the warriors! Stop!"

Hold back the hungry mouths of the millions.

And incredibly the nest did stop, extruding a powerful passivity signal in the next moment. The warriors were ordered first to mass and then to disperse a few moments later. The nest trembled, frozen, in the grip of a coercive power like nothing it had ever known. Chosen read the nest's fear at once and almost laughed; never had a bigger monster freaked out over a smaller mouse. The nest mass had to be in the region of thirty tons of living insects, and he weighed less than a hundred kilos. Then he launched himself into the midst of the nest mind, which squealed to itself in a writhing horror.

"VIOLATION . . . VIOLATION," it howled on the mental plane.

The ultimate horror had been awakened—a trojan horse taken into the nest. An intelligence roaming at will through the memory cores, an intelligence inspired by the nest itself. There was no way to combat it. For the first time in its existence the nest was not in a position to coerce other life-forms. The sheer fright brought on by the realization was enough to push the nest into a chaotic state known to Chitin talkers as "frustration flux." Untreated, it could cause a young nest to break up, certain vizier groups splitting the nest in civil wars.

But Chosen was also in a position to offer the nest what it sought more than all other things but life itself, access to memories and knowledge beyond its own.

Carefully he projected thoughts to the nest. "I can give you the knowing that you seek." Scarlet lemons were bursting on the back of his tongue and eyeballs, a residual effect from the hallucinogen. He blinked them away, still feeling somewhat better, less weak and sick.

Again he projected to the nest. "I can bring you the knowings." And the nest heard him, and the fear was instantly balanced by a tidal wave of hope. Did the captive bring news?!

And he projected the story of Herxx and of the coming of the Arizel tki Fenrille. How the Chitin insect rose to hive the world and, indeed, the entire Solar System that had borne it. Nothing but Chitin and genetically altered Chitin existed. The Chitin hive had constructed star-crossing vessels, vast and relatively slow NAFAL ships.

Chitin crossed the deeps of space. They colonized Fenrille, began the program to hive the planet. All non-Chitin life was to be sterilized, the forests cleared and replaced with Chitin food-crop monocultures. The nests aroused the defense mechanisms of the planet, but even the Woodwose found it difficult to battle the Chitin.

The Arizel tki Fenrille were forced to return from their interuniversal wanderings and defend their homeworld and their forest. After making every attempt to negotiate peacefully with the Chitin, the Arizel concluded that the Chitin hive mind was too obdurate, too self-centered even to consider the concept of negotiation. Accordingly, a black hole singularity was moved by the Arizel and pitched into a tight elliptic about the homeworld of the Chitin.

Zglab the home star was an aged yellow star, close to a period of instability. The sudden appearance of a black hole singularity only a hundred million kilometers away sent Zglab directly into a nova state. The star's outer envelope blew off, enormous fiery prominences were hurled out to the orbits of the furthermost planets of the system, and Herxx, the homeworld, was scorched down to bedrock after the atmosphere burned away in the first hour or so.

Subsequently Herxx itself had been swallowed by the black hole, breaking down into a fine gruel of tiny particles in the accretion ring that formed around the hole while old Zglab wobbled and exploded periodically, from old age suddenly unstable. Of the Chitin insect only the expanding shell of space armadas had remained. The Arizel had systematically destroyed these, expunging the Chitin everywhere except on the planet Fenrille, which had been the insect's downfall. There the Chitin was modified by the Arizel and incorporated into the complex web of life that survived around the Arizel forests on the ring continent, the Hokkh.

The nest absorbed all this; it took time; parts had to be repeated and explained several times. But eventually the nest understood, and a great quaver of misery rose from it.

Chosen projected further concepts. The nest came to know that there were Chitin nests all across the planet. In the Highlands of the central mountains, the Chitin had even been introduced to new habitats by these mammalian bipeds the humans.

There in the highlands the humans "assisted" the Chitin and the Chitin responded by making the communication protein that the nest had discovered tiny traces of on the captives bodies.

"WHO HUMANS? THEN/NOW," the nest mind asked.

And Chosen projected the story of the human occupation of Fenrille. The humans had come by fast NAFAL, in small numbers at first. From a star that might well have been colonized by the Chitin if their space armadas had all arrived safely.

On Fenrille the humans were unable to overcome the highly defensive ecosystems set up long, long ago by the Arizel tki Fenrille. They had then discovered the Chitin and formed a desire for the communication protein which lengthened and enhanced their lives.

This the nest could understand. These poor late evolutes, from a world that had seen many periods of catastrophic climate change and subsequent extinctions, were now dependent on wonderful Chitin communication proteins. They had become symbionts of some kind, but the relationship sounded as if it were stacked in the Chitin's favor.

Chosen flattered the nest, thinking already of the potential for using coercive telepathy. Once suitably programmed such a nest would be a perfect chemical factory, ready to churn out complex acids and protein chains as ordered.

And a great idea struck him. He would coerce the nest into making Alvosterine! The captives need not die!

First, though, he determined to find a way out of the nest. Leaving the Chitin in a state of shock, still numbed by the revelations he had shown it, he maneuvered himself back onto his knees and tried to ignore the stabs of pain he received from the blisters there. When he moved back into the passage that led to the vizier chamber, he found Chi Lin Wei still immobile beneath the trees of memory. He picked her up and half carried her, half dragged her up a sloping adit that eventually narrowed to a gap about two inches across.

"Widen the opening!" and he used his coercive power again. In a few moments workers poured into the tunnel ahead. Furious activity began. A few minutes later the activity slackened, and the tunnel had been widened to a passage about a meter across. It was still tight going, however, and it took considerable effort to pull Chi Lin Wei's body up that tube. Throughout the process she remained locked in a trance, and Chosen felt the sweat down the interior of his helmet again, his knees burned terribly, and he itched all over his body. On the telepathic plane, her mind was curiously blocked, a mental shield of some kind existed around her. When he finally raised her body out of the tube and laid her down beside a relatively slender tree root, he felt dizzy from the exertion, but the synaesthesia was at work again and his fatigue tasted like sugared bean paste and there was a loud clanging in his eyes.

Still she remained unconscious. He whistled in admiration for the strength of whatever mind control method she was using. There was a sound behind him; Zhao six emerged from the hole in the ground having faithfully followed Chosen up the tube. Chosen was thankful that Zhao six was still able to function at all. The man climbed out, blinking, hallucinating wildly, his eyes staring into a fantastic world of moving images that had nothing to do with the deep-shaded greenery of reality.

It was early morning. The eastern light filtered through the forest alongside a breeze. Although it was already edging into the eighties and the morning mists made everything damp, the weather on the surface was a great relief after the heat of the great nest.

Chosen had an uncontrollable urge to rip off the filthy space suit and run to the river to clean his body.

He pulled off the space suit helmet and took a deep breath. Spicy but reviving. He released the nest from coercion and sensed immediately a new consensus in that giant mind—the hate and fear had been transformed into worship. The blinding god that had awoken in the nest had not harmed the nest. Despite its powers, it had simply removed itself and the other captives. The sacred trees of memory had been naked and vulnerable, yet the god had not harmed them in any way. That such absence of malice existed was confirmation of the nest's greatest hopes— that was how it must have been in the old world, where there had been harmony among the nests.

He had laid Chi Lin Wei against a root with her legs stretched out in front of her. After a little while, however, her body pulled itself back into a fetal ball.

Behind them rose one of the nest's ventilation fins, a fan-shaped structure made of sunbaked mud five meters high and almost as long, with an average thickness of half a meter. Millions of air holes penetrated the upper parts of the structure, filtering air in and out of the enormous complex below.

Zhao six squatted beside Chi Lin Wei, drooling from his mouth and nose, a pitiable sight. Chosen dropped the helmet and began pulling off the slimy, befouled rags of the space suit. His battered knees had bled all over the lower part of the leggings, which were crusted. He could only tear them free at some cost to himself.

A black biting fly circled his head, and for a moment he panicked and reached for the helmet again. Then he recalled his coercive power and used it on the fly, which immediately flew away.

Chosen rocked back on his hips and laughed, laughed until tiny tears ran down his cheeks.

31

CHOSEN FOUND A NARROW RIVER CHANNEL NOT FAR AWAY AND carefully washed himself at the end of a root. Then he scrambled back to the others and immediately scanned the Chitin nest under the ground. It remained quiescent, running through the recent wondrous events over and over as it laid down memories on permanent cores.

Chosen broke in, received this time with a warmth, a welcome that was almost ecstatic. The old nest was in a state called "purring" by Chitin talkers, people who for the most part of course had only seen terrestrial cats on a computer display.

Communication was easy; the nest could sense the importance of his need. It understood at once; the spruip fungus was a problem for the Chitin too, something it battled with various antifungal agents, none of which were of use in a mammalian body, not without some redesign. The nest was happy to work on the problem. It would save the god, it had to, for there was no other.

Chosen turned back to Zhao six. He had brought some river water back in his helmet. With this he gently washed Zhao six's fevered face. If the nest could produce an antifungal drug soon enough, they might be able to save Zhao six, but from the little moans that were beginning to break into the babbling and snuffling, the poor man was beginning to feel the early growth of the spore bodies within him. When the fruiting bodies grew, however, then the real agony would begin. In time they would break through the skin and recovery would be impossible.

Already Chosen felt his own nose beginning to run; mucus kept building up in his mouth, and his skin was itching intolerably. The spruip had taken hold. Everything depended on the nest's ability to manufacture chemicals.

After a short rest, he determined to try and awaken Chi Lin Wei. He completed a short sweep of the area about them and drove away all the biting flies. Nothing larger than a sarmer mackee could be detected in his range.

He cast his telepathic sense toward Chi Lin Wei. Her mind was still wrapped in protective fields. As he pressed against them, so they pressed back. Her resistance intrigued him. Obviously there were complexities to this new power.

He focused. The resistance continued, but he was beginning to receive impressions, blurry as if filtered through glue. A mantra, repeated endlessly, BODILOVE, LOVETHEBODY, BODILOVE, LOVETHEBODY. It seemed to swell from the very fabric of the woman's brain; it echoed, rolling and swelling, sighing and breathing.

Chi Lin Wei sat entrenched, far into the "deep state" of Maza practicians, a state which only death or her own will could interrupt. She was impervious to pain or other stimulus.

Finally he sensed something else. Somehow he had penetrated a gallery of memories. His consciousness sifted through them like a net through deep water.

The Chairman, the tall deep-chested man with the beetling brows and the deceptively quiet voice. He appeared again and again. Once it was after her mother and her older sisters had been taken away. She was seven, and she climbed the thick grapevine that grew on the terrace off the palace's top floor, a section where she was made to "play," by herself. Nanny had fallen asleep by her little TV, so Chi Lin Wei climbed the vine. On the roof she found the garden.

The garden covered much of the roof of the great palace, looming a thousand meters above New Baghdad. It was planted with a variety of shrubs, beds of flowers, the style very much in twenty-fifth-century Peking manner, semiwild, with small glades and clearings and masses of flowers in each.

There were also the people, in advanced stages of artificial leprosy, usually chained to a stake hammered into the ground. There was a man with no hands or feet, just seeping stumps that gradually declined toward his knees and elbows. His face was an open ruin, his genitals withered to a putrescent scrap of flesh.

Men, a few women, here and there, in advanced stages of decay but still alive, pitiful, croaking to the little mistress who had climbed up to their dreadful perch.

Then in a clearing she found her sister, Loo Sun, chained to a stake driven deep into the ground. Her face disfigured by a beating, her breath harsh, her eyes wild. Chi Lin Wei turned and ran. In her room, with a cushion stuffed into her mouth, she finally screamed.

Another time, another memory. Her closest friend, her teenage lover, Fei Wong, beautiful Sinoamerican boy, was being taken away. The chairman himself was present with a grim little smile on his face. The doctors wore white. Fei was terrified, he knew he would never come back. She was seventeen; Fei had been her first love. The door closed behind them with a horrifying finality.

A face swam into view. A Chinese face that wept for Chi Lin Wei. Chosen could not tell when or where at first. A wave of powerful emotion, complex eddies, accompanied this remembrance; it resonated in the mind of Chi Lin Wei even now, a century of life afterward. It was a good face, strong, a generous mouth, eyes with a certain flat, staring quality but penetrating, intelligent.

Deng Chao, her lover, coconspirator, the leader of the Hikee faction within the politburo. Always a rival to the chairman but always a trusted rival. They had ousted Koliakov together; their lives had been on the line right next to each other.

Deng had thought, in the end, to manipulate her, use her to help him control the chairman. He had not intended assassination; that *she* had forced on him, gradually. One by one the alternative paths of action were cut off until he was desperate enough to try her scheme.

It failed, but Deng got away from the chairman's private office. No one but Deng and the chairman knew what had happened, but the chairman had risen at the first puff of the gas and, after throwing a table at Deng, had fled through a secret door.

Deng was doomed. He came to her and wept on her bedside until she seized the poison gas spray and directed it into Deng's face, killing him in an instant.

The chairman questioned her carefully after that. In fact he never fully trusted her again; she was never in his presence alone. But she lived; he was at least not convinced of her guilt.

Deng's entire family went to the sharks—a tragic irony in that Deng hated his wife and her children, none of which he claimed belonged to him, and had hardly been in their company more than a day in the past ten years.

More memories burst into Chosen's mind's eye, in fragments, whirling quickly past. He was entering Chi Lin Wei's mind in a new way; this was not the way he had entered the minds of Zhao six or the great Chitin nest.

It was as if the actual consciousness of Chi Lin Wei were absent; he was rummaging through her memories but at an unconscious level, which lent them such a dreamlike quality.

Memories of Luna, first of Moonbase One, hideously cramped,

military discipline in the service of the Party and Military Intelligence. A stifling period of several years' duration.

Other memories too, of Luna City and the sexually extravagant society there. In fact these memories were endless; the woman had lived more than a century on Luna, in a hedonistic retreat that evoked emotions beyond Chosen's understanding.

Then there was a new sensation. The memories were receding; Chi Lin Wei's trance was breaking open. He was penetrating the barriers.

Her question was ringed with rage sign. "Who are you?" It was brief and violent.

He identified himself and broke asunder her meditation state. Her defenses evaporated in the instant.

"How?" was all she could manage to say, though her mind was racing, offering him a salad of schemes and impulses.

She would kill him if it was possible. Use him if feasible. She saw this as a step toward her dream. He shook his head sadly at the scope of this dream, which was nothing less than total domination of Fenrille and the usurpation of control of the supplies of longevity protein from the Highland clans. Chi Lin Wei wanted it all!

But now he had arisen, a new threat piled on the rest. Her hopes had never seemed so far away.

He pushed away, keeping the mind contact. Letting her feel the power a little.

She reacted with a hiss, awaking and getting to her feet with barely a stagger before assuming a karate posture. He laughed. He was dying of spruip, only a few hours from the agony, and she was offering battle.

"Look, that's all very well, but it's irrelevant now. What does matter is that now I know you and I can no longer be harmed by you."

At this her eyes narrowed. She had observed Zhao six; she was virtually alone now with only this odd roundeye boy. And he had changed into a monster! Yet even as she thought about the revolver and getting it into her hands, he read her thoughts and held it up and waved it at her.

"Beat you to that one, I'm afraid."

She hissed. "Get the fuck out of my brain, you monster!"

He laughed at her again. "Stop being so paranoid. I'm not like you. I'm not intent on killing you; in fact I'm trying to save your life along with mine. If you'd just relax we could concentrate on that and forget all these mad schemes of yours."

She gave a cry of inarticulate rage and flounced away trying to blank her mind to give him nothing to see. She ran a mantra through her thoughts, working to concentrate on it and assume a Maza state.

His laughter was forced. He withdrew. She was inexplicable, irrational, and he believed he had seen why. Her life in the home system had been dominated by paranoiac fears. Always she was under surveillance, always aware that the chairman might decide against her and then the men in white coats would come and take her away.

He shivered slightly, although it was already thirty degrees centigrade and extremely humid. His skin itched; he turned his telepathic beam to the nest; his urgency was unmistakable. She would come round, she would have to. Pretty soon she too would begin to itch and shiver.

32

THE HOURS SLID BY, THE NEST WORKING FEVERISHLY, BUILDING the new antifungal agent molecule atom by atom.

Chi Lin Wei had begun to feel the effects. Her nose streamed, her skin itched as if a fiery fury had possessed it. At the thought of the ugly black spore bodies beginning to form in her flesh she wanted to weep.

Eventually she came and sat beside the two men. Zhao six was moaning uncontrollably now. Under his skin, on the chest and abdomen, black points were thrusting up, like obscene acne pimples arranged in radial arrays above the thrusting spore bodies.

To poor Zhao six it was as if he were being slowly impaled on hundreds of needles, working their way slowly through his body. He could no longer move; death was but a matter of merciful hours away. His mouth already wore a beard of foam; soon it would turn red as the body began to disintegrate under the steady onslaught of the spruip. From his lips came disjointed groans, little screams that fluted every so often.

Chi Lin Wei could not bear to look at him. She shook her head as if that would banish their doom. Then she said in a determined voice, "But you should shoot him! Poor Zhao six is dying, the last, my last Zhao. But you must free him of this pain; I cannot bear it; it is beyond my strength to sit here and listen to him. Please, take your gun and finish him off." She spoke as if he were a pet animal of some kind. The tone made Chosen's neck hairs rise. They who came from the home system brought strange ways with them.

Chosen bade her hush. Somehow he found room for hope in his voice.

"Look, the nest may succeed. Perhaps he can be saved. I have heard it said by old deep jungle hunters that people can recover from the spruip up to the point where the skin bursts over the spore bodies. Maybe we can still save him. So I hesitate to use the gun. Of course, if the nest fails us, then I will end his agony. I would do the same for you too, although I feel that you

246

may have to dispatch me, for I seem to be somewhat ahead of you in the course of infection."

Chi Lin Wei stared at him aghast.

"And I came all this way to die like this. My father will laugh until his sides hurt when he finds out. I thought I had finally outfoxed him, you see." She looked at him almost furtively, the habit of centuries. "I tried to kill him, twice, something he never suspected. I tried once, long ago, but we failed, and he never had any evidence of my complicity—no real evidence anyway. But then I tried again, not long before I left the home system, and that time I know he found out. I left traces, unavoidable, I'm afraid." She shrugged.

Naive questions bubbled out of him.

"But why is it like this? I experienced some of your memories, I felt such fear, such terror of life. I do not understand."

She laughed, harshly. He sounded so young! "You cannot know. It would take longer than we probably have left to live for me to even try to explain to you the way life was in the palace. New Baghdad is a large city, but it is a joyless place seething with intrigue. As for my own family, my mother and sisters were taken away one day. I was the youngest by several years. But they went, just like that." She snapped her fingers at him.

"I watched twenty separate families sprout in my father's house. Each came from a new, beautiful young woman of the highest cadre. In a few years each became infected with the treachery of the place and each was removed abruptly by the secret police. I believe most of them were given fairly clean deaths, but my mother and her elder daughters went to the garden. They were the first, you see. He grew more merciful later on. I saw them once, afterward. I cannot describe what I saw—even today I dare not let myself visualize that scene again."

She had an odd, bitter smile. "As for my friends most of them went to the garden of course. And here I am, being devoured by a filthy fungus in another garden." Her bitterness shivered in the green gloom of midday.

"But you survived the palace. Why did you try to kill him after that?"

Chi Lin Wei glowered at him in the grip of strong emotion. "For revenge, for my sisters, my mother; he sent them to the garden too."

"I know, I saw them in your memories, so much pain, so much fear. I—"

"You stay out of my mind!" she screamed. "I survived my

247

father, and if it weren't for you, I might have lived through this too. Yu Zhao was right! You are an agent for our enemy. You are too skillful to be anything else. We should have left you on the starship."

He was amazed, as always when she turned on him.

"This is hardly my idea of a good way to assassinate someone, you know. I mean, even if I was on a suicide mission, I don't think I'd choose the spruip as the means." Heavy-handed irony was lost on her. The hate had returned to her face.

She hunched away from him, trying furiously to blank her mind. But he felt no desire to return to her terror-haunted memories. Then poor Zhao six began to scream in a loud voice. His voice was a terrible cry from the pits of hell.

Chosen turned his attention back to the nest and found a sense of cautious elation. The nest had prepared a drug from a bacterial culture grown in the abdomens of specialized workers. The Vizier Mass had already dispatched workers to bring the substance to the humans.

He looked down at his own skin, where black pinpoints had formed. If the Chitin nest had made a mistake on the toxic side of the delicate equation, he hoped it would simply be a quicker death.

Once again the ground became matted with millions of brown bodies that converged on the humans and ran up their bodies in endless lines to deposit a thin gruel on their lips. Chi Lin Wei had trouble holding still, crushing dozens of workers each time she succumbed to her fears. Fortunately the nest was now more tolerant of the blundering humans.

To Chosen it was just another almost flavorless gruel, forming slowly on his lips and tongue until there was almost a mouthful, which he swallowed, the dosage based on the nest's rough estimate based on Chosen's description of Alvosterine.

After a while the workers withdrew, disappearing back into the nest.

Chosen checked the revolver. There were still shells, enough for all of them.

The effect of the drug would probably show up in Chi Lin Wei first, since she was still far behind the men in the extremity of infection. Whether Zhao six would live was problematical; the spore bodies had stretched the skin to breaking point. The poor man's face was stretched taut, his mouth half-open as he continued to emit strange, disturbed cries. The black dots stippled his face as well; they were growing large.

Soon however Chosen began to feel another sensation, a

discomfort, worse than the itch, and when he moved! He almost screamed as dozens of what felt like white-hot points stung his chest and abdomen. Trembling, he scrutinized his skin more closely. He was about to join Zhao six in hell.

The spore bodies glistened under the skin, still the size of pinheads but growing steadily as his body weakened under the assault of the fungus, millions of his cells dying every second to be devoured by the invader. In time the pinheads would swell to the size of golf balls, quivering on long stalks above his carcass.

They sat with their backs to the roots and said nothing while trying to ignore poor Zhao six's sounds. Once Chosen reached to scratch and felt the hot needles again and had to stifle a scream. It was astonishingly painful; he marveled that such intense agony could be possible. He realized dully that within a short period of time he would be unable to move. Waves of nausea came and went, and gradually it seemed to Chosen Chi Lin Wei's sniffles faded away. She stopped scratching.

At about the same time he noticed that his nose and mouth had dried and the furious itching had lessened a little. He stared at the black spots under the skin. Were they still growing? Would he be able to tell? Then he looked at Zhao six. Here and there bloody matter was seeping from breaks in the skin where spore bodies had erupted. Chosen counted five breaks.

Time passed harrowingly slowly, but the itching abated and was replaced by a powerful nausea. Chosen had nothing to bring up from his already shriveled stomach and could only cough weakly despite the unbelievable agony the moment cost, and lean against the root wall and sob for breath between bouts. Now and then he heard Chi Lin Wei and Zhao six doing much the same sort of thing.

Hours dragged by. The nausea slowly came to an end. Beni was far down in the afternoon sky when Chosen noticed that the black spots under his skin were breaking up, turning red and white in some cases as they became real pimples when the body defense mechanisms attacked the decaying remnants of the fungal nodes.

He would live! He wanted to shout for joy but felt too weak and contented himself with pulling himself upright. The nodes might be dying, but his nerves still screamed at their presence. Any movement at all was agonizing. The nodes, hundreds of them, would degenerate into large infected pustules.

Chi Lin Wei was asleep, and Zhao six still lived—the spore bodies had ceased to grow. But as they declined, bacteria would soon be at work. Zhao six's body would have to make a terrific effort to fight off all these assaults.

They had to have food; so much was obvious to Chosen. The nest then; he would coerce the nest, and it would bring them food.

Chosen surveyed his body, stippled with black spots even in the genital region. His trials had barely begun, it was obvious.

He turned his head slightly to look at Zhao six—hot stabs of pain instantly punished him for it—and he saw the Woodwose standing beside the ventilation fin.

It stood perfectly still. Chosen was staring into eight beady eyes that regarded him intently. He dared not breathe. It was huge, far taller than he had ever seen before . . . except for the 'wose they had passed on the raft. This was the father of 'wose, the great shaggy-trunked, spindly-legged granddaddy of the race of tree guards. It was so close that he knew those huge hands could reach him in less than a second.

Did he dare to try to communicate? Was there any other option? Chosen decided not and flashed a mental probe at the Woodwose before those hands could go into action.

He encountered a very alien mind, a level where a ferocious thought kept blinking on and off like an alarm light. "PEST THINGS (UNKNOWN BIPEDS), EXTERMINATE." Beyond this thought however was a controlling influence. From somewhere in the mysterious mind there was another source of authority. Something was blocking the Woodwose's normal instinctual responses.

He detected considerable confusion. The 'wose felt lost, and very alone, which seemed strange. The great forest was filled with 'wose. Yet this was a lost 'wose, seemingly in the grip of some kind of schizophrenia.

Could he communicate? The thoughts of the 'wose were strong and direct and limited; he pressed for a contact.

"EXTERMINATE, PEST THINGS."

"Not pest things."

"EXTERMINATE, PEST THINGS."

"Not exterminate."

"(UNKNOWN BIPEDS) MOUTHS OF THE MOTHER TREES, EXTERMINATE."

"Why?"

(UNKNOWN BIPEDS) . . ."

"Not pest things."

"(UNKNOWN BIPEDS) PEST THINGS . . ."

"But not pest things."

250

"EXTERMINATE."

It was hard to argue with the Woodwose. And clearly the mental powers awoken in his brain by the Chitin nest were not all-powerful. He attempted to coerce the Woodwose and received nothing but a flash of hate.

But on a deeper level, beneath the Woodwose's conscious mind, something peculiar was going on. Something lurked furtively in the velvety depths of the strange alien mind. A simple kind of mind, very direct, rooted in conceptions that were overwhelmingly alien and hence indecipherable on a cursory examination. The cycle that connected the 'wose to the mother trees was a complex one of many cycles. Leavening life from plant to animal within the wood, endowing the mouths of the trees with their vigor and strength. He received an intense impression at one point concerning "bark" and "barkness," a state of security that somehow conveyed to Chosen a feeling of womblike safety.

Chosen investigated, pushed his probe toward the unconscious, the "dark" regions below. There were many confusions. The 'wose memory was fragmented, everything was wrong, even the color of the sun. But the 'wose obeyed a control, a tiny "voice" that whispered, leaking thought modifiers through into the conscious level.

The 'wose remained still. Chosen cautiously pushed his probe toward the controlling influence. He crossed some mental trip wire and for a moment felt as if he had put his mind into the equivalent of a noose trap. Something pressed "down," compressing his consciousness, holding it tight-focused within the thoughts of the 'wose.

An intricate array of mental compulsions sprang full blown into his mind. Chosen gasped in wonder for a moment. Then sucked in his breath as an Arizel glyph flowered into his mind.

Trickling and gleaming, it twinkled into existence, silvery and quick, alien thought arrayed in such detailed convolution that it was unreadable until it decoded itself, in sequence, thought images welling up from the deepest level of consciousness, taking shapes that slithered around meaning and somehow reacted with his mind to almost instantly translate to human thought patterns. Still the concepts were strange.

Like a snowflake, the mote of consciousness from the Divider melted against the young human mind. That was but the beginning of a process of transfer and then of transformation.

The glyph rang with notes of announcement, the Divider's characteristic descriptive glyph, a tao sign in which black and white subdivided to infinity, connected the announcement with the astonishing "secondary process."

Chosen sat down sharply, not even aware of the stabs of agony from the dying spore bodies. The euphonious "sounds" in his mind were followed by crumbling image clusters that wobbled through his thoughts. A coercion was applied as well— the clusters forced him to attend; he was pricked into awareness. There was an undercurrent of urgency, enormous urgency, a message from very far away, and a terrible doom.

And abruptly Chosen saw the crystal sands of the beach of forever, on the shores of a pink ocean. It was as if he were there, floating above them.

He was drawn across them, and it felt as if he were flying, in a dream. And ahead there was an enormous structure of fanciful towers and crystalline cubes, all in some shining material. A moat ringed it, a drawbridge spanned the moat, and inside the massive gate was a creature. He had no idea what it was, but it was built on the same herculean scale as the castle. It resembled a huge lozenge, dark gray, smooth-skinned, with a forest of slender limbs, incongruously thin structures, that supported it beneath. In other longer limbs that might have been tentacles, it held instruments of some kind that gave off a blue light of singular intensity.

The images of his mind were colored by an intense emotion, which surprised Chosen, since he had decided that this was clearly a message from a great Arizel. They were said to be beyond emotion and physical form, so why was such mournful sadness attached to the visual images? Was the huge, lozenge thing the Arizel in question?

Then the tao signs, forever subdividing black into white and vice versa, reappeared, and a face seemed to form in his mind. It was an austere, alien face that was both wise and quite ferocious. As if a sheep's face had been merged with that of an eagle.

The eyes were overlarge in that head, but they were also reminiscent of fein eyes, and they seemed to gaze into Chosen's eyes or past them and directly into his mind with an astonishing intentness.

"I speak to you from across a great void, a gulf that encompasses distances beyond your comprehension. I speak from an extremity of need and an awareness of a danger to my colleagues of the Arizel tki Fenrille and even to our universe—a terrible threat that must be extinguished. However, I have been taken unawares, am captive, and must perforce coerce you to my aid.

252

You shall be given the instructions. The tertiary process is exacting, but if your heart is true, you shall survive it."

The face appeared to speak to him; the lips moved. Chosen marveled.

Before he could think of a fitting reply, glyph symbols flickered before him in an accelerating torrent that seemed to carry him down a glowing tube of data forms, all inscribed in tiny pictures that shone in silver and gold.

"Accept the dying of the monsters; what they offer is essential," rang in his mind for some reason. He had no idea what it might mean.

The silvery tube sensation picked up speed, revolved, spun, whirled, and opened once more on a "hallway" of glistening adamantine. Chalcedony and purple loadstone rimmed the doors, and in the ways stood the monsters.

Evil-eyed, the bull-face monster opened toward him. He faced it as it bared vast jaws and showed its steely teeth. A sword floated toward his hand, and he took it. The monster roared at him, its teeth clanged together, in its eyes was a distillation of malevolence like nothing he could remember.

A "voice" whispered in his ear. "You must surrender to Bis, for this is that face of unreasoning ego."

The monster had left its bay and tramped on scaled feet toward him. He hefted the sword; this was all there was to defend himself with? How was he to survive?

"Surrender . . ." whispered the "voice."

Steeling himself, he awaited the thing's onrush. Huge clawed hands gripped him and bore him down; the thing opened those jaws and locked them around the center of his body, it shook him, and then opened wide like an anaconda to suck his body into an endless maw.

It closed behind him, and he survived, apparently still hale and able to proceed with the tertiary process.

The tentacloid monster now bore down upon him. He found he had the sword still, though how it had survived ingestion by the bull monster Bis he did not know.

"Foon must be experienced," said the voice. The tentacles reached for him; he was dragged to the beak. The beak was black and shiny, serrated along the cutting edges, which now opened and severed his legs. He felt their loss but no pain, his body was tilted and chopped off in beak-size bites, his head and shoulder being the last. There was oblivion, dark and comforting, and he floated on a wave.

From out of the dark wave appeared an image of himself, a

mirror image but not quite. For this Chosen had an evil smile and eyes that delighted in the misery of others. It held a sword and a mirror and presented the mirror to Chosen's view. He beheld his face within it, but his normal features suddenly distorted, the image of evil was replacing them. Without understanding how or even why, Chosen reached out with his coercive power and tried to stop the evil self. Instantly he felt the mirror in his own hand and felt himself transferred within the false self.

He had lost!

He remembered the voice and composed himself to oblivion. He reappeared on the mirror surface and sprang back into existence whole and well. The evil self shrank into the mirror and disappeared.

And thus did the tertiary process continue, and Chosen never knew how many minutes, hours, or days were consumed by it.

When it was completed, he understood something of the Arizel's pursuit of the Creator. He had command of the projection technique and had experienced the meditative state known as the Husj Kause.

He awoke within his own body, his mind free of the control of the Divider's glyph, and found himself still by the root in the shadow of the nest's great ventilation fan with the Woodwose sitting close by, its immense legs drawn up for its elbows to rest on.

Chi Lin Wei was gone; Zhao six was dead. Had been for some time, it seemed. His own body was covered in sores and worker Chitin that were busily tending him. They brought water and a chewed mush of fruits, and others cleaned the sores, removing the rotting spore body nodes and bacteria.

He investigated further and found the revolver gone and a bullet hole through poor Zhao six's head.

So the poor fellow had almost made it through the spruip, after all that agony, and then his mistress had shot him.

Chosen had a great task to attend to. There was no time to search for Chi Lin Wei, and he could not detect her mind on the mental plane, so she was some distance away already, if she still lived. He would have to search for her later. A great need existed.

He ordered more food from the nest, his strength had to be renewed.

33

WHEN HE REENTERED THE MEDITATION THE QUATERNARY Process began quickly. Scenes whirled past him bearing seed instructions, seed-syllable mantras to evoke and modulate their power. While each evoked startlingly clear visual images, it was as if he saw them with eyes inherently keener than any human being's.

He breathed the seed syllables and experienced the visions. There was a tremendous compulsion to do so; nothing else could be done, no way to oppose them.

In one he sat cross-legged on a mat in a long room with a low, carved ceiling. It was a gallery with a row of small mats, each a splash of primary color beside the blank white wall. The other wall was pierced with precisely placed slit windows, through which shafts of Beni's light shone down on the eager, inhuman faces of the class as they concentrated on the red components of the light of Beni and attempted to control the plexus of Assutava, in which the sexual impulse is encoded in the cerebrospinal system.

The words of power shook the gallery. The drum throbbed, and the long low notes of the brass horns blared on the tower top. With the minds of the great masters actively aiding them, the class concentrated on the rays of Beni. They learned to thread the ways of the electromagnetic maze, shifting through fields to bind the energy of the higher centers issuing commands to the nervous system through the crown center seed syllable. In their minds opened the petals of the million-petal flower.

Chosen, the seeker, moaned with them, accepting the light of Beni. Becoming witness to the fusion of atoms and the underlying principles of the universe in which the four forces work on all space time along the axes laid out by the Creator, that most mysterious superforce or being or unknown of all.

The vision shifted, changed in plastic flow.

Along with two other junior adepts, Chosen climbed to the high ridge in the freezing air. How they were breathing the stuff without technological aid Chosen did not understand. He did understand that he was not in a human body. He sensed wrongness here and there, human arms did not move just so, nor did humans put down feet in quite this way.

He simply accepted that he was receiving impressions from the life of the being that communicated with him through the Woodwose mind. That being had memories of the ancient Fenrille, before the forest, before the great changes.

The others were tall, wide-shouldered but thinly muscled, with bare or shaved heads. They wore skirts of some gray flimsy textile that cut the wind with remarkable ease.

On the bare rocks, flaked away in layers under the relentless attack of sun and snow, the junior adepts sat and began the assumption of control of the Nexus of Vosughada. One by one they began seizing control of their bodily processes, first evaporation rate, then heart rate, and, more gradually, body temperature, all the while breathing long, extremely deep breaths of the cold atmosphere of the heights. Their metabolisms slowed to a glacial crawl. They would not come down until summoned by the abbott's mental call on the glyph plane of deep consciousness. Down in the valley below they could see storm clouds gathering.

Again the image changed.

In a darkened space sat seven adepts. Each held out a hand opened in the gesture of universal acceptance. Above their palms burned the small, holy flames of Puruza. They formed the deep seed syllables, a hum that rang the rocks of mountains. The seventh adept began the translation, the most difficult state of all. The Master warned all against entropic decay. "Discipline your body, or you may lose it. (laugh)" There was a handclap.

As they watched, still invoking the power, the first adept vanished, the air rushing in around him with a heavy pop. The vision ended too.

Again Chosen squatted in a darkened room. He was alone, and before him, floating under his control, burned a meter-high orange flame. Into his mind appeared the great glyphs from the Teacher, known only as Endiclav. His mind vibrated with them in the ecstasy of Arizel communication.

"The Weak Force is the source of troublesome eddies; hew, to the correct vibrational path. Remember always, the goal is back to minus, back to silence. Entropy will penetrate any system that is not perfectly sealed. Entropy must be guarded against above all."

The Master touched his mind and automatically the mantra glyphs appeared in his head and the translation occurred. He floated in an elsewhen, an elsewhere, in a deep void, set in the vastness between galaxies. On one side loomed an elliptical galaxy, spread wide across the dark. On the other, seemingly a little farther away, were two smaller spiral galaxies. Elsewhere, "below" him, there was a smaller bar spiral, so close it seemed spread out like a plate before his feet. Near it was another spiral but edge on, with ragged tatters of luminous gas and stars stretching toward its neighbor. Beyond those were more galaxies, dozens, of spiral and elliptic types.

Chosen realized at once that he floated in the midst of a dense galactic group, probably dominated by the behemoth elliptic that spread across so much of the sky.

With the seed syllables came the knowledge. This was an important place for the Arizel tki Fenrille. For this was the Gungwha point, the place of translation. Set in the midst of enormous gravities, in a balancing point between the monstrous elliptic that sucked the other galaxies, hundreds of them, toward itself—and the monstrous black hole in its center that busily devoured stars by the million every hour—and the large pair of superspirals that orbited the elliptic giant.

Here between the galaxies the fields were balanced. From here then the Masters of the One in Four Forces could launch themselves into the enormous gravity well of the black hole singularity that sat in the midst of the colossal elliptic. With that power at their disposal, the Arizel tki Fenrille had traveled farther than they had ever dreamed possible, discovering a breadth to creation that went far beyond their earlier conceptualizations. But this was the crucial place, the first great Gungwha point.

Surrounding him was simply the protective breath of Welusha, an aspect of the sacred fire Puruza. He could not remain there in vacuum for long. After a moment to reflect, he returned to the universe that contained Fenrille and was guided to the cell by the Master whose mental patterns had been with him all through the process in much the same way that a parent teaching a child to swim would swim close by always within reach.

Between times, during reflective periods when the quaternary process ceased temporarily, Chosen—now simply the Seeker—ate heartily of the special jelly the nest had developed for its god. After an awesome struggle with human biochemistry, the great nest had finally found the perfect food, a jelly much like that given to the young Queens of spring sent forth from the nest every year. Tailored for human digestion with the appropriate mixture of protein and trace elements, it was extremely rich and effective food. To Chosen it tasted like a mix of fruit sugar and a whey curd. After each helping he felt his body respond. Starved, weak, it reacted voraciously. He began to feel good. It was almost better than a pharamol high. As he ate so the nest hummed in contentment. This was perhaps what it had waited for so long in dismal ignorance. It was aware that it was taking part in events that were greater than anything it had ever known before.

And always the Woodwose was there, either sitting close by with its monstrous legs drawn up in front of it or standing unobtrusively beside the tree.

The sores began to heal on the second day. On the third day Chosen approached his own translation and meditation. He had begun to accelerate through the Arizel program, leaping ahead of it more and more as his newly realized powers became integrated into the Arizel teaching. It had been designed for a fein mind, of that he was sure, because with some glyphs came strange, inhuman pseudomemories. Communication occurred within the glyphs, of this he was certain, for the processes were too skillfully knotted together in a mote of almost infinitesimal size for any space to have been wasted on decoration. Yet the responses they aroused in his human mind were surreal. Fear of heights was one, which inexplicably accompanied several of the obscure passages in the tertiary process.

Was it possible that both Ay fein and Arizel were evolutions of some avian form? Another sensation had involved preening, passing inexplicable things through the mouth parts. Had they been feathers?

But Chosen's human mind had already awoken to enormous potential through the gift of the Chitin nest. His understanding spread quickly as the glyphs passed before him.

The last vision differed, as if it came from a much later time. Its style was powerful, different, authoritative. In the great forest the Disciple Divider sat beneath the trees of energy. The light was dim; the forest resounded with the noises of the evening. Nachri were abroad, stirring up some noisy skeep that fled to higher branches with screams of alarm. Disciple Divider had sat there for an aeon, fed occasionally by the Woodwose or the Ay fein. Now the continents were welded together, the dangerous asteroids in the system had been pitched into Beni's outer envelope, and his task was done. Along with millions of others, he was free.

Now he could attempt the enormous equational meditation first codified by Great Master Tshak 404040.

His mind settled into the glyphs of strength, lighting the

Puruza fire within the trees. Permanent translation began and in time was completed as the Disciple Divider consumed his own substance to attain discorporation and join the Arizel tki Fenrille as the entity to be known only as the Divider.

Chosen opened his eyes. The future seemed ordained. To his surprise he found Chi Lin Wei squatting nearby. The Woodwose was invisible, but Chosen could sense its rage and knew it was close by.

Chi Lin Wei had the revolver in her belt. "You're alive," she said impassively.

"Seems that way. Where've you been?"

"Out there." She gestured vaguely. "There's nothing else."

"I see."

"I'm starving," she said, "and I can't eat my Zhao; that would be too much." She reached for the revolver. "I have to eat you." His mind jumped out to coerce hers but found a strange reflective weave. In Maza mind-grip she came toward him, raising the revolver. He got to his feet.

"No, the nest can feed you! It's fed me, how do you think?" But his words caromed off her glassy eyes and blank face; the revolver came up.

He prepared to dodge, to run, aware sickeningly that she was too close and too practiced with weapons to miss. His coercion kept slipping off the surface of her mind; the gun barrel came up only a meter away. She aimed.

And the hand of the Woodwose surrounded her and lifted her bodily into the air. Her scream rented the peace of the evening, and she got off a shot into the Woodwose's shoulder, which maddened it beyond control momentarily. So it ate her. He watched, shuddering, while complex emotions swept over him as its jaws champed rhythmically a moment or two and it swallowed.

Late that night, in the velvety blackness beneath the trees, Chosen was done with the quaternary process. He floated a few inches off the ground.

"... an exercise that the true adept should practice daily, though not to the excess of the show-offs, the sky climbers." He recalled the glyph with ease. When he opened his mental field to encompass the bioenergy in the enormous trees around him, he saw once again the route across the universes laid out for him.

It was time for his testing. His body was healing rapidly, though his skin was stippled with small boils. The quaternary process had given him all that it could, but already his mind, the first of its kind, uniquely different from fein, human, or Arizel, was leaping ahead of the quaternary process.

The glyph would guide him; the trees would provide the energy through the vibrational path. He had received a crash course in the metaphysic of the Arizel, they who had transformed planet Fenrille and then left it to wander the universes.

His purpose was immovable; the Divider had built compulsion into the process. Feeling the hum of power surround him, he submerged his consciousness into the rising glyphs. From the trees he drew on the fire; the vibrational pathways opened.

The mantras for the translation appeared to him. Glyph forms accelerated. He translated, felt the biofield of the forest like some enormous mattress of energy, and bounced himself into a new polarity. Immediately the glyph forms completed the tilt against the three-dimensional axis of the universe, and he slid away in time and space, through a brief vortex that opened momentarily on the great Gungwha point.

His arms were crossed before him, palms upward in the gesture of binary universal acceptance; his legs trailed below, but his entire body was protected by the field of the breath of praba welusha.

Somehow he continued to breathe at the slow steady rate demanded in most of the quaternary process. However, instead of air he breathed the fire of Puruza.

The huge galaxies were awesomely bright. The spirals sparkled with hot blue supergiants threaded like jewels on the background dust and clouds. The glyph from the Divider gave him the gravity primes, and he looked down into the raging heart of the great elliptic galaxy, into regions where millions of close-packed stars blazed together. To that space finally where hundreds of short-lived, enormous superstars coalesced from the pulverized star stuff produced in the torment of the great black hole singularity and its ferocious energy fields.

Myriads of red dwarfs, hundreds of giants, were being torn apart every minute in the chaotic tides on the edge of the accretion ring. For mortal flesh to hover there more than a picosecond risked a riddling with gamma radiation. There was the graveyard of galaxies.

He moved. In those vast vortices he traveled at the speed of thought, hurtling in and beyond the huge singularity that whirled in the heart of the elliptic. There was an intense translation; he was flipped far through the universal topology.

He appeared with a popping sound over the crystal sands of the beach of forever. He dropped four feet to the ground.

The protection of the breath of welusha faded. He was naked standing on cold sand. His skin puckered in gooseflesh; the boils hardened on his skin and began to itch.

The Ring Sun was in full occultation. Only a pale, wan light illuminated the dunes. The air was breathable, odorless, and extremely cold.

He was no longer in the energized state that had taken him through the translation. In fact his levitation power had grown extremely weak. Some kind of damping field was being generated, a field that interfered with all his new abilities to some degree.

He would have to resume normal biological methods of transportation. He cast about mentally, but the sensing was difficult; there was even a fog on the mental plane. He could detect no other life-forms.

In most directions the illumination level was low. In one direction were much brighter lights. He sent his mind forward while his body trudged after it. Something was up ahead, and on the mental plane he felt a completely new sensation. Something angular, heavy, and cold moved there, but it was difficult to perceive through the mental fuzz that seemed to fill that spectrum.

Something about that background noise suddenly gave him the uncanny impression that he was perceiving a herd of artificial brains, all running on binary code!

He climbed several of the immense dunes, breathing hard in the intensely cold air. The sky was incomprehensible to him. The light source was a strip across the middle. There was the blackness of outer space all around the horizon. No stars shone, only a large rectangle, pale gold on the dark that humped a third of the way into the sky in one direction.

Atop another dune he finally saw his destination.

A mile or so ahead stretched a lake of opaque ivory-hued fluid. In the middle of the lake squatted a colossal structure built of some gleaming gray material. It reared a mile into the sky; enormous towers soared above that. It was the Castle of the Numal, built aeons previously by a sentient precursor to the robots. Built in fact in a doomed attempt to keep Numals and *their* creations out.

From the dunes a paved path ran straight to the bridge over the pale lake. Chosen examined the scene carefully and cast around with his telepathic sense. Where was the ancient one? That which had called him here, changing everything that had ever been.

There was no detectable echo of an Arizel mind, and Chosen knew that he would be able to detect such an entity if it was within thousands of kilometers.

Still, it was the place the ancient one had chosen to bring him. That must be where the Arizel had been imprisoned.

The strange artificial force he had felt was concentrated here. But he was separating out various components of it now. The lake, for instance, was not a fluid but a gel creature, a predatory form that would consume almost anything that was placed upon it. This creature gave off a dim moan of misery on the mental level.

Beyond it, in the castle, he could detect other minds, fierce little predatory minds. They loomed through the general fog of emissions as bright vesicles of hunger. Were they the rulers there? Or parasites of some kind? Or just bubbles of fatty consciousness in a general soup?

There was also the Numal, and he recognized it as soon as his consciousness brushed across it and awoke its focus. It was almost as if he trod on the shoulders of a giant the size of a mountain.

Such a greed, such power was unexpected. It flew toward his probe so quickly that although he managed to disengage, he had the uncanny feeling the mind of the machine had detected him, had obscenely caressed his mind and felt its flavor. Now it sought after him in the general fog projected from within the castle.

Inside the castle, indeed, his careless probe had produced a convulsion. The Numal sprang into action, convinced that the mental contact—it was a biological form undoubtedly—had come from the captive djinn field. Communication was in the Numal's grasp if it could only pin down the djinn field inside the bottle and locate its consciousness on the mental plane.

Once communication was established there was no end to the opportunities. Possibly the Numals could yet escape their ancient, dying universe, where even the black holes were fading away year by year and matter was now as precious as life. If there were other universes beyond their own somehow, then their terrible doom could be avoided forever.

The Numal sprang into action on heavy coasters. At high speed it rolled into the instrumentation pocket. A dozen narrow, tubular arms reached out to the controls.

Outside the castle, Chosen decided to move quickly. There was no telling what the contact might produce. Adopting Lavin Fundan's dictum, he seized the initiative. A swift investigation showed that the moat creature was miserable from confinement, not starvation. It was coercible through its pleasure centers. Chosen felt it squirm a little under his coercion, but it was soon content to feel his probe giving pleasure to its primitive brain.

He ran down the dunes, leaping out onto the massive causeway, which he estimated was a hundred and fifty meters wide and yet seemed extremely slender against the walls and towers. It projected out into the lake creature and ended below the drawbridge, which was raised high. The castle was built on a heroic scale. The central towers dwarfed any structure Chosen had ever seen, and the distance between the end of the causeway and the walls was at least a mile.

He looked down. The lake-thing was vast, like some gelid fried egg a dozen kilometers in diameter. With an appetite for any complex chemicals fate cared to offer.

He jumped down, trusting entirely to his coercive powers. The surface started to give ominously; he hurriedly squeezed down savagely on the brute's pain centers. He offered it the previous pleasure, and the surface rebounded to form an elastic skin beneath his feet. He began to trot toward the huge walls.

As he ran, the skin formed in front of his feet, but he kept his coercive control tight on the monstrous organism, aware that without it he would sink immediately out of sight into a digestive pocket that would reduce him to absorbable compounds in a second or two.

The walls grew more impressive the closer he got, until they towered into the sky with the enormities behind them looming above the clouds like the peaks of Mount Fundan. How he was going to climb them was not something he had worked out yet. Still he knew that he must go on; he must enter and release the ancient one who was surely imprisoned in this place.

And within lurked the monster he had seen then, which was most surely the Numal itself.

Eventually he reached the foot of the walls. The moat creature flowed right up to the wall material, a kind of polished ceramic that appeared to offer no handholds whatsoever.

Nearby were the immense workings of the drawbridge, where huge buttresses projected out above the surface of the creature. He wondered if there might be a crack in those hinges through which they might crawl. But he could see no way to even climb up to them, since they were ten meters above him and the wall was as smooth as a mirror.

He closed his eyes and reached for the power of levitation he had developed in the quaternary process. But some indefinable barrier prevented his free exercise of the power. Was it something projected by the Numal? There was no doubting that his adversary was formidable indeed. Exactly how he was going to free the Divider, and from what, he had no idea.

Then he saw a slight declivity cut in the sheer bulk of the wall. Just beyond the drawbridge workings. He ran toward it and found a drain, hacked crudely through the wall material. He might well be able to crawl up inside it.

Over long periods of time the ceramic surface of the wall had pitted through the action of corrosive wastes, and there were many holes and cracks and good handholds. Chosen gazed up into it. How long had he before some deadly liquid was flushed down the tube?

He scrambled up the drain. The handholds were numerous, and he found that he made quite good time. He disappeared into the wall and found that the way sloped gently upward into total darkness.

He detected no life-forms immediately close by, but the ominous mental heaviness of the Numal was not far away, apparently straight up the dismal tunnel.

The climb grew arduous. At one point, when he had been climbing by handholds for what seemed at least a hundred meters, he sensed an intelligence very nearby, something so malevolent and so intently hungry that he cringed involuntarily. And then dared to reach out and examine his find.

A rage to feed, an urge to find food, which might be almost anything that moved, and an awareness that time was short. The young were soon to hatch, and if there was not food they would eat the mother that bore them in her abdomen. The thing moved, hoping to find other moving things nearby. It moved around the pipe, sensing a soft prey nearby, so bafflingly near and yet so far.

With a gasp of relief he realized that the thing, whatever it was, was on the outside of the pipe he was crawling up. Such ferocious intent might well be beyond any coercive power he could muster.

He continued the dreary climb, probing ahead as much as he dared. After a while the way became gentler again. Then it bifurcated. He hesitated then chose the left-hand way. It became very steep almost immediately, then vertical, and there were areas that had been patched at some time. They were roughly outlined by jagged spines of solder.

A light above broke down into three and became brighter as he approached. After another ten meters it became the underside

264

of a grated trap for a sink like a giant's swimming pool. The grate was wide enough to pass his body quite easily.

The sink exposed sheer steel walls in a complete circle around him He sighed. After climbing so far he was confronted again by an impassable wall. Would he have to climb all the way down again and search for another entrance?

Then he saw a plug, a disk of some dark material attached to a cable of jointed metal beads interlocked like the vertebrae of some long fossilized monster snake. As he ran to it, a noise sounded above, a huge noise, with a hissing component. He sensed the Numal's fearsome excitement.

The beads were not difficult to climb, and he soon reached the top and clambered over.

34

IT WAS A SCENE OUT OF AN ALIEN HELL. BEFORE HIM STRETCHED a floor flagged with gigantic gray ceramic tiles. The light was dim except for occasional bright green flashes that emanated from high up. Vast shadowy machinery towered around him. Beneath the light source, which was too bright to look at directly, was spread a vast edifice of scaffolding and tubes that accumulated in its center to a peak several hundred meters high.

That peak was the source of the light, which threw fantastic shadows over the rest of the laboratory. One enormous tube sited a hundred meters above his head and easily ten meters thick arched right across the cavernous room and intersected with the central tower, an array of tubes, flexions, and scaffold braces. Just above the intersection the light flashed.

Menacing green shadows flickered across the alien machines. As he watched, there was a tremendous hiss followed by the unexpected crack of immense electrical energies.

Feeling far too exposed standing by the side of the great drain he had climbed from—and merely a trap set into the floor of the enormous place—Chosen moved toward one of the nearby machines. The mental interference that he had felt before had risen to a din, almost overpowering. To use his new senses at all was a great effort.

It seemed likely that the ancient one was trapped in the center of the enormous group of machines.

After a while Chosen's eyes adjusted, and he made out the ceiling, marked by a broad grid pattern that seemed thousands of meters above his head. He reached the shadows at the base of the machine, which was a simple rectangle that towered hundreds of meters above without lights of any kind. It emitted a hum, low, constant, and when he touched its alloy ceramic skin, he found it was cool but vibrating at the same frequency as the hum. A steeply pitched ramp wound around the outer skin, so he climbed a couple of turns to get a better view of the layout.

He was looking down an avenue that opened onto a central plaza that surrounded the central colossus of equipment. In the central plaza innumerable cables snaked across the tiles, and there was considerable activity among small mobile robots that worked under the glare of intense white lights mounted on their upper carapaces. On the far side of the enormous plaza of robots stood a row of giant machines that looked like broad-shouldered office buildings. To complete the illusion, rows of colored lights winked along their slick, gleaming surfaces.

Beyond these some enormous spidery thing humped up in the dark, perhaps a third of the way to that distant ceiling.

An opening, an avenue between the machines, ran toward the central complex. Down the middle ran a number of huge tubes and segmented conduits.

With the green light flashing stark shadows of himself on the floor behind him, he shifted down the central alley, heading toward the central tower. He passed a maintenance robot, a mechanism that resembled a mechanical crustacean with a dozen delicate working arms. It took apart a junction box and spliced in new cables that it pulled out of an extrusion device that followed it around. The robot took no notice of him, and he passed it without incident.

He was much closer, with about a quarter of the way yet to go to the central massif, when the great green light ceased its flashing. Huge engines whined down. He looked up and saw a dense kidney shape moving within the scaffold tower, something huge.

Then the Numal, on extended roller podia, rumbled back down the access chute. It was time for the Extension Conference. Continued funding for the project was to be judged. The Numal had prepared its presentation very carefully; it left for the conference pod situated in the south tower.

Chosen watched the enormous thing, at least fifty meters tall, glide down a long rampway that lead out of the uppermost section of the experimental tower and descended to the floor about a kilometer away from his position. Its outer skin was a shining gray-purple; small green-and-blue lights winked on the smooth uppermost surface. A number of podia that shone as if they were made of steel were folded complexly across its smooth thoracic region. Chosen wondered if it moved on some kind of antigravity field or whether it was on rollers; its movement was stately.

It disappeared into the maze of huge machines. The robot workers continued their labors, but the experimental tower was quiescent, the flashing green light no longer illuminating the huge room.

Chosen moved forward. It was easier to see his way with the flashing light gone. As he got closer he realized that the tower was nothing more than a laboratory setup on an unprecedented scale.

In fact, high above him, within a mesh cage coated with psionic organism, the bottle that imprisoned the Divider was suspended. All around it hung a halo of probes and manipulators, now temporarily frozen in place.

As he was still unable to try his new teleportation ability, there seemed no logical alternative to climbing the tower in order to take a look. To reach the top involved a seemingly impossible climb until he discovered there were rampways angled through the scaffold structures. Furtively he stole upward.

The way was long and arduous, the metal rampways steep.

From the sheer size of the passageways that closed in around the ramps he judged they had been built for the access of the Numal itself. The walls were a solid mass of pipes, just a few of the millions required to bring the complex nutrient mixtures to the psionic organism and bear away the organism's toxic wastes.

Overhead ran a solid ceiling of tubes of innumerable sizes and purposes. Around him there was ceaseless activity, for although the great apparatus was not in use there were many continuous processes, such as the feeding of the insatiable psionic organism. Pumps labored; valves gasped in chorus.

On the mental plane Chosen detected several zones of mental activity. It seemed he could sense the nearby mental presence of the Numal before it could sense him, for when he concentrated on it carefully he found he could focus on a mid-point between them where he detected the Numal's characteristic mental energies.

Closer to hand he felt the psionic organism, a raw psi receptor, fashioned from some coelenterate colony creature, that could detect activity on the mental plane. It immediately noticed his probe and leapt toward it. The "touch" of the thing was loathsome, and it was very hard to shake off. He had to stop and enter a meditative state in which he dampened down all consciousness to a negligible level before its sucker was finally removed. Afterward, when he resumed his trek, he could sense that it was constantly probing for him. To elude it he had to clamp down his own telepathic search to nothing.

With new concern in his heart, he continued climbing, and

after half an hour's further progress reached the obvious center of the apparatus. Everything was focused on that spot, about two-thirds of the way up the edifice of equipment.

Suspended within the psionic cage floated a tubular container several meters long and at least two wide. As he approached he saw that the roughly spherical cage of mesh that surrounded the space containing the bottle and the Numal's instruments glistened with what at first appeared to be a coat of wet paint, of black or dark purple hue. That he realized was the source of the psionic power he had felt.

And it was the ancient one's prison. It was fashioned from a sparkling material, a metallic glass with some complex impurity. At one end there was an obvious stopper, and from it a thin protrusion or spar emerged that connected to a vertical structural member in the surrounding ring. To reach that spar, however, Chosen would have to negotiate a way around the circular space. He was about 180 degrees distant, and he would have to rely on some precarious handholds and footholds through the maze of pipes and tubes. At the same time he would be in the midst of the psionic organism's field. He prepared himself for an ordeal.

Slowly he made his way around the edge of the space in which the bottle swung, suspended on four long guy wires. He did his best not to look down, for there was a clear drop, hundreds of meters to the floor below.

Complex arrays of tubes and conduits sank into modular mechanisms that were attached to the meshwork. He slid between a pair of large risers and came out onto a massive ramp that led out to an access station beside the bottle. The ramp descended in the other direction through an enormous passageway illuminated by small, bright mercury lamps.

Indeed at the aperture of the passageway, the massive metal plate in the floor bore a conspicuous dent from supporting an enormous weight over long periods of time. Here then was where the Numal squatted during its labors.

Another forty-five degrees around the circle brought him to the spar that held the containment bottle steady in its trapeze of wires. The metal spar was convex on the upper surface and about a foot wide. Carefully he walked out over the long drop and did his utmost to keep his eyes on the bottle ahead. He could feel the sweat running down his temples despite the cold air. The psionic creature filled the mental plane with the equivalent of a hurricane's howl—a moment's lack of concentration and it would pounce on his mind with full fury.

After what seemed an eternity, his right foot reached the

269

flange that rimmed the bottle. The stopper bore a steel butterfly nut about a foot in length. He assumed that the nut had to be turned and grasped the ends. His first effort to move it was fruitless. He repositioned himself with his legs braced against the flange and tried again. Nothing happened. Except that the bottle stirred about suddenly on the guy wires and he slipped and almost lost his footing entirely. For a moment he dangled sickeningly over the drop below.

Concerned that he had tried to turn it the wrong way, he reversed his grip, braced himself again, and heaved. He kept it up while the sweat ran off his body and the chords in his neck started to ache. Still the nut refused to budge, and he concluded wistfully that he needed a tool of some kind; even a steel bar might make all the difference in applying leverage.

Cursing himself for not considering that a bottle stopper set in place by a behemothic Numal might be hard for a two-meter-tall biped to open with its bare hands, he started back across the spar.

There was a sudden rumbling sound coming from the lower passage of the ramp. Steel members groaned around him in the apparatus. The Numal returned.

Fighting down his panic, he devoted himself to keeping his balance and making his way back across the spar. He had passed the halfway mark when he caught sight of the uppermost surface of the Numal, rising into view at the far end of the tunnel. He threw caution to the winds and ran the last four steps to arrive on his hands and knees at the base of the spar at the very moment the Numal's optical devices recorded his presence.

Artificially induced intelligence had been raised to a fine art by the builders of the Numal, but even they had failed, in the end, to conquer the problem of focus selection. Even the Numals' magnificent self-programming couldn't avoid self-focused preoccupation after a victory. Since Numals had first decided to equip themselves with pleasure/pain-from-deprivation loop systems, the move that ultimately doomed their masters, the gap between theoretical efficiency and actual achievement had grown embarrassingly large. Thus the Numal made an error of identification, so caught up in the pleasure of winning renewed funding for the project was it as it rode toward the instrumentation pocket.

But the Numal's mistake was only momentary. At very first impression, it had simply registered annoyance. Vermin at work again, and this time right in the center of the apparatus. The Numal would have to spray again.

270

Then the irregular shape, tone, and texture of the vermin crashed home. The Numal extended emergency podial surface, tilted forward and launched itself like a bullet toward the end of the ramp.

Chosen hurled himself at a smooth pipe that dropped into the depth of the scaffolding. Fortunately for him it was neither too hot to touch nor too cold and he dropped thirty meters in a few seconds.

By then the Numal had arrived directly above. It crashed into its position with a boom that resounded all over the apparatus. The major members swayed, and a chorus of groans and squeals arose from stressed joints and girders.

Sensors, tonguelike modules on the end of articulated stalks, combed across the access spar and examined the containment bottle.

Optical organs on tentacular stalks snaked out in many directions in pursuit of the intruder creature while the Numal's central intelligence was rocked by the revelations of the sensors.

An organic being of an unfamiliar carbon cycle had been there and left secretions, evaporant fluid primarily, of which water was the principal component. The creature breathed the general atmosphere of the laboratory too.

This was an astounding development. First the mental contact, now a creature generated by some unknown means was on the loose in the laboratory. The Numal could only speculate how it had been created, but it was as certain as it could be that the creature was the work of the djinn eddy.

A horrible thought struck the Numal, and a number of appendages leaped to the switches. The screens came on and there, in the bottle, was the djinn field. It had not escaped. Relief swept through the Numal. Excitedly it got down to work. The first thing needed would be a bipedal biped catcher.

35

CHOSEN REACHED THE FLOOR OF THE APPARATUS WITHOUT FUR-
ther detection and began searching for tools. A piece of metal,
something with which to pry that stopper loose. The compulsion
glyph was all-powerful now that he was so close. His teeth
champed nervously together. His mouth was dry; he was using
up his energy reserves at a rapid rate.

Far above him the Numal moved to irradiate the bottle once
more with a high-speed electron cloud and set the acceletron to
work revving up a stream of ionized hydrogen. When it was
played upon the containment bottle, it produced a cellular plasma
within it and turned the containment material virtually trans-
parent. A modest amount of hard radiation was generated, but
not enough to trouble the Numal.

The cellular plasma served to concentrate and isolate the djinn
fields. The Numal suspected the presence of a state of "discomfort" within the field, an exciting possibility. Where discomfort
could be induced, control might be exercised. Control might be
the quickest route to forcing the mental contact that the Numal
was convinced could now be achieved. Intelligence was there,
of that the Numal was certain.

The momentary transparency of the containment bottle was
enough however for the Divider to fire a brief glyph through the
fields that trapped it. The psionic organism caught the glyph full
force and reacted by encysting itself into resistant polyp forms,
throwing the computer program into chaos as it polluted the data
with encystment codes.

The Numal, so grossly insensitive on the plane of mental
reception, caught only a trace of the glyph, before it was gone,
the Divider's characteristic tao-sign division form, white into
black into white forever, but not the message, which was for
the fein adept that the Divider was convinced had come. What
else could have rocked the bottle?

The glyph opened in Chosen's mind with an intense clarity
that was quite paralyzing.

. . . break the bottle; that is all that needs be done. Heroic work is this but essential. Beware the Numal . . .

Then it was gone, and the light had dimmed as well.

Disgust at the state of the psionic organism mingled with eager interest in the new data in the Numal's brain. This contact with the djinn had been intriguingly different from the first. It shut down the beam and began disassembling the psionic organism grid.

But the glyph's repetitive pattern had been caught by the computers and found to be a most complex code. After several minutes' work the program had still no basic idea of what the code was even about, let alone what was in it. This impressed the Numal; such tightness of code in such a tiny package!

It would go at once to the biology lab and make a new psionic organism. At the same time it would hatch some biped catchers. To keep the biped away from the containment bottle while it was absent, the Numal surrounded the bottle with a charged pain field from another kind of organism, a simple multicellular creature floating in a small tank which he activated by clipping it to a feed tube.

Chosen heard the rumbling of the Numal's departure and wondered what it might forebode. It would be best to work quickly; he felt certain that time was precious now. He turned on his heel and went in search of the materials he needed for his new plan. All he had to do was to break the bottle.

Eventually he found a robot cutting and welding cables along a thick steel tube. Other, smaller machines were following far behind it, adding components and linkages to the pattern being created.

About the size of a human coffin, with ten limblike appendages, the robot had artificial intelligence on lines similar to that of the Numal, except that its rudimentary brain, built from biochips, lacked all the higher circuitry of the Numal and the vast resources of Numal memory. Chosen probed at it, sought compulsions. It was difficult; the machine was not intelligent in an aware sense at all. It simply did the tasks programmed into it by superior robots. He gradually worked his way down to the controlling machine codes and found them relatively simple to alter with his telekinetic power, since they involved nothing more than electron flow.

Slowly, with many mistakes, he learned how to program the thing. The pattern of cable modification grew haphazard, ceased. Then he urged the machine to climb higher into the apparatus, drove it to climb to a point above the bottle and there to rest and wait for new instructions.

Chosen climbed partway back up the instrument tower with his remote-controlled tool. He wanted to get it in position before ordering it to begin cutting. Then he heard the Numal returning in a roar of rollers on steel track. It slammed back into the instrumentation pocket. Chosen waited, all his senses searching the space above him.

The Numal removed the pain field–generating organism and pumped fresh psionic organism onto the grid. Simultaneously it opened two carrying cases. From the first one, a trunk about two meters in length, it removed a full-formed biped catcher. From the other, about half that size, it released ten trackers, small ratlike things that ran on dozens of pseudopodia tipped with tiny sucker feet. Both forms employed receptor arrays, cranial surfaces distended like butterfly wings, on which a symbiont psionic form was entwined among arrays of receptor cells. There were no eyes, although the trackers had sensors in their feet.

The trackers scattered, squeaking excitedly among themselves as they raced along Chosen's trail, their psi arrays groping forward for any trace of unusual psionic activities.

He sensed them long before they were in range of him, but he also sensed the one that came behind them and realized he had to move. The biped catcher was bipedal itself, fast and deadly, with four arms and a tubular sensory array that stretched its cranium into a grotesque Medusa of sensors.

Chosen was sure he would not be able to resist this creature physically, certainly not with his bare hands. And coercion would only give away his position to the other things and thus to the Numal itself.

He moved to the nearest black coated tube and slid down it to the floor; his palms and the inner part of his thighs were somewhat burned by the time he reached it, but he gained invaluable seconds. The biped catcher was behind and descending more slowly.

His plan had begun smoothly. Within an hour of dawn the first fein units had slipped deep behind the Kommando lines. Then the mobile command post picked up a message from Young Proud Fundan. The computer accepted a short burst of video images. Cordelia Fundin put them up on the main monitor screen. There was an audible gasp of breath.

Lavin Fundan stared at the pictures in horror hardly able to believe his eyes. Young Proud was crazy, he knew, but this was the work of a monster! He had an overwhelming urge to vomit as he watched his wife, the woman with whom he had built his life, tortured most foully on the screen. No one in the world had ever meant so much to Lavin Fundan as she, except perhaps his son, who was gone, and his daughters, who, he thanked the Creator, were safe in Abzen Valley. To see his wife treated thus laid a chill on his very marrow.

Her screams were harrowing; the rest of the crew in the Command Post had their hands to their ears. Groans and exhalations of disgust accompanied the sound of the whip rising and falling over Fleur's body.

"Turn it off," Lavin whispered, but they were all frozen in place. He whirled and screamed at Cordelia Fundin. "Turn it off!"

Lavin left the tent blindly, head swimming. He was violently ill not far beyond the door. As he leaned against a tree for support, he suffered a wave of frustrated rage so bitter that he wanted to cry out to whatever had created the universe and ordained his fate.

. . . My son is dead . . . what more must I give? . . . What do you demand of me? Why this? . . . The questions burned in his brain alongside those horrifying images.

For a terrible moment he thought of Fair Fundan and wondered starkly if the Fundans were not cursed. Fair had gone beyond the natural way, many times. Her fate had been to see the frustration of her dreams and the realization of another dream. Now Lavin was trapped in the nightmare result of Fair's usurpation of family power two hundred years before.

Am I reacting as she would? For a moment he visualized Fair Fundan, from whom he had sprung entire. She had known great sorrow and lived more than three centuries only to die before her cherished goals had been achieved. Were the Fundans cursed in some fundamental way that put them at odds with the universe?

Young Proud's message had been blunt. Lavin was what Proud wanted, and he was ordered to present himself at the gates of Butte Manor. At which point the Lady Fleur Fundan would be released from torment into the sweet embrace of death alongside her husband.

Fleur lived yet! That much Lavin accepted. He rested his hand on the worn butt of his revolver. He would go, and he would kill Young Proud himself, even if it did mean his life.

* * *

In the end the only way out of Butte Manor had been the underground river. Armada and five others slipped into the waters of a stream that passed under the mountain and emerged as a tributary of the River Uluin. They had lights but no breathing gear, and there were several long passages with nowhere to surface for breath.

Armada counseled a slow but steady approach, traveling down in a group, pausing at each air hole to fill their lungs to capacity with a period of gentle deep breathing.

The water was cold, the way long. Yet after twelve hours underground, they crawled from a low-ceilinged cave into the shocking light of a sunny afternoon on the slopes of the mountains. Around them grew stands of young jik and knuckoo, with clearings everywhere for giselberries and dwarf glob glob. They were above the main valley, looking down into it and across the Uluin and Muld rivers to the green-splashed flanks of Mount Titus.

Armada scouted the slopes around. There was little sign of the New Kommando in their immediate neighborhood. Northward though, in the woods that skirted the mountains below the Skullcap, dark plumes rose above campfires. Out to the west, distantly, they heard the rumble of jet engines at the huge base in Muld.

This absence of the enemy changed her plans. She took the time to hunt down a family of fat-tailed skrin, which she took with her customary accurate handgun fire.

While they ate the skrin, raw, they hurriedly discussed their options. Butte Manor was gone, by now thoroughly looted. Young Proud and the New Kommando had triumphed at last.

Armada believed that only revenge was left to them and that the best place to begin it was at the airfield. They drank from the spring and then set out westward as briskly as they were able.

Rinus Van Relt found his breaking point came when Young Proud ordered him to take the whip and beat the Lady Fundan with it.

"Lord, this is your blood feud, not mine. I would have none of it."

Fleur Fundan stared back at him with a bizarre calmness in her eyes. Van Relt could tell that she wished for death, but tied in the chair, she was helpless.

He waited for the insane rage he expected. Instead Young

Proud turned that queer little smile on him again, as if that was exactly what he'd expected.

"Of course you don't, Van Relt, of course. All right, get out of here then and send in Orik. He can hold the camera."

"Lord, is there any reason to do this again? You have already sent the message."

"What? Of course I must. Have I received any reply? No. So I must carry out my threat. However, I will simply continue the punishment for the purpose of another short holo. At this time I have yet to determine whether a death sentence for the woman is to be carried out or not."

"Surely she has suffered enough. What need is there for—"

"Enough, Van Relt! You must learn to bide your tongue in these matters. I will have no interference." Young Proud's face was suddenly taut. Danger was in the air.

Rinus left hurriedly, not trusting himself to speak again to Young Proud.

Orik, Proud's new, human bodyguard, had until recently been a bull-necked corporal in the Third Division's shock battalion. He was extremely pleased with his promotion and held no qualms concerning his new master's vendetta with the heirs of Fair Fundan. At Van Relt's curt nod, Orik smiled and gave him an obscene wink. "The Master needs me, does he?"

"You find pleasure in this thought, Corporal Orik?"

"None of that guff, messire. I'm out of your precious Kommando now."

Van Relt almost killed him on the spot. His hand went to the revolver at his waist, but he hesitated. After giving him an evil grin, Orik turned his back and went through the door.

Slightly unsteady on his feet, Van Relt made his way to the communications center. He plugged in a terminal in an empty cubicle and logged onto the main line through the Sx Coast retransmission center. Once connected, he switched to the special coded link to the *Black Ship*. He punched in a set of code words and was rewarded with a reply after a half-minute wait.

Van Relt breathed a sigh of relief. It appeared that Alace Rohm was prepared to deal. Rinus quickly keyed in his offer. He would deliver Young Proud and at least twenty kilos of pharamol in exchange for passage on the *Black Ship* and a membership of the Bond.

36

FOLLOWING THE SHARE-OUT OF THE LOOTED PHARAMOL FROM Butte Manor, every man and woman in the Kommando was "gram rich," each having the equivalent of a couple of centuries of extended life. There had been a lot of indiscipline as a result. Small mutinies, attempted hijackings of planes from the landing strip, quite a few murders and many robberies all had taken their toll on Kommando efficiency. Some units had become completely ineffective. So Van Relt had been forced to accede to Young Proud's demands for order, and there had been a crackdown. Young Proud had gibbets set up by squads of those who were to be hanged on them. The bodies were left swinging as a reminder to the rest. Young Proud had also set up a system with hefty rewards offered for information concerning mutiny plots or stowaways or hijacking attempts. Since he was paying in pharamol there had been a torrent of informers and mass arrests. Discipline had tightened to a certain degree, but the problem remained, and most divisional commanders had stopped sending out small patrols, since they rarely came back, the men absconding into the woods and heading for the airstrip. All patrols were being made in platoon strength.

Van Relt ordered a conference of divisional commanders in a room not far from the main gate of Butte Manor. Although the enemy was known to be shattered and dispersed in north Sliverary, Van Relt wanted his force to keep a watchful eye out in that direction. Ever since the battle of Badleck Ridge, Van Relt had nightmares concerning fein surprise attacks. While he spoke to his officers, Rinus tried to keep thoughts of Fleur Fundan and Young Proud out of his mind and he plunged into the minutia of battle detail with a sense of relief.

On the banks of the river Sliverary, hidden in deep underbrush, Lavin Fundan turned to Ng Farr and Chulpopek and told them that he intended to go on by himself. The video signal had changed everything. He would go, alone, to kill Young Proud. He ordered them to take the Impis upriver, into the valleys above

Butte Manor, and there to wait out the war. It was over anyway, and the Fenrille Defense Forces had lost. The *Black Ship* would fill up with its loot and it would leave, so there was no point to further slaughter. Especially since all that remained was a battle over family honor.

He left them and went to the mobile command post, gathered by their horses a few meters away. He dismissed the technicians as well, bidding them to assist Chulpopek in marshaling the fein and pulling out up the river to sanctuary in the hills.

They listened to him in silence, tears brimming in some eyes. Then he was gone, with only Val Bo-Ho by his side.

Lavin loaded a spare revolver, which he tucked into the inside of his sock. He placed a small knife inside the sweatband of his uniform cap.

"Bo-Ho, hero of Brelkilk, you must stay. I must go alone, for this is a mission concerned only with human agony. There is no need for any fein to die."

Val Bo-Ho merely wrapped his kifket in oilcloth in readiness for the swim across the Sliverary. "I will come with you, lord."

"No, Bo-Ho, you will go back to Yunibur's yard and raise your cubs. You are not wanted in this."

Bo-Ho's eyes glowed like coals. "I saw the video too, lord; I belong in this. We must take Young Proud's head before he dishonors all Clan Fundan, men and fein."

Lavin gave up. In his way, Bo-Ho was as stubborn as mighty old Mzsee Rva. Lavin knew he would never shake him off. Therefore, they slipped into the water together a few minutes later and swam across the Sliverary, unseen by the Kommando troops downstream at the pontoon bridge.

On the far bank they paused a moment and listened carefully, then Lavin unwound a small detector cord from his wrist computer to check for photo cells and microcams. Then they vanished into the forest.

A minute or so later the first parties of fein slid into the water and began swimming across. They were followed by more and then by the humans of the Command Post. Among these was Cordelia Fundin, who swam with angry strokes while tears streamed down her face.

Aniki Fundin was swimming beside her, the central processing unit of the battle computer strapped on top of his head, so he was using a breast stroke. Cordelia stayed with him all the way. On the far side she shook out the small ceremonial banner of the first Abzen Impi, a triangle of green cloth with a single golden stripe. She attached it to the aerial of the big receiver she carried in her own pack. With the rest, she headed south and east.

The Fenrille Defense Forces would simply not accept defeat and the death of their commander. Nor could they let Young Proud escape punishment for his treatment of Fleur Fundan. In small groups they continued to swim the river. A wild, dangerous emotion possessed them. There was no singing, hardly any splashing of the water. In fact there was hardly any sound at all but something on the air nonetheless, a scrap of rhyme, a song, a snatch of some ancient fein battle lyric, the wafting scream of the bagpipes perhaps.

In the woods along the freshly bulldozed roads surrounding Butte Manor, Lavin and Val Bo-Ho passed campsites where thousands of soldiers relaxed in the sun. Here and there they found former fein yards. The huts smashed or burnt for fuel, graves dug open and used as latrines.

The troops had been mixing gwassa and alcoholic beverages, not a combination to induce or even permit a high degree of activity. Val Bo-Ho's ear tufts were standing tall by the time they'd passed them.

Using the thickets skillfully, they reached the edge of the trees, near the new road running up to Butte Manor. Ahead was a bare field of fire, covered by the guns in the manor's peripheral forts. Signs warned that anyone moving on the field of fire would be shot without further warning.

The only way forward appeared to be the road, which ran straight to a gap between the Red Mountain and the Shoulder Mountain. The road was busy; heavy trucks lumbered in and out of the manor constantly as the Kommando stripped it of anything of value. In the cleft between the mountains was a checkpoint, and Lavin could see the small figures of troops carefully inspecting vehicles going in and out.

Along the road there were a number of odd question-mark shapes.

"What are they, lord?" Val Bo-Ho whispered.

Lavin gave Bo-Ho the binoculars, the big fein's eyes widened considerably as the question marks resolved into the gibbets of Young Proud, with clusters of hanged men on the ropes.

37

LAVIN AND VAL BO-HO DID SOME SKILLFUL BUSHWORK IN scouting the roads. They examined the problem of getting through the checkpoint from several different angles. They withdrew into the jik forest again to think about it.

Lavin was considering a way of getting one of the big trucks to slow down long enough so they could get on board, when he heard a stirring in the woods behind them. Suddenly hundreds, indeed thousands, of fein, were moving stealthily forward, bunched under the trees on either side of the main truck road. He stared in amazement; such disobedience was unheard of.

An apologetic Chulpopek approached him. "My lord, I'm sorry, but the Impis would not stay behind."

Stunned, Lavin saw that the forest was alive with fein and there were human troops too, hundreds of them apparently. Somehow they'd all infiltrated right behind him, slipping deep into the heart of the New Kommando positions.

The honor they did him was incalculable, he felt his face flush with sudden emotion. He stammered, his voice shaking. "I have to go through those forts. I cannot in good conscience order anyone to accompany me. I do not intend to come back."

"Lord, you will not go alone."

For a long moment he stared into those fein eyes. Ng Farr had come up too. He carried a grenade launcher on his back, had his pistol in his hand.

Lavin laughed. If he'd ever imagined he could somehow spirit an Impi into the heart of the New Kommando, he would've chided himself for fantasizing. But his laugh cut off after a moment. He looked back at them, and his eyes had gone cold. Death hovered over all of them, himself included. And Fleur? Somewhere up that road, inside the great fortress of Clan Butte, his wife was being tortured to death.

"Lord, we should move while we can."

Lavin snapped out of his trance. "Of course, Ng Farr. My apologies to the neilks."

"Your orders, sir," Chulpopek said as he snapped erect to his full six foot five.

"We attack the forts. Head for the road—we will use the road to hit that checkpoint. If they're all as sleepy as the units behind us, we might even have a chance.

Soundlessly the Impi poured forward out of the woods and up the road, alongside the heavy trucks. At first there was simply stunned surprise among the New Kommando. A lot of the drivers were fresh recruits; they didn't understand what the burly fein were doing as they ran past so purposefully in an endless double file on either side of the road. No guns were being fired; the fein seemed less aggressive than athletic, jogging past the trucks up the road. There were men and women too, in the road, all around the trucks, all chugging toward the checkpoint a hundred yards away. Nonplussed, the Kommando drivers looked to each other with raised eyebrows.

The jogging fein were halfway to the checkpoint before the scream of "Fein attack!" rang down from the observer platforms to the gun galleries.

At that point, men and women pulled open the doors of trucks and dragged the Kommando drivers out then raced the trucks forward across the cleared field of fire, simultaneously drawing defensive fire and screening the charging fein. Even when the vehicles exploded, riddled by defensive fire, and gasoline fireballs rolled skyward, the smoke and noise served to mask what was reallly happening.

At the head of that incredible charge came a mad group of Effertelli, fein of a near-mythical village of low status renowned for their drive to win glory on the battlefield even in suicidal charges. Right behind them came Lavin Fundan, Chulpopek, and the rest, sprinting as if they were at a track meet.

The leading Effertelli sent a salvo of grenades into the checkpoint, dropping half the men, who'd been watching the trucks burn. When the big fein came pounding up the road a few seconds later, the defenders, for the most part, were running toward the manor gates as quickly as their legs could carry them.

The first Rinus Van Relt knew of the Impis' charge was the eruption of noise outside the conference room, near the front gates of Butte Manor, where he was working on expanding the patrols to the north of the Sliverary River.

Shouts, a great many shouts. Feet dashing down the halls. He opened the door, the officers crowded behind him.

Unmistakably, not far away, was the sound of small arms

fire, Highlander ordnance—Kelchworth .90-mm machine guns among other things. There was also a hoarse roaring sound that was unlike anything Van Relt had ever heard before but that caused the hairs on the back of his neck to stiffen. "What the hell is that?"

The gray-faced officers ran past. Some men came running in at full tilt.

"What is it?" Van Relt said in a fury, grabbing the first man and spinning him into the wall. Van Relt had his revolver out and trained on the fellow in the next moment.

The man's eyes were wide. "Fein, sir, a whole army of them, at the forts. They came out of nowhere."

More disoriented men were running up to the great gates. The sounds of firing were closer; so was that dreadful roaring. Rinus ran outside, lifted his binox, and scanned the lee side of the Red Mountain. It was speckled with running men, in Kommando fatigues.

Behind them was a solid wall of fein, green pennons waving above them, and as they sprang down the hillside at a gallop, their roaring resounded off the Centro Mountain.

And from the Red Mountain forts rifle fire was striking all around the main gates. Van Relt ran for cover. Once inside he hesitated. Nothing stood between those fein and the gates. Suddenly he knew with dreadful certainty that they couldn't be stopped.

"How did they get through?" He groaned aloud and surrendered to his urge to seek safety. He used a key to open one of Butte Manor's many secret elevators and rode the car to the Command Center. Young Proud and Orik were not there.

Kalman, his adjutant, was there however and extremely agitated. "What news, sir?"

"Ah, yes, Kalman. Get all available units to the front gates. We have to try to stop them."

"Stop who, sir? What is going on?"

"The *fein* army, of course, and Lavin Fundan, who no doubt was driven to this by that message of Young Proud's. You know the message I mean, messire."

"I see, sir." Kalman's face was white.

"Good. Then get on with it, man."

Van Relt slipped back out the door and ran down the corridor. He turned just in time to see Young Proud and Orik bustling into another secret elevator. Orik carried something wrapped up in a sheet.

He sprinted, but the doors closed in his face. Van Relt pounded on them and screamed.

The doors reopened. Young Proud wore a silky smile of pure evil. "Get in, Van Relt."

The doors closed behind them and the lift rose with dramatic speed. A minute later they emerged onto a small platform carved out of the mountain above. A pair of vtol flyers stood ready, including Young Proud's very own Hummbird.

Young Proud bade Orik to put the unconscious form of Fleur Fundan down on the floor. "Draw your weapon, Orik. Point it at Van Relt."

Fleur's body was wrapped in a white sheet. Blood was seeping through, lots of blood.

"Now I want you to draw your own gun, Van Relt. Come on." He giggled. "Of course if you point it at me, Orik will shoot you." Rinus locked eyes with Young Proud, who blazed with an unnamable fury, a dark rage against the cosmos.

"Good." A little smile fluttered on Young Proud's lips. "Now you will shoot Lady Fundan, or else Orik will shoot you. Then we will fly to the Sx Coast and the safety of the *Black Ship*."

"What about the pharamol?" Van Relt said.

Young Proud tittered with glee. "How absurd. There are forty-five kilos in my plane. All prewired with detonax, for which I alone hold the detonator. Are you coming, Van Relt? We have the Galaxy awaiting us."

He struggled. A silence passed between them.

The sounds of the revolver were strangely muted in this high mournful place with its thin cold air. Afterward, Orik emptied his gun into the cockpit instruments of the smaller vtol to discourage pursuit.

The fein had found the newly enriched Kommando troops in the forts with very little stomach for a fight. The outer lines on the Red Mountain fort were taken with hardly a shot fired. The defenders discovered no powerful reason why they should stand and fight. Instead they ran for the safety of the fort on the Out Rock.

The main body of fein came on, so quickly they got mixed in with the fleeing remnants of the defense units from the forts. The men at the manor gates poured fire into both, regardless, but nothing could stop that avalanche of fein who smashed through the lines, reached the walls, bunched together momentarily, and then tore open Aunchus Butte's great gates with their bare hands, roaring the entire time.

284

Inside the gates the fein swept on with a fury that carried them over the defensive barricades despite machine guns, gas, and small arms fire. Where they passed, nothing lived. They took no prisoners.

Lavin Fundan was with the vanguard, watched the gates ripped open with disbelieving eyes, and soon rode the elevators to the Command Post in the Centro. Young Proud was gone; there was no sign of Fleur. In despair Lavin put his pistol to the head of the adjutant who held the command. The man knew nothing.

Then two artillerymen entered with a soldier they'd captured in another elevator. He spoke of a small aircraft platform, on the other side of the peak from the Centro fort.

They ran through the long passages, their breath hot and harsh in their ears, but arrived in time to see a black Hummbird, accelerating southward a mile or so away. Rifles came up, but the range was extreme and the target too small. In a few moments it was out of sight.

On the concrete apron plumes of smoke were pouring from the cockpit of another vtol. Not far away lay a bloodied form wrapped in a sheet.

With a groan of despair Lavin fell to his knees, lifted the weeping cloth, and cradled Fleur to his chest, feeling utterly useless as the tears ran down his face. They wet the dried blood on her forehead, and it began to run. His voice descended to an inarticulate mumble; he could not fashion the words anymore.

Too late! He, who had always relied on arriving in the nick of time, had failed at last, failed the only human he had ever truly known and trusted completely.

He exhaled with a terrible effort. It felt as if his heart would sunder inside his chest and drown him in his own blood. He got to his feet; her body seemed absurdly light in his arms, and though it was one of the most difficult things he had ever done in his entire life, he turned to face the others.

Chulpopek stood forward, aghast, his bloody kifket swinging loose in one big fein paw. He opened his muzzle to speak, saw Lavin's eyes, and closed it again.

Val Bo-Ho stared at him somberly, tried to speak, and failed.

"Out!" Lavin managed at last. They stared at him, concerned for his sanity. His voice rose to a shout.

"Out, quickly, we must get out of here. Young Proud has escaped, and I know he will order an air strike here—nuclear weapons are most likely. This cruel business is designed to blind us with sorrow and keep us here. Until it's too late."

Their eyes widened, mouths open.

"Out," he screamed, "the Black Ship comes, and it brings with it our doom."

Then they turned and ran for the elevator banks.

At the spaceport on the Sx Coast, Young Proud watched Van Relt carefully. Rinus was nervous. Understandable, this was a moment of considerable tension.

The bags beside them were loaded with an eternity of pharamol. Young Proud wondered idly if such a monstrously valuable cargo of contraband had ever before been assembled in one place. A tempting target, indeed. But there was detonax in each bag. If they were double-crossed he would destroy all of it without hesitation. Alace Rohm knew that, and thus he had no worries in her direction. At least until they were aboard the *Black Ship*. And to dispel any likelihood of doubt, he felt the tiny ampoule that was embroidered to the cuff of his flight suit. Queen Alace would have to come to him to negotiate face to face, and then he would sting!

Van Relt was another matter. Apart from his attempts to conspire with Rohm, there was clearly a new insubordination in the man. Young Proud began to believe that it might be better if Orik killed the mercenary quickly, while they were alone.

Then the doors swung open at last, and the Space Marines burst in. He abandoned the idea. Van Relt would live, for a little while longer.

A few minutes later they were strapped in comfortably, their bags beside them in a cabin with no marines present as specified in the deal. Then the boosters on the pinnace exploded into life and the four hundred-ton space boat rose into the sky on a column of fire.

The gee was intense for a few minutes, but after a while the pressure eased then was replaced by weightlessness as they achieved orbital speed and raced toward the *Black Ship*.

"Well, my friends, a historic time. We bid Fenrille farewell. For me this is a moment etched with contradictory emotions. I will sorely miss my homeworld, my beautiful homeworld. I expect I shall never see it again."

He grew silent for a moment, genuinely wistful.

"But alas, I cannot remain here anymore. They who have conspired against me and my Line have made it impossible for me to stay among them. I must move on to a higher destiny. Gentlemen, the Galaxy awaits us!" In anticipation of his new role aboard the *Black Ship*, Young Proud had been practicing

286

public speaking before his mirror every day for months. He was getting quite good at it.

Van Relt, too, looked back down on the blue-green world where he had been born. He too felt mixed emotions though less tinged with regret than any Fundan's could be.

He dragged his thoughts away from such things. The clouds swirled in great spirals over the southern ocean. Fenrille was behind him. Instead he faced unknown perils. These next few hours would be the most dangerous. Their reception just might be a firing squad, detonax or no detonax. His life would hang by a thread during the resolution of the intrigues of Young Proud and Alace Rohm. If she revealed Van Relt's earlier deal...

On the forward screens the *Black Ship* appeared. Slowly it bore down on them. He gasped as he realized just how big it was, a small moon on its own. Already its crescent cut the circular limb of blue ocean and white clouds with an alien horizon of black.

It loomed over them; trailing beneath was the orbital fighters' flight deck, an extended V-winged structure that hung down on a boom projecting between the Fuhl modules.

Then the receptor cradle rushed up toward them and folded around the pinnace, drawing the big boat into the primary docking bay.

Still weightless they floated from the airlock, directly into a waiting elevator that bore them rapidly to the reception area with its comfortable half-gee gravity. Smiling women in gowns of black and dark purple awaited them there. Clearly important officers of some kind, these women were surrounded by a crowd of others, dressed more garishly in normal Neptunian garb.

A tall woman with long straight black hair stood forward. "Welcome," she cried, raising her arms, her gown expanding into enormous butterfly wings with scarlet eyes picked out in the black.

"Well met, Alace Rohm," Young Proud said, putting down his bag and clasping hands with her. Young Proud turned to the ladies of the Bond and bowed low.

"Our mission is accomplished. I have brought a wealth of longevity to the *Black Ship* and its crew." He indicated the three bags. "In here I have more than fifty kilos of the very best pharamol."

There was a roar of approval and wild applause.

"But it is wired with detonax, and I will destroy it instantly if there is any attempted treachery."

The clapping cut off abruptly. They all stared at him intently.

He smiled and purred. "Of course, I know you will keep your side of the bargain." He turned and presented Alace Rohm with a phial of glittering blue crystals.

"A gift to all those present—let everyone taste the first fruits of our defeat of the Buttes and the Fenrille Defense Forces. This is Aunchus Butte's Sunkrystal, the best pharamol of the Butte Clan."

"Excellent," Alace Rohm said with a glittering smile. "On behalf of the entire Neptunian Bond Group, I thank you for your generosity and commend your gallant victory!" Applause began once more, driven by a determined claque mingling in the crowd. Alace leaned close. "I destroyed your enemies as you asked," she said happily.

"Wonderful—for that alone, I will give you an ounce of the best Butte Bullion you have ever seen. We have pharamol of the highest quality, just a glorious harvest. All of us shall live forever."

A cheer went up from the assembled Neptunians. The Nereidan Bond officers applauded enthusiastically and led the crowd in further cheers, carefully rehearsed and orchestrated in the characteristic way of the Nereidan Party. The boisterous Tritonians were careful to toe the new lines. They had all noticed how many of their leaders were missing.

"However I would like to meet with you alone as we have some negotiating to do. You prepared a suite as I requested?"

"Yes, of course, Messire Fundan. It is waiting for you. I will join you there at your convenience."

As he viewed these courtesies on the wall screen in Rohm's private chamber, Ira Ganweek wanted to scream. Instead of welcoming that monster into their midst, they should be putting it out the air lock without delay! Ira prayed, as he had rarely prayed, to an entity he had never really defined in his mind but which in moments like this he called upon for unknown reasons. He prayed the woman would return to her room before she went to meet with Young Proud. She had to be stopped; she could not trust her person in Young Proud's company. Ira shivered. The man was perfectly deadly.

And if Young Proud were to live, he was sure to find out that Ira Ganweek did too, and he would demand revenge from Rohm.

Rohm would do nothing to provoke a clash until she could be sure of safely securing those three bags crammed with pharamol and enough explosive to vaporize it. Which would mean she would give Ira to Young Proud, a thought too horrible to be borne.

The door hissed; Ira's prayers were answered. Alace came in alone. He leapt from his seat.

"Don't go to him, don't ever put yourself alone with him. Please listen to me, I know what I'm talking about. He is incredibly dangerous; he will kill you."

Alace was taking a slim handgun out of the drawer by her bedside.

"I find your concern for my welfare very touching. Never have I had such a loyal bond servant." She gave him a toothy smile. "Perhaps I will find ways to reward you later."

He could feel his life slipping away in the face of her smiling self-assurance. "You don't understand—"

"I understand very well. I must secure that pharamol. That's what we came here for; that's what we fought a war for. A war I just ended, by the way. So I'm going in there, and I'm going to kill those three foolish men and take that pharamol. You see," and she hung over him with that damned smile, "they think they're dealing with nothing more than *a woman*!" She laughed. "That bodyguard is a stupid pig and certainly no fein warrior. I could take his head with my bare hands. He has never met a warrior of Maza."

And for a second Ira wavered, doubt clouded in, but then the face of Young Proud Fundan reappeared in his thoughts. "No, I think you underestimate him. He will have come here prepared; he is insanely dangerous. Send someone else to deal with him."

She laughed mockingly and pushed him away.

"What? And let someone else get their hands on that detonator? One click and we lose fifty kilos of pharamol! No, I do not fear him. His insanity is only further evidence of weakness. Maza will guide me."

And she was gone, and Ganweek wept bitterly from the frustration of it and wondered how long he would have before he met the same fate as the Bond lords.

When the nukes popped, Armada Butte had had the good fortune to be looking in the opposite direction about twenty kilometers south of ground zero. Two of her companions were not so lucky, and they were blinded, possibly for good. With the rest of the sighted, she had watched in awe as the mushroom clouds of three small but precisely targeted nuclear devices rose from the fortress. Their crowns intermingling atop the rolling gray trunks of cloud. At ground zero, the forts of the Centro and the perimeter mountains were gone, fused into the general ceramic of the mountain's surface itself. The great gates of Aunchus Butte had been vaporized, along with the bodies of thousands of dead and wounded who had been lying on the Manor Green. The underground parts of the manor were sealed off with an annealing mixture of molten steel and glass formed from superheated mountain rock.

Within the hour Armada's group encountered parties of battered and dusty fein soldiery, mixed up with Fundan troops and great columns of prisoners from the New Kommando.

Then in a group of men and women on horseback she found Lavin Fundan wearing unfamiliar brown fatigues. A body, wrapped in a sheet, was tied over his knees in the saddle. His eyes bore a hollowness that she had never seen before. He looked as if part of him had died.

"Fleur?" was all she could say.

He nodded, the misery plain. Armada wept for her friend. "Young Proud?"

"Escaped, with a fortune in Butte pharamol."

"Damn them, damn them all and their Peace of the Lamb. Oh, Fleur, oh, my poor lady," and Armada saw the blood and the bullet holes, and on the spot she dedicated her life to finding and killing Young Proud Fundan. Wherever he chose to hide she would find him, somehow.

"There is more," he said sadly. She looked up.

"The old Mzsee is dead, Bg Rva, hero of Brelkilk. I got the news just now from Abzen Valley where they prepare his burial. It seems he fought for Fleur, and must have killed Young Proud's bodyguard, for they found Persimpilges' body as well. But Rva had four bullets in him, so I must lay this too against Young Proud."

Her eyes widened. "But he was so old!" A sob caught in her throat, she laid her head on Fleur's body and wept as she had never done before.

The weary survivors, dusted with soot and ash from the burning, with many walking wounded among them, continued pouring out of Sliverary and heading south to the air base. Strangely, the New Kommando troops they met seemed unwilling to fight and let them pass without hindrance. Here and there they found contingents of New Kommando troops heading for the base as well. It looked as if the Kommando formations were breaking up.

The nuking of the manor had ended their fight as clearly as

any symbol possibly could. Many Kommando soldiers had died under the fireball. Many more would die of radiation poisoning unless they consumed large quantities of pharamol to overcome the effects and repair their cell tissues. As had happened so many times in history, the common soldiers had been betrayed, utterly betrayed, by their leaders.

38

As she entered, Alace Rohm examined the room with watchful eyes. To Young Proud she nodded and smiled graciously while in the puffed sleeve of her gown she felt the reassuring weight of the gun. Her thoughts were confident.

He would not dare anything against her here. Not yet. He would be uncertain, a male on someone else's territory. He was also insane and probably very dangerous, just as Ira Ganweek had said. In time, of course, he would have to be put out the air lock, but that could wait until the pharamol in those cases had been secured for the Bond. Until then she would just have to keep him on the defensive.

Young Proud rose with a greeting. In one hand he bore a glass of champagne. It was a time for celebration. As she approached, the other men rose too, a gesture she found amusing. Ancient courtesy, but these men were uncomfortable rather than assured. Their greetings too effusive. Van Relt was sweating slightly. Her lips curled into a smile.

Close behind them were the suitcases. Young Proud gestured to them and Orik *whoop*ed nervously. Van Relt drank champagne in anxious little sips.

"Will you take some wine with us, Bond leader Rohm?" Young Proud offered her an empty glass. She took it, relieved that he hadn't offered a full one and forced her to refuse.

. . . I will never take a drink from you, serpent! . . .

A Bond servant poured her wine; she sipped and experienced a slight sense of relief. Indeed at that moment Young Proud seemed far from dangerous. He had submitted to a full inspection for weapons other than the detonator device. He seemed almost placid compared to the last time she had seen him in the flesh. By the side of the trail in Sliverary forest.

She would take the offensive, however, from the start.

"So you escaped, messire. To your safety!" She raised her glass. "Safety" was a word calculated to keep them uneasy.

Young Proud was happy to join her. The talk was light, full

of banter and hopes for the future. Young Proud was making a conscious effort to be pleasant.

Alace quickly concluded that Young Proud was ready to try to cut a deal. He would retreat from his earlier position, which had been that he would retain control of the three bags of pharamol forever, doling out the drug in small increments through the years. The crew of the ship would be kept alive forever, and he would feel safe from treachery.

Of course Alace had agreed. She'd have agreed to almost anything to get those bags on board. Now the foolish man probably realized how vulnerable he was and would seek an early generous deal. Hoping to catch her before she had worked out all the possibilities of the situation. Hoping to strike a deal that would still leave him with wealth as well as security.

Alace had plenty of bargaining room, especially since the *Black Ship*'s own forays with the Space Marines had netted half a kilo of pharamol before the assault on Butte Manor. Easily enough to keep all her supporters in a pleasurable haze for months.

She laughed at some sally of the bodyguard's. He had drunk two glasses of wine, was already affected. All the better, should it come to anything. She had barely consumed a third of a glass.

Her own guards were standing a couple of meters back, arms crossed.

Young Proud proposed a toast, some "galactic" nonsense. There'd already been enough of that among the Bond, but Alace touched her glass with those of the others happily enough. Except that Young Proud clunked glasses so heavily that his own broke and carried through to cut the back of her hand. A little nick, a spot of blood, no more. Young Proud's cry was louder than hers, and the bodyguards tensed but did not move.

"Oh no! I'm so dreadfully sorry, Lady Alace. How clumsy of me." He had a white napkin in his hand; he held her hand and pressed the napkin against it. She felt something wet there for a second and it was gone.

He released her. A small pink stain was visible on the napkin.

"Did we stanch the bleeding?" he said solicitously.

"I think so." She found something so awful in his eyes at that moment that she almost ran from the room and ordered the guards to shoot him. When he spoke his tone had changed; there was a new undercurrent.

"Let us sit down and negotiate, Alace, come." He took her hand and led her to a seat.

* * *

The pursuit through the maze of machines had exhausted Chosen. He paced on, down a corridor of smooth metal surfaces. Mirror reflections were everywhere. They made him dizzy. Already his legs felt weak and watery. He could not go on much longer.

The problem had been the first, long pursuit, the race to the nearest machine structure beyond the central tower. He had mistakenly opted for a straight road and thus began a foot race with the biped catcher. He had beaten it to the entrance of the machine by only a few seconds despite a lengthy head start.

Once inside the machine Chosen had given it the slip twice, once on the way up and once on the way down again. However he could not evade it forever, especially when it brought in the little trackers and put them to finding the trail. Again and again it found whatever machine complex he had taken refuge in and pursued him relentlessly.

Chosen had tried to coerce the things but to little avail. All coercion power seemed to do was help the trackers determine more accurately where he was. The big one had a mind of brutal simplicity; there wasn't room for any coercion. The thoughts ran on monotonously. "Find biped, seize biped, bring biped to feed pipe control."

"Feed pipe" was the only thought that ever pricked the emotional surface, inducing a crude pleasure response. There was little else going on in its brain other than bodily control functions. No reproduction processes, no concerns for future or past, no memories; it was blank except for the needs of its task, which involved some complex programming, genes that encoded instincts as well as strength and speed, but it offered nothing expansive enough as a mind for Chosen to get a grip on.

The thing was seven feet high and weighed at least one hundred and fifty kilos. How it could run so fast for so long Chosen did not understand, but he did understand that if it ever got those oversized hands on him he would not escape. It probably had the strength of a bull gzan.

He came to the end of the corridor. Open spaces, lit in weird blue light from some process going on above, surrounded on two sides. On a third were a pair of machine elevators. He flung himself onto the nearest. The machines were weight sensitive, a discovery he'd made in his descent of the first machine tower, where he'd only just eluded the biped catcher.

The lift sprang away from the floor, accelerated and decelerated savagely to a floor thirty meters above. It waited to see if anything was getting on or off.

One of the little rat-size trackers scuttled on and the elevator took off upward once more with a jerk. The ratlike thing let out a shrieking squeal that was shockingly loud for something so small. Chosen dived at it, and it evaded him. He swung at it with fists and feet, finally connecting and driving its leathery little body into one wall. It jumped up and sprang at him, snapping a mouth filled with needlelike teeth. He smashed it against the wall with the flat of his hand. It wriggled and bit him, hard, in the wrist. He seized the psionic butterfly wings over the skull, crushed them in his hands like some overripe fruit. A black fluid bled all over him with a putrid stench.

The elevator jarred to a halt, and the head almost slipped his grasp to bite him again, but he swung it hard against the floor, once, twice, three times. Still it struggled, squirming with horrible vigor.

The elevator took off, and he looked up in alarm, feeling an unmistakable presence. The tracker almost got loose, and in panicky horror he smashed it several more times against the floor. Its struggles ceased, and he threw it in the corner and crouched.

At the next floor the biped catcher was waiting.

When Alace Rohm returned to her suite she seemed unsteady on her feet. The door opened; Ira whirled from his restless pacing and then groaned weakly.

Orik was with her, grinning hugely.

"No!" shouted Ganweek.

"Come along, Messire Ganweek. I've got to put you out the air lock, orders from the top, if you know what I mean."

Ira turned to Alace. She'd been weeping. Her face was reddened, almost swollen. Had she perhaps been slapped? She did not meet his eyes.

He tried to swing at Orik but was disabled with a hard knee to the solar plexus. Orik casually slung the tubby former senator over his shoulder and, pushing Alace ahead of him, left the room.

Outside awaited an escort of Nereidan guards. They formed around Orik and escorted the trio back to Young Proud's suite.

There Orik dumped Ganweek, still gasping, on the floor.

Young Proud Fundan stood with an arm insolently wrapped around Bond leader Rohm's waist. He grinned down at Ira Ganweek.

"Well, Senator Ganweek, you have lived just long enough to

become the object of my first duty as commanding officer of the *Black Ship*."

"What did you do?" Ira turned and screamed at Rohm.

She looked away, seemingly fighting back tears.

"Alace has discovered that she is infected with a rather unpleasant little predatory organism. If she wishes to live she will have to receive the antidote. Of course, only I know the exact sequence required to make antibody for the organism. Which is only natural, since I made the worm myself."

"Oh no . . ." Ira swung his gaze back to Young Proud.

"And now Alace has graciously agreed to appoint me chief executive officer of the *Black Ship*, working in conjunction with the Bond leadership. Don't you think that's wonderful, Ganweek?" Young Proud sounded as if he was only just containing an urge to hysterical laughter.

Ira could think of nothing to say. Young Proud grinned and motioned with his spare hand. "All right, Orik, why don't you work off some aggression on the Senator here, and then we'll all watch him go out the air lock."

Ira gasped as Orik sank a punch into his midriff and spun him around. He was casually hurled across the room, colliding with a chair and toppling over it to the floor. Orik advanced, laughing.

Ganweek felt nothing but nausea as Orik stood over him. He couldn't move, not even as Orik dragged him from the floor and swung a fist that exploded against his face, loosening teeth and sending him back to the floor. Again Orik reached down and pulled him up, only to sink a big fist into his belly and drop him again.

His head whirling, he waited for the end. Orik was coming once more. There was nothing he could do to resist. But Orik's expected grip on his neck never came. Instead there was a new voice. And angry words were exchanged.

Ganweek looked up in time to see an explosive pellet fling Orik across the room in a fountain of blood.

Van Relt had spirited a gun from the holster of one of the guards, and now had it trained on Young Proud's head.

Ira struggled to get some breath into his battered body.

"The detonator, messire, and no tricks!" Van Relt held the gun absolutely steady.

Ganweek scarcely dared to breathe as Young Proud put a hand into his pocket and brought out a small tube. With vast reluctance he gave it to Van Relt.

"Thank you. Now I'm leaving. It's my belief that life will

be longer and considerably happier in this system than it could be aboard this ship with you and the rest of these scorpions. Therefore I intend to leave, with one of these suitcases, which ought to ensure a long and satisfying life, right here. You will both discover that I do not intend to kill you. I'll let you handle those details for each other. Nor will I take all the pharamol. Otherwise you'll have nothing to fight over."

Van Relt seized one of the bags and pushed it across the floor to Ganweek. "Here, Senator, take this bag for me. You carry my bag, I'll save your life. How's that for a deal."

Ira scrambled to comply, scarcely believing that he might yet escape.

"And now, messire and Lady Rohm, if you will just walk ahead, we'll all go down to the docking bay together."

Young Proud stretched his lips in a ghastly smile. "Van Relt. Aren't we forgetting something?"

Rinus looked at him and allowed his hate to show openly. "No, we're not."

"You have no antidote, Van Relt."

Alace gave him a quick look. "You too, messire?"

"He is a master of these things, madame. I will leave him to you and vice versa." Van Relt smiled as he imagined the battle between them in the coming days, weeks, years as each struggled to survive and kill the other.

"You will be castrate, Van Relt!"

"Yes, probably, but I will be alive, messire. Which is more than would have been the case here."

Van Relt prodded his captives toward the door, holding the detonator in one hand and the gun in the other.

In the docking bay Van Relt held the gun on Young Proud and Rohm while Ganweek oversaw the destruction of the computers aboard the orbital fighters and the pinnace. Only a single space boat was left, and it was loaded into the ejection tube. Keeping his gun on them to the very last, Van Relt followed Ganweek into the boat and then swung the door shut on Young Proud and Alace Rohm, who ran for it as the booster jets hissed on and the boat was fired free from the *Black Ship* into orbital space.

39

CHOSEN'S STRUGGLE WAS BRIEF. THE BIPED CATCHER SPRANG into the elevator, which dropped like a stone. It reached out with enormous hands and seized him by the shoulders. The grip was strong. He kicked it as hard as he could straight in the midriff. It felt like kicking a leather-lined wall. There was no response. The thing picked him off the floor and swung him over one shoulder. He battered the psionic butterfly wings, breaking one and leaking putrid goo down the catcher's oily surface. The catcher merely reached round behind itself with a spare arm and caught his wrists and held them as fast as if they were chained to a tree.

The elevator stopped, and the biped catcher ran out and headed down the long avenue between machine towers to the central apparatus and the Numal.

The trip was a nightmare. The thing bounded over the floor just as quickly as it had pursued him. Chosen's heart sank as they passed the robots in the central plaza who went about their tasks without looking up. The central tower loomed above. The catcher ran lightly up the main ramp. It climbed rapidly.

Drearily Chosen saw the Numal's laboratory city take shape below. The huge machines were spread out around them, winking balefully in the dark.

What energy source did the creature use to maintain such endurance? They were moving at almost the same pace that had been maintained on the floor. Chosen wrestled against the arm that held him. There was no noticeable effect.

At last they came to the instrumentation pocket. The Numal excitedly stuffed the feed pipe into the biped catcher's alimentary orifice and put Chosen into a small, cylindrical cage. This it then suspended on a chain, so that Chosen was within reach of the sensors, probes that depended in several hemispherical arrays, within the instrumentation pocket.

The Numal's skin was glistening gray, shading to purple on the upper surface. The skin glistened from some lubricant. Limb clusters with reddish upper surfaces sprouted from cowled pockets where the otherwise seamless surface split open to reveal complex configurations of moving parts shading from glistening yellow to a dark glossy brown.

Things on stalks that could only be eyes and other sensors appeared around the cage. Something whipped in on a segmented stalk and jabbed him with a hypodermic syringe that removed some blood and whipped out again by the time he'd registered the pain. Something else, on a grotesquely narrow limb, a wire, no more, flashed in, yanked out a hair, and was gone. An eye thing like a pink golf ball pressed close. Angrily he slapped it away; it swung and smacked against the side of the cage, righted itself, and wobbled away a safe distance.

The Numal was enormous, almost as tall as a Woodwose and ten times more substantial. Up close Chosen could see the myraid fine lines of definition that striped the monster's sides. He could smell the fishy, chemical reek of the lubrication. He had to fight down truly elemental terrors. This was Jack and the Beanstalk but with the wrong ending. He stared up at the thing; it had no head, no segments, only the smooth lozenge supported on a forest of spindly limbs.

The giant had simply been too formidable. No mere human could have overcome it. Possibly a fein adept would have done better, but Chosen doubted that even the strongest fein could have fended off the biped catcher. Now it looked as if nothing would save the Divider, or Chosen for that matter.

In despair he stared out the narrow-meshed cage at the forest of tubes and instruments.

There, in the center of the pocket's focus, hung the containment bottle, not ten meters away. Could the Divider sense what had happened? Did it realize that all its careful planning had gone for naught? That Chosen had failed?

He looked up and saw the robot cable-laying machine he had programmed earlier. It clung to a boom high above the bottle. He let out an odd groan. Could he reach that far with his psi senses? His telekinetic power did not extend over the distance that his telepathic sensing reached. He had hardly had time to study the powers but already felt as a rough rule that the far sensing was the strongest power and the telekinesis the weakest.

He summoned up every ounce of concentration and focused on the machine. It lay at the very perimeter of his capability; he could just about "feel" the electron flow of its biochip brain. He groped mentally for the machine codes he knew were there. The contact was patchy; there was considerable static.

He remembered his previous program; it had been relatively simple, and indeed the machine code had not been hard to use. If he could just keep contact long enough to shift things about on the electronic level. He had the "feel" and began the task, quickly setting up a new program for the machine.

There came a sudden blast of energy on the telepathic plane and his mind reeled from the mind zap of a new psionic organism.

This was a probe that had been employed many times on the Divider but that had never succeeded in pinning down the elusive Arizel.

But Chosen felt as if a hammer had struck his telepathic senses. All contact with the robot was lost in a howl of alien gibberish. His brain kept translating it to "Here! Here! Here!" endlessly. It was maddening, an enormous alien voice yelling inside his head. He desperately damped down his psi senses to avoid the groping thing that searched for him on the mental plane, but there was no way to stop it, it welled up in his thoughts in as elemental a manner as the tide coming in up the beach. The scream of "Here! Here! Here!" was unnerving; it made him want to scream.

Then he realized it was also guiding another mind, acting as conduit for the Numal's own mental probe. There was contact.

The mind of the Numal was very alien. An artificial intelligence that combined elements of exterior programming and self-programming in considerable complexity. The thinking was mostly inexplicable to a human mind, but not entirely so. The Numal had complex pleasure-pain responses and enormous drives concerned with survival. He could understand something very much like greed at the top of an emotional scale as the Numal increased the contact with the mind of the captive biped. At the images it received in the human memories, of suns, planets, great glittering galaxies, it exulted with a rich joy involving all the pleasure-pain response systems in full positive coupling.

Never had the Numal been allowed such a sensation. This was the happiest moment of its immensely long existence. Indeed there had been suns and galaxies when the Numal first stirred to life. But there had been no stars or galaxies now for upward of thirty billion years. At the thought of young universes, existing in some elsewhere, some unknown region beyond the dying universe, the Numal's survival urge burned at a furious pitch.

The biped of course was proof positive that transportation between such universes and this one was possible. The Numal's excitement was therefore considerable.

Chosen felt probes ratcheting through his memories as the Numal sought data. The contact was without conscious thought transfer; the Numal could not as yet contact the focus of Chosen's mind. The probes felt cold and heavy and brutal and stupid. The Numal remained a machine of some sort, and it retained many of the failings of machines.

Still the probes were hard to resist. Then, contact established, it turned off the brainless psionic organism and its endless screaming cry.

Now the Numal tried to press home the contact. "How? Here come" was the gist of the thought that reached Chosen.

There was nothing to be done but take the offensive. Chosen pushed into the alien mind. Experimentally he hurled human illogicalities at it.

For a moment the Numal mind seemed to stutter, blanked, as if it were clearing its screens. Chosen threw more nonsense at it, rhymes and images of beautiful women, and a few seconds later the Numal turned the psionic organism on again and Chosen found it hard to maintain the focus required to stay in the Numal mind.

The tidal flow between the minds reversed, and the Numal swept back, hungrily feeding on memories.

It read quick confirmation of what the molecular and atomic analysis had already revealed concerning the origin of the biped. A warm-water world and a relatively stable star system. The evolutionary record bore the marks of having been long, punctuated by side steps, the mark of catastrophic extinctions. There was a galaxy in the memories, so young it still formed supergiants, littering its expansive gas fields with enormously wasteful jewellike hot stars.

The Numal sought more than this though. How had the rather watery biped managed to move between universes, and what relation did it have to the captive djinn field in the tank?

Chosen gave up trying to hide from the probes or to blank his memories. They did nothing to stop the Numal. Instead he focused on the psionic organism itself, trying to get past that pulsing exclamation.

The Numal had found fresher memory regions. Here there were inexplicable passages, except that there were certain mathematical concepts that it eagerly pounced on.

Here! Here was the way out! The potential for passage to another universe, where the Numals would survive for aeons to come!

Helplessly Chosen felt the Numal pry things from his memories concerning translation between universes. There was no way of stopping it. Without thinking he tried his coercive power, lashing out at the Numal's mind.

There was virtually no effect. Perhaps a mild discomfort but nothing that would deter the Numal. Desperately Chosen reached for the psionic organism instead. He focused coercion and squeezed as hard as he could. The happy shrieking of "Here! Here! Here!" wobbled, blinked out for a moment and came back on.

Chosen tried again, and this time when the telepathic screaming cut off he drove his mind forward into the brutally narrow passages of the mind of the psionic organism. In a moment he was in control of it, but at the price of having its compulsions run in his own body. His guts voided themselves. His heartbeat became erratic; his arms thrashed against the sides of the cage breaking his left wrist, lacerating the skin, spraying blood and small gobbets of skin around the cage.

But he had managed to turn the organism's power against the Numal, and now he used it to amplify his own coercive power, firing a psychic blast that temporarily disabled the Numal, scrambling the random-access memory system and sending the Numal into bizarre, random behavior patterns. It reversed out of the instrumentation pocket and rolled backward down the ramp.

Chosen abandoned his grip on the organism and it cut off its cry. He ignored the pain; his insides ached; there was a terrible sense of nausea. His arms were a mess, there was blood everywhere in the cage. The pain from his wrist was almost impossible to ignore, but he had to, reach out with his mind to the welding robot where it hung above the pocket. He focused on the machine code, trying to remember what he'd discovered about it earlier, and quickly reprogrammed it.

He fainted.

He awoke to the pain; his wrist felt as if it were on fire. His hand dangled uselessly. Blood was congealing all over his body. Even worse, he was lying in a pool of the contents of his intestines.

The Numal had returned; eyes on stalks examined him intently. Sensors of various kinds were intruded into the cage to sample the materials, the blood, feces, and flesh that had been emitted by the biped.

Unnoticed, the first hawser parted silently under the robot's cutter tool. It began to crawl slowly toward the next.

He took a breath and closed his eyes again and focused and searched for the psionic organism. At first nothing was detected then at last he discovered it. It was considerably damped down. Hardly active at all. With his telekinesis power he opened the switch that controlled it. As it resumed its high-volume scream, he turned it again on the Numal, his body reawaking to thrash horribly inside the cage.

The Numal was not as strongly affected this time; it caught and damped down the psychic power. It was not familiar with such coercion fields, and at first it suffered confusion as Chosen threw erroneous mathematical formulae into its brain. Paradoxes like the Hare and the Tortoise produced impactions in the Numal's random-access memory and led to virtual blackouts in the Numal's mind.

But the robot regained control of itself, it resolved that whatever else was discovered, the brain of the biped would have to be reproduced and experimented with. Clones of the cell tissue should be relatively simple to produce. All the tissues of the biped appeared to be simple evolutions of once-solitary marine animals of a low order. Combined together in a colony form in which one individual served as a bag to hold in a quantity of water, laced with minerals and salts, while another built structural members that were distributed about the inside of the creature. The nervous tissues were the contribution of another organism, and the whole was protected by a complex of single-celled animals that traveled in the seawater alongside respiratory cells.

Much of this biological pattern was familiar to the Numal, but there were twists unique to the captive biped. This was the pattern of slow-evolute worlds in young universes with stable star systems and planets of the right size and position. From such humble beginnings had come the makers of the Numals.

But this life-form had shown exceptional psionic power, not only in strength but also in degree, exhibiting talents previously unknown to the Numals.

A second hawser fell away, and the containment bottle—suddenly freed on one side—swung down to a crash against the side of the instrumentation pocket. The remaining guy wires tore loose, and the bottle broke away and fell to the floor, far below, where it shattered with a sound like a bomb exploding.

Chosen awoke from his faint at the sound. One of his feet was broken. Blood was seeping from a torn ear.

A monad blossomed in his mind. The Divider was free. And very surprised to find a young human, caught in a cage by the Numal.

A human had made translation via the quaternary process? The idea was incredible.

Then the Divider hurled a disabling glyph at the Numal's dull mind. To Chosen there came a glyph sequence begun with the monad, dividing itself white into black forever and followed by the sense of a presence in his thoughts.

"I am the Divider."

"I know." Chosen's reply was vastly different from the Arizel glyph mode.

"You are not like the humans I remember."

"Correct, I have undergone an unusual process."

Where the glyphs rose in the center of thought, taking precedence over everything else, Chosen tried to project, to focus his thought, in inter-English words, in what he visualized as a beam. Certainly the result did not have the feel of expansive power that the glyphs did as they rose in his brain.

"The Numal is temporarily disabled. We must escape it while we can. Will you be able to make translation? I will assist in the quaternary."

"I think so."

"We must begin."

"What about the Numal? It will follow. Its brain probed me. It knows the way."

"I know. I will have to call for help from the other Arizel. We will have to try to trap it here."

They entered the quaternary, the Divider helping Chosen to calm his mind to the consistency of a still pool of water, to ignore the pain of his broken wrist and foot.

It was not easy. The sweat stood out on his head whenever he moved in the slightest. The Divider placed the monad symbol in the center of his consciousness and assisted him in controlling his body, first respiration then the heart and the other organs.

Gradually Chosen managed to obliterate the pain sensations, to float beyond them. As he did so the quaternary process began properly.

A few minutes later they translated together, just as the Numal came out of the dizziness induced by the Divider's glyph.

Chosen reappeared within the mantle of Fenrille's atmosphere and dropped a couple of feet to the ground, a muddy pool in the fidnemed, the great forest. He fell and cried out from the pain in his broken foot.

"My apologies, our aim was slightly off. The distance was great." The Divider's glyph went off in his mind again, popping into existence in the center of consciousness.

The trees around him were crackling with energies.

"Where shall I place ye?"

"You can do that?" Chosen sat in the mud keeping his arms pressed against his chest, wincing each time they moved. His foot throbbed evilly.

"Of course."

"Then to my father in Abzen Vale."

There was a moment of hesitation.

"He is not there."

"Do you sense where he is then?"

"Yes, and more."

The Divider transported Chosen in the next moment, and they appeared in a glade in a forest of Highland trees, jik, and mindal.

Fein and human soldiers, in dusty uniforms, were slowly passing down a trail through the center of the glade.

Lavin Fundan rode a horse in their midst, a bloodstained bundle carried over his knees.

Chosen knew at once what it was.

"My mother is dead."

The Divider was still. Then a glyph rose quietly. "Your mother was Fleur?"

"Yes," Chosen whispered and knelt on the arble. There were tears on his face, hot and wet. The sky was strangely dark; there was the smell of some enormous burning.

And there came a crystal-clear image of his mother, of a Fleur that he had never known, scenes of an Earth in the previous century. Other memories from her early days' struggling on the Sx Coast. They made his heart ache.

"How do you know this?" he asked the Divider aloud.

"Your mother spoke for humanity at the Great Return. She spoke with considerable wisdom, and all the Arizel tki Fenrille formed a high opinion of her. I am sorry indeed to learn that she has died. But your father approaches, and from him I have learned many sad tidings. Great evil has been done here."

Lavin Fundan dismounted and took Chosen carefully in his arms, gingerly embracing the boy who clearly had been badly used.

"My son." Another burden lifted from Lavin's mind. His son lived, his two daughters too. They would support each other now in the absence of their mother.

Chosen felt his father weep and knew not whether it was in joy or sorrow or simply an unbearable mixture of both.

The Divider interrupted with a crisp glyph. "I would hesitate to interrupt, but from what I now understand of the situation, I must seek more data. The death of Fleur is a great sadness, but dissolution is the logical end of all things, even the material of the universes from which we are formed. Therefore it must be accepted along with everything else."

There was a pause.

"Yet do I share your grief," and somehow Chosen and Lavin felt a silver tear drop slowly through the glyph.

"However I also detect unusual gravitic disturbances within the system. From your minds I have an image of a spaceship, a marauder that has wreaked havoc with the human society here."

"The *Black Ship*," Lavin said tonelessly. "Yes, havoc is a fair description."

"The ship is attempting to align gravity fields with which to cleave a path through space-time wormholes. I shall investigate immediately."

The Divider was gone.

"There is much to discuss, Father. I have seen, been, I—" Chosen stumbled over the words, not knowing how to begin.

"There will be time, Son. Don't say anything just yet, but later you will teach me. Perhaps I will even be able to learn. I sense enormous changes."

Hundreds of thousands of kilometers away the *Black Ship* approached the moment of alignment; the Fuhl Drives would be activated and the ship would surge toward a distant star cluster containing several hundred yellow stars with potential planets.

The Divider paced the ship as it moved on a solar elliptic at one hundred thousand kiloms an hour toward the point where the drives would cut in. The Divider observed the murderous hatreds and powerful lusts that beat within the ship.

Far, far away the great Numal completed construction of the protection module and approached universal translation through purely technological means. The Divider sensed its cry of triumph across the universal flux and nudged the Fuhl Drives in the ship into premature activity. The drives achieved a configuration never dreamed possible by those who built them. The engineers had time only to yell a warning to the bridge, and then the *Black Ship* departed normal space time and hurtled into the subvoid.

As it did so it ploughed directly into the onrushing translation module constructed by the Numal, and the two systems engaged one another with the intensity of matter and antimatter. In the wink of an eye a soundless flare of mighty energy bloomed in the subtexture of the universal flux. In a billionth of a second both the Numal and the *Black Ship* were converted into the raw stuff of a new universe, a small one as universes go but an exceedingly hot one, for at least the first fifty million years.

Moments later the Divider returned to the glade in the forest of Muld. Its glyphs described what had happened.

"The *Black Ship* is no more."

"Neither is the Numal."

Chosen felt a terrible perplexity overwhelm him.

"Such enormous events are no longer within my comprehension. My mother is dead, my friend Bg Rva is dead also, I feel nothing but weary. My wrist aches, my foot is unmentionably painful. My heart feels as if it has been carved in two, and now I hear that all our enemies are destroyed."

He got clumsily to his feet, leaning on his father. "I want to go home now. The world is unreasonably tormenting. I don't understand it anymore."

The Divider contemplated this for a moment with more than a touch of agreement. The young human was a new chapter for the old world; the human race itself would transform with the new knowledge. The Divider was convinced of only one thing. The human struggles would never cease; the species was young and wholly unreasonable. The monad flowered in their minds in farewell, and the Divider was gone.

Epilogue:
The Black Ship

IN THE SPACE BOAT IRA GANWEEK BEGAN TO DARE TO BELIEVE that he would survive.

Shortly after they'd accelerated there had been a heavy shock; the boat had lunged forward suddenly. Ganweek had checked the ship computer's inspection for damage and found none. Nor did he find the *Black Ship* on the tracking monitor. The computer informed him that the *Black Ship* had disappeared. Ira suggested to Van Relt that they stop accelerating before they killed themselves. A few moments passed and Van Relt cut the motors and they drifted on in a low elliptic about Fenrille. The sudden weightlessness was unpleasant but considerably better than three gee.

"They really left us?"

"Computer says they're gone. They used the Fuhl Drives."

"What? So close to a planetary singularity? There must have been an accident."

Van Relt turned to stare at Ganweek.

"What would that mean?"

Ira was laughing, a rich bubbling sound compounded of relief, joy, and anticipation.

"I think, my friend dear Rinus, that we are the sole survivors of the *Black Ship*!"

Van Relt nodded, his lips set grimly. Ira's chuckles subsided.

"Of course, I didn't mean—" He waved a hand apologetically.

"We have to avoid the Fundans. We will have to hide for a long time."

"We—" Ira coughed quickly. "—mean *you*, will be rich enough to afford such secure solitude."

"I doubt if I will enjoy it for long. I will take it to my family. At least it will not be wasted."

The old Ganweek charm bubbled to the surface once more. "My friend, I owe you an awful lot."

Van Relt was instantly suspicious.

"Don't come with that guff, Ira Ganweek. I know your reputation."

Ira smiled placidly, grabbed hold of a guide bar to stop himself floating away. "You need hospitalization, and you need it fast, don't you, Van Relt?"

There was a moment's silence.

"Yes. I do."

Ira let another moment go by. "It just so happens that I know a nice little clinic that might be able to save you. It's on the Far Rocks, run by an old, old friend of mine. For a slice of our, I mean *your* pharamol she'll get you immediate treatment." Ganweek put a hand up to his battered mouth. He was still bleeding heavily inside.

"And I will go to the dentist. Find out if he can salvage anything."

Van Relt hesitated for a long moment. There didn't seem any choice. "All right, Ganweek, I'll trust you. But first we land on Van Relt island. It's close to the Far Rocks." He smiled at Ira's abrupt blink of surprise. "Yes, one of those early second-wave families, messire. Never made anything more than just enough to survive on our 'island.' Actually it's a collection of twenty rocks that just rise above the surface. The big storms can be pretty bad out there. But I have a few relatives hanging on to the island, and they will look after our pharamol while I'm in the hospital. That way I'll feel safe, and you and your doctor friend will want to do a very good job of saving me."

Ira bubbled with laughter. "Van Relt, how could you think that I would stoop to treachery? Especially after all we've just been through together."

Rinus Van Relt had to laugh at that. Ira exploded too. They were both giggling like crazed children all the way down into the atmosphere of Fenrille.

And below them, in the deep misty greenness of the great basin of the Bhjum, a Chitin nest made up its mind.

It would go forth and preach the new message. A god had come, a bipedal god from another world. A god that wouuld guide the Chitin back to the technological grace that had been lost so long ago.

A special caste of warrior workers would be produced to take the message to other nests. The work would begin at once. There were millions of nests, all existing in benighted ignorance of the truth. The vizier scrambled in a writhing mass of euphoria at the prospect ahead. It would never be bored again.

About the Author

CHRISTOPHER ROWLEY was born in Massachusetts in 1948 to an American mother and an English father. Soon afterward he began traversing the Atlantic Ocean, a practice that has continued relentlessly ever since. Educated in the United States, Canada, and for the most part at Brentwood School, Essex, England, he became a London-based journalist in the 1970s. In 1977 he moved to New York and began work on *The War for Eternity,* his first science-fiction novel. Published by Del Rey Books in 1983, it won him the Compton Crook/Stephen Tall Memorial Award for best first novel. *The Black Ship* is Rowley's second novel.